THE UNFORGIVEN

'Divide and conquer, brother,' said Calatus, slowing to steer his steed down one of the rows while Annael continued up the main aisle.

Annael fired the plasma talon again, targeting the distant container stacks. The ball of energy smashed into the uppermost container, throwing it into the air in a cloud of twisted shrapnel and molten drops. More las-fire converged on the Ravenwing rider, striking his armour and bike. He turned in the saddle and fired his pistol at the enemy behind him, felling two more, but there were at least another ten sheltering on the high stacks.

It was time to take a different approach.

More Dark Angels from Black Library

• **LEGACY OF CALIBAN** •

RAVENWING
MASTER OF SANCTITY
THE UNFORGIVEN
Novels by Gav Thorpe

LORDS OF CALIBAN
A novella by Gav Thorpe

ANGELS OF DARKNESS
A novel by Gav Thorpe

THE PURGING OF KADILLUS
A Space Marine Battles novel by Gav Thorpe

PANDORAX
A Space Marine Battles novel by C Z Dunn

DARK VENGEANCE
A novella by C Z Dunn

ACCEPT NO FAILURE
An audio drama by Gav Thorpe

TRIALS OF AZRAEL
An audio drama by C Z Dunn

MALEDICTION
An audio drama by C Z Dunn

Explore the origins of the Dark Angels in The Horus Heresy series

DESCENT OF ANGELS
A Horus Heresy novel by Mitchel Scanlon,
also available as an unabridged audiobook

FALLEN ANGELS
A Horus Heresy novel by Mike Lee,
also available as an unabridged audiobook

THE LION
A Horus Heresy novella by Gav Thorpe,
also available as an unabridged audiobook

Visit blacklibrary.com for the full range of Dark Angels novels, novellas, audio dramas and Quick Reads, as well as many other exclusive Black Library products.

A WARHAMMER 40,000 NOVEL

THE UNFORGIVEN
THE LEGACY OF CALIBAN BOOK THREE

GAV THORPE

BLACK LIBRARY

A Black Library Publication

First published in Great Britain in 2015 by
Black Library,
Games Workshop Ltd.,
Willow Road,
Nottingham,
NG7 2WS, UK.

10 9 8 7 6 5 4 3 2

Cover illustration by Paul Dainton.

© Games Workshop Limited 2015. All rights reserved.

Black Library, the Black Library logo, The Horus Heresy, The Horus Heresy logo, The Horus Heresy eye device, Space Marine Battles, the Space Marine Battles logo, Warhammer 40,000, the Warhammer 40,000 logo, Games Workshop, the Games Workshop logo and all associated brands, names, characters, illustrations and images from the Warhammer 40,000 universe are either ®, TM and/or © Games Workshop Ltd 2000-2015, variably registered in the UK and other countries around the world. All rights reserved.

A CIP record for this book is available from the British Library.

UK ISBN 13: 978 1 84970 854 8
US ISBN 13: 978 1 84970 855 5

No part of this publication may be reproduced, stored in a retrieval system, or transmitted in any form or by any means, electronic, mechanical, photocopying, recording or otherwise, without the prior permission of the publishers.

This is a work of fiction. All the characters and events portrayed in this book are fictional, and any resemblance to real people or incidents is purely coincidental.

See Black Library on the internet at

blacklibrary.com

Find out more about Games Workshop and the world of Warhammer 40,000 at

games-workshop.com

Printed and bound by CPI Group (UK) Ltd, Croydon, CR0 4YY

It is the 41st millennium. For more than a hundred centuries the Emperor has sat immobile on the Golden Throne of Earth. He is the master of mankind by the will of the gods, and master of a million worlds by the might of his inexhaustible armies. He is a rotting carcass writhing invisibly with power from the Dark Age of Technology. He is the Carrion Lord of the Imperium for whom a thousand souls are sacrificed every day, so that he may never truly die.

Yet even in his deathless state, the Emperor continues his eternal vigilance. Mighty battlefleets cross the daemon-infested miasma of the warp, the only route between distant stars, their way lit by the Astronomican, the psychic manifestation of the Emperor's will. Vast armies give battle in His name on uncounted worlds. Greatest amongst his soldiers are the Adeptus Astartes, the Space Marines, bio-engineered super-warriors. Their comrades in arms are legion: the Imperial Guard and countless planetary defence forces, the ever-vigilant Inquisition and the tech-priests of the Adeptus Mechanicus to name only a few. But for all their multitudes, they are barely enough to hold off the ever-present threat from aliens, heretics, mutants – and worse.

To be a man in such times is to be one amongst untold billions. It is to live in the cruellest and most bloody regime imaginable. These are the tales of those times. Forget the power of technology and science, for so much has been forgotten, never to be re-learned. Forget the promise of progress and understanding, for in the grim dark future there is only war. There is no peace amongst the stars, only an eternity of carnage and slaughter, and the laughter of thirsting gods.

THE HUNT SO FAR...

Whilst responding to an ork uprising and spreading unrest on the troubled world of Piscina Four, neighbour to the Dark Angels recruiting world of Piscina Five, the Chapter's Second Company, the Ravenwing, and warriors from the Fifth Company uncover a recording made by Chaplain Boreas, former commander of the garrison. It reveals a complex plot involving a cadre of Fallen Angels stealing the gene-seed hidden in the Dark Angels Chapter Keep and covering the theft by wiping out the population of Piscina Four with a life-eater virus. The sacrifice of Boreas and his companions thwarts the plot but allows the Fallen to escape.

Following a lead within the databanks of the abandoned keep, the Ravenwing and their battle-brothers discover a rebel stronghold on the renegade space station known as Port Imperial. The two companies eliminate this threat and in the process Grand Master

Sammael and his officers learn of the presence of a Fallen Angel connected to the world of Thyestes.

The Ravenwing travel to the civil-war-torn world and use the Imperial Commander as bait in a trap for the Fallen. However, traitor legionaries of the Death Guard are involved in the attack and the Dark Angels are forced to retreat. They are eventually able to trace the traitors back to their base and attack, securing the Fallen Librarian called Methelas though they suffer many casualties in the assault.

Returning to the Rock with this captive, the Dark Angels learn that a plot they thought quashed, involving the Fallen called Merir Astelan, is in fact still ongoing. The Master of Sanctity, Sapphon, engineers a deal with Astelan so that the Fallen can prove his protested innocence in return for helping the Dark Angels hunt down the third of the trio of Fallen – Anovel.

This trail takes them to the daemon world of Ulthor, where the Ravenwing and Deathwing are badly mauled and none the wiser for their battle. Seeing little other option, they return Astelan to the world of Tharsis where he had ruled as a bloody overlord for a time – a world he was meant to groom for his Fallen companions to raise a new Chapter of Space Marines. Here Astelan signals for Anovel to join him.

This trap works, luring Anovel to Tharsis, but the Fallen brings with him an ally in the form of Typhus, a powerful warlord of the Death Guard. Anovel's invasion is halted and Typhus's involvement forestalled, but not before Astelan is able to take advantage of the chaos of battle and escape the Dark Angels clutches.

A squadron of Black Knights from the Ravenwing are despatched to run down Astelan, and they pursue him to the ruins of his broken citadel. A fight ensues, during which Astelan is shot in the head and a previously unknown Space Marine reveals himself.

PART ONE
THARSIS

SURRENDER

'You may address me by my title,' said the Space Marine. 'Lord Cypher.'

Annael pushed himself to his feet, pain flaring from his wounded knee. 'Who?' he asked as Calatus moved forward to help him stand. Annael laid his hand on his battle-brother's shoulder and tentatively put some weight on the leg.

'I am the Lord Cypher. I am here to see your leaders.'

'You attacked us,' said Huntmaster Tybalain. His bolt pistol was still levelled at the stranger, a power sword in his other hand. He glanced at the unarmoured Space Marine lying at Annael's feet with half his head missing, and nodded to Nerean. 'Is he alive?'

Nerean crouched beside the traitor's corpse, but the stranger spoke first.

'He is dead. Not even one of our kind can survive a wound like that.'

Tybalain said nothing and looked at Nerean. The

Black Knight nodded his confirmation. 'Stone cold dead, brothers.'

Annael looked at the cadaver and then to the Space Marine that had saved his life. Any gratitude he felt was overwhelmed by suspicion at the Space Marine's unheralded appearance.

'We should call in a Dark Talon to take this one away,' he said, over the squad vox-frequency so as not to be heard by the captive. 'He is clearly one of the Fallen.'

'Why would he give up so easily?' asked Nerean. 'It is a trap of some kind, you can be sure of it.'

'He still has his sword,' said Annael. He studied the way the other Space Marine stood. There was an ease in his stance that betrayed a calm demeanour. He really did not seem at all concerned by his predicament, or else was able to disguise any misgivings. 'This situation is not to my liking at all.'

'Do you want to try to take the sword from him?' said Calatus. 'I fear we shall not do so without killing him, and the attempt would be costly all the same.'

'He certainly dealt with Astelan in swift fashion,' said Tybalain. 'I feel no strong urge to test his competence directly. The name Cypher does not mean anything to you, but it is known to me, in a way. It is a codeword amongst the Fallen, and if we hear it we are to inform our superior immediately.'

'Master Asmodai should learn of this first,' said Calatus. 'It was he that ordered Astelan to be executed. He will know what to do.'

None of the others voiced objection to this and Tybalain communicated what had happened to Chaplain Asmodai. While he did so, Annael kept a close watch on the prisoner. 'Lord Cypher' made no move, remaining as motionless as a statue. He did not even

THE UNFORGIVEN

react when Calatus retrieved the plasma pistol and bolt pistol the stranger had relinquished. Annael looked at the plasma pistol, not recognising the design.

'Old,' said Calatus, turning the weapon left and right. The craftsmanship was exquisite, even to Annael's untrained eye. 'Very old.'

'The Master of Repentance is not happy,' Tybalain reported. He switched to external address. 'We are to await the arrival of Master Asmodai here. You will not move or speak. If you attempt to escape you will be killed.'

Lord Cypher accepted this without a word or gesture, taking the Huntmaster's instruction literally. Annael recovered the bolt pistol that had been taken from him, ashamed that he had been disarmed so easily. The pain in his left knee had dulled, but the wound in his pride at being shot by his own weapon was still raw. He tried putting weight on the leg again to distract himself from his embarrassment and found that he was able to stand, although slightly crookedly. Nerean inspected the damage to Annael's helm and backpack from the traitor's second shot and pronounced that all was well. The bolt had done nothing more than cosmetic harm.

Forty-five minutes passed more or less in silence until the sound of engines grew louder outside the ruins of the Slaughterkeep. A few minutes later Chaplain Asmodai arrived, clad in his full black armour, face concealed behind his skull helm. The paint of his livery was heavily chipped, the exposed ceramite cracked in many places. Clearly the Master of Repentance had been involved in quite a clash.

The Chaplain marched past the assembled Black Knights and stood in front of the prisoner, staring at him for some time. The Fallen made no move of his own and said nothing.

'We are to believe this is Cypher?' Asmodai said eventually, his voice emitted from the external vocalisers of his helm so that the prisoner could also hear.

'My title is Lord Cypher.'

Asmodai whirled around, the blue-gleaming head of his crozius arcanum smashing into the side of the traitor's helm, sending up splinters of ceramite and knocking him to his knees.

'You are no lord!' spat Asmodai. 'You are scum! Filth! Traitor! You do not speak unless directly addressed.'

The stranger stayed down, head bowed, one hand on the ground to steady himself. Asmodai loomed over him, crozius at the ready, but the Fallen remained where he was and kept silent.

'Good, it seems I am understood.' Asmodai stepped back and started to pace, circling the Fallen, speaking aloud as much to himself as to the Black Knights. 'We are to believe that Cypher, architect of a hundred Fallen plots to destroy and dishonour us, is now in our hands. He has finally been caught, nigh minutes after another of his kind came into our custody.'

'Not caught, Brother-Chaplain,' said Tybalain. 'Surrendered. Delivered to us by his own act and admission.'

'You are correct, Huntmaster, the difference is important. As is the timing.' Asmodai stopped beside Cypher. 'Get up!'

The Fallen obeyed, slowly rising to his feet. He kept his hand deliberately away from his scabbarded weapon at all times, giving no sign of threat or even disobedience that the Chaplain could use as reason to inflict more punishment.

'Is it coincidence that you appeared here and now,

arch-traitor? Are we to accept that you have come before us by happenstance? Were you afraid that your accomplice would betray you first? Is that why you killed Astelan?'

'I did not,' said the Fallen.

'You did so, right in front of me.' Annael was incredulous at Cypher's denial. 'Do you call me a liar?'

'Nothing of the sort. I saved your life. I shot the traitor. But that is not Merir Astelan, at least not as I knew him.'

'Nonsense,' growled Asmodai. He knelt beside the corpse and rolled it over. Half of the Space Marine's head was missing, but his face was mostly intact. Asmodai rose quickly and retreated several steps. 'What devilry is this? What have you done with the real Astelan?'

'What?' Tybalain and the others looked at the body again. The Huntmaster shook his head. 'No, there must be some mistake. This is the target you sent us after. It has to be. We found his discarded armour a score of metres away.'

'The mistake was yours, Huntmaster.' Asmodai's voice was icy with scorn. 'You have failed me.'

'We followed the transponder signal you transmitted,' said Annael. 'It led us directly here, Master.'

'There was another signal,' said Asmodai. 'From orbit to the surface. Are you sure you detected no teleport code or energy wave?'

'Nothing, Brother-Chaplain,' Calatus said quickly. 'I scanned the area as soon as we arrived. There were no traces of any such energy expenditure.'

'Then he must still be here!' roared Asmodai. 'Split up! Search the ruins! I want that traitor captured!'

Asmodai remained to keep guard on Cypher while the Black Knights divided to form a search pattern through the remains of the Slaughterkeep. Calatus swept the area with the auspex and declared that there was no human-sized living being within a kilometre, but this did not satisfy the Chaplain.

'Every chamber and dungeon, I want you to look at it with your own eyes and tell me this place is empty. Astelan cannot have escaped.'

Despite Asmodai's insistence, and the confusion of the Black Knights as to how it might have happened, it transpired that Astelan had indeed eluded their clutches. When the squad reformed with the Chaplain the Master of Repentance was beyond irate.

'Where is he?' the Chaplain demanded, pointing his pistol into the face of Cypher. 'Tell me, or by the Emperor I will end your treacherous existence.'

'I do not know,' the Fallen said quietly. 'It has been a long time since I crossed paths with Merir Astelan, I know nothing of his current plans.'

'Then how is it that you happened to be here?' said Tybalain. 'Why did we find you in these ruins?'

'I detected the same incoming transmission that you did,' the Fallen said, obviously choosing his words with care. 'I thought it better that I approached you than you came upon me.'

'Which brings us back to why you have allowed us to capture you,' said Annael. 'What do you want?'

'I must speak with your leaders.' Cypher turned his full attention to Asmodai. 'It is imperative that I see the Supreme Grand Master. Anovel must be stopped.'

'Anovel?' Asmodai's voice was low and dangerous. 'You admit to knowing the traitor? He is aboard our ship and awaiting my attention.'

'He has been captured? Then perhaps all is not lost. We might yet prevent this disaster.'

'The traitor is ours now, his plans have come to naught,' Asmodai assured the Fallen. 'He cannot harm us any longer.'

'I hope you are right, I really do. We must avert this catastrophe.'

'Catastrophe? Disaster? You overestimate the reach of our foes.'

'You are blind to it, Chaplain Asmodai. Do not take lightly what I have to tell you. Your foes seek nothing less than the utter annihilation of the Dark Angels.'

REPERCUSSIONS

Cypher said nothing more as he was escorted at gunpoint to the Deathwing Land Raider Asmodai had requisitioned. Asmodai turned at the top of the boarding ramp and addressed the Black Knights.

'Forget the name of Cypher. Forget this misbegotten traitor and serve your Chapter well.' He uttered the keywords that would place this order into the subconscious of the Space Marines, a hypnotic command rigorously implanted during their earliest training, one that they would be unable to refuse or recall. *'Non memorianda est.* Speak nothing of this moment to another. Speak never of what transpired in the last two hours. Return to Grand Master Sammael and report for duty. Attend to your orders and fight well.'

Thus instructed, the Black Knights returned to their steeds and rode away.

Asmodai stepped into the Land Raider and saw that Cypher had seated himself close to the driver's compartment. He had already pulled down the bracing harness used during rapid assault to lock a Space Marine's armour in place. Asmodai sat opposite but remained unhindered, not wishing to restrict his movements in any way in the presence of the arch-traitor.

'If indeed you are Cypher, as you say,' he said out loud, completing the thought. 'This episode with Astelan is a reminder that your kind are as devious as serpents. What proof can you offer to verify your claim? Why should I not simply extract your repentance now and put a bolt into your head, as you did your accomplice?'

'He was not my accomplice,' the Fallen replied. 'I do not know how I can prove my claim. What evidence would you ever accept that comes from my lips?'

'There is nothing you can say that I will believe,' said Asmodai. He banged a fist against the bulkhead to signal to the driver. He felt a jolt as the Land Raider moved off a few seconds later, the hull trembling with the growl of powerful engines. 'You are falsehood incarnate, especially if you are who you claim to be.'

'So if I am the Lord…' The prisoner checked himself as Asmodai's hand strayed towards the haft of his crozius arcanum. 'If I am the person you know as Cypher, I can be believed even less than if I am not? That is a paradoxical situation, you realise? If I am lying, you do not believe me because it is false. If I am telling the truth, you do not believe because I am telling the truth. How do I defend myself against your accusations?'

'That is not my concern. It is yours. Believe me, your kind become very inventive beneath the caress of my Blades of Reason.'

'If I offer a verifiable truth, would that persuade you?'

'Truth is rarely objective in my experience, except by

its absence. I would save your breath. You will need it for when you scream for forgiveness.'

The stranger shook his head, whether in denial or disbelief it was unclear. After a few seconds he raised a hand, index finger jabbing towards Asmodai.

'Starfire,' said the Fallen.

'What was that?' Asmodai leaned forward. 'What did you say?'

'Starfire.'

'How do you know this word?' demanded the Interrogator-Chaplain, standing up. He swayed slightly as his armour compensated for the rocking motion of the Land Raider. 'What does it mean to you?'

'I am glad that I have your attention, Master Asmodai.' The Fallen lowered his hand. 'I know this word because, as I have already told you, I held the rank of Lord Cypher, a position of authority amongst the Order commanded by Lord Luther.'

'That name is a curse to my ears, even more than your title,' snapped Asmodai.

'I see that "starfire" is known to you, as I hoped. It was the command codeword that activated the orbital defence grid. Merir Astelan, the one you thought I had killed, uttered that word to open fire upon Lion El'Jonson.'

It was possible that the Fallen was lying to Asmodai and had learned of the word by some other means, but the Chaplain doubted it. 'Starfire' had been recorded in the annals of the Lion's sons as the last transmission detected from Caliban before the Fallen had opened fire on their primarch. Astelan's testimony had included as much during visits from Boreas and Asmodai. It seemed an odd secret to pass on the off-chance a Fallen might be captured.

Another matter made Asmodai believe the Fallen.

Although the Chaplain knew that his straightforward mind was incapable of the mental somersaults of Sapphon in being able to think like the traitors, for all that he tried Asmodai could not come up with a reason why a Fallen would pretend to be Cypher. More to the point, why the real Cypher would not attempt to hide his identity.

He activated the Land Raider's comms unit and initiated a transmission to orbit, where the *Penitent Warrior* and *Implacable Justice* strike cruisers were engaged with the enemy flotilla. He coded the signal to Brother Sapphon, the Master of Sanctity, foremost of the Chaplains. It took several minutes for Asmodai's superior to connect and the reply to arrive.

'Brother Asmodai, I thought that you would be returning to orbit to oversee the internment of Anovel.'

'Another matter, more pressing, has delayed me. Astelan has eluded the Black Knights. He is loose on the planet.'

There was no reply for some time. When he spoke, Sapphon was reserved.

'That is unfortunate, brother. I trust that you are organising the pursuit.'

'Alas not, much as I wish to. A third traitor has been apprehended.'

'A third? How many more of these wretches infest Tharsis?'

'We will discover that truth, among many others, when we interrogate the prisoners. The one I have in custody claims to be Cypher.'

Again there was a long pause as this information was absorbed.

'Cypher? You think you have captured the thrice-cursed?'

'I believe I have. However, Astelan cannot be allowed to escape. We must instigate an immediate blockade of the planet and task our Dark Talons and Nephilim to interdict any non-Chapter aircraft. He will not be able to get far, and will certainly not leave Tharsis.'

'You seem to have forgotten an important consideration, brother. We are currently fighting a traitor fleet and a sizeable ground force. We cannot spare neither strike cruiser nor our aircraft to hunt Astelan at this time.'

'I *have* to speak to your Chapter Master,' said Cypher, loud enough to be heard by Sapphon.

'Silence!' snarled Asmodai. 'You will not speak again.'

'Was that him? What does he claim to know that is so important?'

Asmodai turned back to Cypher.

'Answer swiftly, traitor.'

'An attack on your Chapter is imminent. Lord Azrael must be informed.'

'Empty words,' said Asmodai. 'You offer no shred of evidence to back up your claim. Standard protocol is that all statements by the Fallen are treated as false.'

'Can we afford to ignore him?' said Sapphon. 'This is an outlandish situation, there is nothing standard about events on Tharsis. I do not think we can risk being delayed by orthodoxy. Return to orbit as swiftly as possible with your captive, brother. We must discuss our plan of action with Belial and Sammael before we make any decision.'

'There is little to discuss. One of the Fallen remains at large on Tharsis. He must be captured.'

'I concur, brother. But we cannot overlook the importance of your prisoner, if he is who he claims to be. Securing him and returning him to the *Penitent Warrior* safely must be your priority. When we have him in a cell, we can focus our efforts on Astelan.'

'Very well, I shall take that as your command.'

Asmodai cut the link and sat back, watching Cypher. He studied the traitor's armour. It was painted black, like Asmodai's, but whereas the Chaplain's battleplate had a sheen of freshly applied enamel, Cypher's was matt from exposure, even grey in places. The Chaplain could also see small flecks of dark green paint. It seemed that Cypher was not above wearing the colours of both the Legion and the Chapter when it suited his purposes. There was a fine edge of golden trim around the knightly helm, the gilding copied on the rims of the shoulder pads but sparse from wear and damage.

The original decoration of the chest plastron had been removed, and in its place was a skeletal figure with arms outstretched across the breastplate. Skull designs adorned the knees and waistband, and links of chain hung like a belt across the traitor's lap.

A longsword hung from that chain, in a scabbard of black leather and steel, the pommel crimson and gold. There were strange tales surrounding that sword. Tales that Asmodai had heard from the lips of the Fallen and of his battle-brothers. Myth surrounded Cypher as much as the likes of the Lion and Luther, but here he was now, sat in front of the Master of Repentance as solid and real as anything.

Asmodai wondered what truths, what admissions, what myth-shattering confessions Cypher would make beneath the Blades of Reason. The Chaplain knew that all Fallen were equally despised in the eyes of the Emperor, but could not help feeling a touch of pride that Cypher had been brought to him. Almost as much as he dreamed of inflicting his excruciations upon the traitor Rhemell, Asmodai had desired to confront the thrice-cursed.

The traitor would be broken, his secrets revealed and his lies proven false. Asmodai would stand before him and offer him the chance to repent. He would break the Fallen's blade over his knee as the final stroke, the last proof that Cypher was less than nothing and all that remained was to save his soul with acceptance of his guilt.

'I would not,' said the Fallen as Asmodai's gaze returned to the sword.

'You give me orders now?'

The Chaplain stood up and reached out towards the hilt of the blade.

'A warning, not a command,' said Cypher. 'It does not suffer the touch of any. None except its true keeper.'

'It is a weapon, nothing more.'

Asmodai closed gauntleted fingers around the hilt.

Fire burned the sky and the ground fell away beneath his feet. Pain lanced through his body and he saw a snarling face, so close his foe's foetid breath could be felt. They tumbled together, falling from the heavens it seemed. There was a blade in his gut, burning like poison. His own sword fell from his fingers. The pain increased, surging into his head, blinding and terrible.

Asmodai staggered back as he let go of the sword. He had to steady himself against the bulkhead, blinking away the after-effects of the vision.

'Perhaps you should start to heed my words,' said Cypher. 'Not just on the sword.'

Still shocked by what had happened, Asmodai retreated to the bench and sat down. His normal desire to assert control and superiority was overwhelmed by the sense of dislocation that left his thoughts reeling.

The experience had been so visceral, unlike anything he had experienced before. More than a memory, he had lived the moment captured within the vision and for those few seconds he had not known himself.

The memory of what he had seen started to fade, like a dream. Like all Space Marines he had been trained to have near-perfect recall, but just a minute after touching the sword all he could remember was a feeling of betrayal and helplessness. That and the pain. Unconsciously he moved a hand to his midriff, where it was as though a scar was healing beneath his abdominal armour. After another minute, even this sensation had passed.

'Time until rendezvous point?' he demanded of the Land Raider's driver, seeking to steady himself with the physical and mundane.

'Seven minutes, Master Chaplain,' the driver replied.

Asmodai accepted this answer without comment. He looked at Cypher and felt something totally alien. The Fallen always filled him with distaste, with hate, with a desire to avenge the wrongs done to the Lion and the Dark Angels. The loathing was there in Asmodai's gut, seething, wanting to be released, but for the first time since he had ascended to the Chapter another feeling kept the hate in check.

Where Cypher passed, anarchy and war followed. That he would come to the Dark Angels now was a grim harbinger. As he looked at Cypher – for surely the prisoner had to be Cypher and no other – Asmodai could not shake a sense of foreboding.

ARMOURER OF THE SOUL

Sapphon spent some time considering recent events, leaving command of the *Penitent Warrior* to Belial, who had interred Anovel in one of the cells on the dungeon deck of the strike cruiser. The Chaplain retired to the Reclusiam to gather his thoughts, too distracted by the ongoing battle to think clearly while on the command bridge.

The Reclusiam was a high-vaulted chamber on the deck above the dormers of the battle-brothers, located close to the armoury where their suits of Tactical Dreadnought armour were stowed when in transit. It brought a smile to Sapphon to think of the similarities between this chamber and the one a little further along the deck.

In the armoury the Techmarines clad the bodies of the First Company in adamantium, plasteel and ceramite. They loaded and primed their weapons and applied the unguents and blessings of their arcane order so that the machine-spirits of the Terminator war-plate would serve the warriors of the Chapter. In the Reclusiam the Chaplains armoured the souls of their charges with oaths of dedication to the Emperor, and fired their resolve with legends of the Lion's victories and ultimate sacrifice. Just as the Techmarines maintained and repaired the armour that protected the Space Marines, Sapphon and his Brother-Chaplains kept vigilant for damage to the spirit and imperfections in the shield of faith that guarded their minds.

The armourers repainted the bone-coloured enamel of the Deathwing, setting upon it the sigils and markings of Chapter, company, squad and individual warrior. They covered up the burns, scratches and other marks of war, eliminating the scars of history. The Chaplains did no less for the minds of their charges, smoothing away questions that could not be answered, recounting tales that explained away inconsistencies of history, painting over discrepancies and concerns with devotions of loyalty and duty.

And most importantly of all, the Reclusiam was the chamber from which the desires of the Inner Circle were enacted. It was here that the various versions of the Chapter's history were related to the brothers according to their need, rank and experience. From the censers that hung from the ceiling drifted the psychoactive vapours that opened up the hypno-conditioned minds of the Dark Angels, allowing Sapphon to instil the doctrines of faith and remove unworthy doubts and troublesome memories.

Even the First Company, the Deathwing, whose battle-brothers had earned great renown and trust, were subject to such manipulation. Though they had been initiated into the most fundamental secrets of the Fallen – the existence of renegade Dark Angels and the treachery of Luther that had created them – only Belial and a handful of veteran sergeants in the company knew of the corrupting force of Chaos that had turned them, and the identity of the arch-heretics, Luther's lieutenants such as Merir Astelan, Zahariel El'Zurias and the ringleader known only by the title of Lord Cypher.

That Cypher had reappeared now, openly allowing himself to be captured, troubled Sapphon greatly. This fact, the manner of Cypher's capture, weighed heavily on his thoughts as he paced down the aisle between the long devotional benches on which the company sat for benedictions and pre-battle mass. A red carpet underfoot muffled his armoured steps, leaving only the hiss of electric lights and the ever-present rumbling of the engines to break the still of the chamber.

Overhead hung banners embroidered by the Librarium's serfs, the histiographers cataloguing the many battle honours of the Deathwing from the formation of the Dark Angels Chapter to the present day. Two hundred and three banners in black bordered by red, white stitching listing the names of more than nine thousand worlds, space stations, ships, moons and space hulks where the First Company had been victorious, some of them multiple times. In the gloom the writing was barely legible, but it mattered not, Sapphon could recite every single name from memory. He also knew the two thousand, six hundred and forty-eight Righteous Honours omitted from the roll of honour. Actions that had been centred solely on the capture of the Fallen, undertaken by the Deathwing alone.

Three names to be considered for addition to the list:

Tharsis, Ulthor and Piscina. Were these victories? Were they Righteous Honours? Ulthor was easy to discard. It had been a disaster from the instant the company had teleported onto the daemon world. Farce was almost too kind as a description of what had followed. Extricating the company, along with the Ravenwing, could be considered an achievement, but certainly not a battle honour.

Piscina was undecided. Sapphon did not know how the campaign continued in their absence, if at all. Grand Master Belial had petitioned Azrael to declare the world lost and wipe out everything on the surface with Exterminatus, but the Supreme Grand Master had withheld judgement. The expedition to Ulthor had taken Belial and his company away from the theatre of war.

Tharsis was surely worthy. A sizeable fleet and army of renegades had been eradicated, or would be within the next few hours. That those traitors had been lured into attacking Tharsis by the machinations of Sapphon did not undermine the achievement of the warriors in the strike force. It also mattered not to the Master of Sanctity that Astelan had escaped. His recapture was inevitable, even if he had an entire world on which to hide. His was a spent fate. Asmodai would be allowed to administer the final act. Two other Fallen had been captured, including Cypher.

Always there was Cypher, Sapphon's thoughts rapidly coming full circle from their wandering as he knelt in front of the altar. The table was covered with another banner, much tattered and faded, the edges ragged from fire, lasbeams and detonation.

The first battle standard of the Deathwing.

Other Chapters might have suspended such a relic

in a stasis field, preserving it for eternity. Not so the Dark Angels. Their history, as obscured as it was by circles of trust and mistruth, was carried beside them. In the presence of this artefact the warriors of the First Company swore and renewed their oaths, just as the first members of the Deathwing had done ten millennia before. To touch the cloth, to smell the ancient must from its fibres, was to connect with every warrior that had donned the bone armour and tabard of the Deathwing for the last ten thousand years. The stories changed, as did those that told them and heard them, but the inner truths remained constant. The banner served as a reminder to every member of the First Company that they upheld a sacred duty unbroken since the dawn of the Imperium.

Sapphon reached out a gauntleted hand and gently stroked the winged sword icon emblazoned on the standard. It had been dark red once, on a field of black. Now it was a dull orange on a grey background. The colours had faded, but not the glory woven into the fabric as much as the sigil.

A glorious legend. And a second, hidden history no less important.

Looking at the relic banner, Sapphon realised what had to be done, but it was not a decision he could take alone.

'Bridge, this is Master Sapphon. I need a priority coded vox-conclave. Contact Masters Asmodai, Belial and Sammael for immediate exchange.'

'Understood, Master Sapphon. Creating coded conclave for you now. I will inform you when the other Masters have responded.'

Sapphon stood and moved past the altar, eyes passing over the antiquities placed upon the banner cloth.

A goblet it was claimed the Lion had drunk from on his final night on Caliban. A fragment of bone, said to be from a beast of the forests slain at the hand of the primarch's seneschal, Corswain. A shard of crystal-laced metal from the power sword of Grand Master Haradin, who had reformed the Deathwing following the catastrophic events that had seen Caliban destroyed.

Pieces of ancient history, reminders of legacies far greater than a few sacred ornaments. Sapphon had sometimes wondered why the Chapter set such stock by these odds and ends from the distant past, an affectation of remembrance. He understood now. These relics had been present at the beginning, setting in motion a continuum of events that covered the whole arc of the Age of the Imperium, right up to that day, that hour, that minute. All things, every victory, defeat and decision in the last ten thousand years, by Supreme Grand Masters, Librarians, Chaplains, battle-brothers and even serfs, had steered the Dark Angels upon a troublesome course to the present time.

Caught in the glare of this realisation, Sapphon concluded that the past and the present, his forebears and his peers, would not be his judge. Those that came after, those that would inherit the Chapter he left behind, would decide on the right and wrong of his actions.

Had the Lion thought such a thing when he had lifted that silver goblet to his lips, knowing that the coming dawn would see him leave Caliban to join the Great Crusade, perhaps never to return? Had Corswain known when he slew the tainted monster of Caliban's forest that his name would reverberate for ten millennia, his deeds an inspiration to generation after generation of Dark Angels? When Haradin had learned of the existence of the Fallen and instigated the reformation of the Deathwing and Ravenwing, had he considered the possibility that their task would still be continued ten thousand years later?

All grand decisions and actions that had defined the Legion and Chapter ever since, their consequences ultimately unknowable.

The capture of Cypher changed everything. The foiling of the plot between Anovel, Methelas and Astelan was a significant moment also. Decisions made now could frame the Hunt for the Fallen for a century or a millennium.

'Master Sapphon, the coded conclave is active.'

The Master of Sanctity passed through the curtained archway behind the altar and into the smaller chamber beyond. There was a stout desk within, and around the walls many shelves bowed under the weight of books and scrolls. The entirety of the Lore of the Dark Angels, assembled over ten thousand years, starting with treatises from Roboute Guilliman's Codex Astartes on the reorganisation of the Legiones Astartes, to Supreme Grand Master Azrael's interpretations and edicts on the *Tactica Imperium*. Ten millennia of wisdom and battle-rites crowded Sapphon as he accepted the transmission from the strike cruiser's bridge.

'Brother-masters, gratitude for your swift attention.'

'Swiftness is desirable, brother,' replied Sammael. 'I am embarking upon what might be the final offensive of this campaign. This conclave is a distraction from my preparations.'

'One that you will doubtless understand, Brother Sammael, when I tell you that Master Asmodai has captured the accursed fugitive known as Cypher.'

Silence greeted this announcement. Sapphon

remembered his own stunned reaction when he had received the news from Asmodai. He also recalled the questions that had followed as he had comprehended the nature of the revelation and spoke to address them before the others wasted breath giving voice.

'Brother Asmodai is convinced that his prisoner is Cypher, and so I am convinced, as you should be. He is currently stasis-incarcerated and being transported back to the *Penitent Warrior* with Asmodai as escort. He will be placed into further stasis when he arrives. It is absolutely imperative that he comes into contact with no one that has not already seen him.'

'I have instructed Brother Malcifer of the Second Company,' added Asmodai. 'The Black Knights that discovered Cypher and allowed Astelan to escape will be suitably debriefed and if necessary quarantined upon their return.'

'What does that mean?' demanded Sammael. 'Tybalain responded to your orders. He has done nothing wrong.'

'I made no accusation of improper conduct,' answered the Master of Repentance. 'The knowledge of Cypher's presence must be closely contained, as Brother Sapphon attests. To this purpose, Tybalain and his warriors must be sequestered from their battle-brothers. I am confident Malcifer can accommodate this without remark or incident.'

'Astelan has escaped.' Belial's statement was quietly spoken but loaded with a cutting edge. 'This is a grave failure by the Second Company.'

'A terrible consequence of planning and opportunism,' Sapphon said quickly, before Sammael responded to the barbed comment.

'Brought about by your entanglements with Astelan,'

continued Belial. 'I take no pleasure in acknowledging that I warned against this ill-devised endeavour.'

'A matter that you can bring up with the Supreme Grand Master,' said Sapphon.

Asmodai had been in the chamber last, the objects on the table as ordered and regimented as his thoughts. The Master of Sanctity absent-mindedly moved a few things, rearranging the autoquills and piles of datacrystal wafers into a fan pattern. Belial's condemnation did not concern him. Once Azrael was made aware of all the circumstances of the operation he would acquit Sapphon of any misdemeanours. To do otherwise would undermine Sapphon's position and give Asmodai tacit free rein to impose his divisive policies on the Inner Circle and the rest of the Chapter.

'Or perhaps a matter that I will seek to settle personally,' continued Belial, 'in a duel upon our return to the Tower of Angels.'

Sapphon stopped his toying, the Grand Master's threat disturbing. 'By rite, such an event would be held in view of the Chapter. How would we explain the rift between two senior officers? No. It is not possible. It would compromise the sanctity of the Hunt. I forbid any challenge being issued on this subject and will censure any of you that seek such recourse.'

'We stray from the purpose of this conclave,' Sammael interjected. 'If you wish to test authority or blade with each other, please do so without my involvement. Our assault will launch in twenty-seven minutes and there remain many preparations to undertake. The Tharsians are assembling and awaiting my command. Is there any further matter that requires my attention?'

'Our involvement is no longer required,' said Asmodai. 'The longer we remain on Tharsis, the more precarious our hold on the details of this expedition. Our presence will prompt questions not easily answered, and we must not forget that a sizeable traitor fleet remains in the system, even if they appear to be withdrawing.'

'We cannot abandon Tharsis,' Belial replied. 'We will not.'

'We cannot save every world, brother,' said Sapphon. 'The Hunt, this prisoner, must take priority over all other concerns.'

'This world has been placed in jeopardy by your actions, Sapphon. We drew the renegades to this system. We ignited the fire of war, and it falls to us to douse it before we depart.'

'I concur with Brother Sapphon,' said Asmodai. 'We have courted disaster too many times on this campaign. Our surest course of action must be to secure the two Fallen we have in custody and return to the Tower of Angels for their interrogation.'

'They pose no threat,' argued Sammael. 'We must remain as long as required to deter the traitor legionaries of the second fleet. The moment they sense that we are leaving, they will surely return.'

'It is not our two strike cruisers that dissuade their assault,' Sapphon replied tersely. 'They came to Tharsis expecting welcome. They find themselves faced with a fully operational orbital defence system. Whatever prize they sought here, they hoped to obtain through the blood of Anovel and his followers, not their own. They will not be returning.'

'And Astelan?' said Belial. 'You cannot truly believe it is wise to leave him loose on the world he once brought to the brink of ruin with his tyranny?'

'We can learn nothing from him, and the pursuit would continue to expose us.'

'I detest the notion that we would knowingly allow any of the Fallen to escape, but I agree,' said Asmodai, to Sapphon's surprise. 'Cypher's excruciation and repentance, the secrets he will reveal to us, will be an unparalleled achievement for the Chapter. The future success of the Hunt may rest on his testimony.'

'We cannot ignore his claim that there exists a direct threat to the Chapter. We have not yet fully uncovered the extent of the plan we thwarted today. There will be further repercussions and we must consult with the rest of the Inner Circle,' Sapphon replied.

'Your hearing appears to be hampered, brothers,' said Belial, more forcefully than Sapphon had heard in many years. 'I *will not* leave Tharsis to an uncertain fate. Too often in these past months we have vacillated, compromised and allowed ourselves to be blinded to certain truths. The Deathwing will conclude the battle, alone if necessary, to ensure Tharsis's continued prosperity.'

Unseen by the others, Sapphon shook his head, angered by Belial's defiance. It was unlike the Deathwing commander to gainsay the desires of the Chaplains. Now was the most inopportune time for him to declare he served a higher calling.

'The Ravenwing will also not shirk the fight ahead,' said Sammael. 'We have lost brothers whose memory and sacrifice should be honoured with laurels of victory, not hidden in the dusty chronicles of the Inner Circle. Master Belial is right, there are clear foes to destroy and a war to be won. This is the reason for which we were created.'

'Your reticence is noted, brothers,' said Asmodai.

'As is your attempted disregard for the protocols of command, Master of Repentance,' Belial replied with a growl in his voice. 'The First and Second Companies answer to us, not the denizens of the Reclusiam. I would expect such behaviour from Sapphon, but I am disappointed in you, Asmodai. I thought you would desire the prosecution of the enemy.'

'There is no greater priority than the Hunt, Master of the Deathwing,' Asmodai spat back. 'Your disappointment is a burden for you to carry, it is as nothing to me.'

'Let us not end with dissent, brothers,' said Sammael. 'We all wish swift conclusion to this campaign, which has taxed mettle and courage equally. Night will bring victory, I am sure. Let us see what fresh insight the dawn heralds.'

There was a chorus of agreement, reluctant from Sapphon, a single grunt of assent from Asmodai. One by one they broke the vox-link, leaving Sapphon in quiet reflection.

THE CAPTIVE

If he looked to his left, to the north, Annael could just make out the armoured column. Tanks and personnel carriers painted in muted brown and green camouflage flew Tharsian pennants from their aerials. They followed the arrow-straight highway into the wilderness, hidden from view by the hills and undulations of the countryside.

Most of the traitor invaders had been hunted down, but there were still pockets of resistance, some very well armed and consisting of the chemically-boosted and cybernetically enhanced soldiers that had led the attack on Tharsis. Tybalain and his Black Knights were acting as outriders for the tank column heading towards a concentration of enemies that had taken over a town a dozen kilometres north of the capital.

Annael flanked the advance to the east with Calatus, while Tybalain and Nerean patrolled to the west. Land Speeders in the black of the Ravenwing scouted ahead, seeking possible ambushes. So far there had been only the odd straggler, easily dealt with, but Annael remained alert.

'Nowhere to run to, no chance of surrendering, these rebels will fight to the last, mark my words,' said Calatus, riding a hundred metres ahead of Annael. 'What have they got to live for?'

'Not all soldiers have such purpose,' said Annael. 'I discussed as much with Sabrael, back on Port Imperial. That was when his disobedience almost got me killed, but I would gladly accept that sacrifice now if it would return him to the company.'

'You would rather be dead and Sabrael alive?' Calatus slowed slightly, allowing Annael to catch up. 'He abandoned you, brother, and you know he would not wish the same.'

'I think you are wrong. The events on Thyestes changed him. Sobered his mood a little.'

'Too little. He still disobeyed Tybalain's command and paid for his infraction with his life.'

'Perhaps he was right to attack. Did he not embody the spirit of the Ravenwing more than any of us?'

'He was foolhardy and self-interested, traits that belong in no Space Marine.'

'But as a bladesman and a rider, he excelled. A far better warrior than I, his loss would be counted the greater of the two of us.'

'Not by me,' insisted Calatus. 'You ride by my side and I trust that you will guard my back as a battle-brother is supposed to. Sabrael was unreliable, and that makes him a lesser warrior in my eyes.'

Their discussion was curtailed by the sight of a group of buildings ahead, flanking the highway. Huntmaster Tybalain called the Black Knights together and sent word to the armoured column to halt until the small settlement had been investigated.

'*Sable Hunter, Swiftclaw*, keep your distance,' Tybalain transmitted to the pair of Land Speeders. 'Encircle and recon, do not engage unless attacked.'

The gunners of the anti-grav speeders signalled their affirmatives and swept onwards. Under the guidance of their drivers, the Land Speeders peeled apart three hundred metres from the settlement to conduct their scans from opposite flanks. Tybalain raised a fist and gestured for the Black Knights to split to a fifty-metre spread, advancing slowly while the Land Speeders conducted their sweep.

The auspex of Annael's steed, *Black Shadow*, showed around two dozen buildings. The site appeared to be a marshalling yard of sorts, two slipways from the main highway running down ramps into a group of warehouses and living quarters. A small air-dock stood three hundred metres from the road, a cargo-lifter still on the elevated apron. High cranes crisscrossed the entire site thirty metres above.

'Lookouts on the gantries,' reported Brother Casamir, pilot of the *Swiftclaw*. 'Possibly marksmen, no weapons visible yet.'

On Annael's display three red runes blinked into existence, highlighted through the linked telemetry of the Ravenwing vehicles. He looked up at the cab of the nearest crane and focused. His helm's auto-senses took over from his natural sight and magnified the view directly into his optic nerve.

There was a man hunkered down in the cab. Sunlight glinted on glass as he swept his magnoculars after one of the Land Speeders. He appeared to be wearing some kind of facemask, but as the resolution of the auto-senses improved Annael saw that the whiteness was pale, dead skin, the tangle of pipes he had taken to be a respirator dangling directly from the lookout's flesh.

'Augmetics and bionics,' he reported. 'Definitely enemy.'

'Heat traces indicate thirty-plus more targets within the buildings,' said Brother Teraphiel on the *Sable Hunter*.

'Pull back! Pull back!' To the east, the *Swiftclaw* rose rapidly, its anti-grav engines propelling it backwards so that Casamir's gunner could keep the heavy bolter and chin-mounted assault cannon pointing at the enemy. 'Heavy weapons spotted. Missile launchers and some kind of bipod-mounted projectile weapon.'

To the west the *Sable Hunter* also backed away, the missile pods of its Typhoon launchers directed towards the marshalling yard.

'I'm detecting a short-range transmission,' said Nerean. 'Origin point somewhere in those buildings.'

'I have it too,' said Annael, noticing a spike on the radio reception monitor of *Black Shadow*'s display. He tuned his vox in to the frequency.

'...and we will not hesitate in killing him.' The voice was distorted but of a register that made it plain the speaker was a woman. 'You hear me, dogs of the Lion? We have one of your ill-fated sons and we will kill him if you do not withdraw. I am Neira Kamata, the new commander of the Divine Army. The misbegotten Dark Angels have one hour to withdraw their forces from our world or we will slay the hostage. Do not underestimate...'

Annael's vox switched back to the squad channel on an override from Tybalain.

'A lie, I am sure,' said the Huntmaster. 'A desperate lie.'

'What do we do?' asked Teraphiel as the *Sable Hunter* circled the highway, moving out in a spiral to join with the *Swiftclaw*. 'It's an outrageous claim if they are bluffing. They have to know we can verify the status of every battle-brother.'

'It matters not if it is truth or bluff,' declared Tybalain. 'We will teach these traitors that this is a war, not a barter. They cannot negotiate their way out of chastisement.'

'So, we attack?' said Calatus.

'We attack,' replied Tybalain. 'Sword Four, are you receiving?'

'Affirmative, Huntmaster. We are on support stand-by. Do you require a strike?'

'Transmitting coordinates. Designating target Alpha. Full authority strike on Alpha.'

'Data received. Incoming to target. Three minutes until strike.'

Tybalain signalled for them to stop and Annael turned to look south-east, where he knew the Dark Talon fighter assigned to the escort had been patrolling, ready for the strike command. He could see nothing but low cloud for two minutes and then a black speck appeared, quickly resolving into a stub-nosed craft with reverse delta wings. The Dark Talon stooped out of the cloud like a striking hawk, nose aimed at the group of buildings.

'Full attack, follow me!' cried Tybalain as Sword Four swept in on its run. 'Terminate all targets. *Sable Hunter*, *Swiftclaw*, opportunity strike, all targets.'

The Ravenwing picked up speed, their heavy bikes making easy work of the relatively smooth ground that flanked the highway. To their left and right the Land Speeders accelerated past, gaining height. The Dark Talon, just two hundred metres up, soared overhead. The rift cannon in its nose crackled and a sphere of warp energy erupted within the buildings ahead, turning the metal legs of a crane into a crumpled mass. The machine toppled sideways and crashed onto the broad roof of a warehouse, smashing through ferrocrete tiles.

The Typhoon launcher of the *Sable Hunter* belched fire and smoke. A ripple of missiles streaked towards the marshalling yard. Detonations engulfed the closest building, punching through the thin walls and turning the metal roof to slag. The assault cannon and heavy bolters of the *Swiftclaw* spewed fire into the crane cabs, taking out the marksmen stationed there.

Another rift cannon detonation imploded the upper floors of a four-storey habitation block on the road to the landing pad. Sword Four sped over the collapsing building, a dark shape detaching from its hull. The aircraft banked away as the stasis bomb erupted a few metres above the ground, engulfing the centre of the complex in a shimmering time-dampened field.

'I want the leader alive if possible,' snarled Tybalain as the Black Knights hit the highway. 'We will teach Neira Kamata the folly of threatening the Sons of the Lion.'

Following the Huntmaster they skidded onto the roadway ramp down into the eastern portion of the marshalling yard, the plasma talons of their steeds firing bursts of miniature stars into the administration block directly ahead of them. The Land Speeders swept overhead and dived down into the crisscross of ferrocrete and buildings of the western district, their progress heralded by missile detonations, the thrum of heavy bolter fire and assault cannon rounds.

A yellow and black barrier straddled the road ahead but Tybalain did not slow. He rode straight through it. Reaching level ground, the Huntmaster peeled down a wide road to the left with Nerean, signalling for Annael and Calatus to continue straight ahead.

The bubble of stasis energy was shrinking, the crackling globe a few dozen metres in front of Annael, almost out of sight behind the buildings. Sword Four had entered hover mode and was strafing left and right, its hurricane bolters unleashing a torrent of fire into the upper storeys of the surrounding hab-blocks.

Las-fire flickered down at the pair of Black Knights from a window in the second floor of a warehouse thirty metres ahead. The purple beams flared from the armour of *Black Shadow*, leaving welts in the paint but no significant damage.

Annael turned his steed towards the huge doors of the depot and opened fire, blasting a hole in the metal with the bike's plasma talon. A second plasma ball from Calatus made the gap wide enough for the two to ride directly into the main floor of the building. Just as he plunged into the dark within, Annael drew his bolt pistol, riding one-handed through the gap.

The ground floor was filled with cargo containers, each ten metres long, three metres high and three wide. Most were stacked in rows, a broad concourse down the middle, but a few had been left strewn haphazardly, apparently dumped as the facility was being evacuated.

There were figures on top of the container rows, the glint of metal exoskeletons giving them away as they bounded from one stack to the next. Annael lifted his pistol and fired, a salvo of three bolts taking down an augmented soldier on the closest pile. Las-fire replied, bright beams that slashed down to either side of him.

'Divide and conquer, brother,' said Calatus, slowing to steer his steed down one of the rows while Annael continued up the main aisle.

Annael fired the plasma talon again, targeting the distant container stacks. The ball of energy smashed into the uppermost container, throwing it into the air in a cloud of twisted shrapnel and molten drops. More las-fire converged on the Ravenwing rider, striking his armour and bike. He turned in the saddle and fired his pistol at the enemy behind him, felling two more, but there were at least another ten sheltering on the high stacks.

It was time to take a different approach. Accelerating, Annael sped to the end of the artificial causeway, slewing past the abandoned containers in his path. He braked heavily and skidded about at the end, facing the way he had come.

'Sword Four, lock hurricane system to my beacon. Fire for full effect.'

'Please confirm, brother. You wish me to fire on your position?'

'Confirmed! Open fire now!'

Annael gunned the engine and released the clutch, *Black Shadow* leaping forward like a stallion given full spurs. A second later the metal roof of the warehouse erupted into shards while bolt detonations sparked across the tops of the container stacks. Light poured into the gloom through dozens of holes as Annael accelerated, the fire of the Dark Talon tearing into the warehouse from above, tracking his position. As he powered down the depot, the fusillade ripped along behind him, cutting through the warriors taking cover on the containers.

The tyres shrieked and billowed smoke as Annael braked hard, taking the end of the container row at speed; heeling his bike over hard, fighting handlebars that juddered in his grasp, threatening to throw him off. The hurricane bolter salvo from above followed unerringly, a few rounds sparking from the floor behind as he accelerated again, the rest returning as a storm of small explosions along the container piles as Annael gained speed once more.

'Cease fire, Sword Four. Cease fire!' he signalled as he reached the far end of the warehouse again.

A second passed, the last few rounds detonating just a couple of metres away, and then the torrent of bolts stopped. The *crack* of Calatus's bolt pistol sounded strangely tinny and distant in the quiet that fell. Annael looked at his steed's sensor display. He noted seventeen rapidly-cooling signals from those that had been slain. There were still several more active heat returns on the mezzanine level around the warehouse walls, skulking in offices and rest dormitories.

Annael guided *Black Shadow* to a set of open metal steps leading up to the second floor. He was about to dismount when a vox-transmission stopped him.

'We have an armoured vehicle, breaking south-west at speed,' reported Casamir. 'Half-track, transport, turreted heavy weapon.'

'Black Knights, break off for pursuit, target Beta.' Tybalain's orders were issued in a quick but calm manner. 'Land Speeders, Sword Four, continued suppression and eradication of enemy at target Alpha.'

'Affirmative, pursuing target Beta,' said Annael, moving off towards the street. He was already reaching seventy kilometres an hour by the time he burst back out of the warehouse onto the rockcrete street, Calatus just a few metres behind.

KNIGHTS OF THE FIRST COMPANY

His mood soured by the exchange during the conclave, Belial said little as his Deathwing Knights assembled around him on the teleportarium. The five veterans, the very best of the Dark Angels, elite even amongst the Deathwing, knew the Grand Master well enough to remain silent in his presence. Each wore the Tactical Dreadnought armour for which the Deathwing were famed, immense suits of war-plate that dwarfed even their battle-brothers. Over their ivory armour they wore surcoats in the green of the Chapter colours, edged with silver and gold thread.

Unlike the other warriors of the Deathwing, the Knights of the Lion eschewed ranged weapons. Instead they carried heavy maces, the heads adorned with spikes and pierced to allow a vaporous energy to escape from within, causing a pall of greenish smog to follow them. Their master, Zandorael, wielded a flail with three chains, each ending in a censer-like globe that shimmered with a disruption field. Every warrior bore a large shield embossed with the image of the winged angel of absolution, the faint aura of its protective field causing a shimmer across the surface.

Each of the Knights also wore various talismans from the belts of their tabards – keys, eagles, skulls and the like. To most they would seem like simple ornaments, but to one that looked upon them with the eye of the Inner Circle, each told a story of the Knights' achievements in the Hunt and the secrets to which they were privy. Combined with their heraldry on greaves and knee plates, and the extra designs embroidered onto their tabards, these symbols charted the entire life of each warrior and the assorted enclaves within the Chapter to which he belonged.

The Knights of the Lion lifted their weapons in salute as Belial stepped in front of the squad and turned to address them. The ship shuddered for several seconds as the port gun decks opened fire, hurling thousands of tonnes of ordnance at the cruiser that had served as Anovel's flagship. The air was thick with invisible energy, static build-up from the void shield generators running at capacity to withstand the return fire.

'We have seized that which brought us to Tharsis,' the Grand Master declared. 'The traitor is incarcerated and our primary mission fulfilled. An essential but secretive work to be undertaken. Before us stands a nobler task for the warriors of the Lion. It has fallen to us to prosecute the war in orbit while the Ravenwing continue to convey our might on the surface.'

Belial rested his hand on the pommel of the Sword of Silence at his waist. He held his storm bolter in his other fist, the weight of the bulky weapon nothing compared to the strength of the fibre bundles within his armour.

'We are manoeuvring alongside the enemy: one Master Sapphon and Squad Caulderain dealt a blow to, but the foe is not vanquished. We shall be the first strike, aimed at the foe's heart, the ship's reactors. Several other squads are following in our wake, to target weapons batteries and support systems. We cannot destroy a starship alone, but we will leave it crippled, vulnerable to the gun decks of the *Penitent Warrior*. An ideal killing ground for the Deathwing, close confines and deadly melee. My Knights of the Lion, are you ready?'

'For the Lion!' The shout roared from five external address systems. Weapons were hoisted in time to the battle cry. 'For the Emperor!'

Belial was heartened, his sombre thoughts buoyed by the quality of the warriors accompanying him. There were none that could ever match his expectations of perfection, not even himself, but the Deathwing Knights came close to such high measure. The mission at hand was uncomplicated, the gauge of victory simple. It felt good to lead his company into battle, a defiant enemy to slay before him, the finest of the Deathwing at his back.

Inside his helm, he allowed himself a rare smile.

'With me, brothers,' he said, turning and marching onto the closest marblesque plate of the teleporter ring. The teleportation machine aboard the strike cruiser was far less powerful than the systems of the Rock, so only two squads at a time could be transported to their target. Belial had devised a plan of assault that would ensure that the enemy's void shields would be down for long enough for thirty warriors to launch the attack.

As a reminder that the enemy would not willingly

submit to such a fate, the *Penitent Warrior* shook and the lights in the chamber flickered dimly for several seconds. On the deck a hull breach siren wailed. Belial's vox came alive with chatter as the damage was assessed. He blotted out the distraction, checked that his Knights were in place.

'Activating sensorium interface,' he told them, sending the signal.

His view fractured for several seconds as the autosense feeds from the rest of the squad were assimilated by the machine-spirit of his armour. His vision coalesced again as an amalgam image, pieced together from the intelligence gathered by the warsuits of his brothers. Even after years of experience with Terminator armour, Belial still felt slightly nauseated when the sensorium activated, as did everyone.

If he was to describe it, Belial would have said it was like having five additional pairs of eyes whose view changed as his companions moved, alongside five extra pairs of ears that created a soundscape so sharp he could navigate blind without hindrance. He was unconsciously aware of where the Deathwing Knights were in relation to his position and each other, just as natural kinaesthesia told him if he had an arm raised or his fingers curled.

The centre of his sight was focused on his direct autosenses input – what he would normally see. Around the edges were vaguer images from the other Deathwing Terminators, melding together to give a multidimensional view of the area around him. With a sub-vocal command, he swapped the dominant image with that projected by Cragarion's armour. The view blinked out and was replaced by a similar outlook, three metres to his left. He turned his head left, but the view remained unchanged except in the small sub-vision on the top-right periphery of his vision.

'Brother Cragarion, composite test.'

The Deathwing Knight complied, turning his helm towards Belial. The Grand Master looked at himself from the side and slightly behind. He pulled free the Sword of Silence and held it aloft, seeing the smooth action from Cragarion's perspective.

'Auto-sense systems integration check positive.' He told his armour to revert the view to normal. *'Bellum machina dominatus positivia. Gratuis armorium et Adeptus Mechanicus.* Commencing augury data merge.'

Each armoured suit also contained a scanning array the equal of any hand-held or vehicle-based device employed by the other battle-brothers of the Chapter. On activation, the Tactical Dreadnought armour bathed its surroundings with thermal, motion, pressure, electromagnetic and sound detectors above and beyond the inputs from the auto-senses. This was the third and greatest use of the sensorium suite, so that any enemy within a three-hundred-metre radius could be detected, extending up to a kilometre if the members of the squad were separated.

It had been unfortunate that the sensorium had been excessively burdened by the warp-reality overlap on Ulthor. Had his company been functioning at full capacity, Belial had no doubt they would have taken the daemonic fortress and avoided the costly and shameful retreat that followed. He had already written an exhaustive report on the matter to be given to the Techmarines when the expedition returned to the Rock.

'All systems configured,' the Grand Master announced. He pointed his sword to the hooded and robed attendant manning the teleporter controls. 'Begin teleportation.'

Arcane purple and blue energy leapt from the coiled transmitters arranged in a horseshoe around the back of the teleporter ring. The whine of archaic transformers and the crackle of cables filled the chamber, the armour of the Knights gleaming in the flashing light.

'Imperator protectivis.' Belial whispered the invocation, a habit from his childhood that all the years with the Dark Angels had never quite eliminated. It was an entreaty to the Emperor to watch over him in the coming voyage, and it had returned to Belial's mind just before his first teleport. *'An nostrus equivocum celestiates magna. Expeditus ave honorum Imperator Rex.'*

The teleporter energy reached its crescendo just as the last syllables slipped from Belial's lips. He felt lifted, his mind soaring away from his body. The sensation seemed to last for minutes, but it was in reality an instant before his body followed and the *Penitent Warrior* disappeared.

TRUTH WITHIN A LIE

It was easy to see where the enemy transport had exited the marshalling yard. A four-metre section of chain-link fence had been toppled and wide track marks ploughed up the muddy ground beyond, heading away from the highway. The haze of exhaust smoke still lingered in the soft breeze.

Tybalain and Nerean had reached the hole in the fence first and were a hundred metres away by the time Annael and Calatus came upon the scene. The Land Speeders flitted overhead, guns firing, to continue the fight against the remaining enemy in the warehouses. The distinctive sharp *crack* of Sword Four's rift cannon punctuated the clatter of heavy bolters.

Riding over the broken fence, Annael thought at first that the escaping transport was simply heading cross-country, but after fifty metres they came upon a rutted track, churned up by recent use, which curved southwards into a stretch of forest. The Huntmaster and his companion were almost under the eaves as Annael and Calatus turned onto the uneven road and followed.

Eagerness pushed Annael to accelerate hard. Eagerness not just to overhaul his companions and be present at the battle, but to revel in the simple pleasure of riding over open ground beneath the sky.

'Too often of late have we been confined to corridors and streets,' he remarked to his battle-brother. 'To give steeds full release has been a rarity.'

'Too true, brother,' replied Calatus. 'It bolsters the spirit when the hunt becomes literal!'

Annael laughed. 'Sabrael would have had some quip at this point. I fail in that regard.'

'Aye, I'll grant you that his humour was often timely. But as much as it was uplifting, his wit deserted him often in other ways.'

They reached the cover of the tree canopy, the track sloping downhill as it curved gently through the woods. Annael could smell the oil and smoke from the steeds of his squadron-brothers, strong enough that he knew he had gained distance on them. Ahead the road took a long turn to the left, and he saw an opportunity to make up even more ground.

He leaned the bike to the left and bumped off the track into the mulch and dirt beneath the trees. He felt the tyres slip for a second and gunned the engine for more grip, twisting the handlebars to steer around the thick trunk of a tree.

'Where are you...?' Calatus did not complete the question, but wrenched his bike after Annael's. 'The spirit of Sabrael lives on, it seems. Who knew that stupidity could be infectious?'

Annael barely heard his companion's complaint. He

was concentrating hard, view flicking between the trees directly in front, the flicker of black shapes along the road further ahead and the blip of the sensor return on *Black Shadow*'s display.

With smooth movements he guided the speeding bike between the thick boles of the trees, bumping over roots and stones. He could see on the scanning monitor that Calatus had dropped back, unwilling to match Annael's speed. Annael wondered if Calatus was right, that he was somehow compensating for the loss of Sabrael with this foolish behaviour. He decided he did not care. The Ravenwing were expected to display bravery and daring, to perform the impossible.

He hit the track hard, almost thrown from the saddle as the grip of the tyres found solid purchase, dragging him across the heavily-rutted surface. He glanced back and saw that Tybalain and Nerean were about a hundred and fifty metres behind. Thick black smoke from the traitors' armoured carrier hung like fog across the track, though the vehicle itself was not yet in sight.

Taking the next curve at top speed, leaning hard into the bend, Annael almost lost control of *Black Shadow*. Wind had drifted rotting leaves across the track, making it slick. He felt the bike slipping out from under him, wheels bouncing across the uneven ground. He slammed his foot into the dirt, digging his heel into the earth as an anchor against which he could lever, dragging the bike back under control. His injured knee throbbed with fresh pain and damaged fibre bundles in the back of the joint sent warning signals through the armour systems but he held on.

He righted his steed as it hit a straight stretch. The transport was three hundred metres ahead, slowly drifting from one side of the track to the other as the driver tried to maintain control at sixty kilometres an hour.

Annael accelerated hard, making the most of the straight and the fresh ruts left by the carrier's tracks. He quickly closed the gap to two hundred metres. A flash of muzzle flare from on top of the broad transport alerted him a second before a hail of laser pulses flickered past.

'Turret weapon is a multi-laser,' he told his companions as he jinked to the left to avoid another stream of red bolts.

Black Shadow's auto-targeter for the plasma talon was trying to get a motion lock on the speeding transport, but the bumpy track and swerving vehicle took the task beyond the small machine-spirit. Annael fired out of instinct, the plasma bolt slamming into the back of the transport. Metal buckled beneath the strike but the vehicle was not visibly slowed.

The gunner was beginning to get in his aim as another volley of multi-laser fire streamed down the road. Annael was still gaining, but slower now due to weaving left and right to elude the sporadic bursts of las-fire. A glance at the display showed that his companions were still a hundred metres behind.

The road started to curve, presenting more of the transport's flank to Annael. Additional armour plates had been bolted onto the sides, but the tracks were still exposed. Annael fired the plasma talon again, getting a glancing hit on the track housing. Suddenly thick black smoke billowed from the track unit, engulfing Annael in darkness. His auto-senses flickered through various spectra and thermal modes while flashes of las swept along the road.

Annael's vision settled just as a flurry of bolts caught

him across the right arm and shoulder, searing along the ceramite of his armour. He almost lost his grip on the handlebars and was forced to slow to regain control. The smoke was thinning as whatever gear or engine he had hit burned out, but the track was becoming more winding, forcing both the transport and its pursuers to slow.

Seeing the gunner lining up for another shot, the six barrels of the multi-laser pointing right at him, Annael accelerated again, shortening the range so that the salvo sped over his head. He rode hard, until the turret could not depress enough to target him. Just ten metres behind the transport, Annael knew that if the driver braked suddenly he would slam into its back.

The road dipped beneath them and Annael felt a second of weightlessness as *Black Shadow* left the ground. The transport landed heavily and more smoke spewed from the engine grille. Narrowly avoiding riding straight into the back of the armoured vehicle, Annael pulled around to the left and dragged free his corvus hammer.

He saw the road curving sharply even as he swung the hammer. The gleaming beaked head smashed through the outer track apron, the twisted metal stripping links. Metal showered Annael as he braked so hard he almost threw himself over the handlebars.

Still shedding links, road wheels grinding against the ground, the carrier was unable to make the turn. It ploughed over the raised lip of the track and into a tree, riding up until the trunk snapped under the weight. Annael saw the gunner in the open turret flop sideways in his hatch, spine snapped by the impact.

Remembering Tybalain's demand that the leader of the group was to be taken alive, Annael slewed to a halt and dismounted. Corvus hammer in one hand, bolt pistol in the other, he advanced.

The front hatch slammed open and a figure staggered out. A male in grey fatigues, some kind of bionic augmentation plugged into his left shoulder and neck. Obviously not the speaker on the vox-link. Annael fired and the bolt tore apart the traitor's head.

Annael heard the creak of another hatch and looked up as a figure emerged beside the turret. She was tall, muscles bulging with stimulants, white hair cropped to a peak. There was a vox-unit implanted in her face, replacing the cheek and ear, a short aerial jutting back from the cranial adaptation. Her torso was protected by a hauberk of overlapping black scales, heavy gauntlets with spiked knuckles on her fists, her feet shod in knee-length boots with metal banding and thick buckles down the side.

Neira Kamata hissed and leapt at Annael from the roof of the transport.

He moved back a step and swung his corvus hammer, using the haft as a weapon. It caught the descending traitor in the chest and flung her against the side of the transport with a loud clang. Dazed, she fell forward, into Annael's rising boot. The cyber-implant shattered as she flew back again, crashing into the armoured vehicle. She slumped into the dirt, barely conscious.

Annael noticed the growl of engines and turned to see the others slowing to a stop just a few metres away. Tybalain was quickly off his steed. Annael stepped back and allowed the Huntmaster to see the prisoner.

'Neira Kamata, as you requested, brother-sergeant.'

Tybalain hauled the woman to her feet. She spat blood across the face of his helm and was thrust hard against the transport as punishment.

'Die, Imperial dogs! I will tell you nothing!'

Tybalain holstered his pistol and grabbed Kamata's head in one hand. His fingers squeezed and she screamed.

'Far stronger foes than you have told us everything, Kamata. Your lord is dead, your army scattered, your fleet destroyed. All you can hope for is swift release.' Tybalain moved his grip, taking his captive's wrist in his gauntlet. Again he applied just the right amount of pressure and elicited a shriek of pain. 'Tell me where you have the captive and you will endure no more.'

Kamata looked at him and Annael could already see the defeat in her eyes. She sagged, eyes downward.

'I never had him,' she confessed.

'I thought as much,' said Calatus.

The prisoner looked over at him and grinned savagely, bloodied teeth on display.

'I said I did not have him. I do not know where he is, but my comrades will make him pay in suffering for the affront he has caused them. If the Dark Angels do not leave Tharsis within the hour, his remains will be returned to you.'

'Where is he?' growled Tybalain. Bones cracked in Kamata's wrist. She drew in a snarling breath.

'In the city,' she gasped. 'I don't know where. Safe. Hidden.'

There was truth as well as pain in her gaze. Tybalain nodded and extended his arm, pushing her against the hull of the vehicle, hand plunging through breastbone and internal organs. With a last wheeze, the traitor died. The Huntmaster ripped free his bloodied hand and let her body fall to the ground.

'She believed there is a hostage,' said Calatus. 'There could be some truth to the story.'

Annael looked down at Kamata's corpse and for the first time in a long while he wondered who she had been. Normally he would not spare a second thought for the lives of traitors, but there had been something about her honest defiance that had struck him. Had she willingly joined forces with the rebels or been lured into servitude with false promises? She had clearly lied about being the new commander of the traitor army. An act of arrogance or desperation? Kamata had capitulated easily enough to Tybalain's demands, it was likely she had been grasping for hope from the moment the Dark Angels had struck.

'She was telling the truth, for sure,' he said. 'She hoped that we already knew about the hostage and was relying on us believing that she had him.'

'She was mistaken,' said Calatus. 'Fatally so.'

'A sentence merely commuted since she sided with anti-Imperial elements,' said Nerean. 'Justice has been served, vengeance has been enacted.'

'But what of the possible hostage?' said Annael.

'A mystery easily solved,' said Tybalain. He returned to his bike and gestured for the others to mount their steeds. When they had done so, Tybalain wheeled away from the wreck of the transport and headed back towards the highway depot.

'Sword Four, Land Speeders, status report,' the Huntmaster transmitted.

'All enemy neutralised. Local forces are moving forward to secure the shipping yard.' There was a pause and a touch of humour entered Casamir's tone. 'What's left of it.'

As the squadron emerged from the woods, Annael saw several columns of smoke rising from the remains of the cargo station. Several buildings had been levelled in their entirety and others were in flames. Tharsian infantry were advancing, supported by their armoured vehicles, but Annael knew that if Casamir reported that all enemies were dead, it was definitely so.

'We shall uncover the nature of this hostage story, one way or the other,' said Tybalain. The vox signal wavered as he routed his transmission through his steed's systems to contact one of the strategion technicians on board the *Implacable Justice*. 'This is Huntmaster Tybalain. I need a full force casualty notice, with reference to all lost personnel.'

'Request received, Huntmaster. Compiling report.' There was a pause while the information was collated from the battleforce data-stream. The Black Knights reached the highway and roared past the slowly moving armoured vehicles of the Tharsians, only stopping when they had moved half a kilometre beyond the burning waystation. Another minute passed before the strategion sent his reply. 'Combined losses are seven Second Company battle-brothers killed in action, thirteen attended by apothecarion personnel. First Company casualties are as follows. Three slain. Two in apothecarion review.'

'Report received, *Implacable Justice*.' Tybalain turned in his saddle and looked at the rest of the squad. 'No hostage. The whole story was a lie.'

'That seems strange,' said Annael.

'Stranger than one of our brothers being taken alive?' said Calatus. 'I know which reality I think the more credible.'

'The woman, Kamata, believed there was a hostage. We all saw it. Which means that someone else told her there was a hostage. What purpose does such a falsehood achieve? Why would anyone perpetrate such a mistruth to their allies?'

The others were silent for a while, and Annael realised the awkward nature of the topic he was delving into. As Black Knights, they were privy to secrets from the history of the Dark Angels that had not been revealed even to other members of the Ravenwing. The majority of the battle-brothers were not even aware of the existence of the Fallen and their part in assisting Horus in the destruction of ancient Caliban.

'Myriad are the deceptions of the enemy,' Nerean said eventually. 'If we were to expend thought in unravelling such mysteries we would be philosophers, not warriors. There are few enough hours in each day as it is, without pondering the imponderable.'

'I think Brother Annael has a point,' said Calatus. 'Another thought occurs, also. We reported Sabrael dead, but as yet no body has been recovered. Perhaps there are others that were lost in the fighting, their demise assumed rather than confirmed.'

'A possibility,' conceded Tybalain. Again the vox crackled as the Huntmaster boosted his signal. '*Implacable Justice*, casualty report clarification needed. How many brothers killed in action have been visually or telemetrically verified?'

'That will take some time to clarify, Huntmaster. We will have to contact the reporting sergeants and analyse the tactical data-stream.'

'I am a patient man,' replied Tybalain.

'Of course, Huntmaster. Apologies if I implied to the contrary. I will assemble the report for you as swiftly as possible.'

While they waited, Annael watched the Tharsians taking possession of the half-ruined marshalling yard. Sword Four had departed to continue its air cover while the Ravenwing Land Speeders buzzed back and forth above the local troops, guns at the ready to provide immediate overwhelming firepower.

There had been little contact between the armoured column and the Black Knights, and Annael wondered what the Tharsians thought of their superhuman allies. From their point of view it might seem as though the Dark Angels had brought this war upon their world, rather than arriving at an opportune time to help in its defence. Annael knew little of the strategy involved, but there had to be good reason Grand Masters Belial and Sammael had brought the task force here for the timely intervention. Doubtless it was intelligence gathered at the horrific daemon world, or perhaps even from the Fallen warrior captured by Sammael's company on Thyestes.

It gave Annael some extra satisfaction to think that the latter might be the case. It was proof of the just cause of the Hunt. Capturing the Traitor Space Marine on Thyestes might have led to preventing the devastation of Tharsis. The Tharsians could never know the truth of how the Dark Angels had arrived at such a timely moment, that would be disastrous, but to return to a world that had been so ravaged by the crimes of one of the Fallen and see it guarded safe against the violent intentions of another…

It almost made the disappointment of the failings at Piscina bearable.

Annael's downward turn of thought was interrupted by a reply from the technician in contact with Tybalain.

'Huntmaster, four casualties reported as killed in action are as yet unconfirmed,' said the serf. 'Brother Sabrael of your squadron, along with Brothers Orius and Garbadon, and Sergeant Polemetus of the First Company.'

'Gratitude, *Implacable Justice*. Transfer last known locations of the brothers and their beacon telemetry frequencies.' Tybalain disconnected from the long-range broadcast and addressed his companions. 'We shall see if Annael and Calatus are correct, and one of our missing brothers has been taken by the enemy. Brother Casamir, rendezvous at my position and relinquish your Land Speeder. Annael, you are coming with me. Let us see if you remember your gunnery training.'

TELEPORT STRIKE

The sensorium was alive with signals from the instant Belial materialised aboard the enemy ship. The white flare from the containment fields of three plasma reactors almost blotted out every other signature in the vicinity. Against this glare he could dimly perceive hundreds of life signs. The sensorium took several seconds to adjust to the proximity to the ship's reactors and engines, during which time Belial surveyed his surroundings by more conventional means.

The Grand Master and his Deathwing Knights had landed exactly where he had chosen, in a broad, high gallery that ran for several hundred metres between the port and starboard engine decks and intersected ahead with the reactor chambers. Everything was bathed in an orange glow from battle lighting.

The plain metal decking and bulkheads were in considerable disrepair, corrosion and damage evident wherever he looked. Through the wide archways that ran the length of the corridor he could see banks of monitoring servitors – shrivelled half-humans wired into the myriad systems of the heavy cruiser's engines.

The sensorium gained some clarity, dimming the signal from the plasma shields so that Belial could see the crew in more detail. The rows of servitors were marked with lines of grey dots, stretching for two hundred metres behind him and three decks above and below. There were brighter spots from overseers and tech-priests walking the ranks, currently heedless of the enemy that had just arrived on their ship.

'Onward to the objective,' Belial told his warriors, pointing his sword at the two sets of high doors that ended the large passage. 'Kill everyone we encounter.'

The sensorium picked up a fresh spike of energy, a dozen decks above and to starboard. Another followed to port. These were the Deathwing squads tasked with inflicting as much damage as they could to the gun decks. A third and a fourth would be targeting the void shield generators above the plasma chambers, but it would be another half a minute before the teleporters had recharged.

A siren announced that the crew of the flagship had been alerted to the presence of intruders. A reedy voice barked orders over an address system, in some argot that Belial did not recognise. He assumed it was from the pirates that made up the bulk of the fleet, though part of him wondered if the language had a darker origin, somehow connected to the daemons of Ulthor. There seemed no sign of obvious Chaos infestation, but he was prepared for the worst.

The doors shattered beneath the blows of Barzareon and Deralus's maces, revealing a tight knot of corridors and winding stairways around two open elevator shafts. Belial led the squad on, the body lamps of the Terminator suits bathing the confines of the ship in pale fluorescence.

Suddenly a flood of signals boiled towards their position from the decks above and below, streaming along the stairwells like ants.

'Barzareon, Galbarad, rear defence.'

The two Knights peeled away from the advance and turned back. At the edge of his vision Belial could see the first of the ship's crew coming into view through Barzareon's link. They wore grimy grey, blue or green coveralls, barefooted. He saw only men, heads shaven to the scalp, red tattoos of interlocking circles marking the exposed skin.

They were poorly armed, most with nothing more than lengths of pipe and tools to wield, a few with long, axe-headed boarding gaffs that they could barely carry. Some had knives, either crude but properly-fashioned daggers or sharpened splinters of metal with rag-woven handles. All were emaciated from lack of food, eyes sunken and dark, skin jaundiced.

The moment the crew at the front of the wave laid eyes upon their foes, their impetus faltered. Seeing the armour-clad giants they had been sent to confront, the determination in their eyes quickly became desperation. The patter of feet on the metal grille of the deck slowed, and some tried to turn and move back but found their path blocked by those behind.

From Galbarad's point of view an overseer with a crackling electrowhip could be seen behind the first few dozen indentured crewmen. He snarled something, trying to urge on his reluctant charges with snaps of the whip.

Barzareon did not wait for his foes, but ploughed

forward, his mace smashing through a handful of bodies with one sweep. The protestations of the slaves became panicked screams as the Deathwing Knight carried on, pushing through the mass of frantic humanity, pulping their bodies underfoot, his shield crushing them against the walls of the corridor while his mace obliterated anything it touched.

There was little enough for Galbarad to do except follow in his battle-brother's wake, ready to exterminate any crewman fortunate to survive the onslaught.

Belial's attention was drawn back to closer matters when he reached a wide ferrocrete stair that led down to the causeway running around the reactor chambers. A fusillade of las-bolts and shotgun rounds met his descent, flickering and ricocheting harmlessly from his warsuit.

His storm bolter barked in reply, the first salvo of rounds cutting down three foes. These were better equipped than the slave-fodder that had come up from the depths, formed into coherent groups around heretic tech-priests wearing stained red robes. The soldiers wore scarlet like their masters, their padded jerkins and scaled kilts in contrast to black open-faced helms, steel-banded knee-high boots and gloves that glinted with spikes on the knuckles. The crewmen stood and knelt along the curving corridor, using girders and columns as cover. Some bore chainswords, perhaps as a badge of rank, and a few had gilded stripes on their helms, which Belial took to mean they were deck officers of some type.

The corridors opened out into a massive domed space at least a hundred and fifty metres across. In the circle formed by the surrounding raised platform of decking, the three reactors were arranged in a triangle, heavily reinforced egg-like structures whose top thirds were visible from this level. Several kilometres of cabling and pipes looped and coiled around the power plant and like the approaches to the chamber there were signs of poor maintenance everywhere. Exposed wiring let loose fountains of sparks and leaking connectors on coolant pipes and heat exchanges vented icy vapour and steam.

The energy field projected from the Grand Master's iron halo flared into life as another torrent of fire erupted around him. Zandorael moved past the Grand Master as Belial opened fire again, the stream of bolts ripping into a group of foes on the leftward curve of the causeway. Cragarion and Deralus followed just behind their master, shields lifted to deflect the incoming fire.

Belial continued firing to the left while the Knights advanced to the right. The tech-priests were not so brutal, or perhaps unthinking, as the slavemaster had been, and the ring of red collapsed back from the advancing Terminators, still firing.

Belial reached the bottom of the steps. He adjusted his focus to see what was happening with the rearguard, assuring himself that Galbarad and Barzareon had little to concern them. The corridor was awash with blood, choked with the bodies of slain deck-workers. Of the overseer there was no sign, his whip lost in the gory mass. Galbarad glanced across to his companion and for several seconds Belial could see Barzareon, the off-white of his armour almost lost beneath a sheen of crimson.

The flagship suddenly thundered, the dome overhead buckling to send slivers of metal and ferrocrete raining down on the exposed reactors. Although the Terminators were unaffected, the ship's crew were rocked by the impact, some of them losing their footing as they scrambled away from Zandorael and his companions.

'*Penitent Warrior*,' Belial snapped into the vox. 'Cease firing at the aft section. Reactors are highly unstable. I am standing right next to them!'

'Profuse apologies, Brother Belial,' Sapphon replied. 'We have been taking some damage ourselves. A hit amidships has caused a targeting metriculator error with one of the macro-cannons.'

'Shut it down,' said Belial. 'Concentrate all firepower on the secondary bridge and prow sections. We do not need to suffer casualties by our own hand.'

'Shutting down the battery now, brother. The Lion guards us.'

The Grand Master increased his stride, powering towards the rebels that continued to fire at him from the left. Unlike those confronted by the Knight Master and his two warriors, these traitors held their ground, firing desperately with lasguns and shotguns. His energy field a shimmering aura of red around him, Belial fell upon the closest group with the Sword of Silence.

Belial was one of the foremost blademasters of the Chapter, and had defeated nearly all challengers since he had been inducted into the Dark Angels ranks. The ship's crew were little more challenge to him than the straw-stuffed dummies he had, as a child, attacked on the training fields of Bregundia, when he had been a squire in the Society of the Ebon Star. The Sword of Silence parted raised rifle butts, arms and necks without hesitation or favour, rendering Belial's victory a simple matter of mathematics and time.

A tech-priest held his ground before him, his left arm replaced with a scythe-fingered claw that gleamed with a power field. Beneath his hood, his face was masked with bronze and gold, a tear-like ruby studding the left cheek – a curiously emotional adornment for one who had been a member of the Adeptus Mechanicus.

Though his weapon posed more of a threat than the daggers and bayonets of the crew, his skill was no greater. Belial parried the first swiping blow, the clash of weapons unleashing a miniature storm of lightning. Not wishing to waste any time in the conclusion of his mission, Belial turned his wrist and thrust, lancing the point of his blade into the throat of the tech-priest. He withdrew the sword and the dead adept slid to the ground, half-decapitated, artificial windpipe hissing air like a broken valve.

The tech-priests realised that if they retreated they would allow Belial free rein on the reactor deck. This was unacceptable, so they bellowed orders in metallic tones, physically restraining some of their warriors from retreating. Despite the crew's bolstered enthusiasm, this resurgent offensive was no better than the defence, and Belial shot twenty or thirty foes over the following minute, dissuading any further assault.

Across the sensorium, he could see that Zandorael, Cragarion and Deralus had finally run their prey to ground, cornering several dozen crew against a trio of pipes, each higher than a man was tall, which cut across the surrounding causeway to aft, linking the reactors to the main engines. The green glow from their flail and maces gave the carnage an otherworldly air, clouds of emerald fumes swirling and twisting with each swing of a weapon.

The sensorium alerted Belial to the arrival of a

conveyor a few metres ahead of him, descending from one of the upper decks. The telescoping doors rattled open. The tech-priests and their soldiers parted to reveal the occupants of the transport cage.

Two hulking figures almost filled the doorway. Belial recognised the monstrous ogryns they had once been, but little remained of the abhumans' natural bodies. Pale blue flesh was ridged with subcutaneous bony implants and their veins stood out like cords, pulsing with near-toxic levels of stimulants and steroidal compounds. Their heads were encased in steel helms, just a slit left for them to see, their squinting red eyes visible within. Their hands had been removed, on the one replaced with circular chainblades, on the other a drill-like appendage and a power hammer.

In the small gap between their bulk, Belial saw their handler. She too was dressed in Adeptus Mechanicus robes, but there was armour beneath her vestments, pale grey and made up of overlapping scales. Belial glimpsed the blue glow of a plasma containment field – a pistol in the magos's hand.

'Finally,' Belial said to his companions, lifting his blade with a flourish, 'a foe that might test me.'

A MISSING BROTHER

Under Tybalain's control, the Land Speeder glided to a halt beside a tangle of wreckage that almost blocked one of Streisgant's streets. Annael turned the heavy bolter to cover the upper storeys of a shell-pocked building to the left, then swung it to the right towards the main avenue. The area was deserted, but the instinct for alertness was ingrained into every cell of his body.

'This is definitely the place,' said Tybalain, dismounting from the hovering Land Speeder. On the *Swiftclaw*'s scanner flickered the tracer beacon of Sergeant Polemetus's Tactical Dreadnought armour, indicating a point somewhere just behind the twisted metal and cables. 'Casualty report has the sergeant failing to teleport back to orbit with his squad but none of them saw him fall.'

Tybalain pulled aside a jagged sheet of plasteel. A smoking engine block fell free. Annael could make out the shape of three walkers in the mangled ruin, each nearly twice the height of a Space Marine. Their frames bore holes from bolt detonations and the distinctive molten-edged folds where a power fist had torn at them. There were other signs of damage: the slash of a power sword, the blackened, sticky residue of burned promethium from a heavy flamer.

'He's here,' announced Tybalain, shouldering aside one of the burned and broken war machines. A multi-barrelled laser like the one on Kamata's transport flopped uselessly on its mounting as the Huntmaster heaved at the wrecked walker some more.

The bone-coloured armour of Polemetus was stark against the dark ferrocrete road. Annael could see the red of the Dark Angels insignia on his shoulder plate, and the golden winged skull on his chest. A piece of armoured leg lay across him, severed at the top with a neat blow from a powered blade. That blade was still in his hand. There was no sign of his head.

'Definitely dead,' said Annael. 'May his shade be honoured for his valour.'

'Honour his shade,' Tybalain murmured in reply, stepping back from the corpse. 'That leaves us with Sabrael and Orius to confirm.'

'The closest is the position we last saw Sabrael,' said Annael, scrolling the navigational display on the console in front of him. He studied the schematic data. 'Some of the invading forces are still holding out between here and there. The Tharsians were outflanked when our brothers in the Deathwing pulled out with their prize. It looks like they're content just to contain the enemy.'

'That shall be our next objective,' said Tybalain, climbing back aboard the Land Speeder.

The whine from the anti-grav engine increased as

the Huntmaster took them above the pile of wreckage, joined by the throatier roar of the thrust engines. The Land Speeder darted forward, the gloss black of its armoured hull reflecting the sky. Smoke clouds were clearing above, leaving a vibrant indigo in their wake. It was late afternoon and the local sun was just over the tops of the buildings, gleaming from thousands of shattered windows.

Annael continued to track back and forth with the heavy bolter, one eye on the scanner, the other ahead. Tybalain steered the skimmer with the casual ease of several decades' experience, flitting along alleys barely wide enough to accommodate them, turning at speed into broad marketplaces and racing across battle-scarred plazas.

They came across groups of civilians picking through the wreckage of their homes. Most stopped and stared as the Dark Angels sped past. Some cheered, a few waved, but many were just dumb with shock, staring with vacant eyes at the gods of war in their midst.

Annael noticed that most were young, less than thirty years old, except for a few womenfolk. The oldest men would have been youths when Astelan and his Sacred Bands interned and slaughtered millions as he ruled from the Slaughterkeep. A lot were younger still, fortunate not to remember those harrowing times in any detail.

Generations lost, Annael considered. Perverted to a barbaric cause by the Fallen or slain for their opposition, or even their apathy. Streisgant had been built anew but the wounds of the turmoil were written deep into the people of Tharsis. They would take generations more to heal, and fresh wounds had been opened by this latest war.

'Curse the traitors, curse all of them,' growled Annael. 'May their souls burn in eternal agony for the woes they have heaped upon these people.'

'They will,' Tybalain assured him. 'As soon as our blades and bolts deliver them to that hell.'

A few moments later Annael detected the metronomic crash of an artillery piece not far away. It seemed to be firing point-blank, judging by the time between the *crack* of its fire and the thunder of the shell's detonation. He looked around and saw a plume of wind-blown dust rising over the buildings ahead and to the left. Correlating this with his scanner data, he saw that the traitors were holed up in a habitation block ten storeys high, overlooking several manufactorums and workshops in which the Tharsians had made their stand.

'Sabrael fell on the boulevard on the opposite side of that hab-block,' he told Tybalain. 'If we continue on this road and swing–'

'No need for a lengthy detour,' said Tybalain, slinging the Land Speeder into a tight climbing turn over the roofs flanking the street they were following. They continued to ascend, flitting through billows of steam escaping from a sprawling laundry works, churning vortices in their wake as the Huntmaster accelerated.

A warning sounded from the auspex, detecting an incoming projectile. Tybalain was already jerking the control column to the right as Annael looked up to see a missile streaking down at them from the upper storeys of the hab-block. The projectile whistled past a few metres to their left and detonated on the roof of the laundry.

Annael traced back the trajectory in a second and swung the heavy bolter around. He opened fire, steady bursts of four rounds each. The explosive-tipped bolts punched into the ferrocrete wall around the window from which the missile had been fired and exploded in the room within.

The artillery piece, somewhere off to the right, fired again and a chunk of the building's corner three storeys up fell away into the street. Exposed pipes gushed water and severed power lines hurled sparks after the debris.

Now that they were closer, Annael could see the criss-cross of las and tracer fire between the lower levels and the Tharsian troopers holding ground in the surrounding complexes. Tybalain steered the Land Speeder down to ground level, barely a metre clearance beneath them as they screamed along the main road past the hab-complex. From here Annael saw the piles of dead by the doors into the hab-building, dressed in the fatigues of the Tharsian militia, the casualties of failed assaults.

'What are you waiting for?' snapped Tybalain. 'Targets of opportunity, open fire!'

Snapped out of his reverie, ashamed at the momentary loss of focus, Annael let his embarrassment become ire. He unleashed a long salvo of fire from the heavy bolter, tearing along the second-floor windows with a storm of bolts. He saw flashes of pale, pain-wracked faces in some of the windows, the bricks and frames spattered with blood.

With the buzz of a gigantic hornet, the assault cannon opened fire under Tybalain's control. Annael felt the shock of the sudden recoil slowing the speeder in midair, such was the torrent of projectiles unleashed by the rotary cannon. A cluster of stained-glass windows on the ground floor – the local chapel, it seemed

– disappeared in a welter of flying coloured glass and spinning masonry shards.

Tybalain reversed the jet flow hard, swinging the Land Speeder around in a tight U-turn. They had come to a hover opposite one of the hab-block's entrances. The short flight of steps was red with dried blood, three bodies sprawled by the thick wooden doors.

'Suppression fire, second floor,' Tybalain snapped. He switched his vox-unit to external address. 'Warriors of Tharsis, reclaim your lands from the traitor filth! We of the Dark Angels stand proud to be counted amongst your allies.'

Annael opened fire again, short bursts into each window above the entrance, quickly moving from one to the next and back again. Tybalain turned the doors to matchwood with a burst from the assault cannon and then churned a few thousand rounds into the surrounding rooms, the armour-piercing ammunition tearing holes through the ferrocrete.

A Tharsian officer had taken the lead, confidence buoyed by the presence of the Angels of Death. A platoon of militia followed the sword-waving Tharsian across the road, plunging up the steps with bayonets fitted to their lasguns. Renewed fire sprang up around the Land Speeder as the Tharsians poured on everything they had, covering the attack of two more platoons dashing across the road.

Not all made it. Bullets and lasbeams sprang out from the upper floors, cutting down a quarter of the Tharsians in the open. Annael did his best to return fire with the heavy bolter, as Tybalain manoeuvred from one group to the next.

The attack warning sounded again, but this time Tybalain did not have time to evade the incoming missile. It struck the *Swiftclaw* on the engine pod just behind Annael's head. His armour blared alerts as shrapnel and fire engulfed him.

The *Swiftclaw* spun sharply to the left, turning three full circles before Tybalain was able to equalise the thruster outputs. Annael leaned sideways and looked back so he could evaluate the damage. Smoke leaked out of cracked ceramite and the buckled armour plate beneath. The fire soon sputtered out, doused by internal regulator systems. There was a speckling of frost along one side of the jagged gash.

'Coolant system pierced. We won't be able to achieve maximum speed without overheating.'

'We have done enough here,' said Tybalain, aiming the Land Speeder down the street. 'Let us see what has become of Sabrael.'

Annael fired a few more bursts into briefly-glimpsed figures on the third and fourth floors while Tybalain concentrated on keeping the Land Speeder moving straight, boosting the power on the anti-grav plate to compensate for the damaged engine. The *Swiftclaw* rocked slowly from side to side as though riding a wave, making it difficult for Annael to maintain any accuracy, but he poured what fire he could into the visible enemy before they broke away at the end of the main street.

A sharp left took them under a rail bridge and then they climbed over the peaked roof of the station terminus building, narrowly avoiding its clock tower. Beyond lay the long boulevard that would take them to Sabrael's last known position.

Three hundred metres out, Annael knew they should have picked up his battle-brother's telemetry signal. There was nothing on the scanner. On its own this meant nothing, as the beacon in their armour suits was often one of the first systems to cut out in the event of power loss or damage. However, in the context of the hostage situation, Annael felt a mixture of hope and annoyance. Hope that his brother – his friend, he admitted – might be alive, spoiled by the annoyance that Sabrael would dishonour them all by allowing himself to be captured.

They found the exact spot where the Black Knights had turned back from their attack on the orders of Asmodai, and Sabrael had continued on to confront an enemy transport on his own. Tybalain slowed as they turned the next corner. There was a small crater in the road, surrounded by pieces of black-enamelled armour. Four bodies, or pieces of bodies, were scattered further out, bloodied and burned.

'It looks like he used the terminus protocol,' said Annael.

'Not so,' said Tybalain, bringing the Land Speeder to a hover next to the site of the detonation.

The Huntmaster dismounted and picked through the wreckage for a couple of minutes. He returned, holding a broken piece of fuel tank.

'It's all from his steed, no pieces from his battleplate,' Tybalain said, tossing the debris away. 'The corpses are Tharsian youths. Sabrael must have been taken and his steed activated its anti-tamper terminus command. The Tharsians most likely thought they had found something worth looting and the bike detonated its plasma talon core.'

The Huntmaster pulled himself back into the driver's position, but he laid his hands on the console rather than taking hold of the controls. His head was dipped for some time, deep in thought. Eventually he straightened and grabbed the steering column.

'It seems our wayward brother is alive, but possibly not for long.'

BLADE VERSUS BEAST

Belial moved to intercept the augmented ogryns before they could exit the confines of the conveyor cage. He fired his storm bolter at the closest monster, the rounds tearing chunks out of its rivet-pierced flesh. The damage was superficial, a thick layer of fat and slabs of muscle preventing the bolts penetrating to any depth.

There was a particular art to fighting in Terminator armour, using the impetus of attack to overcome the bulk of the war-plate. Belial was well-versed in this style of fighting and raised his blade to slash at the wounded ogryn as he passed. The Sword of Silence connected with the elbow of his target, severing the arm to send its whirring chainblade clattering to the deck.

The ogryn barely noticed, lunging with its other arm as it stepped out of the conveyor, the teeth of its circular saw screeching across Belial's left shoulder pad and marring the crux terminatus displayed there. Belial's attention was fixed on the next ogryn, which was struggling to get past its companion.

The Sword of Silence flashed towards the abhuman's chest but deflected from the glowing head of the ogryn's hastily-raised hammer-hand. Sparks flared across its pale chest and Belial's plate. Its spinning drill met the Grand Master's charge, the diamond-glinting point slamming into his abdominal armour.

The blow nearly stopped him on the spot, his next step faltering, leaving him vulnerable to the ogryn coming up from behind. Belial shifted his weight and twisted, the flat of his blade knocking aside the chainblade aimed for him. He fired his storm bolter into the gut of the ogryn with the drill embedded in his armour, shredding more flesh and the underlay of bionics and organic enhancements. He allowed himself to be pushed by the beast's drill-fist rather than let it dig into his war-plate further, turning almost into the creature's embrace to slash the Sword of Silence down its thigh.

Thick blood spilling from the parted femoral artery, the ogryn reeled back, tearing its drill free in a fountain of ceramite shards and metal splinters. The one-handed ogryn slashed its saw again, but Belial's iron halo burst into life, the power field absorbing the force of the blow, dissipating it harmlessly.

This unfortunately left Belial vulnerable to the magos's plasma pistol. She opened fire, the ball of energy flickering between the two brutish bodyguards to slam into Belial's already weakened left shoulder. The pauldron split apart, shattered by the bolt of plasma. The release of energy and sudden loss of weight on one side sent him reeling. He brought up his storm bolter and fired back out of instinct, the weapon's targeter allowing him to aim at the tech-priest even though he was looking away.

The bolts ripped through her robe but seemed to blunt themselves on the armour underneath, their detonations charring the red fabric but causing no harm to the magos. Undeterred, Belial spent a second to analyse the situation of his squad. The Knights had almost wiped out the tech-priests and crewmen they had trapped against the energy exchange pipes, but they would have to come the long way around the gantry to assist their Grand Master.

Annoyed that he had not yet eliminated one of his foes, Belial reassessed his strategy even as he parried another swipe from a spinning sawblade aimed at his head. He slammed his storm bolter up into the chin of the ogryn, breaking the jaw and cracking tusks. This gave him half a metre of space to sidestep, using the brute's body to block the angle of attack from the other.

One-on-one for a moment, Belial made good use of the time. The Sword of Silence carved deep welts into the ogryn's flesh, the gleaming blue power sword cutting through the bone under skin as easily as it could part steel and ferrocrete. Four times he struck these scything blows, opening up the monster's chest to expose its breastbone and ribs. Belial finished with a flourish, straightening his arm to plunge his blade through the ribcage and into the massive heart.

He wrenched the Sword of Silence free and barged his shoulder into the toppling ogryn, sending the dying monster staggering backwards into the magos who had been trying to get out of the conveyor.

Belial took a calculated risk, stepping to the left past the falling ogryn, into the confines of the conveyor. It left him with little room to retreat or manoeuvre, but granted him an extra second to surprise the magos. Two articulated iron tentacles sprang from her back, trying to seize hold of Belial's weapons with grasping claws. He cut the mechanical claw from one and fired his storm bolter between the magos's shoulder blades, hoping her armour was not as strong from the back. It was, and as before the salvo impacted on her without causing injury.

She turned, aiming the plasma pistol.

Belial closed the gap, slapping away the pistol with his storm bolter so that her shot pierced the side of the conveyor. He punched her in the face with his sword-hand, buckling a respirator implant across her mouth and nose. He saw her eyes widen in shock as her air supply was cut off, panic in her gaze.

Her momentary hesitation was more than enough time to smash his storm bolter against the side of her head, knocking the magos to one knee. A heartbeat later, the Sword of Silence arced down, decapitating with a single stroke.

A gleaming hammer caught him full in the face, sending him staggering back across the conveyor cage. Sparing no glance for its fallen mistress, the surviving ogryn stepped into the cramped interior, its drill tearing through Belial's tabard to skitter across the winged sword blazon on his chest.

There was barely room for Belial to swing his sword, and all he could manage was a raking slice across the shoulder of the ogryn. It grunted, perhaps in pain, perhaps anger. Scarlet eyes glared at the Grand Master from the depths of the bucket-like helm.

The ogryn seized Belial in a bear hug, lifted and smashed him against the rear of the conveyor. The attack did little actual harm, but his storm bolter was pinned to his side and his sword equally useless in his raised hand. It stepped back and rammed him into the wall again, buckling the metal.

The Grand Master kicked, driving his heel into the inside of the ogryn's knee. The monster's leg buckled as it twisted, giving Belial an opportunity to get his feet on the floor again, though the ogryn did not relinquish its desperate grip.

Thrusting with both legs, Belial managed to drive back his attacker, forcing it to trip over the corpse of its dead companion. The ogryn let go as it fell, unable to fight the instinct to put out a hand it no longer possessed. The drill was no help, deflecting from the hard deck as the ogryn pitched backwards.

Belial used his momentum to seize the ogryn's neck in the crook of his elbow, broken chin locked between the thick plates of his armour. He twisted, trying to pull the monster's head free, but could not gain enough leverage.

It rolled but Belial kept his hold, moving onto the ogryn's back to pin it to the floor with the weight of his Terminator armour. With no proper hands to steady itself, the augmented brute could not push itself up and moaned helplessly, bucking like a stallion being broken.

Belial dragged the creature's head back further and pulled his gleaming blade across its throat, sawing through metal-sheathed windpipe and reinforced tendons. Blood bubbled rather than sprayed, thick like oil.

The ogryn shuddered and collapsed underneath Belial.

'Grand Master!' The tone of warning in Galbarad's

voice caused Belial to instinctively switch his viewpoint to the Deathwing Knight's.

Galbarad needed to offer no further explanation for his concern. A small mountain of dead crew and lower-deck slaves was heaped in the passageway leading back to the main concourse, but over the mound of mashed corpses Belial spied several heavily-armoured, bionically-enhanced figures, illuminated by the glow of plasma weapons.

'Hold for two minutes,' Belial told his rearguard. 'Zandorael, Cragarion and Deralus, meet me at the entry to the plasma chamber.'

He switched back to his own view as he turned right and headed to rendezvous with the rest of the squad. A flicker of his right eye highlighted the strategic display. A schematic of the ship imposed itself over his view, several dark red runes marking target objectives for the other Deathwing squads. Most had a red slash across them, indicating they had been destroyed, but the void shield generators remained operational.'

'Sergeant Caulderain, report assault status.'

'Two casualties, already teleported back to the *Penitent Warrior*. Progress slow, regretfully report unlikely to achieve objective, enemy massing.'

'Understood. Withdraw to the strike cruiser to prevent further losses.' Belial changed the vox-channel to contact his Knights. 'Zandorael, Cragarion and Deralus, reinforce the rearguard. We must secure the main concourse for teleportation, there is too much interference from the plasma containment field inside the dome to receive a lock signal. I shall join you shortly.'

He barely heard their affirmatives as he focused his attention on the three plasma reactors. The main containment vessels were heavily shielded, and even if he could penetrate the force fields the vessels themselves had walls two or three metres thick. He needed to interrupt the power exchange to the void shield generators without causing an instant meltdown that would most likely consume everybody aboard the ship, including more than two dozen warriors of the Deathwing.

His gaze returned to the exposed cables and shoddily-repaired coolant pipes that crisscrossed the middle part of the chamber. It was impossible to tell what conduit led where in the rat's nest of tubes and wires. He fired the last three rounds from his storm bolter, punching several holes in one of the vents atop the closest plasma case. He reloaded and fired again, emptying a dual-magazine of bolts into the surrounding web of connectors and exchanges.

'*Penitent Warrior*, can you monitor power flow to the void shields?'

Sapphon's reply returned a few seconds later.

'Yes, brother, we are reading significant fluctuations in the recharge rate.'

'Good. Initiate extraction sequence.' He did not wait to hear a reply. A sub-vocal command changed the vox-transmitter to company address mode. 'All squads prepare for immediate teleport extractions, in sequence as briefed.'

He checked the status of his Deathwing Knights. All had suffered some damage to their armour, Galbarad and Barzareon quite heavily, but it was only the latter that had been injured. Across the telemetry of the sensorium Belial could tell that the Knight had only partial use of his right leg.

'Push forward to the teleportation point,' Belial ordered, emptying another full magazine of bolts into the plasma energy system. He turned and broke into a lopsided run, the absence of his left shoulder plate and the damage to his chest plastron affecting his suit's balancing systems.

The Deathwing Knights had retaken the archways leading to the main passage but a torrent of fire – plasma, lascannon and missiles – streamed down onto them from gangways to either side and the open archways leading to the engines.

'Lock shields, advance ten metres,' Belial barked as he joined them. He fed another magazine into his storm bolter and fired back at the rebel crew thronging the gantries above.

The Knights did as commanded, raising their shields to form a line shoulder-to-shoulder just a few strides onto the concourse. The fields of their storm shields overlapped, creating a shimmering wall of energy in front. Belial fell in behind them as they advanced in step, bullets and las-blasts flaring from the barrier of their shields in a constant thrash of released energy.

On the far left and right, Barzareon and Deralus slowed, allowing the shield wall to curve slightly and protect the flanks.

'*Penitent Warrior*, do you have our signal?' Even as Belial asked the question, a beam from a tripod-mounted lascannon sliced down from the walkway on the right, piercing the energy shield to burn through Deralus's breastplate. The Knight fell sideways to one knee, his shield tumbling from his grasp before he toppled face first to the deck. Belial could see a hole in the back of Deralus's war-plate.

'Faint, intermittent signal, Grand Master,' the crewman of the strike cruiser told him.

'Do it!' growled Belial as more enemy fire converged on the weakening shield line, stray rounds pattering from the armour of his brethren. 'Activate extraction teleport!'

The inside of the ship glimmered with a purple aura, the Deathwing Knights at the centre of the glow. Belial felt himself sinking again, mind slipping free from mortal body. A brain-jarring moment passed and then the squad was deposited back aboard the *Penitent Warrior*, appearing on the teleportation plate arranged in a static tableau just as they had been aboard the flagship.

'Grand Master, we need the teleporter for Squad Ardeon,' announced the retainer at the controls.

Belial understood his meaning immediately and sheathed his sword. Barzareon was the quickest of the Terminators to comprehend his intent. He tossed aside his shield to grab the arm of Deralus while Belial took a leg. They dragged the badly wounded Terminator free of the platform so that the serf could recharge the cells and bring in the remaining Deathwing squad.

Leaning over Deralus, Belial inspected the damage and the wound beneath. It was severe, and the Knight's suit was transmitting a faltering life signal.

It was not yet time to count the cost of the mission. First Belial needed to know the measure of success.

'Brother Sapphon? Enemy status?'

The crackle of the activating teleport echoed around the room as Squad Ardeon reappeared. Belial noted that they too were carrying one of their brethren between them. He waited intently for the reply to his question, knowing that the Deathwing had paid a high price in its battles of late and could ill afford more casualties.

'Severe damage to starboard batteries,' Sapphon confirmed. 'Void shields still inactive. Plasma drives partially functional. Congratulations, Belial, you've given us a sitting target. We are closing in for the kill.'

ANNIHILATION

Clad in his Chaplain's black armour, Sapphon stalked the command bridge of the *Penitent Warrior* like an all-seeing shadow. He simultaneously assessed three streams of information; from the Ravenwing assault preparations, the progressing teleport attacks by Belial and the Deathwing, and the ongoing duel of gun decks between the strike cruiser and the rebel fleet's heavy cruiser flagship.

Though his particular strengths and aptitude had taken him into the ranks of the Chaplains, Sapphon was a Space Marine with centuries of battle behind him, and possessed more command experience than most general staff officers across the Imperium. He was perhaps not as adept as Belial or Sammael, but the fight with the heavy cruiser proved that he was far superior to the enemy's captain in the absence of Anovel.

'They should be pounding us with twice the rate of

fire,' he remarked to the ranking non-Space Marine bridge officer, Lasla Chirpet. 'Poor discipline on the gun decks.'

'True, Brother-Chaplain,' said the deck-captain. 'I am sure that a squad of Deathwing marauding through their batteries is also causing them some consternation, master. For all that, they still outgun us by a margin. It is taking nearly all of our firepower to simply keep their void shields overloaded.'

'And they the same.' Sapphon glanced at the mission chronometer that had started on the instigation of Belial's teleport attack. The First Company warriors had been aboard the enemy ship for three minutes and twenty-four seconds. Sapphon and the crew of the strike cruiser were under orders to retrieve any Terminator whose signal they could detect at the five-minute mark. Any remaining aboard were to be presumed lost and Sapphon would evaluate whether to continue the starship battle or withdraw out of teleport range.

'Helm, reduce inclination by four degrees,' Sapphon announced, checking the relative positions of the ships on a battle schematic. 'Starboard eight degrees. Keep us to starboard and below their guns, the Deathwing are focusing their attack on the lower starboard gun batteries.'

'Aye, Brother-Chaplain,' the three serfs at the helm controls chorused. One of them turned his head to confirm the order. A youth no more than seventeen or eighteen years of age by Terran standards, his hair was shaved to the scalp. His sleeveless green robe revealed one of his arms to be badly crippled, twisted almost to a ninety-degree angle at the elbow. A token of a mishap during his initial training. 'Inclination minus four degrees, starboard eight degrees.'

A concentrated salvo of fire from several operational gun decks erupted from the opposing flagship. Lasla bellowed for the brace warning to be sounded before Sapphon opened his mouth. A second later, clarions rang the length of the strike cruiser, alerting the crew and the few Deathwing warriors that had remained on board.

Sapphon refused to grab the brace bars that were set behind each of the command positions. It was his duty to display implacable composure in the face of the enemy. He folded his arms and waited for the shells and rockets to strike.

It started as a rippling shudder towards amidships, moving in the direction of the prow. The vibration picked up speed and intensity as it travelled, becoming a growling rumble by the time it enveloped the command bridge situated atop the dorsal spar of the warship.

The *Penitent Warrior* rocked as attitude thrusters misfired during the bombardment, causing the strike cruiser to roll to port a few degrees. Damage warning sirens blared into shrill life around Sapphon as one of the communications stations fell blank from loss of power. The attendant at the console looked around, forlorn, at the row of empty screens and silent speakers.

'Brother Nemeus, please attend,' Sapphon said calmly. The Techmarine who had been standing at the back of the bridge came forward, his three servitors clumping across the deck behind him, faces slack, their extremities replaced with a variety of basic and powered tools.

Nemeus's red armour was a stark contrast to the black of Sapphon and the dark green robes of the attendants. It matched the colour of alert lights that sprang into life as he inserted a diagnostic spike from his war-plate's vambrace into an aperture in the communications station.

'Primary relay overload,' Nemeus reported, speaking more to himself than the Interrogator-Chaplain. Content that the Techmarine knew exactly what to do, Sapphon allowed Nemeus to drift out of conscious thought, along with the clank of ratchets and hiss of a solder torch.

'Master Sapphon, the *Implacable Justice* is requesting permission to pursue the departing renegade battleship.' Lasla showed no sign that he, or any of the crew, realised that the battleship he referred to was the *Terminus Est*, flagship of the despised traitor legionary Typhus. This much Sapphon had learned from Asmodai's brief account regarding what had happened with Astelan. Nor did the deck-captain of the Ravenwing strike cruiser know the true nature of the enemy vessel, as evidenced by the request.

The presence of the *Terminus Est* added a new layer of intrigue to the plot of the Fallen that had been thwarted and Sapphon would have ordered the pursuit in a heartbeat if there had been more vessels at his disposal. He would be tempted even now, with just two strike cruisers and a dozen or so system defence ships, but for the fact that the *Penitent Warrior* could not disengage from its duel with Anovel's heavy cruiser.

As reminder, the bombardment cannon fired again, the projectiles racing across the display on the main screen. Magma warheads exploded across the hull of the enemy warship. A blaze of fire from the gun decks followed, shells slamming into the prow sections of the heavy cruiser.

To break away now would be to maroon the Deathwing aboard the opposing starship, an unforgivable breach of trust. Similarly, regardless of the hazards in pursuing the *Terminus Est*, the Ravenwing strike cruiser had engaged other elements of Anovel's fleet – vessels that would be left free to target the *Penitent Warrior*.

'Signal to the *Implacable Justice* to remain at current station,' the Chaplain told Lasla. 'Continue to implement containment strategy.'

Much of the Fallen's pirate fleet had been destroyed in the minutes following Astelan's pre-emptive decision to open fire. Expecting welcome from the orbital stations and platforms of Tharsis, the renegades had been caught in vicious crossfires and torpedo salvoes. The arriving strike cruisers had formed the lid of the box, interposing themselves between the assailed vessels and the route out of low orbit.

The debris from the fighting was starting to form a ring around Tharsis, plasteel and frozen water and metres-thick ferrite plates joining the millions of micro-asteroids surrounding the world. On the surveyor displays an even more complex pattern emerged – sprays of heat and radiation, the radio echo of final transmissions and dissipating plasma swirling around the physical debris.

The *Implacable Justice* was pursuing a pair of enemy corvettes, which were hoping to dissuade the strike cruiser from attacking by staying close together. Deck-Captain Pichon had been left in charge, a more experienced starship commander than could be boasted by many vessels in the Imperial Navy. Pichon and the crew of the Ravenwing's transport were doing an admirable job of ensuring the *Penitent Warrior* and the enemy flagship could conduct their duel without interference.

The orbital stations of Tharsis had reaped quite a toll early in the attack, opening fire at Astelan's command against the unprepared fleet of Anovel. Now they formed an effective barrier against which the *Implacable Justice* was able to force the smaller ships it pursued. Unable to turn and head for outer space and not daring to risk the fire of the defence stations in lower orbit, the pair of corvettes were inevitably being run to ground.

'Lord Sapphon.' The voice of the communications attendant drew the Chaplain's thoughts back to his own situation. 'Master Belial has been teleported back to the ship.'

Sapphon checked the chronometer. Four minutes and forty-three seconds. There was little to be gained by waiting another seventeen seconds, and lives could be lost.

'Teleport stations, activate full retrieval,' he commanded. 'Gunnery systems, open fire at full tempo. Helm, bring us to torpedo launch distance.'

The bridge officers broke into action, relaying orders, coordinates and target specifics to the relevant crews in the bowels of the vessel. Attitude engines burst into life, checking the *Penitent Warrior*'s momentum. The battle lighting flickered as the two teleportaria simultaneously brought back the remaining squads of Terminators, temporarily usurping the power output of the plasma reactors.

'Brother Sapphon?' Belial's vox signal was routed through the internal systems. He was safely back on board. 'Enemy status?'

Sapphon already knew the answer to the question, but reviewed the latest augur data streaming across the displays.

'Severe damage to starboard batteries,' he told the Master of the First Company. 'Void shields still inactive. Plasma drives partially functional. Congratulations, Belial, you've given us a sitting target. We are closing in for the kill.'

The *Penitent Warrior* broke away from the heavy cruiser, stalling its inertia to allow the target vessel to slip ahead by several thousand kilometres. Its own engine output disrupted by the Terminator assault, the enemy flagship could do nothing but arc slowly to port, trying to bring the bulk of its operational gun decks to bear.

All the while, the dorsal bombardment cannon kept up a relentless fusillade against the opposing ship. Shells created to breach surface fortresses and obliterate star bases pounded into the crippled cruiser. Each impact sent clouds of atomised armour and superstructure spraying into the void.

'Master, torpedo failsafe distance reached,' reported one of the weapons serfs.

'Load both tubes, melta warheads.' Sapphon consulted a sub-screen just to his left. 'Zero spread. Helm, angle us to bearing mark-oh-seventeen. Engines to ahead standard. Launch on my command.'

While the huge torpedoes were lifted up to the firing tubes, the *Penitent Warrior* increased speed once more and turned, keeping inside the arc of the curve described by the route of the enemy. The prow of the Space Marine vessel edged ahead of the target's trajectory, the intersecting points of the torpedo flight and the enemy course picked out in red on a weapons display in the bottom right corner of the main screen. Numbers counted down the time to optimal launch.

'Master, weapons crew report torpedoes loaded. Tubes sealed. Ready to launch.'

Sapphon acknowledged the report with a nod.

'Remain on course.' He switched to the command vox. 'Brother Belial, are you en route to the strategium?'

'Thirty seconds, brother. Give me thirty seconds and we will watch these traitors burn together.'

'I think we can stay our hand for that long, brother.' Sapphon strode to the front of the command auditorium and turned to face the deck officers and attendants.

'The situation brings to my mind an ancient quote. No one remembers who first said these words, but you should mark them well. They have not been forgotten in ten thousand years for good reason.' The Chaplain paused as the doors hissed open to admit Belial. The master of the Deathwing's Terminator armour was scorched and cut in many places, the painted heraldry flaked and charred. His helm was in his hand, his face set with grim determination. Despite his efforts to mask it, the commander seemed out of breath, as if he had been running hard to get to the bridge in time. 'Hail to Master Belial, and the First Company. By their effort and sacrifice we have earned victory this day.'

A resounding shout filled the strategium, a wordless commendation to the warriors and commander of the Deathwing. Belial accepted the praise with a grudging nod.

'You were making a speech,' he said to Sapphon, taking up the command position at the centre of the strategium.

'I was,' said Sapphon. His gaze moved across all that were in the chamber, meeting the gaze of each and every serf and Space Marine present. 'The enemies of the Emperor fear many things. They fear discovery, defeat, despair and death. Yet there is one thing they fear above all others. They fear the wrath of the Space Marines!'

Belial directed an inquiring look at Sapphon, technically his subordinate until the Chaplain saw fit to return command to the Grand Master.

'Hereby witness that I rescind authority of command of the *Penitent Warrior* to Grand Master Belial.' He nodded and smiled at his fellow officer, and waved a hand towards the tactical display. 'All is in order. The torpedo room awaits your will, brother-captain.'

'Launch torpedoes,' the Grand Master growled without ceremony. 'We'll send these scum to the void.'

They followed the progress of the immense projectiles as they hurtled across the vacuum towards the heavy cruiser. The main sensor arrays damaged during Sapphon's attack, their engine power reduced by Belial's assault, the officers commanding the traitor vessel detected the incoming missiles late, and lacked the ability to do anything but execute the most rudimentary evasive manoeuvre.

A few hundred kilometres from their target, the torpedoes shed their warhead sheaths, dispersing hundreds of armour-piercing melta charges. The cloud of munitions engulfed the heavy cruiser thirty seconds later. Every warhead erupted into a short-range radiation blast intense enough to penetrate metres of ferrite, plasteel and ceramite. Each was enough to make a small breach, but in their hundreds they punched through the aft section of the cruiser in a red wave, shearing almost halfway across the decks.

Already punished to the point of breaking by the bombardment cannon shells and gun deck salvoes, the heavy cruiser was in no state to weather this latest assault. Stanchions snapped and decks collapsed, the back third of the vessel tearing away as spasming engines and secondary explosions pushed the prow up and to starboard while a reactor breach spewed plasma to port, twisting the doomed cruiser amidships.

In another minute, the ship had torn itself in two, fires raging along the forward section while plasma swallowed the aft.

'Vengeance is ours,' Sapphon declared.

'Tactical report,' Belial barked, sparing no time to mark the achievement. 'Target priority assessments. There are others awaiting our retribution.'

A BROTHER'S CHOICE

When they reached the rendezvous coordinates in the outskirts of the city, Annael saw that the other two Black Knights were already present. Calatus and Nerean waited astride their steeds, with Casamir and his gunner, Eladon, on their borrowed mounts. Tybalain had picked a small square intersection between three roads, overlooked by high hab-towers pocked by shells and las-fire. The auspex relayed the presence of several hundred life signals, and as the Land Speeder approached Annael could see terrified faces peering out of shattered windows. The area had been reported secure, cleansed of enemies, but Tybalain followed procedure and circled the area twice while Annael kept the heavy bolter primed to fire at any target that presented itself.

Bringing the skimmer to a halt beside the squadron, Tybalain jumped down from the driver's seat and motioned to Casamir.

'My thanks for the lending, but I prefer the feel of my

steed to the seat of your carriage,' said the Huntmaster.

'Remember that the next time you run into a blocked street, Brother-Huntmaster,' replied Casamir as Annael alighted to relinquish his post to Eladon. 'We have received orders from the Grand Master to assist the attack being launched through sector fifteen in the canal quarter.'

'I have also received such command, but wait a moment, brothers.'

Casamir and Eladon stopped before they reached the *Swiftclaw*. Tybalain activated his vox, connecting the transmission to the external address so that they could all hear the exchange.

'Grand Master Sammael, this is Tybalain with an urgent force deployment request.'

'Received, Huntmaster.' It was strange to hear Sammael's voice issuing from Tybalain's helm. 'Make your request.'

'We have subdued enemy forces that claimed they had captured a battle-brother. I have conducted an investigation and believe this is true. I reported Brother Sabrael dead, but there is no sign of his body. I request that a strike force is readied to punish the perpetrators of this affront.'

'You have a confirmed location, Huntmaster?'

'Not yet, Grand Master, but we will acquire intelligence while the strike force is assembled.'

'The purging of the enemy army is ongoing, Huntmaster. We have suffered heavily of late, nearly half our strength. We cannot afford these distractions.'

'A threat has been made, Master Sammael,' Annael cut into the discussion. 'Brother Sabrael will be executed if our forces do not leave Tharsis. Compliance is impossible, so we must rescue Sabrael.'

'It is a matter of honour,' Tybalain replied.

'There is much to mar the honour of the Second Company of late, Huntmaster. If we fail to drive the enemy from Streisgant, we shall bear a far greater shame in the eyes of our First Company brethren. Sabrael's foolhardiness has cost him dear, but it is a fate of his own making. You will continue to join with the assault force assembling for the strike through sector fifteen.'

'Grand Master, I ask you to reconsider,' said Tybalain. 'We can ill afford another blow to morale.'

'That is a consequence you will have to bear, for allowing Sabrael to break rank. Losing more warriors in a rescue mission would be vanity, brother. I have given my command.'

The link was broken from the other end and Annael shook his head.

'This feels wrong, brothers,' he said. 'You know that Sabrael would be the first to aid any one of us, despite his flaws.'

'He would be the first to disobey an order, that's for sure,' said Nerean.

'This seems to be an issue for your squadron, Huntmaster,' said Casamir.

'We'll leave you to your... discussion,' said Eladon, turning back to the Land Speeder.

'Sabrael was Ravenwing as much as he was a Black Knight,' said Annael. 'He is battle-brother to us all.'

'The Grand Master did not leave any room for interpretation,' said Calatus.

'The order was clear but our duty is not,' argued Annael. 'Brother Tybalain is right, we need to consider the extent of our losses. Even our Huntmaster, may the Lion watch over him, cannot claim a greater skill with blade or more adroit employment of steed. For all his indiscipline, Sabrael is a boon to the squadron.'

'In your opinion,' contested Calatus.

'In the opinion of Brother Malcifer, the Grand Master and several other superiors who have been well aware of Sabrael's mercurial behaviour but have not striven to break him from his nature.'

Annael remembered seeing Sabrael astride the Grand Master's jetbike on the occasion they had come upon *Corvex* aboard the *Implacable Justice*. The thought that Sabrael pictured himself as being Master of the Ravenwing in the future had horrified Annael at the time, but recent events had made Annael reconsider his objections.

'Another moment of your time, Casamir, Eladon,' Tybalain said, causing the pilot and gunner to turn back. 'I cannot order you to accompany us, but I am asking, as one brother to another.'

'We're going after Sabrael?' said Annael, his mood lifted by the Huntmaster's decision. 'You are willing to ignore the Grand Master's command.'

'We will seek fresh intelligence,' said Tybalain. 'Another captive might reveal what we want to know. I promise nothing more.'

'Why should we risk the wrath of the Grand Master?' asked Eladon.

'As Huntmaster it is within my purview to elevate you to the rank of Black Knights,' Tybalain replied. 'I would happily do so, with the endorsement of my squadron, if you were to assist in the recovery of one of our number.'

'A posthumous rank is of little value, brother,' said Casamir.

'The promotion will be immediate, and we all have

to die at some point,' said Tybalain, returning to his mount. He swung a leg over and settled into the saddle while Annael made his way back to *Black Shadow*. 'Your Land Speeder would prove very useful in the task ahead.'

The crew of the *Swiftclaw* looked at each other and there was a pause while they communicated over their isolated vox-channel, unheard by the Black Knights. Judging by the body language, Casamir was the more enthusiastic of the two, but whether for or against Tybalain's proposal was impossible to tell. Eventually they both turned back to face the Black Knights.

'We agree,' said Eladon. 'We will help you.'

'And you will bestow the rank of Black Knights on us now.'

'Welcome to the brotherhood of the Black Knights,' said Tybalain, holding a fist across his chest in salute. The rest of the squadron followed suit. 'We will establish the formalities later, I give you my word.'

'Are there oaths to swear?' asked Casamir.

'Many,' replied Tybalain, 'but only one I demand of you at this time. Whatever you hear, whatever you might see, whatever you might learn, you must swear never to reveal to the rest of the company, nor to any member of the Chapter except for an officer or member of the Deathwing. When you became Ravenwing you swore to uphold the secrets and lore of the company. Now do the same for the brotherhood of the Black Knights.'

'I swear by the Lion, the Emperor and my soul, to uphold the secrets and lore of the brotherhood of the Black Knights,' the two Space Marines intoned simultaneously.

'Welcome to the brotherhood,' said Nerean.

'Let us hope it is not a decision you regret,' added Annael.

'Very well.' Tybalain signalled for the newly promoted brothers to board their vehicle and addressed the rest of the squadron. 'We need to find where Sabrael is being held. It must be in one of the contested sectors, fifteen, sixteen or twenty. The Grand Master's offensive is about to tear through fifteen and sixteen and if Sabrael is there they will find him. We must take a prisoner who can tell us about sector twenty.'

'Wait, Huntmaster,' said Calatus. 'You have not asked us.'

'Asked you what?' said Tybalain.

'Whether we are willing to disregard the Grand Master's orders. Sabrael was a liability even before he was captured.'

'You think we should abandon him?' said Annael. 'Forget that it is Sabrael. Would you grant that boon to our foes, to say that they slew a Dark Angel?'

'It will be a boast of the moment, swiftly ended when we wipe out the last of these heretic scum.'

'I did not ask because I did not think there would be debate,' said Tybalain. He looked at his Black Knights. 'Was I wrong? Did I misjudge the mettle of the warriors I lead?'

The question was left hanging, along with the implied accusation within it. Annael broke the silence that followed.

'We are the only Black Knights left after the losses of this campaign. We cannot allow another of our rank to die simply for the sake of pride.'

'Pride?' Calatus growled the word. 'Ask Sabrael the meaning of pride when we find him.'

'You will come?' said Tybalain.

'Yes, Huntmaster, I will come.'

'And you, Nerean?' said Annael.

'Brother Tybalain is correct,' said the last Black Knight. 'It is redundant to ask.'

'Follow me!' barked the Huntmaster. 'Casamir, scout us the quickest route to sector twenty.'

'Aye, Brother-Huntmaster,' the pilot replied.

The small force left the intersection, the bikers following the lead of the Land Speeder. Within two hundred metres, Casamir had accelerated out of sight, but the signal from his vehicle remained on *Black Shadow*'s scanner.

'How do you propose we locate a suitable target for capture?' asked Calatus. 'We could round up dozens of these scum and not find one who knows Sabrael's whereabouts.'

'Though she overstated her position, Kamata knew, and clearly had some authority over her group,' said Tybalain. 'A lieutenant in the wider scheme. We shall locate an enemy force, identify the leaders and extract them for interrogation.'

'That should be simple enough,' said Annael. 'It is the reason for our existence.'

'As you have it, brother,' said Tybalain. 'Casamir, I want you to coordinate with the *Implacable Justice* to identify the most significant enemy presence in sector twenty.'

'And if they ask why I want to know? We are supposed to be embarking on a mission in sector fifteen, Huntmaster.'

'Remind the strategion that you are a battle-brother of the Chapter and his superior. The Chaplains will be interested to hear of his reluctance. I do not think he will require further encouragement.'

'It seems unworthy to threaten serfs, Brother-Huntmaster,' said Casamir.

'We are disobeying the orders of our Grand Master, brother. It is too late to quibble about the details.'

'Of course, Huntmaster. I shall find us a good fight to pick.'

The invasion and subsequent Dark Angels counter-attack had encompassed nearly the whole city, so that as the Black Knights rode westward through the battleground there was barely a street or building that did not show some scar from the fighting. In places whole districts had been flattened, either by the orbital bombardment or the Tharsians shelling their own homes to drive out the occupying enemy. Elsewhere there were little las-burn or bolter marks to show that a war had been raging for the fate of the metropolis.

With most of the fighting having moved away from the centre, survivors emerged, some clearly shocked by what had occurred, watching dumbly as the Black Knights rode past. Some of the citizens had started trying to clear up in the aftermath of the brutal exchanges, picking through the rubble, trying to piece together lives as broken as the buildings they had lived in.

Dusk was coming, the daylight fading quickly to twilight in this part of Tharsis. Some parts of Streisgant were lit by the phosphorescence of street lamps, others dark except for lanterns and candles glowing fitfully through dirty, cracked windows and broken shutters.

There were groups of scavengers roaming the darker streets, like those that had been slain by the terminus detonation of Sabrael's steed. Though they skulked in the ruins and shadows, Annael's auto-senses picked them out as clearly as noon sun. The looters and leeches scattered at the sound of the approaching

Space Marines, disappearing into cellars and sewers like startled rats.

Gunfire crackled in the distance, the boom of bombs and artillery lessened now that the enemy columns had been shattered and only isolated pockets remained. Fires burned from broken energy lines and incendiary ammunition, patches of orange against the deepening purple sky, lighting the underside of the thick smoke clouds that swathed the city.

Annael could hear the staccato rhythm of heavy bolters and the burr of assault cannons as Ravenwing Land Speeders heralded the attack gathering momentum to the east. Though he could see nothing of the battle, by sound alone he recognised the hiss of tornado missiles and the particular *thump* of Thunderhawk battle cannons.

That the sounds were in the distance when he should have been in the thick of the fighting gave Annael a few seconds of regret. He cursed Sabrael for his headstrong nature and for lacking the decency to get killed by his foolishness. The Ravenwing rider kept his momentary reservations to himself, knowing that they would pass when the squadron located a clear quarry to pursue and he had something else on which to focus his energy.

HIT AND RUN

While much of the city had been quiet after the cataclysmic events of the day, the approaches to sector twenty were busy with people still fleeing from the foe. Tybalain led the Black Knights from the main road into one of the side streets but after another two hundred metres the press of people made it impossible to proceed any further.

'The crowd extends for over a kilometre,' reported Casamir. 'Nearer thirteen hundred metres, across sectors nineteen and twenty-one.'

'Clear us a path,' growled Tybalain. 'We have no time for a detour.'

'Clear a path, Huntmaster? You want me to open fire on Imperial citizens fleeing for their lives?'

Annael was not sure if the pause that followed was due to Tybalain reassessing his intent or surprise that Casamir might think he should issue such an order.

'Use your external address, brother.' The Huntmaster's

tone became more exasperated. 'Get the crowd to disperse from your position and we will come to you.'

The Huntmaster activated the clarion of his steed and the other Black Knights followed his lead. The blare of an ascending siren split the crowd for a few metres, the breach opening like a tear in fabric as the riders advanced. The refugees stared at the passing Space Marines with a mixture of hope and resignation, fear and happiness. Many were bloodied, their clothes ragged. Faces were smeared with grime from their desperate escapes. Those that had been worst affected shuffled out of the path of the Dark Angels with stumbling, listless steps, their vacant gazes following the armoured Space Marines without comprehension.

After a few minutes the mass of humanity ended abruptly, leaving empty streets and buildings. Seven hundred metres ahead a broad perimeter roadway divided the bulk of Streisgant from the industrial zone that formed most of sector twenty. The broad encircling highway was like a cut across the suburban landscape. On the inside rose tall, windowed towers of hab-blocks, steepled Administratum cloisters, Ecclesiarchy temples and many-domed tithe chambers. On the periphery stood a forest of smoke stacks and steam vents, raised transitways and roads on ferrocrete legs, arching plasteel bridges and fuming furnace works.

Like the city the riders left behind, the industrial zone had not escaped the fighting, though the full vengeance of the Emperor's warriors had not yet descended upon the area. A refinery blazed, belching a noxious black cloud into the sky. Fire from ruptured gas pipelines lit arcing travelways with a cerulean gleam. Warehouse windows were shattered and the roofs of storage depots several hectares in size had gaping holes from the random fall of shells. The surface of the road was littered in places by debris and glass – little hindrance to the heavy bikes of the Ravenwing except where whole facades had toppled, and in one place where a shell or rocket strike had severed a bridge support and brought several thousand tonnes of ferrocrete down on a railyard.

Annael saw a bright spark of bluish-white lighting up the sky half a kilometre from their position. Simultaneously *Black Shadow*'s auspex sounded a tone to alert him to a considerable energy discharge and Casamir was on the vox.

'By the Lion's shade, that was close!' A stutter of heavy automatic weapons fire and the zip of laser blasts could be heard, both over the vox-link and echoing down the factory-flanked street. 'I have some enemies. I was not expecting them to have a plasma cannon. Withdrawing to await orders. Transmitting target data.'

'That rules out approaching undetected,' said Nerean.

A schematic of three buildings appeared on *Black Shadow*'s screen. One was an open depot, much like the marshalling yard where they had rooted out Kamata. The two flanking buildings, one to the north-east and the other to the north-west, were smaller, Casamir's scan showing each had a dozen or so internal rooms over three floors. Heat data was vague, but showed a concentration of enemies on the upper floors of the two outbuildings, with little in the warehouse itself. A bright spot in the eastward tower showed the position from which the plasma cannon had fired.

'Remember the mission,' said Tybalain. 'We are not here to conquer, but to extract. *Swiftclaw*, suppressive fire on the western structure. Operational centrepoint will be the eastern tower. Calatus and Nerean, perimeter and containment. Annael and I will conduct the extraction.'

The Ravenwing warriors confirmed their orders and Annael added his own affirmative response. Another thirty seconds brought them in sight of the *Swiftclaw* as Casamir brought the Land Speeder rising up over the roof of a building neighbouring his target. A torrent of fire burst from the assault cannon and heavy bolter, ripping along the uppermost row of windows. When the first lasbeams and bullets of counter-fire erupted from the lower floors, the *Swiftclaw* dived quickly, obscured from the view of the enemy in a matter of moments. Strafing sideways the Land Speeder adjusted position by a few metres and then rose again, targeting a different part of the facade for several seconds before using the intervening building to shield itself from the redirected fire of the enemy.

The Black Knights squadron swept along the road beneath the Land Speeder, travelling on from the target for half a kilometre before turning along a connecting road to come back at the objective from a perpendicular angle of attack. Calatus and Nerean accelerated and took the lead by twenty metres. They opened fire with their plasma talons the instant they were within range, sending sparkling blasts into the lowest storey. Braking hard, they added salvoes from their bolt pistols while their bike weapons recharged.

Tybalain and Annael sped past, moving towards the target building at high speed. Annael sent another ball of plasma through the ruins of the main door, its detonation star-bright in the darkened confines. For an instant Annael saw the figure of a mechanically-augmented woman with a large-calibre rifle at an adjoining window. The apparition disappeared as the searing plasma cloud vaporised the rebel sniper.

The Huntmaster veered in front of Annael and activated his steed's grenade launcher. The projectile arced up into the second storey and for a second nothing happened. Bringing their bikes to a screeching stop in front of the door, the two Ravenwing Space Marines dismounted in one fluid motion, pulling free their corvus hammers as they did so.

Above them the stasis grenade erupted, a flickering field of non-time engulfing the room over the entrance.

More plasma from Calatus and Nerean accompanied them into the building, the shots directed on both sides of the stasis grenade's effect. Inside, Annael found himself in a narrow hallway, a set of steps leading up at the far end, two doors to either side of the corridor. The walls were covered with a pallid green, the floor tiled with large brown ceramic squares. It was dark inside, whether by design or accident. Annael's auto-senses adjusted, turning the world into a ruddy swathe of dark reds and muted oranges.

'Up,' barked Tybalain. 'We seize the high ground and if we do not find what we seek, we shall search on the descent.'

Annael offered no comment and pounded towards the steps. Glancing through the first door on the left, he saw the charred remains of the sniper, the tiled floor melted into ridged sworls, the walls bleached white. He passed some kind of workshop to the right, with lathes, vices and die-presses. The next chamber was an archive storage room filled with shelves and boxes, and on the opposite side the open door revealed a food preparation area. Annael assumed that the building was some kind of shift house for the workers in the depot.

His armour-boosted legs took the stair in three strides, bringing him to a landing that ran back to the front of the building. It was decorated with the same paint and tiles as the ground floor, but only two doorways came off the landing, both of them shut with white plastek doors.

The stasis field was shrinking, but in its grip crouched at the window were two robe-clad rebels, a tripod-mounted anti-tank gun held between them. One had a bionic limb, a crude claw more than an arm, the rifle held fast against his shoulder. The other was leaning forward looking out of the window, his astonished look visible through the eyeholes of a grey mask sculpted in the likeness of a leering face.

'Keep going,' said Tybalain. He took two steps along the landing and vaulted over the banister onto the next flight of steps. As Annael followed, the metal rail bending slightly in his grip, a fragmentation grenade bounced down the stair past him. He glanced back to see it clatter across the landing and then stop mid-bounce as it met the edge of the temporal effect.

A group of foes were emerging onto the uppermost landing as Annael reached the top step. He was accustomed to the strange mixture of chemically-altered bodies, crude exoskeletons and stimulant-fuelled stares that met him. Tybalain was already halfway to the nearest door. His bolt pistol shattered the leg of the woman stepping onto the landing, the detonation twisting the bracing wired into the joint.

The sound of the frag grenade going off below announced the collapse of the stasis field, followed by the screams of the anti-tank rifle crew as shrapnel ripped into them. Annael had no thought to spare for them, his attention focused on the enemies at hand.

Tybalain moved past the woman he had injured, thrusting his hammer into the chest of the next foe. Annael followed his Huntmaster, his boot connecting with the chin of the wounded traitor as she toppled forward. Her head twisted violently and her eyes glazed before she hit the floor.

'Search right,' Tybalain commanded, smashing his bolt pistol across the face of another rebel soldier. The man fell backwards, a gash of blackish blood opened across the green-tinted skin of his forehead.

Annael ducked a chainsword swung at his head and blocked the return blow with his arm, his attacker's exoskeletal frame clanging against the ceramite of the Dark Angel's war-plate. Annael struck the man in the chest, sending him into one of his companions. The Black Knight followed up, punching another foe into the wall to clear space to the door on the right.

Someone grabbed him from behind, throwing their arms around his helm, legs wrapping around his thigh like a constricting serpent trying to crush him. Alchemically boosted muscles strained against Annael's armour to little effect.

Turning, Annael threw himself backwards and he crashed through the plasterboard wall with his assailant attached. Dust and debris fell around the Space Marine as the dazed rebel's grip slipped. Holstering his pistol, Annael grabbed the man's arm and pulled him free, slamming him to the floor, a massively over-muscled shoulder dislocated by the throw. The man howled and tried to roll away. Annael's boot came down on his thigh, shattering the bone.

In an instant, Annael took stock of his surroundings. An overseer's office. Ahead the wall had half-collapsed, a picture frame broken beneath the remains of the plasterboard. To his right, a desk below the window at the front of the building, which had been upturned to create a barrier. Two men were at the window with blunt-nosed lasguns, returning fire at Calatus and Nerean.

Behind him the wall had a long shelf stacked with regulation tomes, personnel data-files and order books. Incongruous given the current situation, a brightly coloured blown glass bauble was used as a paperweight to hold down a sheaf of transparencies at one end of the shelf.

On his left were a pair of glass-fronted wooden cabinets containing more gaudy ornaments and a delicate set of shoddy, mass-produced porcelain Ecclesiarchy figurines depicting various saints in their grisly martyrdoms – shot, decapitated, disembowelled and otherwise gratuitously violated. Annael was struck by their contented smiles and cheerful colours, in particular the obscenely bright red of splashing blood.

He almost didn't see the figure crouched between the display cases, his body heat masked by a head-to-toe bodysuit armoured with flexible plates, face concealed in a helmet fashioned in the likeness of a wolf's head.

The figure snarled and leapt as Annael registered the danger, a gleaming power knife in one hand, the fingertips of the other sheathed in serrated blades.

Annael stepped into the attack and caught the traitor in a bear hug, the power knife and fingerblades rasping against his backpack. He spun with his assailant's impetus, grip tightening until he felt his foe's ribs buckling, air pushed from his lungs. With his free hand Annael broke the man's wrist, the power knife clattering to the floor. Manoeuvring to get a better grip, Annael crushed the man's other fingers in his fist, breaking every bone and tearing ligaments. His captive howled and writhed but could no more break free than a truculent infant could escape the grasp of a parent.

'Possible target secured!' Annael told Tybalain. He smashed his head into the face of his struggling captive, cracking open the wolf-mask and crushing the nose of the pale-skinned warrior within.

The soldiers at the window turned, only now reacting to Annael's surprise entrance. One of them pitched to the floor, half her head missing from a bolt fired from outside. The other raised his lasgun as Annael broke into a run.

'Rapid extraction with target,' Annael announced to his companions. 'Cease fire!'

The rebel at the window did not open fire, perhaps realising he might hit Annael's prisoner. The accelerating Space Marine barrelled into him like a locomotive, all three fighters crashing towards the window together.

Annael jumped at the last moment and plunged through the glass feet-first. He landed heavily but safely just a couple of metres from *Black Shadow*, with the prisoner couched in his arms. The lasgun-wielding rebel was less fortunate, hitting the unforgiving ferrocrete headfirst, his skull popping and neck snapping. Annael smashed the butt of his hammer into the side of his captive's head, dazing him further. As he swung a leg over the saddle of his steed, the crash of more splintering glass heralded the arrival of Tybalain. Stowing his corvus hammer, the prisoner dragged across his lap, Annael grabbed the handlebar and accelerated away, glancing back to see that the Huntmaster was empty-handed. The squadron leader vaulted onto his bike and followed, barking an order for the Ravenwing to withdraw.

Las-fire and bullets followed them along the street until they were out of range. The *Swiftclaw*'s guns covered their exit, the tempest of fire from its heavy bolter and assault cannon dissuading any foe from pursuit. They covered half a kilometre and then Tybalain called the squadron to a halt in the shadow of a huge water tower.

Annael pulled up alongside his Huntmaster and slung his captive to the floor. The man rolled to his back and groaned, helm falling away to reveal a face marked with the scars of implant surgery and facial reconstruction. His teeth were steel points fastened into flesh, his ears replaced with bionic receivers. A bulge on the side of his neck revealed the presence of a subcutaneous vox-caster.

'Obviously a leader of some rank,' said Annael. 'Modified for high-level communication.'

The man groaned, some semblance of alertness returning to his eyes. Tybalain dismounted, hammer in hand. The prisoner tried to rise but was pinned back to the floor by Tybalain's weapon, the power field switched off. The Huntmaster knelt, one knee resting on the captive's chest. He moved the head of his corvus hammer to the side of the man's face. When he activated the weapon, a blue power field enveloped the hammer's head and crackled across the rebel lieutenant's flesh, melting skin and fat, causing sparks to fly from his artificial ear.

The rebel screamed until Tybalain deactivated the hammer.

'It is time to find out what you know,' said the Huntmaster.

THE HAND OF JUSTICE

Asmodai walked down the ramp of the Thunderhawk gunship, the huge overhead lamps of the docking bay gleaming bright spots on his ebon armour. He was just a few strides from the gunship when the pilot closed the boarding ramp and took off, the heat wave from the plasma drives washing across the Chaplain. In a few seconds, the Thunderhawk was gone, returning to its missions on Tharsis through open bay doors secured by the blue glow of a power field.

Every gunship the strike cruiser possessed was in action on the world below. Asmodai hurried towards a door in the bulkhead to his left, his footfalls echoing in the cavernous space. The door was barred by a lock, concealed with the skull-seal of Caliban centred on the heavy security portal. Taking one of the ornamental keys that hung from the rope belt of his tabard, Asmodai made two swift adjustments to the talisman, revealing a transponder. Activating the device, he stepped back.

The door seal split apart to uncover a runepad with thirteen buttons marked with the old alphabet of Caliban, used in many of the most ancient texts of the Chapter. Asmodai entered the codeword that he had learned on being accepted into the Inner Circle, each unique to the individual members. A faint green light confirmed the validity of the code and the bulkhead sighed open.

Beyond was another flight deck, far smaller than the one beside it, no more than ten metres square. It appeared on no plan of the strike cruiser, its purpose known only to the Deathwing and Ravenwing that used it. Its outer door was a slit barely large enough for the arriving Dark Talon to enter. Sliding into the opening, the aircraft came to a halt on pillars of plasma, hovering in place while the pilot affirmed that there were no unauthorised personnel present.

The Dark Talon dropped onto the landing zone depicted by the winged sigil of the Ravenwing – the only place such a symbol appeared on the *Penitent Warrior*, the only chamber where the Second Company were allowed.

The Dark Talon settled onto its landing gear and the whine of the engines died down and eventually fell silent. Wheezing hydraulics lifted up the tail boom of the aircraft, revealing an arched hatch sealed with several lockbars. The outer rim of the door was rimed with frost, a side effect of the stasis field within passing through the vacuum of space – water particles trapped in time had frozen on the exposed edge of the stasis chamber. The chamber itself was located just behind the cockpit, powered by the same arcane warp core that fed energy to the rift cannon mounted in the nose of the craft.

THE UNFORGIVEN

A short set of steps extended from the back and folded to the deck. Asmodai ascended and scraped ice from the central lock panel. He took another key, one of only six that existed – the others were in the possession of Sapphon, Ezekiel, Belial, Sammael and Azrael. Originally there had been eight keys, Asmodai had learned, but two had been lost over ten thousand years of fighting. Only the most senior members of the Inner Circle could open the stasis cells. The keys contained a unique crystal centre, the formation of which resonated with an emitter inside the stasis lock. Only the Keys of Devotion could conduct the signal across the divide and unlock the bars.

The background buzz of the field generator died away and after several seconds the cell door opened a few centimetres to release a cloud of vapour into the cool interior of the bay. Asmodai grabbed a handle and pulled, retreating down the steps as the door swung open.

Cypher stood inside the chamber like a corpse in a sarcophagus, head bowed, arms held to his chest as if in prayer.

'Move,' said Asmodai, knowing that the stasis field effects had already worn off. 'Come here!'

Cypher looked at Asmodai. With slow, deliberate movements he disengaged his helmet. Hanging the helm on his belt, he pulled up the hood of his robe and descended towards Asmodai, walking with slow strides. Asmodai grabbed the front of the prisoner's robe as he reached the last step and dragged him onto the deck, tired of the Fallen's attempts to display power and control.

'You are nothing,' Asmodai told Cypher. 'All that you once were has been wasted. Your plans, your ploys, your lies, schemes and alliances, they have failed and come to nothing. Your existence is meaningless. When you come to realise this you will be prepared to atone for your sins. But not before!'

Asmodai looked into the shadow beneath the hood and saw Cypher staring back at him, showing no signs of amusement. There was the faintest hint of a glitter in his eyes; a reflection of a gleam from Asmodai's armour, the Chaplain told himself, nothing more. Asmodai pulled the prisoner away from the Dark Talon as the stasis cell closed and the engines built to a roar. In half a minute the craft was gone, returning like the Thunderhawk to the final battle for Streisgant.

'Will you disarm?' said Asmodai, pointing to the sword hilt protruding from the scabbard at Cypher's waist.

'Will you try to take it from me again if I refuse?' said Cypher. 'Or perhaps order some menial to do so for you?'

Asmodai considered the question. He had no desire to experience the unsettling vision that had assailed him aboard the Land Raider. The Chaplain weighed this against the protocol that demanded that all Fallen be disarmed and removed from their armour as soon as they were in secure custody. A faint smile had crept onto his captive's lips, but the humour had not spread as far as his eyes. Normally Asmodai would have responded to such mocking with a short but intensely violent episode. Such outbursts usually forestalled any further attempts at ridicule. The Interrogator restrained himself with effort, knowing that not only was Cypher trying to elicit such a reaction, this was a prisoner like no other.

When he had been younger, first elevated to the rank

of Interrogator and made aware of Cypher's existence, Asmodai had heard the other Interrogator-Chaplains discussing their methodology in the event they were the ones to capture and admonish the legendary Cypher. Asmodai had scorned such debates, accusing his brethren of fantasising. He had asserted then that Cypher would be treated like any other Fallen, no better and no worse. Now that he found himself in that enviable position he knew two things. Firstly, that Cypher did require special treatment and a unique approach. He would have to work closely with Sapphon to ensure both mind and body were equally vexed. The prospect of such a cooperation made his mood darker still.

The second thing he realised was that the fantasies of the other Interrogators would not have worked. None of them possessed, or had possessed, the combination of brutality and determination embodied in Asmodai.

He came to the conclusion that he was procrastinating, second-guessing himself and his captive. This reaction annoyed Asmodai even more than Cypher's attitude. He had allowed himself to be awed, only a little, but enough.

He punched Cypher in the face. It was a quick jab, nothing more, but it knocked the Fallen down by the shock of it.

There was blood on Cypher's gauntlet as he pulled it away from his face. Asmodai looked down and saw the same on his hand. It was reassuring to see such a thing, evidence of his prisoner's mortal frailty.

'You can keep the sword,' Asmodai said as Cypher got to his feet. 'If you attempt to draw it you will be slain. No threats, no bargaining. If you lay a hand on that hilt death will follow on swift wings.'

'I understand,' said Cypher, his tone sincere.

'Fortunately I have as much desire to wield this blade as you do, but it is my curse and honour to bear it.'

Asmodai kept his eye on the prisoner and sent a short, wordless vox-burst, coded to be picked up by the Deathwing squad that stood outside the other door to the internment chamber. The door hissed open a few seconds later, revealing Belial and three Deathwing Knights. The armour of all four warriors bore the scars of the recent battle aboard the enemy flagship.

'Wait here,' Belial snapped at his men as he stepped into the chamber. He turned and closed the door. The lock light flicked from green to red again, indicating the chamber was secure.

'You do not entrust this information to your Knights?' said Asmodai. Like Sammael's elite, the Deathwing Knights knew of Cypher's existence and importance, if not his true nature.

Belial said nothing and strode past Asmodai. He did not wear his helm, his eyes fixed on the Fallen.

Just as the Deathwing commander reached for his blade Asmodai realised Belial's intent. The Sword of Silence flashed free from its scabbard and Asmodai had only a heartsbeat to react.

The Interrogator-Chaplain launched himself at Belial, one hand reaching for the blade of the Grand Master's sword while the other dragged the crozius arcanum from his own belt.

The Sword of Silence crackled as Asmodai's fingers closed around the weapon. Pain seared up the Chaplain's arm and he saw rather than felt his fingers and thumb falling away. Though he had lost his hand, the interruption had been enough to deflect the Grand Master's blow.

As Belial turned, faced twisted with hatred, Asmodai

lashed out with his crozius. Belial parried the blow easily – Asmodai was no match for the master swordsman, but he could not let the Grand Master attack the prisoner without cause.

'Cease this madness!' Asmodai bellowed.

'You protect *him*?' Belial snarled back. 'The Damned One. The Cursed of the Dark Angels. The Lion's Bane?'

Asmodai shoved Cypher aside with his mutilated hand as Belial moved to strike again, intercepting the Grand Master once more. Belial stayed his blade a centimetre from Asmodai's head.

'It is too dangerous to allow him to live,' said Belial, his voice strained by conflicting, rare emotion. 'We risk too much bringing him aboard. He will only die beneath your blades all the same. You must forego your bloody pleasures this one time.'

'That is not the point!' roared Asmodai, affronted by the notion that he was no more than an executioner. 'He must be allowed to repent. His death condemns or exonerates his soul. I take no pleasure from the grievous harm I inflict. It is necessary to arrive at the unvarnished truth. Blood washes away the lies. Do not dare to call me a murderer, Belial!'

The vehemence of Asmodai's rebuttal caused the Grand Master to pause. Asmodai was incensed and did not relent.

'Is that what you think of me? A maniac, good only to slay our prisoners? Am I held so low in your regard that you would deny me the opportunity to extract the repentance of one we have held in such vile humour for ten millennia?'

'He will manipulate us, bend our thoughts to his will. See what ruin Astelan wrought upon us and how easily he escaped, with simple words and opportunism. It is a mistake to allow him onto this starship, and I would no more let him set foot upon the Rock than I would invite an enemy army into the Tower of Angels.'

'It is not your decision,' Asmodai insisted with gritted teeth. The Chaplain knew that if Belial still decided he wanted Cypher dead, there was little – nothing, he admitted – that he could do physically to prevent it. But he would not be bowed by veiled threats. 'Would you raise your blade against me, Grand Master of the First Company? Am I to be your foe as well?'

'If you decide to stand in my way, you place yourself against me,' Belial replied, taking a step, his sword raised.

'I give you one last chance to submit to my will, brother.' Asmodai did not say what he intended. Belial lunged at him, the tip of the Sword of Silence directed at the Chaplain's shoulder, aimed to disarm rather than kill.

Asmodai swept up his crozius barely in time. The Grand Master's blade sheared through the Chaplain's pauldron, missing the shoulder within. Pulling back his blade, Belial readied for another blow. Asmodai could see in the Grand Master's eyes that this time there would be no leniency.

'*Et spiritu vexatus!*' Asmodai shouted in desperation, using the words that had been implanted into the mind of every Dark Angel as a failsafe against this treachery. The message could be transmitted mentally by a Librarian also. Never again would a Dark Angel turn on his own.

Belial stumbled, face screwed up with pain at the verbal trigger. More calmly, Asmodai continued. '*Libertaris non, Belial. Tu esta dominatus voxilis. Tu pacifica et somnalis.*'

The other Space Marine sagged in his armour, eyes glazing. Asmodai's incantation had caused Belial's catalepsean node to misfire. Normally the implant allowed a Space Marine to relax one half of his brain at a time, remaining semi-functional whilst effectively asleep. Now the malfunctioning organ was rapidly activating and deactivating the Grand Master's synapses, effectively rendering him into a hypnogogic state.

'You should not have seen that,' said Asmodai, looking at Cypher. The Fallen's expression was a mixture of concern and curiosity. 'If you speak of this to anyone...'

'You'll kill me?'

'I have never claimed to be a complicated man.'

'What will you do with him now?' Cypher asked, stepping forward to inspect the stunned Grand Master more closely.

'That is no concern of yours,' Asmodai replied.

The truth was that Belial would be roused by another set of keywords, which would also erase his memory of the incident. In time, he would naturally construct a false memory to cover the gap, prompted by certain key elements inserted by Asmodai before Belial awoke.

He motioned for Cypher to walk towards the door. When the two of them were next to the portal, Asmodai hitched his crozius and used his remaining hand to activate the door lock. The door opened and he pushed Cypher into the corridor beyond.

'Take him to stasis cell four,' he instructed the Deathwing Knights.

'As you command, Brother-Chaplain,' replied Zandorael. The Knight Master looked at Asmodai's fingerless hand. The blood had already clotted and the

Chaplain's armour had stemmed any pain from the wound. 'What happened, brother?'

'A mistake,' said Asmodai, and shut the door.

THE WAYWARD ANGEL

Annael was impressed by the mind-work of Tybalain. The Huntmaster had been right about the rebel lair being located in sector twenty, and the captive taken by Annael had not required much inducement to reveal the exact location.

The *Swiftclaw* was conducting a low-intensity scan of the area while the Black Knights waited a kilometre away from their target. Casamir provided a running commentary while his gunner stayed alert to immediate threats.

'The manufactorum is an assembly plant, ground floor only on the main building, four-storey administration structure attached. We have three ingress routes to the west, thermal scan shows marksmen in the over-zoom bridge to the north have that covered. Detecting low-rate pulse feeds, probably trip detectors on the road approaches. North access is cut off by a canal, nearest bridge looks to be the main highway, two kilometres north-east. They have a gun emplacement station covering the canal regardless. Two, perhaps three mounted weapons.'

There was a pause while the Land Speeder circled. Casamir kept his distance and maintained a low speed to minimise the chance of detection. If the rebels had an inkling that they had been discovered they might bolt or try to kill Sabrael.

'Shall we take another vote on whether we still want to rescue that Lion-forsaken rogue?' asked Calatus. He had accepted the mission with good humour after voicing his arguments. It was the manner of the Black Knights to exchange frank truths with each other when necessary, but to harbour no malicious consequence of those opinions. As a brotherhood within the wider Ravenwing it was essential that they trusted each other without reservation.

'It would not surprise me if we found the idiot drinking recaff and throwing dice with the rebels,' replied Annael. 'He has a knack of exploiting situations to his advantage.'

'Fortune favours the fool,' said Nerean. 'And there are few fools greater than Sabrael.'

Any further exchange was cut short by the continuance of Casamir's report.

'Still no obvious sign of where they are holding Sabrael. We have heat clusters at various points in the plant, but that could be idling machinery, power armour or just a fire to keep them warm. We would have to get closer to uncover the finer detail.'

'Negative, *Swiftclaw*,' said Tybalain. 'Mission security is paramount. Continue wide sweep.'

The Land Speeder pilot recommenced his description, transmitting the vague scan data to the steeds of the Black Knights squadron. Annael watched as a sketchy, three-dimensional image coalesced on the display, grainy detail added every few seconds with each pulse of the *Swiftclaw*'s surveillance systems. After another half minute, the rebel lair and surrounding buildings were mapped out, likely sentry points and enemy groups highlighted with floating red icons.

Annael immediately noticed a particular pattern to their dispersal.

'They appear to be concentrated on the ground and first floors,' he said.

'Fearing orbital or air attack?' suggested Nerean.

'The reason is unimportant,' said Tybalain. 'It is a weakness we can exploit.'

'If our steeds had wings or we had a gunship, perhaps,' said Calatus. 'I do not see how it favours us without.'

'We have other means to part ways with the ground,' said the Huntmaster. 'Casamir, what would be your maximum altitude with four extra crew?'

'Hitch a ride on the *Swiftclaw*?' Annael laughed, but his brothers did not share his humour.

'A highly exposed target,' said Calatus. 'One good shot would see us all drop, vulnerable to every gun in the surrounding buildings.'

'A fourth-storey roof would be attainable, Brother-Huntmaster,' confirmed Casamir.

'If they fear the skies, they will be holding Sabrael as far down as possible,' said Annael. 'Basement, sub-levels. Anything of that sort, *Swiftclaw*?'

'Extensive basement and sub-basement structures beneath the main plant and linked to the accompanying structure. Pipes, energy cables, storage space, a jumble of conduits, chambers and passageways. Once we launch the attack, I can perform a low-altitude pass and perhaps pick up something more definite.'

'Affirmative, *Swiftclaw*,' said Tybalain. He dismounted and the others followed. Annael was reluctant to leave *Black Shadow*, fearing something might happen to his steed in his absence. He patted the saddle and left one hand on the fuel tank as he awaited instruction from the Huntmaster.

'Are we sure of this course of action, brother?' said Calatus. 'To risk the lives of six brothers to reclaim a single wayward soul seems a poor exchange of effort for reward.'

'No order has left my lips,' snapped Tybalain. 'If you did not wish to accompany us, you have come a long way for nothing.'

The Huntmaster and the Black Knight stared at each other for several seconds, before Calatus bowed his head in deference.

'Your will is my command, Brother-Huntmaster,' Calatus said. 'No order need be voiced.'

The growl of the *Swiftclaw*'s engines reverberated down the street and they turned towards the approaching skimmer.

'It is fortunate that we have expended most of our ammunition reserves,' Eladon told them. 'We should be just within the weight boundary.'

The sound from the anti-grav plate became a moan as Annael and Calatus climbed onto the boarding steps on either side of the Land Speeder. It increased to a loud whine to compensate for Nerean and Tybalain, the *Swiftclaw* dipping slightly before resuming its place a metre above the ground.

'Are you positive you can put us on the roof?' asked Annael.

'Yes.' Casamir's tone made it clear he did not appreciate Annael's question. 'Everybody secure?'

After receiving their affirmatives, the Land Speeder pilot took his machine into a vertical climb, rotating the nose towards the target.

'Straight in and out,' he said. 'I'll set up a distraction attack on the east side once you are on the roof.'

The speeder rose to about ten metres, just enough to clear a cluster of power cables stretching along a line of pylons beside the road. The nose dipped and the thrusters eased them forward, a little more than walking speed.

'Can you not dawdle?' said Nerean. 'The enemy are bound to see us if we meander into their midst.'

'I have almost no trim or roll control, let's not make this any harder,' Casamir replied, his mood tense.

They crossed several streets and manufactoria, moving through clouds of steam and smog from exhaust stacks, the ground below lit by idling forges and the gleam of lamps through bulls-eye-glassed windows, the headlights of abandoned ore movers and cargo haulers. Perhaps to conceal their presence, the invaders had doused the street lanterns in the processing plant and surrounding buildings. Rather than hide their whereabouts, the blot of darkness made it clear that something was amiss in the area.

It also meant that the *Swiftclaw* moved almost invisibly, the black-hulled craft a shadow against the smoke that swathed the sky. The wind carried away the noise of the protesting grav-plate. Unseen and unheard, the Black Knights alighted on the roof of the target building.

Annael was the first to land, his armour absorbing the impact of a three-metre drop. He had his bolt pistol in hand, but it was his combat knife in the other that would be his weapon of choice on this operation. It was key that the enemy did not know they were compromised until it was too late.

The roof was made of plasteel sheeting that sagged under his weight.

'Disperse,' he hissed to the others. 'Fragile surface.'

He moved a few paces so that the others could spread out, distributing their weight more evenly.

'I see no ingress point,' he told them, looking around. 'No stairs or conveyor.'

'Heating spill shaft here,' said Nerean, kneeling beside a grille-topped pipe that extruded about a metre from the slight cant of the roof. 'Let me just see if...'

He fell silent and pulled the pipe with one hand. It resisted and then slid upward. An extraction unit followed, leaving a metre-square hole in the roof material. Tybalain moved to the edge while Nerean set down the piece of machinery. Taking the lip in both hands, the Huntmaster pulled, peeling back the roof like the lid of a rations tin. Moving backwards, he opened up a gap large enough for a Space Marine to drop through.

Nerean went in first. Annael heard the *clump* of his battle-brother landing and the tread of his boots as he moved around the top floor.

'Abandoned,' Nerean declared. 'Not even being used for storage.'

Tybalain, still holding back the roll of plasteel, gestured for Calatus and then Annael to descend. They quickly formed a defensive perimeter and were joined by the Huntmaster. Annael missed the auspex of *Black Shadow*, but even without its enhanced systems, he could see that the floor was mostly one open space, crisscrossed with ducts and pipes from the environmental and communications systems situated on the floors below.

'Stairwell,' announced Tybalain, from the north-west corner.

A dull rattle broke the still. Though dampened by the walls, the sound of the *Swiftclaw*'s heavy bolter was unmistakable. Between fusillades, Annael could hear exclamations of shock from the floors below, and the sound of running feet came up the stairway.

They followed Tybalain down a level. The third storey, from what Annael could see through the open door on the landing, was divided into several illuminators' stations, split by chest-high partitions and bookshelves. The easels and magnifiers of stencillists and the pict-capture devices of the crystographers had been left undisturbed, along with the sheaves of reports and archives the administrators had been transcribing.

The sound of descending soldiers on the stairs below faded away. Tybalain started down the next flight, followed by Nerean and then Calatus. Annael was bringing up the rear. While the others continued down, he stopped just before the landing. He heard the scuff of feet and muttered cursing.

A moment later a blue-skinned soldier, head shaven, body bulging with boosted muscle, stepped out in front of Annael. The rebel's attention was fixed on the large-calibre automatic weapon he was carrying in one hand, and the drum magazine he was trying to slot into place with the other.

The *clump* of Annael's stride brought the renegade spinning around, mouth opening to shout a warning. Adrenal stimms gave the man preternatural speed, but he was still not as swift as the Dark Angel.

Annael's knife stabbed up into the man's throat,

sliding effortlessly through his enemy's windpipe, cleaving up through tongue and soft palate to fix the dying man's mouth shut. The base of Annael's pistol grip smashed into the man's temple, shattering bone, killing him instantly.

'Target slain,' he reported to the others. He paused, listening intently. 'No sign of any remaining, I think he was the last.'

He caught up with them on the next floor, but Tybalain moved on without pause until they had reached the bottom. The stair had brought them to a vestibule area, a broad door flanked by two high arched windows. The flicker of muzzle flare strobed through the coloured glass and the panes rattled with every discharge from the Land Speeder's assault cannon.

'No entry to the sub-levels,' said Calatus, who had been checking the space beneath the ferrocrete steps.

'Casamir, we need a basement entrance point,' said Tybalain.

They waited several seconds for the reply, eyes and ears straining for any sound of the enemy close at hand. There was none; it seemed the building had been emptied by the *Swiftclaw*'s diversion. Casamir replied, the background zip of las-fire caught in the transmission.

'I have your position. There is a service elevator in a docking bay seven metres to the south. It goes down one level.' There was another pause and through the windows came the bright flash of an explosion. 'Frag warhead, minimal damage. Fire control systems activated. The service elevator takes you into the connecting duct with the main facility. Head east, there is a branching point, the second one that turns north again. I am reading a strange thermal cluster. Could be a generator, but it looks worth investigating.'

'Acknowledged, proceeding to target point,' said Tybalain. 'Maintain attack for thirty seconds and then break off. We will be in the sub-levels at that point.'

'Confirmed, Brother-Huntmaster.'

They followed Casamir's directions, moving from the stairwell via a short corridor into a cage-like storage pen and through into the loading bay. The metal shutters were closed, the conveyor doors open. Tybalain stepped into the elevator, followed by Annael.

'Wait!' said Annael, holding up a hand as Nerean was about to step aboard. He pointed to the plate above the door indicating the maximum load weight. 'We will have to descend two at a time.'

Nerean took a step back and Annael slid the door closed. Tybalain pulled the lever and they made their rattling descent. When the conveyor had touched the bottom, a bell chimed outside.

Annael wrenched the door open and stepped out quickly, pulling his knife free, aware that the elevator's bell might attract attention. He was in a corridor only a little wider than the elevator, which ran for a few metres and then met a larger passageway cutting perpendicular across the end. Thin glowing wires set into the ceiling cast a jade light across the sub-level.

Without needing any command from Tybalain, Annael strode forward and stopped at the junction. He checked both ways.

'West runs about thirty metres, east ten metres and then turns. No activity.' In fact there was very little at all in the corridor. A pipe ran along the joint between the wall and the ceiling, dripping at a few broken seams, leaving a mouldy growth on the walls. The sound of the drops echoed starkly in the silence. Down here, nothing could be heard of the Land Speeder's attack or the rebels' response.

'Move to the turn,' Tybalain said, as he sent the elevator clattering back up to collect the others.

Annael obeyed, long strides taking him swiftly to where the corridor bent thirty degrees north-east.

'Forty metres, I can see another conveyor at the end. Two doors on the left, wheel-locks. Three branching corridors on the right.' Annael stopped, his auto-senses filtering something from the air. He boosted the olfactory receivers and audio conductors, his vision dimming slightly while the system compensated. 'I can smell sweat, gun oil, explosives. Picking up breathing, multiple respirations per second. Footsteps!'

The pad of feet grew louder and a shadow emerged from the end of the corridor Casamir had indicated. Decisive action and surprise were the key tactics of the Ravenwing, whether mounted or on foot. Annael responded without thought, dashing forward with pistol and knife at the ready.

The man that stepped out of the passage looked surprisingly normal, in comparison to the heavily augmented warriors that made up the bulk of the enemy force. He wore loose grey trousers and a long blue coat, a tattered forage cap jammed onto a head of white hair. Annael was still several metres away when the rebel turned his head towards the sound of the onrushing Space Marine.

The traitor gave a shout of warning and brought up his lasgun.

The *crack* of Annael's bolt pistol sounded loud in the confined space, as did the impact detonation that split the man's head apart.

Annael had seconds to make the most of the enemy's shock and confusion. He threw himself around the corner into the side-tunnel, cracking the ferrocrete as he rebounded from the far wall. Ahead, the metal door at the end of a ten-metre corridor was closing. Annael loosed off as many rounds as he could, the bolts sparking from the hatchway, but the door slammed closed with an ominous clang.

He reached the door, slamming his shoulder into the ferrite, the reverberation of the impact accompanied by lock bars scraping into place.

'Melta charges,' he told the others. 'We have to breach.'

Calatus had the melta bombs and ten seconds passed before he arrived at the barred door. Annael stepped back to allow his companion to work.

The Black Knight placed three charges, one at each hinge and one about two-thirds of the way in where he judged the interior lock to be located. Waving for Annael and the others to back away further, Calatus pulled a priming pin from each charge and rapidly retreated.

Three seconds later the melta bombs detonated, vaporising the metal of the door. The hatch continued standing, but the hinges and the wall around them had been turned to blackened slag and dust.

Annael heard shouts from inside the room beyond – panicked yells.

He pushed past Calatus, about to raise a boot to kick the door, when the hatch fell towards him, clanging to the floor in a swirl of charred motes and dissipating vapour.

In the doorway stood Sabrael. He wore his armour, except for his helm, and there was fresh blood sprayed across his chest, his gauntlets ruddy with gore. Half a dozen corpses lay mangled in the storeroom behind him, hearts and throats ripped out. Annael could see another door open behind his battle-brother, almost ripped from its mountings.

Noticing the direction of his gaze, Sabrael stepped back and looked at the dead men.

'They made the mistake of trying to kill me,' he said quietly. 'They really should not have opened that door.'

Annael grinned inside his helm and stepped forward, offering a hand. Sabrael took it and they stood looking at each other. Calatus intervened, stepping between them to break the handshake.

'Brother Calatus, it is s–'

Sabrael's intended witticism was cut short by Calatus's fist crashing against his chin. Dazed, Sabrael reeled back and Calatus followed, throwing another punch that slammed against the side of Sabrael's head. Annael leapt forward, taking Calatus to the ground. The two of them struggled for several seconds as Calatus tried to rise again.

'Enough!' The stern command from Tybalain separated the two grappling Black Knights. 'Show some discipline, both of you. We are still in enemy territory.'

'Thank you for your intervention,' said Sabrael, extending a hand in gratitude.

The Huntmaster ignored him and looked around the room. On a table was the Blade of Corswain, lying in its scabbard. Tybalain pushed past Sabrael and took up the sheathed sword in one hand.

'I was about to…' Sabrael's protest died as Tybalain turned round, one finger raised to silence him.

'When we return to the Chapter it will be decided whether you may retain the swordsman's honour. Until then, you have forfeited the right to bear the Blade of Corswain. That you risked its loss is evidence enough that you do not deserve it. However, it will not be my judgement, but the Supreme Grand Master's.'

'Of course, Huntmaster,' said Sabrael, bowing his head in submission to Tybalain's command.

'If you have any honour, you will not contest its confiscation,' the Huntmaster added.

'The shame you have brought upon yourself, the squadron and the company is monstrous,' said Calatus, pushing himself free from Annael's grip. 'If you have any honour, you will seek the penitent's fate at the next opportunity.'

The Black Knight stalked back to the corridor, where he received a nod of agreement from Nerean. Sabrael said nothing as he turned and helped Annael to his feet. He looked pensive as he retrieved his helm from a shelf and fitted it to the collar of his war-plate.

The penitent's fate – death in battle.

PART TWO
PISCINA

END OF AN AGE

'If I might ask, what does that mean, Chapter Master?'

Colonel Brade looked up at the giant warrior who stood next to him in the cratered remains that had been a roof terrace on the Imperial Commander's palace. The ranking officer of the remnants of the Piscina Free Militia looked haggard, his skin loose where he had lost considerable weight in a short time. His uniform was carefully pressed, the collars starched stiff, but such treatment could not hide the stains and wear of recent months. The de facto ruler of Piscina Four looked weary beyond caring.

'You might ask, colonel, but I feel no inclination to answer,' replied Azrael.

The Supreme Grand Master of the Dark Angels stood in his full war panoply, his dark green armour embellished with gilding and gems, his personal standard affixed to a pole that extended from his backpack. He wore the Sword of Secrets at his belt, which banded his robe about his waist, the cloth the bone-white of the Deathwing to mark his passage through the First Company.

He glanced down at Brade and then returned his gaze to the broken city that lay about the palace. Kadillus Harbour was less a metropolis and more a ruin. It had never fully recovered from the invasion of the ork warlords Ghazghkull Thraka and Nazdreg. The uprising and ork resurgence of the past year had brought down everything that had been rebuilt and more. Tactical squads from the Chapter and specialised Free Militia units were using flamers and pyrobombs to cleanse the shattered remains of the city, to ensure no ork spores remained.

The spires of the ancient Chapter Keep that had once dominated the eastern part of the city had been flattened, not by the greenskins but the Techmarines of the Dark Angels. Nothing remained of the old stronghold.

The Basilica that had once belonged to the Chapter, site of the fiercest fighting in the city between Ghazghkull's orks and the Third Company, still stood, a hollowed shell. It seemed a sacrilege to pull down such an honoured structure, so he had deigned to let it remain as testament to the bonds that had once held Piscina and the Dark Angels together.

Beyond the curtain wall – itself a jagged shadow of its former defiance – were the East Barrens where any number of ork nests remained to be uncovered. In the opposite direction was the ocean, the only part of the region untouched by the orkish taint.

'You can't just leave, Chapter Master. The war isn't over!'

'This war will never be over, Colonel Brade, until the regiments of the Emperor's Astra Militarum arrive with such numbers that every square kilometre of Kadillus Island can be scoured. I thought once that my Chapter had achieved this end, but I was wrong. Your forces are experienced and well-equipped now, enough to keep the threat under control until a task force can be mobilised by the Adeptus Terra.'

Azrael could not tell the colonel his reasons for leaving Piscina, any more than he could inform him that this disaster had not been brought about by orks, but the intervention of a handful of Dark Angel renegades from the dawn of the Imperium. It sounded so ridiculous to think of the Hunt in those terms. Azrael almost wanted to tell Brade the truth, just to see his incredulity. That was out of the question and the Supreme Grand Master reined in his whimsy, regaining his composure. Of his expression nothing had changed during the internal debate and Brade continued regardless.

'If the Dark Angels remove their liegehood from Piscina, what will become of us? We have scant resources for our people, with the docks in ruins, the mines just as unworkable.'

'The Priesthood of Terra will find a place for you in the grander scheme of the Imperium, colonel. It is done, there is no turning back my decision. You must learn to survive without the patronage of the Dark Angels. Far lesser planets and people have done so for millennia, I do not doubt that Piscina Four will endure long into the coming centuries.'

Azrael did not say how close Piscina had come to having no future at all. It had been a difficult decision to cut Piscina loose from the demesne of the Chapter, but an event two months earlier had left him only a far worse alternative.

* * *

The door terminal chimed, announcing the arrival of Master Belial. Azrael waited for a few seconds, finishing his briefing notes for the next phase of missions into the East Barrens of Kadillus Island. He looked around the chamber, sparing a glance for the view of the world below through the great arched window to his left. A globe of mostly blue ocean and dark clouds, the glimpse of grey and green continents brief.

These rooms had hosted the commanders of the Dark Angels for generations. He was far up in the pinnacle of the Tower of Angels that Azrael knew once had been Aldurukh, the keep of the Order on Caliban. Lesser towers and fortifications as well as star docks and launch bays spread out across the asteroid that now served as the fortress-monastery of the Dark Angels, spilling yellow, red and white patches of light across the barren rock. Tradition held that these rooms had been used by the Lion himself.

The walls were hung with banners showing the heraldry of successive Chapter Masters, Azrael's taking pride of place above the chair and desk at the far end of the chamber. Countless worlds had been saved by orders issued from this chamber, and countless again were the foes slain and the brothers lost in those wars. Azrael's only concession to that history was a skull of an eldar pirate, polished to a gleam and inscribed with curses and catechisms to torment the soul of the creature it had belonged to. He had learned many things on becoming Supreme Grand Master, reading the old texts of the Lion and gleaning what he could from the Dark Oracle in the dungeons beneath the Rock. The eldar had once controlled an empire across the stars, but had lost it. The severed head of the eldar warrior was reminder to Azrael that the Dark Angels clung to a similar precipice and a moment's respite would see them fall into the abyss of damnation.

He looked up, noted that Asmodai accompanied Belial, and waved them forward. He watched the two of them carefully, wondering why Asmodai had chosen to join Belial in the petition. The Master of Repentance made no secret of his dislike for Azrael's appointment of Sapphon to the position of Master of Sanctity. Was this another opportunity to exert pressure on his Chapter lord? The timing was inconvenient, to put it mildly.

'You understand that our campaign on Piscina is ongoing.' *The Supreme Grand Master focused on Belial who had called for the audience, eyes as dark and hard as granite.* 'All three of us have duties elsewhere.'

'I will be brief, Grand Master. I think that we waste valuable time and resources trying to reclaim Piscina Four from the ork infestation. With the Rock in orbit we possess the weaponry required to obliterate all life on the planet, and should do so before casualties amongst our ranks become excessive.'

'I am surprised that you of all my warriors are prepared to abandon Piscina Four without a battle. You have already striven so hard to guard this world for the Chapter and the Emperor, why give in to the counsel of despair now?'

'No despair, Brother Azrael, only a long-delayed acceptance of the consequences of my failures many years ago. Had I succeeded in eliminating the ork threat properly at its arrival the current situation would not have developed. That I did not has allowed the orks to gain a grip on this world that no effort of the Chapter can prise away.'

'I see.'

The Supreme Grand Master stood up. To mask his annoyance he started to pace back and forth behind his chair. He stroked his chin, feigning deep thought, while he mastered unwarranted feelings of betrayal. When one held sway over the Inner Circle it was too easy to give in to paranoia and the belief that every disagreement was but the first pebbles that heralded a coming avalanche of treachery.

Just as every Supreme Grand Master secretly harboured the hope that he would usher in an age after the Hunt had finished, they all had been prone to an underlying dread that they would preside over the ultimate collapse of the teetering edifice of lies and obfuscations that the Dark Angels had become. From his position atop the mound of falsehood and misdirection, Azrael could clearly see how precarious was the position he held and the foundations beneath it. And Asmodai was just the sort of individual that would happily see the Chapter fall upon itself if it proved him righteous.

Belial took this as an opportunity to argue his case further and Azrael said nothing to stop him.

'We cannot accomplish this task alone without ignoring other battles that require our intervention. The longer we spend on this lost world, the more danger to other planets of the Emperor. The Piscinans have been rendered useless as allies, would you have us wait until forces from the Imperium arrive to assist us?'

Asmodai shook his head, thumping a fist into his other hand.

'Impossible! All three of us know that the Fallen interfered with Piscina during the stewardship of Chaplain Boreas and his companions. We risk knowledge of their existence spreading beyond the world if outsiders become involved in the campaign.'

Azrael stopped and turned a warning look towards the Chaplain, his hands moving to clasp each other behind his back. Talk of the Fallen earned a fierce scowl from the Supreme Grand Master.

'You suggest that I destroy the population of an entire world to keep secret the existence of the Fallen? An act *that will earn us further investigation and suspicion, no doubt. Sometimes I think you desire a confrontation with the Imperium, Asmodai.'*

'There is precedent, Brother Azrael. And the presence of the orks presents far more justification than has sometimes been offered.'

'If there is evidence of the Fallen to be removed, it will be removed. If I listened to your counsel, every world where even rumour of the Fallen is found would be left a lifeless wasteland.'

The Deathwing commander stepped closer to his superior, darting an equal look of annoyance at the Master of Repentance. Azrael did not react, but noted that the two were not of perfect accord. Neither of them were experts at the internal politics of the Chapter and both had come with an honest petition to make. Belial took a breath and weighed his next words carefully.

'The Piscina System is tainted, we can no longer recruit from here with any confidence. If we become mired in a war against the greenskins we compound the failure of my earlier campaign.'

Azrael's eyebrows rose in surprise.

'Your campaign? Your failure? Did you not hold back the orks sufficiently to stop the world being overrun, and did not the entire Chapter under my command conduct the intended annihilation? You would embroil us in intrigue with the Imperium and throw away millions of lives because of your impossible quest for perfection?'

'Apologies, Supreme Grand Master. Our failure. And it is not perfection I seek, it is simply an absence of error. Our warriors spend days in the Reclusiam pondering their failings and atoning for their deficiencies. Those of us of higher rank must hold to an even stricter code.'

'The reasons are irrelevant. We cannot place ourselves

in higher moral authority than the people we are sworn to protect. If there is atonement to be made, should it not be painful? Should it not involve sacrifice? You suggest the easy route, thinking there will be no repercussions, no regrets.'

Belial struggled, the truth of this statement undeniable. It was no secret that the Grand Master of the Deathwing vexed his flesh with acidic tattoos so that he would better remember the price of perceived failure. For the most part it was an entirely desirable – admirable – trait in a commander but now the First Company's master was becoming intolerant, perhaps finding undue alliance with Asmodai's hard-line beliefs. For all that Belial agreed with Azrael's sentiment, equally he could not hide his consternation at this apparent refusal.

'And I see from your expression that there is some other purpose for wishing swift conclusion to our war in Piscina.'

Directly confronted, Belial showed renewed dilemma in his expression. Azrael had guessed correctly that a more personal motive steered the counsel of the Deathwing commander. Belial sighed heavily.

'There were reports of the Beast, sightings a few thousand light years from our current position. It would be a better use of our might to strike down the creature that dealt the fatal wound to Piscina than to remain here and mire ourselves with the scraps left behind.'

Azrael had heard these reports that Ghazghkull was on the move again, but they were no more substantial than a hundred other rumours about the warlord since he had returned to the hives of Armageddon to lay waste to the world that had been the site of his previous great defeat. The Chapter Master regarded Belial evenly, letting neither angered temper nor indulgent forgiveness colour his demeanour.

'So it is to be revenge, is it?'

'*I would prefer you not cheapen my motives with such terminology, Supreme Grand Master. It is justice, is it not, to punish those guilty of the crimes? The Beast killed Piscina, we are simply putting the planet out of its misery.*'

Azrael paused before speaking, about to argue out of habit, out of necessity, but confounded by Belial's argument. He sat down again, another act that bought him a moment's grace to think more clearly. He steepled his hands to his chin and rested his elbows on the report-strewn desk. He looked at Belial for some time and saw honest desire, and then moved his gaze to Asmodai, who had watched the exchange in uncharacteristic silence.

'It is a bleak day when the Adeptus Astartes must weigh the life and death of a whole world, an entire culture that has supported and praised them for generations. You are both dismissed.'

'Are you refusing my proposal, Supreme Grand Master? Am I to conclude that my plan does not find favour in your eyes? You will not conduct Exterminatus?'

'You have made sound arguments, brother. I will not decide the fate of a world in a moment.'

Exterminatus had been out of the question, on practical accounts if the moral reasons were not enough. As Azrael had told the pair of officers, wiping out all life on an Imperial world invited scrutiny he did not desire. Weighed against this had been the equally legitimate argument that the Dark Angels were tarrying far longer than was feasible. There would be no swift end to the problems of Piscina, and the Adeptus Terra were better able to deal with those problems than a Chapter of Space Marines.

'It could be years before they respond, the Adepts of Terra,' complained Brade. 'Even if the astropaths send signals now, they will not receive them on the Throneworld for months more.'

'I have already sent transmissions notifying the High Lords of my decision,' Azrael informed the Free Militia commander. 'My personal psygnia was attached to the broadcast, to ensure it receives the swift attention it deserves.'

'The High Lords?' Brade was clearly vexed by the realisation that Azrael dealt with such powerful, semi-mythical creatures. He was used to dealing with the faceless, endlessly bureaucratic ranks of the Administratum.

'Of course,' said the Chapter Master. 'The surrendering of sovereign Chapter domains to the Imperium is no small matter. I expect that a great deal of attention will soon be brought to bear upon Piscina and its people, and its rulers. Be sure that all is in order when the agents of the Adeptus Terra and Inquisition arrive to audit your conduct.'

The veiled threat pierced Brade's bluster and a fresh look of horror crossed his face.

'Inquisition?' he whispered. 'Here?'

'If I were you, colonel, I would welcome such a thing. I will leave a report that highlights your exemplary behaviour, both in the current crisis and during our earlier dealings with Ghazghkull. Praise like that will earn you a general's rank in the Astra Militarum if you desire it, or perhaps officially confirm you as Imperial Commander of Piscina, dispensing with the charade of your coup and puppet-governor.'

'Puppet?' Brade was genuinely offended by the intimation and bridled before Azrael, stiffening to his full height and staring the supreme commander of the Dark Angels in the eye. 'I have nothing to fear from the Inquisition, Chapter Master Azrael. Can you say the same?'

'The Inquisition have never been a problem for my Chapter, colonel. Remember, we are the First, the Dark Angels, the Emperor's Own. Do not make me regret penning my report in such favourable terms.' Brade sagged again, his moment of fortitude evaporating. 'As an appointed representative of the Piscinan authorities, you are duly informed that the Dark Angels Chapter of the Adeptus Astartes rescinds all ties to the worlds of the Piscina System. As outlined in the *Justices Astartes*, the *Liber Mortis Angelica* and the Codes of Imperial Governance, I exert the right for all oaths, allegiances and tithes to revert from the sovereign control of the Dark Angels Chapter to the Adeptus Terra, overseers of the Imperium in the Emperor's name. *Acquieset finalis*.'

Brade paled even further as the finality of these words sank home.

'Brother Bethor,' said Azrael, looking to the Space Marine who stood at a tall flagpole near the edge of the roof. At the top of the pole flew a black banner with a golden Imperial aquila upon it. Beneath fluttered a pennant, black, marked in white with the sigil of the Dark Angels.

Taking up a silver cord hanging from the pole, Brother Bethor lowered the standard of the Dark Angels. He removed it from its toggles, folded it thrice and presented it to Azrael with a bow. Azrael took the flag with a solemn nod and held it for several seconds before passing it back to the Chapter Standard Bearer.

'Is that it?' said Brade, looking around. 'I expected more... pomp. Grandeur?'

'Do you feel this a moment to celebrate, colonel?' Azrael swept a hand towards the encompassing city.

'Would you like to announce to all and sundry that your liege-masters are departing, never to return?'

'No, I suppose not,' said Brade. 'Not yet. The Free Militia draw strength from our alliance. I will not rob them of that, not yet.'

'Our business is concluded, in all ways.' Azrael turned away but spun back and extended a hand of friendship to the colonel. Surprised, it was several seconds before Brade clasped it in return. 'I would have had this another way if I could, Colonel Brade. You have my sincerest regards and respect, and I wish you every success in the forging of a new age for Piscina. You will be a worthy Imperial Commander.'

'Thank you,' said Brade, clearly humbled by the Space Marine's unexpected praise.

Azrael said no more as he turned on his heel and marched away, Bethor matching his stride beside him.

'The deed is done,' said the Standard Bearer.

'Yes. It is time to implement the extraction strategy.' Azrael did not look at his companion as he voiced the consequences of his decision. 'Within four hours, for the first time in thousands of years, there will no more be a Dark Angels presence on Piscina.'

THE HIDDEN CHAMBER

Asmodai descended the ramp of the Thunderhawk, his step echoed by the Deathwing Knights behind him. They flanked two prisoners, both manacled with magno-cuffs and hooded with eyeless cowls made of plasteel chainmail. Anovel had been divested of his armour, Cypher not. It annoyed Asmodai that he was reluctant to strip the arch-renegade of his wargear, but the memory of the sword's vision was burned into his mind. He did not know the full properties of the blade, or its provenance, but if the myths were true that it was the Lion Sword, weapon of the primarch, it was possible his last moments were etched into the ancient metal in some arcane fashion. He had spoken to Ezekiel about the matter but even the Chief Librarian had been reluctant to psychically probe the sword.

Beneath the cowls both Space Marines were gagged and further blindfolded, to ensure there was no possibility of communication between them. A Deathwing Knight, in ivory-coloured robes rather than armour, stood between them to further restrict any possibility of them passing a message to each other.

They were halted by a pair of large gates, wrought from black metal in the design of a winged sword that was mirrored on each side. Asmodai looked back, past the Thunderhawk, into the gulf of space. The spread of stars was slightly out of focus, distorted by the banks of energy shields that protected the Rock. Piscina's star was no larger than his fist, dwindling imperceptibly as the fortress-monastery powered away from the abandoned world. They were outside the orbit of Piscina Five, Piscina Four just a blue speck barely visible in the light of the star. Five more days would see them at the gravitic boundary of the system, where the pull of the star was weak enough to allow a warp jump.

It had been fortunate that the expedition had arrived in Piscina a scant few days before the Rock was due to transition to the warp. Azrael had decided the Chapter would move on to battle the emerging threat of a Varsine Bloodflock tearing across the Phyleaides Cluster seventy light years away. Though Ezekiel had despatched psychic transmissions concerning the imminent return of the Ravenwing and Deathwing – though no word of their special captive could be risked across the warp – the two strike cruisers had outpaced the astropathic message. Such were the vagaries of warp communication and travel at times.

Azrael had decided against Exterminatus, a decision Asmodai thought weak but predictable. Even without knowing the events on Ulthor and Tharsis, the

Supreme Grand Master had chosen to compromise rather than take decisive action. The Chaplain had not spoken to Belial since the *Penitent Warrior* had jumped in-system, but he knew that the Deathwing commander would bear the news with his usual phlegmatic manner.

The Master of the First Company followed his Knights from the Thunderhawk, Ezekiel and Sapphon with him. Sammael and Malcifer had arrived at the Rock three days earlier, the Ravenwing's transit through the warp slightly swifter than their brothers in the Deathwing. Asmodai could see them as the gates opened, standing beside Lord Azrael.

The prisoner and escort halted as they reached the bare stone paving outside the dungeon entrance. Belial and his companions passed them, the Grand Master of the Deathwing with eyes only for the Supreme Grand Master. Asmodai had ensured that Belial knew nothing of what had happened with the arrival of Cypher, and they had not spoken since departing Tharsis. Their last conversation still troubled Asmodai.

Belial was still in the semicomatose state induced by Asmodai's psycommand words. The Interrogator-Chaplain approached and whispered in the Grand Master's ear.

'Somnalatus exaunt.'

Belial straightened but there was still a glassy, faraway cast to his gaze. His catalepsean node was returning to normal function, but in the next few minutes Belial would be capable of interacting with the Chaplain, and also highly susceptible to any prompt or implanted thought. Asmodai chose his words carefully.

'Master Belial, do you understand what I am saying?'

'Yes,' *the Deathwing commander mumbled.*

'Do you recall what happened before sleep took you?'

'Yes.'

'Tell me what happened from the time that you left your chamber to meet me.'

'I assembled the escort squad as protocol dictates, mustering at the second guard chamber of the cell deck.'

'What were you thinking?' Asmodai asked.

'I was concerned with the procedure of the incarceration. The prisoner is highly valuable and extremely dangerous. It was not the time to allow for any mistake.'

'And your thoughts towards the prisoner at that time?'

'I was not considering him as a person, simply a prisoner, an object that required careful handling. I did not have any thoughts towards him beyond that.'

'You arrived with the escort party and waited at the door for my command, is that correct? How did you feel then?'

'That is correct. I was expectant, curious to see what the arch-renegade looked like. Anticipation, a little apprehension that I did not welcome.'

'What happened next?'

'When I entered, when I laid eyes upon the prisoner, I felt hatred boiling inside me.'

'At that exact moment when you saw him?'

'Yes. I realised that he had to die. I did not want my Knights to see what I was going to do, nor give them the chance to intervene. I closed the door. I moved to kill the prisoner with my blade and you protected him.'

'Why did he have to die?'

'I am not certain.'

'Not certain? You showed no reluctance to slay him. You were possessed by conviction. Why did he have to die?'

'It was an instinct, an overwhelming urge. He is the arch-renegade, the *traitoris principe* and death was his punishment.'

Asmodai could see comprehension begin to return to Belial's eyes. He had to act swiftly.

'The prisoner misspoke, insulting the Chapter and the Lion. He provoked you.'

Belial's brow wrinkled in confusion but he parroted the line a few seconds later.

'The prisoner tricked you into drawing your blade and tried to take it from you.'

Again Belial, words faltering, recited the line.

'I intervened to assist you and my hand caught on the exposed blade.'

'He sliced off your fingers,' said Belial, looking down at the Chaplain's ravaged hand. That was a good sign. The Deathwing commander was starting to create the false memories himself, picking up the narrative implanted by Asmodai. The more he imagined for himself, the better the memory would sit in his mind.

'That is correct.'

'I came to your aid and restrained the prisoner.'

Asmodai bit back the instinct to correct this assertion. He suppressed his pride and allowed himself to be pictured as the victim in the exchange.

'That is also correct.'

Belial nodded, almost fully awake again.

'You will not remember us having this conversation, only the events as you have related them. You have just sent the prisoner away with the escort and are going to inform the apothecarion of my injury. Do you understand?'

'Yes, I understand.'

'Mnemonis dialogis non memorianda est.'

Belial came to consciousness like a man resurfacing from being beneath the waves. He looked around the flight bay and then back at Asmodai, his gaze straying to the wounded hand.

'*Apothecary, this is Belial. Master Asmodai is on his way for treatment. Digital loss. Inform the armoury master, active prosthetics will be required.*'

Asmodai flexed his artificial fingers, the movement still feeling stiff and unnatural. The Techmarines had removed his whole hand – easier than attaching individual digits – weaving the old tendons, reinforced with muscle fibres similar to those used in power armour, around a metal and plastic skeleton. Black tubing acted as veins and capillaries. The bionic was covered with a thin sheen of blood, though he had been assured that would dissipate as the biowelding healed fully.

The ruddy glow of lamps flickered off thousands of skulls adorning the walls and ceiling of the vast sepulchre, gleaming in eyeless sockets and shining off polished lipless grins. Many were human, but most were not: a mix of subtle, elongated features, brutal, bucket-jawed aliens, eyeless monstrosities, horned, twisted creatures and many other contorted, inhuman stares looked down upon the assembled Dark Angels.

The solitary toll of a bell brought the assembled guard to attention, both officers and Knights. The great gates in front of the prisoners opened inwards, another clanging of the bell drowning out the hiss of hydraulics and creak of ancient hinges. When the gates were fully open Belial gestured to the escort to advance. Under their prompting, Anovel and Cypher marched across the threshold into the dungeons of the Rock.

Azrael's hood was raised. Nothing could be seen of his expression.

'Brother Malcifer, lead the escort to the prisoners' cells,' he said, his voice quiet, the softest of echoes returning from the walls of the dungeon vault. 'The rest of you will remain with me.'

Asmodai peeled away from the group with Belial, Sapphon, Ezekiel and Sammael to either side of him. They waited for further instruction from their lord, who followed the progress of the captives into the depths. When the last sound of footfalls had passed, the Supreme Grand Master turned silently and led his senior officers to a set of steps winding up from the entrance tunnel.

Asmodai had never seen the stairwell before – he had always come either by shuttle or gunship, or down the steps located a few dozen metres further into the Rock, which descended from the Lower Reclusiam of the Tower of Angels that soared above them. He glanced at his companions and saw that they were similarly intrigued, the existence of the steps known previously entirely to Azrael. Only Ezekiel remained unmoved, his eyes fixed on the Lord of the Dark Angels.

The stair did not ascend far, thirty steps in all, and brought them into a space illuminated by a dim, flickering light. Asmodai judged the chamber to be just below the Great Library where candidates for the Inner Circle were tested, and the successful were given their tuition in the innermost mysteries of the Chapter.

There was a curtained archway to one side, probably leading to another secret entrance in the Grand Library. The room was round, a star inlaid in twelve alternating red and black points in the stone floor. Azrael stepped onto the white circle at the centre of the design and turned to face them. His officers halted just short of the star, looking around the chamber.

Asmodai turned his gaze towards the ceiling and saw another star above, the colours reversed so that red was above black and black above red. The centre was formed by a large crystal that glimmered with pale light. It was inscribed with a ten-pointed star, and inside that another star with eight points, then six. The last, no larger than the tip of Asmodai's finger, had four points.

He detected a subtle intake of breath by his companions and he returned his gaze to the rest of the room. In the shadows at the edge of the chamber he saw diminutive figures, no taller than waist-high. There had to be two dozen of them, swathed in dark robes that hid any sight of the form within. Eyes gleamed like embers beneath their cowls.

Watchers in the Dark.

They had always been around the Rock, and Asmodai had never questioned their existence. They were as much a part of the Dark Angels as the green armour and the robes of office. The Watchers had been there when Asmodai had first been brought into the Chapter and a rarely seen but unremarkable sight ever since.

It struck him now as odd that their presence had been so disregarded by everyone. Outsiders simply assumed that they were child serfs or some kind of Adeptus Mechanicus servitor-creation specific to the Chapter. Asmodai had never given them much thought until now.

His speculation was interrupted by Azrael.

'This is the Hidden Chamber. A banal name for a place of such importance.' The Supreme Grand Master turned a full circle, arms wide. 'Within these walls the first Inner Circle convened.'

'To discuss Guilliman's Codex Astartes and the break-up of the Legion,' offered Sammael.

'No,' Azrael replied bluntly, completing his rotation.

He pulled back his hood, revealing a face with dark eyes, gaunt cheeks and furrowed brow. 'That is a lie. One of several likely to be exposed over the coming days and months. We were told the Inner Circle came together to discuss the formation of the Chapters, but that event predates the Inner Circle's inception by several decades. Thus I have found in the private library of my position.'

Asmodai looked as Azrael raised a hand and gestured to his right. The Watchers had parted and where there had been a plain wall there was now an archway leading into a small book-lined chamber. Sapphon took a step forward, entranced by this apparition.

Several Watchers gathered between the Master of Sanctity and the library. They made no noise, said nothing, but their eyes glimmered a little brighter, though they revealed nothing more of their faces. An air of oppression, of chastisement filled the chamber and Sapphon hurriedly stepped back, muttering an apology. The Watchers parted again, their eyes dimming.

'Do not think that this is the only secret library in the Rock,' Azrael said with a lopsided smile. His gaze roamed across them all, and settled on Ezekiel. 'I know that you each have records and tomes peculiar to your positions, and only one of us has access to copies of them all.'

Asmodai wondered how Azrael had learned of the collection of lore volumes in the crypt of the Upper Reclusiam – databanks that expanded with every interrogation of the Fallen. He realised that the Lord of the Chapter was speaking generally, and did not know the location or contents of these additional knowledge banks. The intimation that the Chief Librarian knew the contents was a trifle unsettling, however, although it was obvious, now that he considered the possibility.

'The Inner Circle was first drawn together to discuss a new and terrible threat to the Chapter. The existence of the Fallen.' Azrael paused to allow his words to sink in. 'Swallowed by a great warp storm as battle raged for Caliban, the traitors that had turned on the Lion were thought destroyed for a generation. Our predecessors had believed the rebels annihilated by the tempest they had summoned to aid victory, torn apart by the same energies that had ripped asunder our home world. And then the first of the Fallen was found and the truth of their scattering became known.'

'Why would such a thing be kept secret?' asked Belial. 'We all know the purpose of the Inner Circle.'

'I cannot answer that, because the records do not show, at least not to me,' Azrael replied. 'Many reasons for acts in the distant past have been lost. The shock of the revelation, the creation of the Hunt, these matters preoccupied the officers of the Chapter. The first Inner Circle consisted of twelve Grand Masters, the Chapter Master of the Dark Angels and his peers that ruled the eleven Successors of that time. From that first enclave the decision was made to pursue the Fallen with all vigour and secrecy, and the rule of the Inner Circle was disseminated to all the Chapters of the Unforgiven.'

Asmodai gritted his teeth at mention of the secret name held by the descendants of the Dark Angels Legion. He despised the appellation, for it assumed that the Dark Angels were guilty of the sins of the Fallen. He did not cleave to that philosophy though many did, and preferred to think of the Dark Angels and their Successors as the Vengeance of the Lion, not the bearers of a hidden shame.

'Why reveal this to us now, Master Azrael?' asked Ezekiel, who knew much but clearly not everything. His bionic eye shone red as he glanced at his brothers. 'It is the capture of Cypher, is it not?'

'It is.' Azrael moved a few steps and stopped at one of the points of the star, facing his library. Asmodai followed, an odd compulsion drawing him onto the point two to the left of the Supreme Grand Master. The others took up positions around the device, Ezekiel on the right hand of his lord, Sapphon directly opposite. 'Cypher holds the key to our salvation. And our damnation.'

Asmodai glanced down and saw that he was flanked by two Watchers in the Dark. So were the others. Their diminutive escorts bore identical articles. The one on the right of each warrior carried an empty silver goblet. The Watcher to the left bore a slender dagger.

'You must all swear a new oath today. Rather, you must swear a very ancient oath, sworn first in this chamber and only by six more groups since.'

'What oath could bind us to greater secrecy than we already have sworn?' asked Sammael. 'By what power higher than the Lion and the Emperor could we swear?'

'A good question,' Azrael said. 'Our honour has been staked in the sight of the Emperor Himself, so what further demand could be made? The first Inner Circle were more pragmatic. They swore a blood oath, that death would find them if they broke their word.'

The Watchers beside the Supreme Grand Master moved in front of him and turned, the one with the knife presenting its weapon. Azrael took the golden blade and held it to his palm while the second Watcher in the Dark held up the goblet beneath. A stream of crimson filled the cup as Azrael drew the blade across his hand.

'With this blood I seal my lips. With this blood I still my tongue. I hold faith with my brothers present today that all I shall learn about the Dark Angels, the traitors of Luther and the breaking of Caliban will never be passed to another. Should I break this oath, shall my lips be sealed and tongue stilled for eternity.'

When Azrael had returned the dagger to the Watcher, the two creatures moved away, disappearing into the shadows. One by one they each repeated the blood-pact, until it was Asmodai's turn. Out of instinct he sought to replicate Azrael's deed, but realised that he held the knife in his left hand, ready to slice the palm of his new bionic.

He paused, taken aback by this, alarmed that this was a bad portent. He tried to dismiss the notion and swapped hands, quickly pulling the blade across exposed flesh. He was too hasty, the cut deeper than he wished. He hid the mistake, putting his hands behind his back when the Watcher had collected a goblet of blood, grasping the cloth of his robe tight to help his genhanced blood stem the flow.

'So your life will be forfeit if you break the faith that has been sworn today,' said Azrael. 'Now I can tell you that this is not the first time Cypher has been captured. It was he that caused the first conclave of the Inner Circle to gather. He presented himself at the very gate we have just left, demanding audience with the lords of the Chapter. Another six times has he been in our grasp, yet on all occasions he has escaped retribution for his betrayal.'

The Supreme Grand Master looked each of his lieutenants squarely in the eye, his jaw set.

'We will not make the mistakes of the past. There will be no in fighting, no personal agendas and no cross purposes. My will, my word, is absolute and any that choose to think otherwise will be held *instantly* accountable.' He took a deep breath, his point made. When the Supreme Grand Master continued, his voice dropped to a determined whisper. 'The future of the Chapter, of all the Unforgiven, has been placed in our hands and we shall not squander it.'

DARK PROPHECIES

Watching the others leave, Azrael understood their bewilderment and frustration. He had related everything he had learned about Cypher from the ledgers of the Chapter Masters, and it was woefully little. The position of Lord Cypher had been shrouded in mystery throughout the history of the Order, and such secrecy had endured for the warrior bearing the title at the fall of Caliban. Despite clear opportunities to subject Cypher to excruciation at the hands of the Interrogators, Azrael's predecessors had singularly failed to do so, unless some record was kept in one of the other hidden libraries he had spoken of.

Of the previous seven occasions of Cypher's incarceration, four had resulted from the rebel presenting himself to his captors. The three remaining circumstances were vague, the reports of dubious authenticity, so that Azrael suspected the encounters had been arranged by Cypher but the chronicler was reluctant to admit as much.

He wondered how he would write this latest entry into this particular tale.

Similarly, the reports were unclear on the manner of his departure. Escape from the Rock was impossible, yet Cypher had found freedom seven times before. Azrael had instituted new security regimes and guard doctrine as soon as he had learned from Sammael of the arch-renegade's capture, but he feared it was not enough. Earlier Chapter Masters must have tried similar strategies, without success.

The only other connecting theme between the encounters was their timing. Every appearance of Cypher happened just before a pivotal moment in the Chapter's history – the eve of a great victory or defeat.

There were many missing elements of these accounts too. Supreme Grand Master Cariontis had not disclosed why he had despatched the entirety of the Third and Fourth Companies to Trangenia, where they had been wiped out at Clevinger's Pass by unknown assailants. Equally, Master Dameus shared nothing of the instinct that had guided him to move the Rock to the Akartier System where it met with several of the Successors to intercept a sizeable traitor legionary force breaking out of the Eye of Terror. Again and again, calamity and triumph were presaged by Cypher's arrival.

Azrael had to know which it was this time. There was only one source that could tell him.

He turned around and saw that the Watchers had anticipated his desire. The wall behind him was broken by a slender arch, beyond which the Deep Stair led into the bowels of the Rock. Half of the creatures had already descended, the rest remaining as escort to the Supreme Grand Master. They held small lamps that glowed with amber light, but still nothing could be seen of their faces. All that showed of them were hands, mostly hidden by the voluminous sleeves of their robes, gloved in a material so black it might have been woven from the shadows in the cosmic depths between stars.

Not for the first time, Azrael wanted to know what was beneath the hoods. Even as the thought entered his mind, he felt he was being observed, the presence of the Watchers becoming suddenly obtrusive and judgemental.

It was always there, that last secret, a subtext in every memoir and chronicle he had studied. The Watchers in the Dark had been part of Caliban, part of the Order, but there was nothing to suggest that they were anything other than true to the Lion. Like those that had borne his title before, Azrael simply had to accept the Watchers as what they were – guardians of an older mystery he would never unveil.

'Your secret is safe,' he told them, not even sure they could hear or understand him. Communication was more primal, a shared instinct or desire, a subtle entwining of thoughts.

The Watchers in the Dark were shadows again, as unheeded as the material of the Rock itself. Azrael started towards the revealed stairs and remembered the first time he had descended them.

The dream returned. Seven days had passed since the mantle of Supreme Grand Master had passed to Azrael. Seven nights had come and gone, each bringing with them the same nightmarish apparition.

The tower stood on a hill, broken, windows empty, battlements crumbled.

A flash of lightning, highlighting a face in the lowest slit, hands clasping bars. A plaintive howl split the night air, from no wolf or animal, unleashed from a human throat.

The sky reddened, with flame not a new dawn. An inferno rose up from the ground, its sound the cackle of laughter, the movement of the bright fire like grasping fingers. It surrounded the tower, throwing ruddy light onto ancient stones.

The moans and cries of the man in the tower were piercing, his agony as the flames consumed him more visceral than any experience Azrael felt in waking. In the shrieks he felt his own body burning, his flesh stripped away, soul bared to the licking flames.

He was in the tower, he realised. He must rescue himself.

For the seventh time, Azrael awoke on the cot. The chambers of the Supreme Grand Master seemed strange, still new and awkward. He ran a hand over his chest, wiping away waxy sweat. His fingers followed the ridges and whorls and holes of battle scars, feeling the rigid surface of the black carapace beneath a layer of leathery skin and fat.

By the doorway, a Watcher in the Dark stood, regarding him silently, the glow of red eyes sharp inside its hood. It turned away and walked into the outer room.

This time Azrael followed, finally understanding the summons of the dream.

The Watcher waited patiently as Azrael pulled on his bone-white robe and belted it tight. Symbolic and real keys clattered together, along with the talismans of lamps and hourglasses, amulets of swords and angels' wings. Centuries of service rendered into symbols with hidden meanings.

Barefooted he padded after the diminutive creature. The chamber door swung wide at his approach, though he voiced no command nor bade the locks to open.

I am still in the dream, he decided.

The sense of unreality continued as he stepped out into

the corridor. It was dark. Not just shadowed, but utterly black, save for the glitter of bright eyes lining the passage to his left. The row of light points headed towards the Great Library.

His escort produced a torch from somewhere. It burned with white flame, but its illumination did not reach the lines of creatures flanking Azrael's path, creating a deeper darkness in which they hid.

The Watcher in the Dark led him on, until they came to the huge double doors of the Great Library. Azrael moved towards the portal but found it barred against him, the Watchers refusing to part ranks. Something – not a sound but some other instinct, a twitch on the nape of his neck – caused him to turn.

In the wall, where he knew there was bare dressed stone, an archway had appeared. The keystone was moulded with the winged sword symbol, its blade broken. The sigil of the Deathwing, Azrael knew. But in this context he realised that it was not for the Deathwing that the icon had been created – the First Company merely borrowed it from a far older time.

Steps led down into the darkness, and into that gloom the Watcher disappeared.

Hesitantly, he followed, just about keeping the dim flicker of the Watcher's brand in view.

The steps continued for some time and he passed doors and archways, but his guide continued straight down. He would explore these hidden depths given time, but he knew that his present destination lay at the bottom of the stair.

He reached that point and found the Watcher waiting for him. There were lit torches in sconces on the walls, lighting the near end of a rectangular chamber no more than ten metres wide but disappearing into darkness thirty metres away. Azrael proceeded down the hall and more brands burst into life to either side, lighting his path by a few metres at a time.

Iron doors, riveted and reinforced, locked with heavy bars, lined the hall. Azrael heard only the sound of his steps and felt only the beating of his twin hearts. He knew these cells were empty.

The torches brought him to the last cell, set into the end of the hall. There was no door here, no bars. A shimmer of energy three metres by three metres obscured whatever was within, but Azrael could make out the outline of a man, arms upraised as if pleading with unknown gods.

He realised that the Watchers in the Dark had joined him, clustered around him in a semicircle, as though stopping him from retreating from that cell.

The figure inside was unmoving and it occurred to Azrael that he was looking into a stasis field. He could not hear the slightest buzz of power, though, and he wondered if the field was physical in origin at all.

The field dimmed and cleared, revealing the cell's occupant.

He was tall and broad, for a human, though not as large as a Space Marine. He wore a ragged kilt of stiff leather, revealing that he had undergone extensive augmentation and alteration. Azrael could clearly see the ridged tubes and reinforcements around muscles and bones. The man's skin had a slightly jaundiced cast to it, evidence of extensive stimulants and steroidal boosters – piping inlaid between his shoulder blades and sprouting from the small of his back paid testament to surgically implanted reservoirs for these substances.

The prisoner had his back to Azrael but his face was in profile. Noble of bearing, but contorted in a pained expression, eyes cast up to the heavens in despair. The glitter of cybernetics lay in his eyes and there were auto-sense-like receivers inserted into the back of his ears.

The field snapped off.

'...and rightful restitution shall be made! I beseech you, heed my cries, master!'

The man's lament faltered away, his head cocking to one side as he turned towards Azrael.

'Ah.' The prisoner looked surprised. 'A new one.'

'A new what?' demanded Azrael.

'A new Lord of Aldurukh, of course. What did they call you? Thy name?'

'Azrael,' he replied without thinking.

A smile twisted the man's lips, but there was little humour in his eyes. He flinched suddenly, at some thought or sight unknown to Azrael. The prisoner started to whisper, in no tongue that the Supreme Grand Master recognised.

'What did you do with the Lion?' the man suddenly demanded, face contorting into a feral snarl.

'The Lion is dead,' Azrael said.

'Of course.' The captive slumped, shaking his head. His voice dropped to a whisper. 'That's what they want thee to think. But he hears my pleas, I know it.'

'Who are you?' Azrael demanded.

'Thou know not?' The prisoner looked crestfallen at this revelation. 'Some of the others realised straight away. I am disappointed. Your angels gave me many titles. Your predecessors spat many epithets in my face, but my name is Luther.'

That had been the first time, but not the last.

Without the Watchers to open the path, Azrael descended by a slightly different route, coming to a huge iron gate sealed with a silver lock in the dressed stone wall beside it. He unsheathed the Sword of Secrets and pushed the blade into the locking mechanism. There was a sensation of warmth from the weapon and the lock opened with a clatter of hidden gears and bars. He withdrew the sword and the gate swung open onto the corridor that led to the abandoned cell block.

Azrael came to that cell again, a plain wooden chair set facing the haze of the stasis field. A cluster of Watchers waited in the shadows. Inside, Luther was hunched forward on the bench at the side of the cell, his hands making fists in his lap. What could be seen of his face was a mask of anguish, teeth bared, droplets of spittle from his lips suspended in mid-fall.

Azrael sat down, and as if this was an instruction the stasis field flickered and died.

'...burning twin moons of life and death, sundering from the world of men...' Luther's rant died away as he realised time had moved on. He sat up and looked at Azrael with uncomprehending eyes.

'Welcome back,' said Azrael. 'Four hundred and thirty-eight days have passed for me since we last spoke. Or thereabouts. Warp travel makes it hard to keep track of precise dates.'

The Lord of the Dark Angels had discovered that it helped Luther settle if he was given some sense of the passage of time. From the Dark Oracle's viewpoint his life had become a stuttering existence of minutes at a time, each period of activity no more than an hour, eked out over ten millennia. Context made the architect of the Calibanite rebellion more coherent. For a short time, at least.

Azrael had read the earliest records of the Dark Prophecies, and it was clear that Luther had never been sane, not from the time he surrendered to the forces of the Lion and was placed in the stasis cell. Even so, his grasp on reality had slipped more and more with each passing century. Azrael considered himself fortunate if he gleaned four or five sentences of cogent thought from his captive.

'The visions,' said Luther. His eyes filled with intelligence and recognition. His voice was deep, assured, authoritative. It was the sort of voice Azrael could see himself obeying. The voice of a leader.

The Dark Oracle was a psyker of prodigious talent, though he had never possessed such abilities in the service of the Lion. A gift from the Chaos powers, the old chronicles proposed, in reward for heretical loyalty. Despite his mental puissance, he had never once used his abilities in aggression against his captors.

'What about the visions?' the Supreme Grand Master asked quietly, leaning forward, arms resting on his knees.

'They break mine intellect, Azrael. I sensed the query in thy thoughts. The answer is yea, the visions take a toll upon my mind.'

'You seem lucid enough now.'

'A serpentine piece of string to which I cling, how depressing. It will slip from my fingers soon.'

'You already know why I am here. What can you tell me about Cypher?'

'My Lord Cypher? He is dead. Slain by the hand of the Houndlord who bore my master's blade.'

'You know that is not true. Cypher was saved, as were the other Fallen. What does it mean? Why has he come here?'

'My Lord Cypher returns to me?' A look of hope passed across the Dark Oracle's face, but was swiftly replaced by a mask of paranoia. 'My companion in treachery, the goad and the hand of my darkest will. He knows that I must confess. But he cannot hear it.

Only the Lion can give mine absolution! Only the Lion can name my penance!'

Luther's words devolved into growling and muttering, a mix of archaic Imperial Gothic, High Gothic and ancient Calibanese. Azrael would usually wait for the fits to pass but anxiety forced him to be hasty. Every minute Cypher was in custody was time that the Chapter could be moving towards a catastrophe.

'Why has Cypher come here? Why now?' Azrael demanded, standing up. 'What does Cypher want?'

Luther fell silent and stood up as well. Though Azrael knew for a fact that the heretic was not even as tall as a Space Marine, at that instant the Dark Oracle seemed to fill his cell. The shadows crowded close about Luther, the lamps in the outer chamber guttering. Azrael sensed agitation from the Watchers in the Dark and realised that several more had appeared.

In the gloom, Luther's eyes were silver points, like distant stars.

'The fall of Caliban approaches!' the Dark Oracle declared. 'The sky will burn and the ground will tremble and a world will die!'

'That is an event ten thousand years past,' said Azrael. It was not uncommon for the Dark Oracle to lament his actions of the rebellion. Sometimes this yielded valuable information, but the digression was unwelcome now. 'Caliban broke a hundred centuries ago. Cypher. Tell me about Cypher.'

'The herald sounds the clarion. The dark heart stirs and all will be broken asunder. The past, present and future, that which was, is and will be, united again.'

Luther's gaze moved away from Azrael, no less piercing, but directed towards a spot on the wall, seeing something that was not smooth-cut stone.

'I have wronged thee, my Lord! My transgressions are beyond the counting, my wrongs innumerable. Hear my confession, master, and release me from their torment of guilt. I demand justice, punishment for my sins, and the release of my soul! Why won't thou heed my pleas? Thou listen but do not reply.'

The Dark Oracle fell to his knees, sobbing.

'He cares not for my lament. Hard as the stone, unfeeling. I will whisper it, and shout it, and whisper it again. I failed you, master. I failed you.'

It was obvious that Luther would be no more use at that time. The shimmer of the stasis field returned the instant the thought occurred to Azrael, freezing Luther in a pose of obeisance and petition, hands clasped and imploring, staring at the wall as though his master was before him. Crystalline tears welled in his desperate eyes.

'A madman,' Azrael muttered, turning away. The circumstances gave a venomous edge to the Supreme Grand Master's thoughts. 'I hope the Lion's shade torments you in your sleep, you traitorous dog.'

PENANCE

The penitent's robe chafed. It was meant to. It vexed Annael as much as the harsh cloth itself, to think that he had been engineered to endure all manner of pain, to survive wounds that would slay lesser mortals, and yet a simple linen tabard could irritate him so thoroughly.

The robe was light grey, bereft of any insignia or design. Despite his physical bulk, this rendered him virtually invisible to his battle-brothers. He ranked beneath even the serfs and knaves. Only servitors were lower in the Chapter's hierarchy, considered materiel rather than people.

He knelt on the floor of the Black Reclusiam, the chapel set aside for the Ravenwing on those rare occasions when they spent time in the Tower of Angels. The long benches were as old as his armour, the varnish peeled and cracked as he applied another coat of lacquer with a coarse brush. More varnish than wood remained, he thought.

It was the only time he and the other Black Knights were allowed in the Black Reclusiam. Amongst their many bans was sharing the devotionals and recitals conducted by Malcifer for the rest of the company.

He had expected penance, had even desired it. But this penance was like no other he had experienced. No Dark Angel could wholly avoid spending time in the penitentium now and then. Whether caught by the vagaries of the Chapter's arcane lore or the notoriously fickle demands of the Chaplains – or worse still, the unflinching application of the Rites by Asmodai – it was expected that every battle-brother would spend time in the Reclusiam to acknowledge his sins. Time was spent transcribing the annals of the Chapter or reciting aloud canticles of doctrine and war-prayers. A few days, a week or two.

The Black Knights had disobeyed their Grand Master, the fact could not be denied. Even so, the Black Knights' incarceration seemed harsh to Annael. From the moment they had returned to the *Implacable Justice* and presented themselves before Chaplain Malcifer and Grand Master Sammael they had been sentenced to penitent status indefinitely. Only on return to the Rock had they been permitted to perform duties outside the penitentium.

It was serf-work mainly. Scraping the algal build-up from the environmental humidifier intakes. Scrubbing walls and floors. Assisting the Techmarines with oily unguents that stained the fingers. Helping the refectora prepare the nutrigruel, carboloafs and vitamead for the warriors of the companies – nearly a thousand mouths to feed, with the Chapter wholly assembled for the first time in years. The penitents themselves ate in their solitary cells, forbidden from mixing with the other battle-brothers.

Most of it was drudgery, pure and simple. Some of it was dangerous, to a degree. Sabrael and Annael had been sent out into the void to chip ice crystals from a failed plasma exchange, protected by nothing more than antiquated environment suits, attached to the Rock by frayed tethers. Sabrael had quipped that their superiors wanted the Black Knights dead, but Annael had not shared his morbid humour.

The menial tasks were meant to give the penitents time to think on their transgressions and come to repent them. It was not punishment, but opportunity. Freed from the concerns of the battle-brothers, the penitents had the time to focus on their redemption.

So three-quarters of each day was spent. Another five hours were used for study and transcription, the absorption of knowledge, the repetition of the edicts and strictures the slabs on the road to understanding and absolution.

One hour was set aside for sleep and another for two meals and necessary hygienic matters. Annael was used to routine, every Dark Angel was. In that respect, the penance was nothing to endure.

What Annael hated most was the humiliation.

The details of the Black Knights' crimes were not shared with any other, and any rumour would be ruthlessly crushed by the Chaplains. The good deed performed by Annael and his companions was unknown to the rest of the Chapter. All they saw were grey robes. Transgressors. Tainted and honourless. Annael was bidden by oath to offer no dispute to any accusation or insult levelled at him by his brothers. He was not to speak to them, not even the Supreme Grand Master. Only Malcifer was to communicate with the penitents, the voice and ears by which they would be guided back to their righteous place amongst the ranks of the Dark Angels.

This fact chafed Annael as much as the robe itself. They had saved Sabrael! Yet not a word was he allowed to utter in his defence, ashamed and dishonoured before all.

He had endured the curses of 'turnword', 'sliptongue', 'slywound' and 'skainbreak', and without reply. When Brother Varidetus had called him a 'stinking oath-wretch' and split his lip with a punch, Annael had accepted this pronouncement in silence. He would harbour no resentment to Varidetus – Annael had inflicted worse on penitents in his time. It was not only permitted, but expected. The punishment of the body went hand-in-hand with the vexation of the soul.

'Your brush falls idle, Annael.' Malcifer approached along the gap between the benches, his black robe dragging across the floor Annael had swept at the start of the day. He wore no mask, but his face was just as lifeless. The continual omission of 'brother' was another subtle but piercing chastisement. 'I trust that you were so wrapped in sorrow for your abandoned brothers that it quite overwhelmed you.'

'My abandoned brothers?' Annael moved to stand up but a gesture from Malcifer kept him on his knees.

'The First Company that you chose to ignore while you pursued your personal goal.'

'I did not abandon them, but time was of the essence.'

'It was indeed, but time does not twist at your behest any more than your superiors receive their orders from you. There was a mission, in which you were called upon to participate, and in your absence you brought greater risk to the lives of your battle-brothers.'

'But we saved Sabrael!' Finally Annael was able to

speak the words out loud. It did not make him feel any better, now that the deed was done.

'The result justifies the defiance, does it?'

Malcifer's sharp words made Annael realise how petulant the protest sounded. The words seemed hollow, failing to capture the sentiment he had intended.

'A brother's life was directly threatened, Brother-Chaplain.' How could he explain? How would Malcifer, the embodiment of discipline and adherence to the strictures of the Chapter, possibly understand? 'Are we not meant to act to preserve our brothers?'

'The matter was brought to the attention of Grand Master Sammael and he disapproved of any such act. You disobeyed not only his desire, but his direct command. You can claim no ignorance of the crime nor cite any reason that supercedes a superior's order.'

'How much longer must we pay penance?' Annael asked, returning to his labour at a gesture from the Chaplain. 'I am sorry that we had to disobey Master Sammael.'

'You misunderstand the intent of your penance, Annael.' Malcifer turned his back on the Space Marine but did not walk away. 'It is not a punishment, to be meted out from me to you to balance a scale that has been skewed. This penance is for a crime that borders on treason, and save for execution no punishment could be weighed against such sin.'

'So what must I do?' Annael laid aside the brush and looked up with desperation. 'I am sorry.'

'A meaningless word.' Malcifer looked back, brow creased with anger. 'Your apology does not match the spirit in your heart, so save your tongue from the burn of platitudes.'

'But I *am* sorry, Brother-Chaplain.'

'*Sorry* is an expression of guilt. Your admittance of the facts of your transgression does not equate to repentance. Do you believe you would act differently if presented with the same situation again?' Annael paused and Malcifer seized upon the hesitation. 'Your equivocation speaks volumes more than carefully-crafted words! You do not regret your actions, and admit no wrong in them. Until you do so, you have not repented and so there can be no forgiveness.'

The Chaplain walked away up the aisle, head bowed in disappointment, hands clasped behind his back. Annael watched him depart, and only when he heard the hiss of the doors sealing closed did he snatch up the brush and throw it at the wall, spattering the bulkhead with red lacquer.

He instantly regretted the act. Someone – probably him – would have to clean up the mess, and he had defiled the sepulchre of the Ravenwing.

There was no point in simply telling Malcifer what he wanted to hear. The Chaplain was experienced enough to detect the slightest falsehood. Even if that were not the case, Annael could not bring himself to utter an untruth. He did not believe that rescuing Sabrael had been wrong, and events proved that. To admit otherwise would be a tremendous act of cowardice, for his principles but also for his friend.

HALF-LIFE

The hissing, whirring machines, the stench of antibacterial agents and whitewashed walls meant that he was in an apothecarion. After a few seconds' contemplation of this fact, analysing the background noise and vibrations, the smell, the sounds from beyond the glass door in front of him, Telemenus concluded that he had been returned to the Rock.

He could see himself – what was left of his body – in the door of a metal cabinet polished to a mirror-like finish. He was on a life-support stretcher, nothing more than a head, half a torso and his right arm. Where his guts and legs had been was a mess of tubes, pumps, blood-scrubbers and stimm-feeds.

The glow-globe above was a warm yellow, leaving blotches of darkness in his eyes when he looked away. It was strange to think that even his vision had been damaged, though he had suffered no blow to the head.

'Such is the intricate nature of your physiology,' the

Emperor said. The Lord of Terra manifested Himself as a small star-like reflection of a sun, in the curved shade of the lamp beside the life-support cot. There was the faint hint of a skull at the centre of the miniature sun, while the Emperor's corona swayed and flared like hair in a strong wind. 'A finely honed but delicately balanced system. Without certain agents previously introduced into your bloodstream by organs that are now missing, your visual acuity has returned to that of a normal human.'

A figure appeared at the glass screen of the door – a serf in white orderly robes. He saw that Telemenus was awake, nodded encouragingly and then departed.

'I was in stasis,' Telemenus said, though he kept the words inside his head where only the Emperor could hear them. 'I wonder what happened after Ulthor.'

'Do not concern yourself with wider events. Your immediate fate must be of more concern. Your body is crippled but you must convince the Apothecaries that your mind is still fully functioning.'

With some effort, Telemenus moved his hand to his chest.

'I will do all that I can to continue to serve. I swore an oath to fight for You until my death. I will cleave to that oath if I can.'

'Your will is strong. That much is proven by the fact that you still live. Brother Ezekiel himself declared so. The Chapter makes use of even the most grievously wounded. Only despair will rob you of the chance to serve Me further.'

'That You have chosen me banishes all despair, Master of Mankind. I take strength from Your indulgence. With Your wisdom to guide me and Your will to sustain me, there is no test I fear.'

There was more movement at the door and a white-robed Apothecary entered, followed by a Space Marine in the red tabard of the armoury – a Techmarine. Telemenus recognised both – the former from the Deathwing, the latter by the bionic appendage that had replaced his right arm and the plasma scars up the side of his face.

'Brother Temraen, Brother Adrophius,' he welcomed them. Telemenus smiled. 'Excuse me for not standing.'

They took the joke with thin smiles, their lips at odds with the concern in their eyes. Telemenus regretted his flippancy, wondering if being so dismissive of his condition made him seem less stable.

'How do you feel?' asked Temraen.

It was an odd question. Telemenus hardly *felt* anything. There was not much left of him to feel. He decided that honesty was the best approach.

'My hand is slightly numb,' he said, waggling his fingers. 'My eyesight has diminished also. Breathing seems laboured and I am fatigued.'

Temraen accepted this status report with a nod. He hummed a hymnal as he checked the gauges on the life-support cradle.

'That is nothing unusual,' the Apothecary said, making further notes on the data-slate in his hand. Telemenus desperately wanted to know what Temraen was writing, but said nothing, afraid that undue interest might be taken as paranoia. 'The loss of your third lung and secondary heart will have that effect. I am compensating with mechanical and alchemical solutions, but we will have to wean you off their assistance eventually. You can function with what remains, but it is better to let your system adapt over time. Any side-effects of the suspended animation induction?'

'No.' Telemenus looked at Adrophius. 'How can I be of assistance, brother-armourer?'

The Techmarine crouched and looked closely at the scars and scabs of Telemenus's wounds. Expressionless, he stood again and received the Apothecary's slate to study for a few seconds.

'Difficult,' said the Techmarine, though Telemenus did not know the question to which this was obviously the answer.

'What is difficult, brother?' asked Telemenus. He became sharply aware of the increased beep on one of the machines attached to him as his heart started to race. He turned his attention back to Temraen. 'What have you been discussing?'

'Apologies, brother,' said Adrophius, focusing on Telemenus for the first time since entering the room, as if he had only just noticed him. The plasma scars on his face, a deep red weal from chin to ear, formed strange spirals as Adrophius smiled. 'I have been assessing your suitability for prosthetic enhancement.'

'Can you rebuild me?' Telemenus asked. He knew that the armourium was capable of bionic wonders at times.

'No,' was the Techmarine's blunt reply. 'The arm is no problem, of course. Full lower limb replacement is possible. Artificial organs, perhaps with some gene-replacements, are always available. But not all together. Too much nerve and circulatory damage to sustain the cybernetic systems.'

'Neural conductivity might also be an issue,' said Temraen. 'It would be too much for your brain to lay new pathways, especially after the infection you suffered. There was slight necrosis in your right hemisphere.'

'Even if we could patch all of those augmetics and

prosthetics together, your movement, your reaction times, your coordination will all be compromised.'

'A danger to your battle-brothers,' added Temraen. Telemenus was not thankful for the clarification but kept any bitterness he might feel suppressed.

'What can you do?' he asked. He caught the flicker of the Emperor in the corner of his eye and remained calm, fighting a rising desperation. 'How can I continue to serve the Chapter? The Emperor? Only in death does duty end. I am not dead!'

'If the damage were less extensive I am sure the Master of Recruits might have been able to make use of you,' said Temraen. 'I understand that your marksmanship is excellent. Perhaps there is still a training role for you, even if you can no longer demonstrate your skills physically.'

'Stop listing things I can't do!' snapped Telemenus, losing his patience. He bit back another angry retort and tried to calm himself. 'Tell me what I *can* do. Please.'

'Gunnery, most likely,' Adrophius told him. 'You might never be able to pick up a bolter again, but that marksmanship can still be useful. We can map your neural systems onto a gunnery interface. Predator turret, perhaps? You are Deathwing, they are always looking for good gunners for their Land Raiders.'

'A sponson gunner?' Telemenus tried not to sound deflated. It was, after everything, a miracle he would be able to do anything.

'Subject to a full evaluation,' warned Temraen. 'The Master of the Apothecarion will assess your suitability for return to battlefield duties.'

'If not?' Telemenus did not really want to know, but had to ask. Better to learn now what his fate might be.

'Assignment to a warship gunnery position, if there is one available,' said Temraen. Being wired into the targeting systems of a strike cruiser's weapon batteries was a dubious honour, but better than the Apothecary's next suggestion. 'Or maybe integration into the Rock's defence array.'

'I understand.'

There seemed to be nothing more to discuss and the two Space Marines left after Temraen had checked a few more of the life-sustaining systems.

'I have to prepare for the worst,' Telemenus said to the Emperor. 'Oaths sworn demand that I accept whatever duties are assigned to me.'

'A worthy outlook.' The Emperor grew bright, moving along the blades of scalpels arranged in a row on a shelf just above Telemenus's right shoulder. 'Your tenacity and dedication are a credit. Be sure that the Master Apothecary sees that. The chance to fight at all is better than nothing.'

'Better than death?'

'You will know that only once you have experienced it.'

A mischievous thought crept into Telemenus's head.

'If anyone knows that, it is You. *Imperator Mortis Rex*. How was death for You?'

'Painful,' the Master of Mankind admitted. 'But not without its benefits.'

The apparition of the Emperor shimmered into nothing, leaving Telemenus alone. The room felt flat without the presence of his creator. Grey and empty.

'Only in death does duty end,' Telemenus whispered out loud.

He looked up at the scalpels and the shelf they were on. He stretched out a hand, fingers clawing for the edge of the shelf. He knew the shelf would not take much to break, even in his weakened state, toppling the surgical knives within reach.

He withdrew his hand, disgusted with himself. He stared at the blank ceiling, trying to imagine what it would be like to be a gunner in one of the Rock's batteries, never leaving the Tower of Angels, and in all likelihood never again seeing battle.

Eventually exhaustion, and perhaps more of Temraen's coma-inducing elixirs, claimed him and he fell into a deep sleep.

CYPHER'S TESTIMONY

'You are not an Interrogator.' Cypher issued this conclusion as the door closed behind Azrael.

'I am not.' The Supreme Grand Master sat down on a stool, opposite the bench to which the traitor was chained. 'I can fetch one if you prefer. Asmodai. He is very dedicated.'

'I noticed. Your robes, Deathwing, with officer markings. But I have already met Grand Master Belial. You wear no badge of the Librarium or Reclusiam or armourium. That leaves only one option. I am honoured, truly, Supreme Grand Master Azrael.'

The cell was silent while Azrael studied Cypher. The renegade had his hood drawn back, head resting against the wall in an attempt at relaxation, but his eyes were intent and never left the Lord of the Rock.

Azrael allowed the silence to endure for a few more minutes, face impassive as he waited to see if Cypher would speak. The renegade held his tongue.

'You told my Chaplains that you had an urgent message for me, for the Chapter.'

'For the Legion...' Cypher whispered.

'I am here. You are here. We should conclude this portion of your visit swiftly and then we can proceed to your excruciation.'

'If it were that simple, we would all rest easier in our sleep.'

'This is your first and last caution. I have no interest in this matter. If I tire of your presence I will leave and not return. Asmodai and Sapphon and Ezekiel will wring the truth from you using whatever means they care to try. It will be painful, shaming and terrifying. You might not break, but you will suffer. Either way, if you do not tell me why you are here, if the next words from your lips are not an explanation of your presence, I will get up, open that door and leave you to their cruel attentions.'

A twitch, small but noticeable, moved Cypher's right eye. A glance towards the door for a fraction of a second before he returned his gaze to Azrael.

'It concerns the traitor, Anovel,' said Cypher. He leaned forward and made to place his hands in his lap, but the shackles clamped to his armour did not allow him to move them past his waist. 'The plot with Astelan, Methelas and Typhus is more than it seems.'

'No doubt. Will you unravel this mystery for me?'

'As best I can, but despite what you might believe I am not the architect. I have been deceived by my allies.'

Azrael was not sure whether Cypher's frankness was a genuine response to the threat of torture or simply playing for time. He had the feeling that the Dark Angels would learn more from an open conversation than extraction by force. Initially, at least. He would indulge Cypher for a few minutes.

'He believes he is telling the truth,' Ezekiel's voice buzzed through the comm-bead in his ear. The Chief Librarian observed the exchange psychically, unobtrusively monitoring Cypher's thoughts.

'Continue,' said Azrael.

'I led the attack on your Chapter keep on Piscina Four,' Cypher admitted. Azrael fought the instinct to take a sharp breath. He forced himself to make no reaction at all, though a slight narrowing of Cypher's eyes indicated that he might have already seen or heard some response Azrael could not suppress. 'You look surprised, but I am sure the account of Colonel Brade left you in little doubt.'

'My surprise was due to your open admission to the crime of killing innocent novitiates, as well as their trainers, and unleashing the life-eater virus in an attempt to wipe out the planetary population.'

'I did no such thing!' Cypher looked genuinely aggrieved at the suggestion. 'Methelas was the architect of that particular attempt at genocide. I did not know until we had departed and he boasted of what he and Anovel had done.'

'Again, he believes that is the truth,' Ezekiel reported. 'He has not revealed all that he knows, but what he has claimed is true to his knowledge.'

'Why did you come to Piscina Four?'

'So I have been returned to the scene of the crime?'

Azrael bit back a reply, annoyed with himself for revealing this scrap of information.

'We are leaving the system,' he said.

'For the gene-seed, you already know that. It was my part of the bargain, to supply the genetic material that would form the basis of a new generation of legionaries. Astelan was to seize Tharsis. It was perfect.

Remote, but technologically capable. I did not expect him to be so... rigorous in his enthusiasm to cleanse the world of opposition.'

'Another genocide you did not participate in? How convenient.'

'Let us put aside these mortal notions of morality, Supreme Grand Master. You forget the history of the Legion whose name you have taken. Genocide was not uncommon during the Great Crusade, and the Lion you laud so much was accomplished at its application. Compliance was rarely gained peacefully when he led the Legion.'

'Tell me about Tharsis, and the gene-seed,' said Azrael, keen to stay on the topic of Cypher's plotting rather than broaden the conversation to older times.

'It was to be a new home world, the start of a new Legion from the combined efforts of Dark Angels and Typhus's Death Guard. I believe there was some further assistance from a former Emperor's Children Apothecary, a deviant called Fabius Bile.' Cypher paused and flexed his fingers as if to return some feeling to them.

'You claimed that there was more to the plot than you have said, and that the Chapter was under threat.'

'I did, and it is, but the exact nature of that threat I cannot say. I genuinely do not know some of the details. I believe Anovel has betrayed his allies in order to secure leadership of the new force for himself. That is the extent of my knowledge.'

'He is lying,' warned Ezekiel.

Azrael stood up and turned towards the door.

'Where are you going?' Cypher demanded. 'Why are you leaving?'

'You are lying to me,' Azrael replied without turning around. 'I will waste no more of my time with you.'

'Wait!' Cypher shouted as Azrael took a step. 'Wait!'

'Why?' Azrael looked back over his shoulder. 'So that you can spin more half-truths for me? My Chaplains have the patience for these games. I do not.'

Azrael had reached the door when Cypher spoke again, as though the words had been torn from him.

'It is a horrifying plan, and would see the Dark Angels destroyed, their legacy ruined. The ruins of Caliban, that's all I know. Anovel was going to take Typhus and these new legionaries to the Caliban System.'

'Caliban?' Azrael turned slowly, masking his concern as his hearts beat a little faster. 'What business does Anovel have with our dead world?'

'I do not know, for certain, but I can find out,' Cypher assured him. 'I will help you turn Anovel.'

Azrael left the cell, thoughts whirling. He closed the door and stood in the corridor outside, head bowed in thought. Ezekiel joined him, expression pensive.

'He was telling the truth, at the end,' said the Chief Librarian. 'He was worried by what Anovel might be doing. I sensed that he desperately wanted to stop Anovel.'

'We cannot put them together, not after the disaster with Astelan.' Azrael shook his head, depressed by the options available to him – take Cypher at his word and ignore the threat he posed to the Imperium or allow the Chaplains their time-consuming and inconsistent methods.

'Allow the meeting.' Ezekiel rested a hand on Azrael's shoulder to reassure him. 'Astelan is protected by some psychic ward we could never break, but there is nothing that has stopped me sensing the secrets inside Cypher's mind.'

'Have you discovered who he is?' said Azrael.

'That would require a far deeper scan, one that he would be aware of. Is that what you wish me to do?'

'Not yet. There will be time enough for such answers when his excruciation begins. For the moment it would be better if we leave him unmolested. We shall allow the pretence of cooperation while it serves us.' Azrael looked back at the cell door, picturing the warrior within. The Fallen disturbed him. His confidence was not the posturing that Azrael had seen in so many other traitors. There was surety in his thoughts. Azrael nodded. 'Tell Sapphon to arrange the meeting. Asmodai is not to be informed. I need no further debate at this time.'

'I commend your decision, brother,' said Ezekiel, his bionic eye glowing red in the gloomy passageway, the psychic glint of gold in the other. 'Repentance is earned, not given. It requires effort and sacrifice, and no small amount of risk, if it is to be of value.'

Azrael looked at his Chief Librarian and remembered the accounts of how the young Ezekiel had been found – imprisoned and alone on a world that had been held in the sway of the Dark Gods. That he had undergone horrific treatment due to his abilities had been clear, and he had withheld retribution against his captors by refusing to use them. If there was any Dark Angel alive that knew about effort and sacrifice, of the mental strength to endure the barrage of trials each day brought to the members of the Inner Circle, it was the warrior Azrael had accepted as his closest advisor, and in some small part as his friend.

'Thank you, brother,' he said, replicating the gesture of Ezekiel, hand to his shoulder in a gesture of unity. 'A storm comes upon us but with your aid I will chart the fairest course back to safety.'

'With you to lead us, brother, we gladly follow into the tempest.'

Ezekiel broke away and marched off along the corridor, leaving Azrael alone with his dark thoughts.

THE TRAITOR STRIKES

There was to be no repeat of the mistakes made in the handling of Astelan, that much Sapphon had sworn to himself. He had received his instructions from Azrael, via Ezekiel, without complaint but he harboured many misgivings in secret. There would be no concealed communications and they certainly would not be left alone together.

Armed with what he had gleaned from Azrael's conversation with Cypher, Sapphon began by confronting Anovel alone. If he could confirm any of Cypher's testimony, and perhaps convince Anovel that his secrets had already been divulged, it might be possible to avoid bringing the two of them together at all.

One of the guard rooms in the lower halls of the Rock had been cleared, providing more space than the cells of the dungeon. The chamber had been emptied of all furnishings save for the banner with the Chapter symbol on the wall opposite the door and two benches, now with the addition of bars to which the prisoners could be chained.

Anovel had already been secured when Sapphon entered. He had typically Calibanite features – narrow cheeks, dark hair cropped short and sunken brown eyes. His thin lips were set in a look of determined defiance, brow creased by a scowl as he scanned the room. He wore a sleeveless robe of dirty white linen, his wrists bound by bronze-coloured manacles secured by a length of chain to the bench. The bench itself had been bolted to the stone of the floor in a dozen places.

Two Deathwing Knights flanked the Fallen, clad in bone-white power armour for the occasion. Sapphon dismissed them with a word and waited until they had gone before he met Anovel's gaze.

'We captured Cypher.'

This simple declaration elicited a rapid series of emotions from the prisoner, all written across his face in a succession of expressions. First there was scepticism, then doubt, then anger and then doubt again. Eventually Anovel mastered himself and his frown of distaste returned, jaw moving as he ground his teeth.

Sapphon smiled.

'I see that it is a name known to you.'

'A title.'

'What was that?' Sapphon was taken aback by the interruption.

'Lord Cypher is a title.' Anovel met Sapphon's stare. 'A revered position of the Order.'

'The Order no longer exists. The title is meaningless. As is your resistance.'

'The Order lives on, in our hearts and minds.'

Sapphon did not reply to this immediately.

The Order, the knightly organisation that had been

ruled by Luther and then by the Lion, had been destroyed along with Caliban. Most of the Fallen had mentioned it during their confessions, the majority had been members – even those that had originally hailed from Terra had been accepted into the ranks during Luther's rebellion. Anovel had been the first to claim that the Order had somehow survived, even if only in spirit. Sapphon was in two minds whether to pursue this new course of inquiry or stick to his original track.

'Cypher is intimately acquainted with your plans, and has proven very helpful,' he said, deciding to continue on the theme with which he had opened. 'Piscina Four, Port Imperial, Tharsis. He has been involved every step of the way.'

Anovel said nothing and continued to glare at the Chaplain.

'I am here to inform you that we are not interested in the details of your confession, we have them already. You are not here for intelligence, but as a first and last opportunity to repent the sins you have committed and earn yourself a swift and honourable demise. When I leave this room, that offer is ended.'

'You know nothing of honour, bastard of the Lion.' Anovel spat on the floor and sneered.

'Probably not. It would be wise, however, to keep a civil tongue when you are with my fellow Interrogator, Asmodai. He is less tolerant of such abuse. We have forsaken honour in our quest for the truth. A quest that can free your soul from the damnation that currently ensnares it. I really am here for your sake, not mine.'

'Allow me to signal my appreciation,' said Anovel, his hands forming an obscene gesture. 'You cannot open your mouth without lies spilling forth.'

'Let me tell you of lies, friend Anovel. You have been deceived. Betrayed. We know that you made a bargain with Typhus to secure his Death Guard a new home world. You were once an Apothecary and would be guardian of the gene-seed for this new Legion. Gene-seed, in fact, that you and Cypher stole from our Chapter Keep on Piscina Four. The Sacred Bands of Tharsis and the "Divine" of Port Imperial were to be the first batch of recruits. In the meantime your world would be protected by engineered soldiers provided by the adepts of Fabius Bile. His biomechanical alterations are particularly distinctive, combined with the blessings of the Plague Lord whom you serve with Typhus.'

The certainty on Anovel's face was slipping as Sapphon continued the litany of facts the Chaplains, Ravenwing and Deathwing had unearthed in the last year.

'We captured Methelas as well, you see. The corruption in him is grotesque, I am sure you'll agree. But despite your fair appearance I am sure that we would find the Mark of Plague upon you somewhere if we looked closely enough. Perhaps inside...'

Anovel's posture changed dramatically as he leaned away from the Interrogator-Chaplain, his eyes returning to their search of the room, seeking some exit that did not exist. Clearly Cypher's additional information was correct, to a point.

'Astelan was captured more than fifteen years ago. He told us about Port Imperial but we could not find it, until we learned of its precise location from another traitor in your ranks. Your vile trick at Piscina Five did not work. Our battle-brothers were strong and refused to leave the keep in further pursuit. They sacrificed themselves to stop the *omniterminus* virus from spreading. Someone left us a clue in the databanks, a spoor to follow.'

'You lie!' Anovel bellowed, in desperation rather than defiance. 'We swore oaths of brotherhood to each other. We would be the founders of the Death Angels, a new beginning for us all. None of the Order would betray that trust.'

'They all betrayed that trust!' snarled Sapphon in reply. It was time to let Anovel see exactly what would be the penalty for further refusal to cooperate.

Sapphon smashed a fist into Anovel's jaw, almost knocking him from the bench. As he righted himself, the Chaplain unleashed a punch with the other hand, flattening the Fallen's nose into a bloody mess. He stepped back, panting.

'You have one chance to spare yourself further pain and humiliation. Either Cypher or Methelas, or one of your many lieutenants we captured at Tharsis, will tell us your intent at Caliban. It is in our code to allow you the first right to make this final confession. You say we know nothing of honour, but we know that it is you that forsook it ten millennia ago. If you wish to restore it, if you wish to save your soul from the dark abyss, you must make this last admission. If you refuse, you will be dealt with and we shall learn what we need to know from the others.'

A sly smile crept across Anovel's face. He wiped his split lip with the back of a hand and spat blood.

'You are lying about having the others. They would not confess to something they know nothing about. It would invite only further punishment when their falsehood was revealed.'

'So you admit that there is a plan at Caliban? There is something to conceal?'

Anovel shook his head but his sudden surge of confidence was punctured by the realisation that he had been caught by the simplest of traps.

'I am not lying. If you want further proof, I can offer it.'

Sapphon moved to the door and spoke to the two guards outside. The door swung outwards to reveal Cypher, clad in his war-plate, hood down, hands manacled before him with the length of chain dangling to his knees.

'No!'

Anovel heaved at his bonds, the muscles in his arms like boulders as he strained against the chains and bolts. After several seconds he sagged, falling to his knees with his arms stretched behind him by his chains.

The Deathwing Knights led Cypher into the room while Sapphon closed the door.

'Wait,' he told the Knights as they readied the chain on Cypher's wrists. Sapphon had no intention of letting Cypher and Anovel speak. It was enough that the Fallen Apothecary knew that the Chaplain was not lying about having Cypher in his possession. 'Take him back.'

The two renegades looked at each other. Sapphon heard and saw nothing untoward, but Anovel's expression changed from anguish to one of resignation. He pushed himself to his feet with a surge, a loud cracking as muscles railed against chain, snapping the bones in his wrists and hands so that they slipped free.

Cypher twisted, dodging the grasp of the Knights as they rose to their feet. With a deft movement he looped the chain of his manacles over Anovel's head and twisted his body, lifting the other Fallen from his feet over his shoulder. Sapphon heard the snap of vertebrae from several metres away and knew it was too late even as the Knights overpowered Cypher and took him to the ground.

Sapphon dashed along the chamber as one of the Deathwing Knights repeatedly clubbed a fist into the side of Cypher's head and the other pulled apart the links wrapped around Anovel's throat. The Fallen's face was already purple and his head lolled unnaturally to one side as he was rolled away.

'Get him out!' Sapphon roared, jabbing a finger at Cypher, who was still conscious, barely. He was laughing quietly as blood streamed from half a dozen cuts to his face and head.

Kneeling beside Anovel as Cypher was dragged away, Sapphon knew there was no point calling the Master of the Apothecarion. No mortal force would save Anovel now. As the Interrogator-Chaplain watched, the curse of Anovel's infernal pact with the Lord of Decay manifested. His skin turned to dry flakes and fell away from evaporating flesh and fat. Muscles withered into a dry husk like ancient tree roots and organs sagged, his chest and belly flattening in a few seconds.

Disgusted, Sapphon retreated, one hand clamped over his mouth as a cloud of yellow dust escaped the corpse's lungs and puffed in a cloud from Anovel's open mouth.

He bumped into someone and turned sharply in surprise.

Ezekiel was there, one eye a golden orb of blazing energy.

'Witchery,' the Librarian said calmly. The eye dimmed and focused on Sapphon, and the lenses of the bionic replacement of the other adjusted with a whirr and a click. 'I will ensure the remains are cleansed properly. You will need to speak to Brothers Cragarion and Galbarad about the strange events they have witnessed today. There is also much to be explained to the Inner Circle, Brother Sapphon.'

'Lord Azrael must be informed of what has happened.'

'He will be.' Ezekiel sighed, a sad look on his face. 'This is most unfortunate. Along with the misadventure involving Astelan, it seems that of late you have erred greatly in your endeavours.'

'But I was under orders from the Supreme...' Sapphon's voice trailed off as he understood what was happening.

With Belial and Asmodai both looking for signs of weakness in Azrael, this was no time to drag him into a fresh failure. More than ever, with Cypher captured and some plot unfolding that threatened to doom the whole Chapter, the Inner Circle required stability. Sapphon was already a marked warrior, his record far from blameless. Another transgression on his part would almost avoid remark had it not involved such a high-profile prisoner. Sapphon bowed his head, accepting his fate.

'I was acting of my own accord in bringing Cypher and Anovel together. I hope the Supreme Grand Master will see fit to forgive my error of judgement.'

CONFESSION AND REJECTION

Seeing Sabrael in his full regalia as blademaster took Annael by surprise. The Black Knight stood amongst several other warriors of the Ravenwing, his robes black, a golden sword emblazoned on the chest, the hood edged with red and silver thread. The Blade of Corswain had even been returned to him, despite the threat from Tybalain that Sabrael would never carry the artefact weapon again. He looked as if the events in Streisgant had never happened, laughing easily at his own wit while the other warriors shook their heads in mock disappointment at some poor jest.

As his surprise subsided, Annael felt a stab of anger. It had been Sabrael's hot-headed behaviour that had led to his capture and the subsequent need for a rescue mission. Now he had been returned to the company, forgiven, and Annael was still being punished.

He leaned on the handle of the mop he had been using to clean the deck outside the Land Speeder bay, wondering what silvery words Sabrael had slipped from his tongue to earn early release from his penance.

As one of the Ravenwing warriors turned, Annael saw that it was Casamir. He was not in the robe of a Black Knight – apparently his confirmation as a member of Sammael's elite had not yet been ratified – but he was clad nonetheless in Ravenwing robes, instead of the penitent's garb he had last been wearing.

Annael wanted to march over to them and demand how they had bought such leniency. He was stopped only by the thought that to speak to anyone save for Malcifer was another transgression that would simply set back his cause. As much as it pained him to watch his companions returned to the brotherhood, he could not get involved.

Casamir ignored him and passed into the armoury bay when the group split, while Sabrael headed in the opposite direction, not even casting his gaze towards his friend. The others walked past Annael with scowls. Brother Zafaen almost strode into Annael, forcing the penitent to push himself into the bulkhead to avoid the collision.

Annael cast his gaze downward, avoiding any accusation of confrontation with the battle-brothers. When they were gone, seized by a fit of anger, Annael snapped the mop in his hands and tossed the pieces along the corridor with a snarl.

He instantly regretted the action, wondering what would have happened if anyone had seen. It was a childish act, unbecoming of a Space Marine. He swiftly retrieved the splintered parts, took up his bucket and headed back to the store chamber where they were kept. Stowing the mop and pail, Annael headed up through the Rock to return to the Reclusiam of the Ravenwing.

Malcifer was there, kneeling in front of the altar table, head bowed. The Chaplain looked around at the breathless entrance of Annael. Seeing the frustration written across the Dark Angel's face he stood up and held out a hand. He beckoned Annael to approach.

'You are grievously vexed, Annael.'

'I wish to repent,' the penitent replied, falling to his knees in front of the Chaplain. 'I committed a grave act of disrespect to my brothers and superiors. I acknowledge the shame it brought upon me, and beg the forgiveness of you, my mentor, so that I might return to my brothers in honour.'

Malcifer looked at him for some time, lips pursed in thought.

'Why do you repent?' he asked.

'My soul burns with the shame of my sin. If there were a way, any way I could scour this feeling from my flesh, I would do it.'

'The scorn of your former brothers is a harsh blow to weather. You understand why they disdain the penitent so much?'

'I have no honour. The penitent's robe is a symbol of my guilt for all to see.'

'For *all* to see?'

'I wear my status upon my back each day, Master Chaplain. What could be plainer to see?'

'So you accept the punishment of your peers?'

'And my superiors,' Annael added hastily.

'And do you think you have made sufficient amends to those that you have wronged?'

'Amends? I do not understand.'

'The duties you carry out, they are a service to the Chapter, to the brotherhood of the Dark Angels. In performing them you make restitution for the offence to their honour.'

'I wish to restore my honour, Master Malcifer. What more must I do to prove I am sorry?' The anger returned, but Annael was careful not to direct it at the Chaplain. 'Others have been forgiven, I saw them today. Sabrael, the catalyst for my dishonour, wears the full robes again. Casamir, fellow penitent guilty of no lesser crime, stands garbed as a battle-brother beside him.'

'Do you wish that Sabrael is held to greater account?'

'I do not understand.'

'Do you consider your dishonour to be the fault of Sabrael?' The question was quietly asked, but Annael was not fooled by Malcifer's apparent civility and innocence.

'A series of events occurred directly as a result of his actions.'

'Speak plainly!' Malcifer's rebuke caused Annael to flinch. 'A "series" of events? At least give voice to your crime. You must take responsibility for it. You disobeyed your Grand Master! You pursued a personal desire above the needs of your commander and your battle-brothers. Do you think that Sabrael is guilty for your loss of honour?'

Annael did not know what else he could say. Malcifer gave him no longer to compose a reply.

'Do you remember what I told you of repentance?'

'I do. I sincerely wish we had not disobeyed the order of the Grand Master.'

'Do you feel guilty for what happened? Do you accept the blame, solely and on yourself?'

'I...' Annael could not lie. Malcifer was trained to spot the slightest falsehood and Annael was not accomplished at subterfuge. 'I feel that in the circumstances my choices were limited.'

'Do you deny that you were instigator of this sorry affair?'

'If Sabrael had not been captured, events would have run very differently.'

'And your Huntmaster? What of his guilt?'

'He took the lead. It was natural to follow.'

'Yet you spoke out to convince your brothers to act with you. You appealed to their brotherhood, corrupted it to your selfish goals.'

'That is not how it happened!'

'That is exactly what happened!' Malcifer bellowed in reply, making Annael cower before the righteousness in his voice and manner. 'By your testimony and others. You hoped to rescue Sabrael from the moment you discovered that he had been taken. Would you have been so vehement in your arguments for the sake of Sergeant Polemetus, or Brothers Garbadon and Orius? You wanted to rescue a friend, one with whom you share a closer relationship than with your other brothers. It clouded your judgement and it clouds it still.'

'What do you want from me?' snarled Annael, his anger breaking through like water rushing through a breached dam. 'Why won't you accept my apology and answer my confession?'

'What have you confessed?' Malcifer said, voice almost a whisper. 'That you feel guilty? That you want your punishment to end? Shall I tell you why Sabrael wears the black of the Ravenwing once more?'

Annael said nothing, stewing in his frustrated impotence. Nothing he did or said would change Malcifer's mind. It seemed the Chaplain had chosen to push Annael to the limit, though why he did not know.

'Sabrael apologised in person to both Tybalain and Sammael. He had agreed not to contest the Blade of Corswain at the next trials. He knelt before this very altar and swore anew the oaths to his Chapter and company. Most of all, he accepted that he was not deserving of forgiveness. He did not plead or try to bargain or rationalise his act. He accepted his weakness of character and thanked me for my forbearance on previous transgressions.'

It did not matter, to Annael's mind. Sabrael was always able to spin his words as a weaver creates beautiful cloth. From Annael's mouth the same claims made by his brother were like the crude canvas of his penitent's robe. Malcifer was deaf to his intent, his desperation.

'In short,' said the Chaplain, 'he repented. He sought no return to honour, no cessation of punishment, just the simple act of forgiveness from those he had wronged. He did not try to earn it or buy it, he simply allowed himself to hope for it.'

'Do you not hear me? Have I not professed my guilt enough for you?'

'I told you before that your guilt needs no confirmation. Your regret is based upon the application of your penance, which you yet insist on viewing as temporal punishment rather than spiritual opportunity.'

The rage would be held in check no longer. He dared not lay hands on his superior. Instead, with a wordless shout Annael seized the closest bench and threw it across the Reclusiam. The pew crashed into the wall, splinters showering one of the battle-trophies hanging there, a standard from the Ullissa campaign four thousand years old.

'I'm sorry,' he gasped, realising what he had done. He

fell to his knees again, hanging his head in shame. 'I am unworthy.'

Malcifer showed no sign of anger. His expression had become that of a benevolent older brother.

'Trust me, Annael. I am watching. I am listening. You are making good progress, but do not dwell on what you have done or what you are doing. Study the doctrine of the Chapter and resolve what you will do. The key to redemption lies not in the past but the future. Admit your failings and seek to balance them in thought and deed.'

The Chaplain walked away, heading to the main door. Annael felt broken, exhausted more than if he had been fighting for weeks on end. It was almost impossible to contemplate carrying on, returning to the others to bear their barbed words and sneers of derision.

Almost, but not wholly impossible.

Annael pushed himself to his feet and took a deep breath. The future, Malcifer had said. His first task was to clean up the mess he had made of the shrine. Fighting back the weariness in his soul, he turned towards the door, straightened his back and settled his shoulders.

He would endure.

CENSURED

'I do not defend my actions with claims of success,' said Sapphon, 'but I would ask the members of this council to review in full the transcript of what occurred. Before he died, Anovel confirmed much of what was alleged by Cypher. That they had been in collusion was already likely, and Anovel's acts on seeing the other Fallen provide incontrovertible proof that they were in cohort with each other.'

'And incontrovertible proof that you overstepped your authority once again, Master of Sanctity.' Belial glowered at Sapphon, who made every effort not to look to Azrael for support. It had been the vote of the Supreme Grand Master that had made Sapphon the Master of Sanctity and the reason was now becoming clear. Sapphon would willingly compromise himself for the good of the Chapter, even if it meant falling on his sword when required.

The Deathwing commander was going to continue

but Sapphon had already heard enough and decided that even if he was going to take the fallout from Azrael's decision, there was no reason not to go down fighting.

'I have every authority, *Grand Master*, in the remit of my rank.' He gritted his teeth, giving extra vehemence to his words. 'I am the Master of Sanctity, the spiritual guardian of the Chapter. On Tharsis and Ulthor I bowed to your authority in strategic and military matters. In affairs of the soul and the Fallen, you do not command, you obey.'

Belial faltered, cowed by Sapphon's uncharacteristic bullishness. The Chaplain looked around the table and saw that the other company captains were equally taken aback. Setting an example with Belial, thought by many to be a natural successor to Azrael should fate unfold in that direction, reminded the rest of the Inner Circle of their place in the hidden organisation of the Chapter.

'Whether the right to do as you did belonged to you is not under discussion.' This came from Master Eradon, the Tenth Company captain. Alone amongst the Inner Circle he sported a beard, blond and cropped short. He tugged at the facial hair as he continued. 'How you exercise that authority on behalf of the Chapter, and whether you should retain it, is the cause for this conclave. A succession of poor decisions have dogged your elevation to Master of Sanctity, and perhaps that is an appointment that must be reviewed.'

All present turned their attention to Azrael. He sat at the head of the table, hood raised so that nothing of his face could be seen. He said nothing and waved for Sapphon to continue.

'For the benefit of all, might I remind the council

of the words spoken by the Supreme Grand Master during the last full conclave.' Sapphon glanced at Azrael who leaned forward, disapproval on his face as it was revealed by the movement, no doubt sceptical about Sapphon's reasons for dragging up his past utterances. The Master of Sanctity tried to provide what assurance he could with a glance before he activated a vox-servitor by his side. The half-man started to speak, mouth opening and closing monotonously, nothing more than a flesh puppet. From its slack lips emerged the recorded voice of Azrael.

'Let it be known that the war on Piscina progresses swiftly to conclusion with the might of the Chapter ranged against greenskin and rebel alike. However, the conflict has much delayed us in the pursuit, as I suspect was intended by those that instigated the attacks on Kadillus and the destruction of the fortress here. The gene-seed was stolen by Anovel, I conclude, and to what end we already know. I consider the thwarting of this plot to be of the utmost significance, while the Ravenwing and Deathwing can stand ready for fresh duties.'

Sapphon allowed these words to sink in before continuing.

'"The thwarting of this plot to be of the utmost significance" was the Supreme Grand Master's assessment of the situation. I accept that errors were made in the prosecution of this duty, but contend that despite these setbacks we succeeded in eliminating the threat posed by the machinations of Cypher, Astelan and the others. They are dead or in our custody, there is no possible way in which their plans can be carried out.'

'Astelan is still loose,' said Sammael.

Sapphon was surprised. He had expected the

accusation from Asmodai. As it was, the Master of Repentance was strangely silent, perhaps keen that the manner of Astelan's escape, and Asmodai's part in it, was not reviewed again. Though there had been no formal discussion, the members of the Inner Circle from the ranks of the Reclusiam were upholding their mutual honour.

'You voted with me to use him as a lure on Tharsis,' Sapphon replied quickly.

'I did, and it was a mistake. I will admit that in front of my peers. Can you do the same?'

If it had been another Master than Sammael that asked the question, Sapphon would have suspected a trap of some kind. The Master of the Ravenwing was as independent of thought as his company was rigid of command, and had no alliances and no obvious agenda within the Inner Circle. Even so, it left the Master of Sanctity in a difficult position. To continue to defend a decision that looked to have gone wrong would make him seem pig-headed. To admit it was a mistake would invite censure.

'We lost Astelan, but we gained Anovel and Cypher. On balance I believe we made the correct decision.'

'Cypher gave himself up,' said Sammael. 'I would hardly list that in our achievements of that day.'

'Would he have been there had we not brought Anovel and Typhus?' countered Sapphon. The question was left hanging.

'And on balance,' Belial picked up the thread of the conversation, 'do you believe allowing Cypher contact with Anovel was the correct decision?'

Again, Sapphon had to resist the instinct to look at Azrael. He masked the urge by looking at the Dark Angels assembled, meeting their gazes, accusatory, neutral and supportive. His eyes rested on the Supreme Grand Master for a second and then turned to Belial.

'It was a mistake. Poorly conceived and executed without forethought. Allowing Cypher to kill Anovel removed a lever which we could have applied during his interrogation. At the least we should have spent more time beforehand exerting traditional methods on Anovel to see what he might reveal.'

Belial opened his mouth to speak but Sapphon raised a hand to silence him and turned to Azrael.

'As I understand it, this conclave was mustered to discuss what we are to do with Cypher. It seems to be moving towards a trial by hearsay. If I am to be charged with transgressions against the Chapter, let them be plainly known.'

'We must understand what has happened with Cypher if we are to chart a new course,' said Ezekiel. 'No accusation has been made, brother.'

'In which case might I present some conclusions I have drawn from this unfortunate incident?'

A nod was the only reply from Azrael, who settled back into his chair, face disappearing into the shadow of his hood once more.

'Cypher allowed himself to be captured precisely to silence Anovel. He knows exactly what the plan-within-the-plan was going to be. Anovel was killed because of his complicity. I saw the look in his eye as his neck was broken. He was resigned to the fate, willingly laying down his life to protect Cypher.'

'Or possibly the plan,' said Asmodai, speaking for the first time since arriving. 'We cannot ignore the possibility that Tharsis was simply a diversion or staging ground, and that whatever was due to occur at Caliban might yet come to pass.'

'How could that be? We have the prime conspirators here,' said Sammael. 'Unless you believe Astelan capable of continuing the plot on his own.'

'Typhus still lives,' said Sapphon, 'and who can say how many Fallen are involved, directly or at the periphery? Master Asmodai is correct, we must proceed as if Cypher's warning is genuine.'

'Voluntarily believe the lie he spun to gain access to Anovel?' Belial sounded exasperated. 'How much further down this blind alley do you wish to drag us?'

'It makes no sense that he would be captured unless he believed he had a means to escape,' said Master Balthasar. The captain of the Fifth Company held out a hand towards Ezekiel. 'Brother-Librarian, how is it that you did not detect any murderous intent from Cypher?'

'I scanned him only passively. There are techniques to mask one's thoughts from such casual detection. You all know some of them, such as reciting the battle hymnals, visualising maintenance routines, other exercises that occupy the conscious thought. Cypher used such a technique to disastrous effect.'

'This motivation seems unlikely,' said Master Eradon. 'Why silence Anovel at the cost of one's own freedom? Cypher cannot escape the Rock, he has made his last mistake.'

Sapphon could say nothing of what Azrael had revealed in the Hidden Chamber, of the previous seven occasions when Cypher had been in custody and yet managed to regain his freedom. Nor could any of the others privy to that knowledge, and so it left them without evidence to argue against the seeming impossibility of Cypher getting away from the Tower of Angels.

'I concur,' said Lexicanium Merlith. 'We are in danger of creating ghosts out of thin air. We are treating Cypher with too much respect. Strip him of his armour, apply brand and blade and see how willing he is to suffer for this supposed ploy.'

There were nods and murmurs of assent from others around the chamber. On the face of it, the Inner Circle was prepared to believe the threat had ended. Master Eradon, the Scout Company captain, voiced as such.

'I propose a vote. The motion is that the latest expedition of the Ravenwing and Deathwing has recovered the primary conspirators in a plot to seed a new force of traitors on the world of Tharsis. In defying this they have taken valued captives in the Hunt and also protected the future stability of the sector. Does my summary find approval with this conclave?'

'A vote is called,' Azrael said. 'The conclave will make known its will. White signifies support for Master Eradon's assertion and the conclave is concluded. Cypher will be submitted to all the usual means of excruciation. The Rock will continue to its current destination and the Chapter shall divide into such campaign forces and companies as required by its forthcoming commitments. Black signifies disagreement. The conclave will continue until a different course of action is determined and a fresh vote taken to approve it.'

The lights flickered out, leaving the participants in pitch darkness. In his left hand Sapphon had the black ball, the white in his other. It occurred to him that there was little to be achieved by continuing the discussion with the full Inner Circle. Whatever happened next with Cypher would be of the most clandestine nature. Although he disagreed entirely with Eradon's assessment, it made no sense to drag out the proceedings.

Finding the channel carved into the surface of the conclave table with the fingers of his right hand, he allowed the white ball to slip from his grasp and roll to the receptacle at the table's heart. The black he slid into a gutter at the edge of the table, destined to be gathered with the other discarded votes in front of Azrael. He listened to the sound of the balls clicking and rolling through the mechanism of the table.

Silence fell. The vote was concluded.

The lights came on at a hidden command from Azrael. The Supreme Grand Master activated the counting mechanism and the crane arm swept out to the central receptacle and retrieved the votes within. Azrael separated the balls into two slots before him.

'The white outweighs the black,' Azrael announced. 'Master Eradon's proposal is approved. We shall recommence our usual duties.'

Only then did Azrael look at Sapphon. The Master of Sanctity saw the intent that the matter was far from concluded. Sapphon replied with the subtlest of nods while the others left the room. Whatever he needed to do next, even if he had the tacit approval of his lord, the Master of Sanctity would be acting entirely on his own and would be expected to bear full responsibility.

As it always is, he thought.

UNDER SCRUTINY

Sapphon watched through the grille of the cell door as Asmodai plied his bloody talent on the body of Cypher. The Fallen had submitted to having his armour removed without argument, though Asmodai had issued a stern warning regarding the sword – a warning issued with such vehemence that Sapphon might have concluded Asmodai was wary of the blade, if such a thing were possible.

With the same meekness, Cypher suffered the blows and cuts laid upon him by Asmodai. The Interrogator-Chaplain seemed inspired, eyes alight with the challenge of breaking the will of the thrice-cursed. Sapphon had seen him many times before, in a semi-hypnotic stupor most of the time. Now Asmodai was relishing every moment of the excruciation.

It was just the first few hours of what promised to be a very long process, but even so Sapphon was impressed by the stoic silence of the prisoner. His body was no stranger to injury. The scars that crisscrossed and punctured his flesh were testament to millennia of battle.

Cypher lay on the slab and stared at the ceiling, looking at some faraway place in his own mind. He barely flinched as flesh was parted by blades and skin seared by brands.

Sapphon was no stranger to these cells and the activities for which they existed. It was rare these days that he took up the cruder instruments of interrogation, preferring instead to use manipulation of the soul and psyche, and the talents of the Librarium, to prise the secrets from those that came to him. Unlike Asmodai, he was interested more in the secrets of the Fallen than their confessions. Perhaps that was why he lacked a single black pearl to his name – the reward given to a Chaplain for each Fallen brought to repentance. When they had revealed their secrets to him, when they were ready to admit their sins, Sapphon lost interest and was willing for others of the Reclusiam to complete the bloody deed.

Despite this experience he found the spectacle of Cypher's excruciation bordering on the uncomfortable. The Fallen was barely present, only the odd grimace to show that he felt anything at all. In contrast, Asmodai was a grunting, snarling, bestial thing of the shadows. Not once had the Interrogator asked a question in the hours since his arrival. These opening stages were not about the truth, they were about demonstrating the pain that was to come, the pregnant threat of the dire instruments lined up on the shelf next to the captive. It was the proof that any and all measures would be used without mercy.

If there was any expression on Cypher's face, it was sorrow. A profound sadness in his eyes, brought about by whatever imagined vista he looked upon rather than his current plight. Looking more closely, Sapphon realised why the scene did not sit right in his mind. Cypher's twitches and lip curls of pain had nothing to do with the ministrations of Asmodai – the Fallen's reactions were purely to slights occurring in his mind.

All this contributed to his unease, but there was one other thing that gave him misgivings about the current situation and he resolved that he should speak to Asmodai about it. Given the delicate balance of affairs both with Cypher and the Inner Circle, Sapphon wanted to be as honest as he could with the Master of Repentance.

Sapphon entered quietly, earning a glance from Asmodai. The Master of Sanctity gestured to his fellow Chaplain and indicated that they should step outside. Asmodai wiped his hands on a bloodstained cloth and followed Sapphon back into the corridor.

'Have you ever witnessed the like?' said the Master of Sanctity when the door was closed and the grille shuttered.

'Never,' admitted Asmodai. 'Aside from his physical resistance, he seems to me as one that has no more left to lose, nothing worth defending. The Fallen cling to their lies and betrayals as definitions of themselves, and are only too eager to spout their vile beliefs to those of our calling. He makes no defence, raises no objection to his treatment.'

'Perhaps he thinks he deserves it?'

'That would be remarkable. It would also be against every impression he had given me so far, up to the murder of Anovel. He has secrets, every Fallen does. He killed his ally to keep us from learning them. Maybe he is certain he can resist all excruciation.'

'Or he has another plan,' said Sapphon, dropping his voice to a whisper. 'You recall his history, as Azrael related it?'

'You think his manner stems from confidence that he will escape?'

'We must consider the possibility. There is also one other matter I wish to bring to your attention.' Sapphon opened the grille again and stepped back. 'The far corner, on the left, where the shadows from the brazier fall.'

Frowning, Asmodai looked into the cell. He stepped back in shock and darted a look at Sapphon.

'I have never…' The Master of Repentance was lost for words, stunned by what he had seen.

Sapphon said nothing as he closed the slit, glimpsing again what he had seen a few minutes earlier. In the darkness of the corner were two embers, eyes in the shadow. A Watcher in the Dark.

'It is without precedent,' he said. 'Never has a Watcher shown any interest in an excruciation before.'

'None that exists in our records,' Asmodai added quickly, obviously referring to the journals spoken of by Azrael. 'Perhaps there is an account elsewhere. Could the Watchers be the means of his escape?'

'I would rather not speculate. But it is clear to me that we must pursue a different strategy. Physical incentives are having no effect, no matter how deftly applied.'

Asmodai shook his head, brow furrowing.

'You are going to talk to him, yes?' the Chaplain growled. 'Do you learn nothing?'

'I must,' Sapphon said with a shrug. 'But we must be of accord this time. I require no oath nor will make any demand by my rank. I want you to listen and apply your own assessment. You are wrong about me,

I do learn, and so I rely upon you to stop my judgement being led astray. We will listen together and we will decide what to do together. Will you grant me that grace?'

Asmodai was almost as shocked as when he had seen the Watcher. His stare searched Sapphon's face for any sign of treachery, but found none. The Master of Sanctity had been entirely earnest in his approach. After accepting the blame for the fiasco with Cypher and Anovel, on top of the machinations with Astelan, Sapphon needed Asmodai as an ally not an enemy.

'The Supreme Grand Master needs us to find answers, and swiftly,' Sapphon added. 'What we learn must be for the ears only of those that Azrael entrusted in the Hidden Chamber. Do you agree?'

Asmodai glanced at the cell door, thinking of the captive within, and then nodded in reply to Sapphon's question.

'The vote of the conclave was in error,' Asmodai said. 'The scheme we unearthed might well be continuing and our only key to its mysteries is Cypher. I expect I could bludgeon the truth even from such a reticent soul, but your methods may prove swifter. The Supreme Grand Master cannot afford to pander to the niceties of the Inner Circle.'

The Master of Repentance opened the door and signalled for Sapphon to enter.

'I will wait here,' Sapphon heard the other Chaplain say as he closed the cell door.

Cypher was looking at Sapphon intently, his eyes following him as he moved around the slab-like table and stood beside the Fallen's head. Blood spilled from dozens of cuts and there was bruising around the chest and ribs – there would be no evidence of either in the morning, due to the quick healing of a Space Marine's physiology.

'I am sorry,' said Cypher, surprising Sapphon. 'The death of Anovel was regrettable. Dishonourable.'

Sapphon was not sure how to respond to this. He had expected more silence, not an admission of guilt, despite the obvious nature of the crime. Beneath a crimson mask, Cypher's face seemingly showed genuine contrition.

'A trap was being set,' Cypher continued. 'Anovel was just a pawn in a greater scheme.'

'You told me he was going to betray his allies.'

'He was. In fact, he has. The deed is done, his death changes nothing except to silence him.'

'But you know his secrets, I think. Secrets that condemn you.'

'I am condemned already by history,' Cypher replied. He glanced away. 'The list of charges you bring against me is long indeed, is it not?'

'You are the thrice-cursed,' said Sapphon. The epithet seemed trite, irrelevant now that he was face to face with the man it had been placed upon. Calling one's enemies bad names seemed a petty act, but so useful for inciting the necessary hatred in others. 'I appreciate your candour. Let us start with the most fundamental questions. Do you deny that you took part in the rebellion against the Lion?'

'That is of no importance, Master Sapphon. We could trade words for a lifetime concerning my allegiances and still be in discord. You are just following the form of your colleague, Asmodai. You may invite him in if you wish, what I have to say needs to be heard by you both. I needed to know that you would listen.'

Sapphon looked towards the door and gave a nod

to Asmodai looking in through the grille. For some reason the Master of Sanctity then glanced to the corner where the Watcher had been standing, perhaps seeking permission or reassurance. He did not know why. Whatever the cause of Sapphon's curiosity, the Watcher in the Dark had vanished. Whether this was implicit approval of the current proceedings or entirely unrelated, Sapphon could only guess.

Asmodai closed the door with a firm hand and waited on the threshold, not trusting himself to move within reach of the bound Fallen. His displeasure at being apparently summoned was already writ in his reddening face.

'Choose your next words very carefully,' said Sapphon.

'Perditus,' said Cypher.

'Is that a curse?' snapped Asmodai.

'A world,' Cypher said, resting his head on the stone table. 'One that I first heard of during the time you now call the Horus Heresy.'

'What is on this world?' demanded Sapphon.

Cypher smiled with genuine warmth of recollection.

'The key to Horus's defeat and the salvation of the Dark Angels.'

REPULSED

Deep in the heart of the Rock was the chamber of the Master of the Forge, head of the Cult Mechanicus amongst the Techmarines of the Chapter. He was the driving force behind the machinery of the Tower of Angels – literally. On ascending to his rank, each Master of the Forge forsook an independent life and became part of the systems that controlled the Rock, a conscious biological intelligence monitoring nearly the entirety of the Dark Angels fortress-monastery. This ranged from plasma reactor to void shields, environmental stabilisers to the artificial gravity network. It also included the extensive security systems of the Tower of Angels, meaning that very little passed unnoticed by the Master of the Forge.

Such surveillance made it necessary for Sapphon and Asmodai to approach Sammael in clandestine fashion, arranging to meet the Grand Master of the Ravenwing in the Hidden Chamber now that Azrael had revealed its location.

They rendezvoused just after the first sermons, when Sapphon had completed the mass for the Deathwing and Sammael had finished the hymnals with the Ravenwing. The chamber was devoid of features and Watchers, even the inscription on the floor and ceiling concealed in the absence of the Supreme Grand Master. Had anyone by some miraculous coincidence stumbled upon the chamber by accident, it appeared utterly uninteresting – perhaps an old storeroom for the dungeons.

'Interesting,' said Sapphon as he stepped across the threshold into the empty room. Sammael was already there, pacing impatiently where Azrael's library had been revealed. 'Greetings, Grand Master. Our apologies for engaging in subterfuge again but we must speak on a delicate matter.'

Sammael stopped and looked at both of them.

'When the two of you come together as one voice, I know it is time to be concerned.'

'It is true that we rarely see eye to eye, Brother Sammael, which should tell you of the importance of our request today.'

'Request?'

'We need you to take the Ravenwing to the Perditus System,' said Asmodai. 'As soon as possible.'

'Impossible.' Sammael shook his head. 'Azrael has already issued orders to my company for when we arrive at the Phyleaides Cluster. The *Implacable Justice* is to conduct initial scouting operations against the Varsine to establish their strength and disposition.'

'A secondary consideration,' said Asmodai, earning himself a frown from Sapphon. 'We have intelligence that Perditus hides a secret from the Chapter's ancient history.'

'A secret? I have never heard of Perditus. What is the source of this intelligence?'

'A recent interrogation of the Fallen, Methelas,' Sapphon said quickly, before Asmodai could respond with the truth. The Master of Repentance opened his mouth to deny this but shut it again without protest. 'Perditus is a small Adeptus Mechanicus station that houses a powerful weapon which may be used against the Dark Angels in the near future.'

'Why come to me rather than the Supreme Grand Master?' Sammael stared at Asmodai. 'It is not like you to circumvent the Inner Circle, brother.'

Asmodai looked uncomfortable. Sapphon knew he could not answer on his fellow Chaplain's behalf without raising Sammael's suspicions further. The Master of the Ravenwing had a keen nose for intrigue even though he was virtually incapable of it himself beyond the basic secrecy required by the Inner Circle.

'We do not wish to make another blunder in full scrutiny of the Inner Circle,' Asmodai replied eventually, seeking some truth he could fix upon. 'The claim by the Fallen must be investigated but we would rather not distract the entire Chapter.'

Sammael eyed both of them and then shook his head again.

'Do not think me a fool,' said the Second Company commander. 'This claim comes not from the lips of Methelas but from Cypher. It is writ clear on your faces that you conspire and it occurs to me the source of your intelligence must be held in doubt or you would go directly to Lord Azrael.'

Sapphon exchanged a look with Asmodai, who seemed relieved that their pretence had been ineffective.

'Your insight is as acute as ever, brother,' said Sapphon.

'But let not the source detract from the possible value of the knowledge.'

'How can I not?' Sammael, jaw clenched, turned away and flexed his neck, trying to relax. 'He tricked you into allowing him the opportunity to kill Anovel. He allowed himself to be captured by my Black Knights. There is some hidden purpose to this, and I will not place my company directly in the line of fire. From Port Imperial to Ulthor to Tharsis my Ravenwing have suffered casualties. I will not risk the rest of my warriors with such an obvious trap.'

'*Your* company? *Your* warriors?' spat Asmodai. 'They are Space Marines of the Dark Angels, not some personal household troop!'

'And yet above me, the only authority to which they bow is the Supreme Grand Master,' Sammael snapped, turning back. 'If you wish to go to Perditus, it must either be with the whole Chapter or you must convince Azrael to issue an order that despatches my company to almost certain extinction.'

The Master of the Ravenwing stalked past them towards the secret stairway down to the dungeons. He stopped at the top step and looked back.

'To preserve the honour of your positions, I will grant you the courtesy of one day to make good this arrangement with Lord Azrael. After then, I will approach him with what has transpired today and I expect him to demand full censure from the Inner Circle. How dare you try to drag me into your conspiracies and lies!'

Sammael stormed down the stairs, leaving Sapphon and Asmodai looking at each other.

'That could have gone better,' said the Master of Sanctity.

'If we had been open from the outset and not attempted

deception, do you think he would have been persuaded?' asked Asmodai.

'The Ravenwing have been hurt of late, he is not wrong. Sammael feels the pain of his company and his caution is understandable.'

'The Ravenwing are ever the first blade drawn, the first weapon thrust towards the enemy. It is their lot to face the strength of the parry alone. If Sammael has lost the daring on which we rely, his company is no longer suited to its purpose.'

'Keep such thoughts to yourself, brother!' Sapphon grabbed Asmodai's arm in a tight grip. 'We may not yet have made Sammael an enemy to our cause, but if you attack him he will defend himself at our expense.'

'This is why I detest these games of half-truth and misdirection,' said Asmodai. He pulled his arm free. 'I agree with Sammael, we must approach Azrael and speak plainly of what we have learned. You are too close to this mess and I freely admit I am too belligerent. Let the wisdom of the Supreme Grand Master prevail.'

'How the times change us,' Sapphon said with bitterness. 'You challenge Azrael at every opportunity but now you scamper to hide beneath his mantle.'

'I will accept no weakness from others. I swore no oath to uphold our agreement, you made that clear. If I see no reason to continue with this concealment there is nothing to prevent me making known what has happened.'

'You need a reason to investigate a probable threat to the Chapter?' Sapphon stepped close and dropped his voice, even though they were alone in the Hidden Chamber. 'In ten thousand years Cypher has only come to us eight times. Eight times! That's less than once in a millennium! We will never have this opportunity again. And you want *another* reason to go to Perditus?'

Asmodai thought about this for a few seconds and conceded Sapphon's point with a solitary nod.

'Context is paramount,' said the Master of Repentance. 'And we must create the correct context for the other Masters of the Hidden Chamber.'

'The Masters of the...' Asmodai looked around the room. 'You have named our little cabal?'

'It seemed appropriate.' Sapphon shrugged. 'Do you have a better suggestion? The Innermost Circle, perhaps? The Hub?'

'You busy yourself with strange thoughts at times, Sapphon. I do not envy you the machinations of your fertile brain. If you wish to call our grouping the Masters of the Hidden Chamber, that is your business. I will trouble myself with greater matters, such as how we are going to convince our brothers to accept an expedition to Perditus.'

'That will be my concern, brother. I will assemble the Hidden Masters.'

'I prefer that. It is shorter.'

'Then we have accord.'

A LAST GAMBIT

'He seems…' Sapphon was not sure of the word to use to describe Cypher's behaviour over the previous hours. 'Cooperative? Forthcoming?'

Azrael looked at Sapphon from behind his desk, hands laid flat on the wood. The Supreme Grand Master seemed calm, despite the intrusion by Sapphon. Azrael stood up and seemed to regard his personal banner, hands behind his back.

'We cannot change our destination to Caliban, not on the word of a traitor and proven liar.'

'I understand, master. He must know this, and yet he still insists that we must act. Our fate lies at Caliban, he claims.'

Azrael inhaled deeply. He did not turn around, but his voice became taut.

'Each day I must weigh impossible decisions, Sapphon. To uphold my oaths to protect the Emperor's domains and to prosecute war against His enemies, or to hold to those secret oaths I swore to the Inner Circle to prosecute the Hunt for the Fallen until we have erased the stain upon our honour.'

He turned, still not looking at Sapphon, and lifted a few sheets of printed flexitrans from his desk.

'Thousands have died in the last hour, across the Phyleaides Cluster. The Varsine Bloodflock is in full migration. Four worlds have already lost millions. The Emperor's loyal servants, slaughtered by xenos filth. Millions more will die even if we could stem the Bloodflock this minute. The regiments of the Astra Militarum do what they can but they are too slow to chase down the Varsine. The Imperial Navy is stretched too thin to protect every system. We must find and destroy the worldnest or whole sectors may be lost.'

Now he looked at Sapphon, with intensity not anger. 'You want me to delay our intervention on the untrustworthy assertions of an admitted traitor?'

Sapphon met his Chapter Master's inquiring look with a regretful one.

'Yes,' he said. 'How many millions more will die in the centuries to come if the Dark Angels do not survive to protect them? How many *billions* if, as Cypher claims, the Unforgiven will be destroyed in their totality? Not by aliens, or heretics or mutants. By the Imperium. By our fellow Space Marines. Civil war, Lord Azrael. On a scale we cannot imagine.'

Azrael said nothing, his look demanding more from Sapphon. The Lord of the Rock wanted to be convinced, but had not yet been given sufficient reason to act.

'Once in ten generations, turmoil such as this tears at the Imperium,' said the Master of Sanctity. 'Aside from a few of our most revered warriors interred in the sarcophagi of their Dreadnoughts, there is one alone that has witnessed all of these events. He is in one of our cells and requests an audience with you.'

Sapphon leaned across the desk, resting on his fists.

'This is not one of those days when you must weigh the Hunt against our broader duties. Today the Hunt and the protection of the Imperium are the same. I do not ask that you act, merely that you listen. I could relate Cypher's arguments here and now, but it is better that you look into his eyes and listen to his voice, not mine.'

'And if I remain unconvinced by his testimony?'

'We kill Varsine and I speak no more of Cypher.'

Azrael considered this, laying down the reports from Phyleaides back on his desk, using his finger to neaten the pile.

'Very well,' he said. 'One last audience.'

The two of them made their way down from Azrael's chamber near the pinnacle of the Tower of Angels into the depths of the dungeons in the Rock beneath. They reached the stretch of corridor where Cypher was imprisoned, nearly a quarter of a kilometre long, and empty of all other Fallen.

'Where are the Deathwing that should patrol these passages?' demanded Azrael as he noticed the guards' absence.

'I am sentry alone,' said Asmodai, emerging from the shadows of one of the watch chambers adjoined to the tunnel. 'We can trust no other.'

'You approve of my visit?' said Azrael, surprised.

'The salvation of the Dark Angels could be at hand, Supreme Grand Master. Others may misunderstand my motives, but the erasing of the ancient shame has always been my goal.'

'I see,' said Azrael. He looked at the closest cell door. 'He's in here?'

The two Chaplains nodded in reply.

'He says he will only speak to you alone,' said Sapphon.

'He is restrained,' added Asmodai. 'He presents no danger.'

Azrael darted an aggrieved look at the Master of Repentance and opened the cell door. Silhouetted against the glow of embers from within, the Supreme Grand Master stopped on the threshold.

'I will listen to what you have to say.' His words were addressed to the cell's inhabitant, not the Chaplains outside. 'If you persuade me you are telling the truth, I will act on your assertions. If I am unconvinced, I will have you executed. Are you willing to submit to these terms?'

There was a pause that seemed to last for some time to Sapphon, but must have been only a couple of seconds.

'Yes.' Cypher's voice seemed distant.

Azrael pulled the door closed with a thud that resounded along the empty corridor. Sapphon and Asmodai looked at each other and retired to the guard room to await the decision of their lord.

THE CANKER OF DOUBT

The pick shrieked as its head rebounded from the metres-thick ice clustered around the coolant exchange. Annael hefted it back over his shoulder and swung again. The ferrite tip caught in a jagged crack and split a chunk of ice a metre thick. The outer part fell away to the decking at Annael's feet. He crouched and tossed it aside. Stepping back, he lifted the pick again.

He had laboured for twelve hours and twelve hours more would not tire his superhuman muscles. The monotony of the first six hours had threatened his sanity. It was as though he had been locked in with his own thoughts just as he had, metaphorically speaking, been locked in the coolant exchange ducts by his penance.

Into the seventh hour he had started to daydream. He had thought at first that his catalepsean node had been triggered, causing half of his brain to slumber. In fact it had been caused by something far more prosaic – boredom. A concept almost alien to the Space Marines, whose lives were filled with training, duty and attendance to their brothers even when not in combat.

His idle thoughts had little space to roam. His childhood was an indistinct blur, his earliest recollections of any depth coming from his days as a novitiate of the Chapter. For the next four centuries he had been a battle-brother of the Dark Angels. A warrior cast in the mould of the heroes of ancient times. An unrelenting life of bloodshed and honing deadly skills.

Such experiences left little to the imagination. Flights of fancy were heresy.

Yet somehow Annael's unencumbered mind had managed to find a place to wriggle free of catechisms and hymnals, bolter drill and armour maintenance doctrine.

He had imagined a forest. The trees of dead Caliban, where the Lion had hunted great beasts and earned himself the rank of Grand Master amongst the knights of the Order. Annael had pictured himself as a knight of the Order serving beneath the Lion, joining him on the Great Hunts. They had been lauded and feasted on their return to Aldurukh, the very tower beneath which his tireless arms now swung again and again and again.

The Lion was magnificent – an amorphous individual in his daydream, his features reminiscent of Lord Azrael and Belial and Malcifer and Sammael – the resemblance not simply superficial, as the primarch combined the authority, resilience, wit and daring of all four. Annael felt joy just to stand in the Lion's shadow.

He had dreamed of destriers. Hardy-bred steeds of

flesh and bone rather than plasteel, the forefathers of *Black Shadow* and the other bikes of the Ravenwing. Whimsy distracted his thoughts at this time, to wonder if the machine-spirit of *Black Shadow* had been offended by Annael's actions. Did the steed share in his shame, shunned by the other bikes and speeders of the company until its master made penance?

Even in the fantasy of his daydream, Annael could not escape the crushing humiliation of his punishment. In the depths of his despair, he found the means to make himself feel even more wretched – he dreamed that he had disappointed the Lion.

The Grand Master of the Order looked on him with benevolence, but there was also dismay in the primarch's eyes. Annael felt that gaze upon him and there was no greater punishment that could be meted out.

He wept, his soul torn apart by the thought that he had failed the Lion.

'Annael.' A hand touched him on the shoulder. 'Annael!'

He looked up through tear-filled eyes. For a moment his vision swam and he thought he looked on the face of the primarch. It resolved into the features of Malcifer, crouched over him with concern knotting his brow.

'Master Chaplain?' Annael croaked. He realised that he must look a sorry state – curled around the pickaxe like an infant, head resting on a lump of ice. He sat up, wiping a hand across his face.

Malcifer stood up and Annael sprang to his feet, embarrassment coursing through him. He tried to stand to attention but hours of lying on the ice had numbed his muscles and he stood lopsided, silently cursing his weakness.

'Do you know why I sent you here, Annael?' the Chaplain asked.

'To clear the ice from the coolant exchange, Master Malcifer,' Annael replied.

Malcifer gave him a condescending look.

'That ice has been here for millennia. Do you really think it needs to be cleared?'

Annael thought about this, his gaze moving from Malcifer to the jagged frozen liquid and back again.

'To break my spirit?' he ventured.

'What use is a Space Marine without spirit? Come, Annael, what has happened to you in these last few hours? Speak from your soul.'

'I dreamed that I failed the Lion,' Annael confessed.

'Just a dream?'

The Dark Angel looked deep into Malcifer's eyes. Trying to interpret this question. He gained no insight from the impassive stare.

'A realisation,' Annael said eventually. 'Acceptance of what I have done.'

'And what have you done, Annael?'

'I failed. I brought shame to myself, to the squadron, to the Black Knights.'

'And how did you feel?'

Annael bowed his head and looked at the floor.

'Less than worthless. It was not that the Lion was angry with me. Or even that he was disappointed. There was something else.' He looked at Malcifer and gritted his teeth. 'He gave me a particular look. It seemed as though he no longer trusted me, and it was the most grievous wound I have felt.'

The Chaplain folded his arms and nodded, but said nothing. Annael realised he was supposed to continue. Rather than attempting to marshal his whirling thoughts, the Black Knight gave voice to them as they occurred, trying to find some sense in the stream of ideas.

'If the Lion does not trust me, nobody will. The bond of brotherhood, my honour, the oaths sworn, they were all meaningless in that instant. Once broken, never repaired. No word I could utter could heal that injury, could mend that fracture. All that I had done before was as naught. Dust scattered by the wind. All that I would do was tainted, marred by the doubt of my lord.'

The anger Annael had felt for weeks was no longer in his breast. He tried to find it, the spark of outrage that he had been treated so poorly, but nothing of his defiance remained. Something else was missing too. He looked sharply at Malcifer, confused by the sensation.

'I do not feel sorry,' Annael admitted.

'Oh?' Malcifer rubbed his chin with the back of his hand. 'Why is that?'

Annael tried to articulate the feeling. He started several times before he could find the right words.

'It no longer matters what I did. The deed was unimportant. The betrayal…' He felt the confession stick in his throat. A look at Malcifer, open and honest, forced it out. 'I was a Black Knight. I was to be above reproach. Others looked to me for inspiration, for guidance, for honour. We disobeyed… That is, *I* disobeyed Sammael, and in that act I cast doubt on his commands. If the Black Knights are above obeying orders, why not the other Ravenwing? What of the commands of the Supreme Grand Master, the instructions of the Chaplains? Loyalty is not flexible. Obedience, true obedience, is absolute.

'Doubt is a canker. You have warned us so many times

that perhaps I no longer heard the sermon. When Sammael issues an order to me, will there be doubt in his thoughts? When the other brothers see me, will doubt erode their respect for the position I occupy? Even my squad-brothers, even with Sabrael, though we acted in concert, can we trust each other again?'

Malcifer accepted this with a thoughtful nod. He stepped towards Annael and his hands moved to the Space Marine's, lifting them to Annael's chest. Annael felt the intensity in the Chaplain's stare as though it was the glare of a Land Raider's lamps, blinding him with its strength. He felt that strength flowing into him, his fists clasped in Malcifer's hands, the beating of his twin hearts suddenly fierce in his chest.

'What do you have to say to me, Annael?' asked the Chaplain.

Annael felt as though his soul was burning him from the inside out, flushing cleansing flames through his body. Dishonour, shame, weakness. Everything that he reviled, everything that he hated about himself that he had not accepted, it was all purged. The greatest punishment had been within and it was strength, not weakness, that brought it forth.

'I repent,' he whispered, lowering to his knees. He kissed the Chaplain's knuckles and closed his eyes.

'Do not be afraid. Declare it to me. Let the universe know the mettle of your soul, Annael.'

'I repent,' he said again, louder. He felt a tug from Malcifer, lifting him to his feet. He opened his eyes and saw that the Chaplain was smiling. Annael grinned, astonished by the emotion flooding through him. He had thought this moment would be sombre, a dour instant of indignity and disgrace. Instead, he lifted his voice in a joyous shout. 'I repent!'

'Truly you do,' said Malcifer, stepping away. His smile was replaced by a sincere expression, and the gravitas spread to Annael, his own happiness fading to a more sober mood. 'Welcome back, *brother*.'

ANCIENT DEEDS

Cypher had been moved from his interrogation chamber to a detention cell. There was very little difference – the absence of the Chaplains' excruciation implements and the fact that the prisoner was chained to a cot rather than a slab. Even so, it irked Azrael that Cypher had managed to dupe not just Sapphon but also Asmodai into alleviating his circumstances in promise of knowledge. The Supreme Grand Master had huge reservations about the Master of Repentance's attitude, but he had thought he could always rely on Asmodai to give short shrift to any of the Fallen. Apparently he had been wrong.

'Your doubt is obvious, and I cannot blame you for harbouring such sentiment.' Cypher stood, his ankle manacled to the leg of the bed. He spread his arms in supplication. 'The consequences of our last meeting were drastic.'

'An understatement. They were appalling.'

'And you will never believe another word I say.'

Azrael hesitated, remembering what he had told the Fallen before entering.

'I am dubious of every word that falls from your tongue. But I promised I would give you this last chance to vouch for the usefulness of your continued life. On my honour, such as is left of it, you have my word that I am not wholly deaf to what you have to say. I will give you fair hearing.'

'You claim to have little honour left, but you have never broken an oath, nor have you done anything less than your utmost to uphold the name and standing of the Dark Angels. You would have been a fine seneschal to the Lion.'

The Supreme Grand Master tried hard not to let this praise affect him, but the sincerity in Cypher's voice made it impossible not to feel a small swell of pride. Azrael pushed it to the back of his mind.

'Empty words.'

Cypher's lip turned down and he looked away, sighing. Azrael did not speak, but he chose not to harry the prisoner to continue. The Fallen was deep in thought.

'The dishonour was not yours,' he said, still staring at the floor. 'Whatever misdemeanours you feel you have perpetrated in the cause of the Hunt, you have atoned for a hundredfold by your dedication to the Imperium. The crime was not yours, not any of the Dark Angels that now bear the burden of shame.'

'No, it was you, and the other Fallen. You turned on the Lion. That act is the wellspring of our dishonour.'

'And yet you carry that shame as though your robes were made of lead. I have met many of those you call Fallen. Some are vile creatures, like Methelas, who have descended into the pits of the darkness. Some retain their honour, caught up by good faith in bad superiors, given no chance to make amends for being used and discarded. Some are twisted, but believe in all their soul that they were on the right side of the argument. Many were willing, but many were not.'

'I would expect you to make apology for your fellow traitors.' Azrael crossed his arms. 'I hear nothing that exempts you from our condemnation or merits any comment.'

'I ask for another indulgence, Lord Azrael.' The Fallen's use of the title confused and irked Azrael. It was uttered with respect, or seemed to be, but sounded alien from the mouth of this treacherous dog.

After a few seconds Azrael realised that Cypher was being literal, asking for permission to continue. The Supreme Grand Master waved for him to carry on speaking.

'To understand how your brothers might be saved, you must understand the journey that has brought you here,' said the renegade.

'So you are to recite to me the history of my own Chapter?'

'Not at all, but to remind you of the part I played in it. Whatever the chroniclers have recorded in secret, I can tell you much of what has happened and what it is that you seek to repent.' Cypher sat down and indicated for Azrael to do the same – there was a stool beside the door. Azrael ignored the invitation. 'I have stood in the Hidden Chamber. I have walked the Forever Passage. I have in my time seen most of the Tower of Angels, as prisoner or guest.'

'Yes, that is a matter I would have you clear up for me. How do you intend to escape this time?'

'I do not.' Cypher sat forward, earnest. 'The Rock is

a void-borne fortress, escape is impossible. I intend to leave your company the same way I left the company of seven prior Supreme Grand Masters. With your permission, perhaps even your blessing.'

Azrael laughed, shocked by this incredible assertion. Cypher smiled, sharing his humour.

'I am going to let you go, is that what you are telling me?'

'Yes.'

It took a few more seconds for Azrael to control himself. As the last of his laughter died away, the Supreme Grand Master sat down.

'Tell me, thrice-cursed, what wisdom you have for me. What do you know of the atonement of my gene-brothers that I do not?'

'It was not the turning of the Fallen that sealed the fate of the Dark Angels for ten thousand years. If you could see with eyes undimmed by the lies of your forebears you would know the truth, see the last ten millennia for what they are. Nearly half of the Legions joined Horus. They have been forgotten, their memory denied to the common people of the Imperium, their primarchs half-whispered names of devils and slain traitors.

'And there were those within the Legions recorded as loyal defenders of the Emperor that did not remain true to their oaths. They split with their brothers and gene-fathers, for Horus or personal gain, or were tricked into selfish acts by promises from the agents of the Dark Powers.'

'There is rumour of such in the oldest annals,' said Azrael. 'It does not compare to the crimes of the Fallen.'

'No, it does not. But also, the fact that your ancient records contain such knowledge proves that the other

Legions that suffered such treachery in their ranks were of no mind to conceal it. Those that remained loyal used the evidence of deserters and defectors to reinforce their dedication to the Emperor. But in the annals of the Space Wolves and the Ultramarines, in the spoken mysteries of the White Scars and the halls of records on Baal Secundus, where does it speak of the Fallen?'

'Nowhere!' Azrael was alarmed by the thought that the Dark Angels great secret might be known to anyone outside the Unforgiven.

'A secret kept for ten thousand years. Not strength drawn from division, but shame. A shame multiplied every day by your denial to the Imperium and yourselves. The crime for which you must atone is not the turning of the Fallen, but the decision to conceal it. That first lie, that the Dark Angels had remained loyal, told to the primarchs of your brother Legions. Years later, a second lie, even greater than the first, told to your own warriors. When I returned to warn that the Fallen were not dead, I hoped for openness, but instead my news was greeted with distrust and secrecy. Every lie begets a new secret, every secret begets a new lie. If you capture all of the Fallen, if this moment I was to repent every sin I have knowingly committed against the Lion and the Emperor, your shame would not be ended. You carry it in your souls, not the Fallen.'

Azrael resisted the urge to get up and strike the corrupted Dark Angel, and shook with the effort.

'Why do you take such umbrage at my words?' said Cypher. 'Dismiss them as the ranting of a Fallen. The seeds of doubt sown wildly by a traitor. You cannot argue, because in your soul you know what I say is true. Every warrior that bore your title, Supreme Grand

Master, carries the guilt not of the Fallen but of every Chapter Master that has chosen a path of deceit rather than honesty.'

'And that would save us? To confess to ten thousand years of manipulation and secrecy? The Unforgiven would be declared *Excommunicate Traitoris*. Not even our cousins in the other Chapters would side with us. All of the Imperium and the Adeptus Astartes would hunt us down.'

'And your pride would force you to defend yourselves, rather than meekly accept your execution as you should. Deluded to the end that you were in the right, a curse on the Imperium spat from the lips of the last Dark Angel to die to a righteous blade.'

'And what is this to do with you and Astelan and Caliban? Is it your blade that will hunt us?'

'You misunderstand me. I would save you and the Imperium this fate. No good comes of forcing the truth into the light. Only by your own admission of guilt will you ever be free.' Cypher stood up, a hand extended towards Azrael. 'No matter what you think of me, I am a Dark Angel too. The same gene-father's blood runs in our veins. We are so alike, creations of the Emperor, but your blindness sets us light years apart.'

'You think that I would trust you?' Azrael asked.

'No,' said Cypher. His expression was fierce as he continued. 'You must never trust me! There is no oath that I will keep, no power that I can swear by that you can hold me to. I *am* the thrice-cursed, liar, traitor and enigma. The more I assert I am telling you the truth, the less you should believe me.'

'But you ask me to believe you now? How can you say such a thing and then expect me to stay here and listen to your lies?'

'I am not asking you to believe *me*. That would be fruitless. Open the door.'

'What?' Azrael glanced towards the heavy cell door.

'Please, I am chained, I cannot escape. Open the door.'

Azrael, frowning, stood up and did as he had been asked. He swung the cell door out, revealing the corridor. The Supreme Grand Master stepped back in shock. Instead of the empty passage he had been expecting, he was confronted by dozens of glinting red eyes in the gloom.

Watchers in the Dark, at least thirty of them.

The air was filled with the same sense of dislocation he had felt when he had been taken to see Luther for the first time, as though a fog hung across his senses. He glanced to the left, seeing the flickering light of the lanterns in the guard room where Sapphon and Asmodai waited. Azrael could see them now, talking to each other, but moving with extreme slowness, their gestures changing by tiny degrees, lips opening and curling with tectonic speed.

To the right the corridor stopped abruptly, two hundred metres short, and a huge hydraulically-locked door barred further progress.

'They wish us to follow.'

Azrael turned at the sudden voice at his shoulder, hands rising to protect himself, but no attack came. Cypher rubbed feeling back into his wrists, his bonds laid out behind him on the bed and floor.

'Not my doing,' the Fallen said quickly, lifting his hands in surrender as Azrael took a step closer. 'It was their act.'

Azrael thought he understood the strange nature of the Watchers now, or at least had an inkling of the source of their power. Space was something they could rearrange at will, creating stairs and corridors and gaps between walls whenever needed. He had no doubt the portal was real, somewhere else in the Rock, but for convenience they had brought it close for him.

'Do you know what is inside?' Azrael said, looking at the forbidding door in front of him. It was reinforced with heavy bands. Ancient symbols of the machine cult were etched into the metal, with no sign of tarnish or weathering. 'Is this what you were going to tell me?'

'I have no idea what this place is,' confessed Cypher. 'I answered only the urge from our small friends, an instinct that we needed to meet again.'

'Then there is only one way to find out,' said Azrael, striding forward. The Watchers parted before him.

HEIRLOOM OF THE LION

The door opened with a hiss, swinging inwards to reveal a metal-lined hall within. For an instant Azrael thought he had seen the chamber before, but the memory would not stand still for scrutiny, constantly changing in slight details. It was a dream, he realised. One that had come to him again and again but not until now had he remembered it.

Like most of the dungeon beneath the Tower of Angels, the cathedral-like space was lit by electric lanterns, at least fifty of them casting a yellow glare across the hall's contents. The walls, nearly a hundred metres apart, were covered in stacks of machinery and monitors, so that the bare metal was hidden behind banks of dials and levers and flashing lights and coils of cabling and pipelines. The precise position of each mechanism seemed slightly out of place, ajar with the dream-memory.

Gantries and walkways, steps and ladders were

arranged around something that had always appeared as a blur in his dreams, with sensor probes, monitoring dishes and scaffolding further enmeshing the centre of the warp device.

The thing itself was there, clearer than anything else. A sentience, or at least semi-sentience that had been quietly calling to him for a century and more. It was a perfect sphere of marbled black and dark grey, with flecks of gold that moved slowly across its surface. Ten point six seven metres in diameter – how he recalled the exact dimensions the Lord of the Rock did not know – it was made of some exotic material beyond comprehension.

Two protuberances extended from the sphere, one at each pole, each only a few centimetres long. The rounded nodules touched against circuit-covered plates stationed above and below the device, which in turn were linked by a dizzying web of wires and cables to the surrounding machines.

Azrael could feel the thing regarding him with some alien sense. He was not sure how he could tell, nor how the warp device could sense him in return. He looked at it and felt another flash of memory. Savage humans clad in red rags, wailing and screaming praises to the sphere. He brought death to them, slaying dozens.

'Careful, brother!'

Ezekiel's sharp words cut across Azrael's daydream, bringing him back to focus on the reality of where he was.

'How did you come to this place?' he asked the Librarian.

'By the same manner as you,' Ezekiel replied. He glanced back at the crowd of twinkling eyes in the darkness outside the doors. 'I was summoned. It seems I arrived just at the appointed hour. You are correct, this thing perceives us. It is psychic, connected to the warp, but in no way I have ever encountered before. I sensed its energies leaking into your mind, but I cannot penetrate its depths.'

'Nor will you ever,' said Cypher. 'No probe or drill or psychic exploration has ever revealed its mysteries.'

Azrael noticed a corpse, almost invisible amongst the tangle of cables on the floor. The body was that of an old man. More than old, ancient. His skin was as thin as paper over fleshless bones, hair and beard so long that they must not have seen a blade in all of his life.

There was something in the back of the body, a pipe that snaked into the darkness, another set just below his neck.

It was then that Azrael heard the faint flutter of a heartbeat amongst the buzz of machines and the crackle of charging power cells. He hissed in disgust as the dead man's chest began to rise and fall. He would have sworn that the old man had been a cadaver, no breath or pulse in him, but now the frail body twitched.

He sat up, moving jerkily like a badly-controlled marionette. The eyes were glassy, the limbs moving stiffly. With a glance at the alien orb, Azrael saw the golden motes moving more swiftly than before, forming brief patterns in the dark swirl.

'You have returned.' The man's voice was cracked, barely audible, devoid of emotion, his face featureless. A hand raised and waved erratically.

'What?' said Azrael, snarling as he turned on Cypher. 'What abomination is this?'

'It is not of my doing,' said the Fallen. 'Your predecessors imprisoned it here rather than returned it to Perditus as they claimed.'

'You make no sense. What is it?'

'It is called Tuchulcha. That is about all that I can say, and that it was pivotal to the Legion during the Horus Heresy. It can be very cooperative, though it is disturbing to deal with.'

'It's a daemon,' said Ezekiel.

'Not strictly true, young Ezekiel,' the servitor-avatar croaked, turning its withered form towards the Librarian. 'I am a lens, you could say. It no more makes me a daemon than looking through a window makes you glass.'

'What are you?' said Azrael, stepping forward until he was within arm's reach of the puppet-servitor. He could not imagine that the animated man did not suffer somehow from this ordeal, and flexed his fingers at the thought of snapping his neck to end the mockery of life.

'I am Tuchulcha, Lord of Angels.' The corpse-servitor looked up with rheumy yellow eyes. It took a couple of seconds for Azrael to realise that the warp-thing was using the title in address to him, not in reference to itself. 'I am the everything. Everywhere. I was once Servant of the Deadly Seas. I was a friend of the Mechanicum. For a time I was ally to the Lion.'

'You are evil,' said Cypher. 'You thrive on turmoil and bloodshed.'

'Some have tried to destroy me, Lord of Angels. Physically, it is impossible, nor should you desire it. All things desire me. The one they call Typhon covets me, but I am not what he thinks I am. I do not wish to be destroyed.'

'Typhon?' Azrael looked at Cypher for an explanation.

'Calas Typhon, once First Captain of the Death Guard. You curse him as the one called Typhus.'

Azrael's mind whirled. Ever since his ascension to the Deathwing he had grappled with mind-bending tales from the time of the Horus Heresy, of secrets and lies within lies and secrets. There had been no mention in any of the annals of the existence of Tuchulcha. Azrael studied the machinery around the warp device, his eyes narrowed.

'Why did they bring you here? Those that came after the Lion?' Azrael looked at Cypher again, feeling more out of his depth than at any point in his long life. He detested the fact that he was at the mercy of the mercurial renegade. 'What did they intend?'

'They coveted me. All things covet me.' The corpse-puppet grimaced, pulling back cracked lips and revealing toothless gums in an attempt at a smile. 'I am desirable.'

'They feared releasing it, I would guess,' said Cypher.

'Guess? I thought you know this thing?'

'Of it, that is all. I did not know it was here. The Watchers told me. Showed me. I felt it, through them. However it is that they communicate.'

'What do you want?' Azrael asked Tuchulcha, addressing the orb rather than the servitor. 'Why have you been revealed now?'

'I want to make you happy.' Azrael saw that the puppet's gaze was not directed at him, but at Cypher. 'I thought I did. You do not seem happy. Why are you not happy?'

'Ignore it,' Ezekiel said quickly, stepping in front of Cypher. He darted a worried glance at Azrael – an expression the Supreme Grand Master had never seen before on the face of his Chief Librarian. 'We must find some way to destroy it.'

'You cannot.' The servitor let out a dry laugh. 'If I could be destroyed, I would not exist. If you wish to be rid of me, all you have to do is take me home.'

'Perditus?' said Cypher.

'I am not handing this abomination back to the Adeptus Mechanicus,' said Azrael. 'I have no idea what it is, but it is clearly too dangerous to allow it to be free.'

He looked at Tuchulcha, wondering what was inside that strange globe, where it had come from and who, if anyone, had made it. 'Why Perditus, what is there for you?'

'Salvation.' The servitor sagged. 'Release. For all of us. But not Perditus. Home. The world you called Caliban.'

Azrael could not speak for several seconds, mastering his anger at this assertion. In his place Ezekiel spoke.

'Caliban is no more, destroyed. You must know this if you knew the Lion.'

The puppet-corpse tilted its head to one side.

'It does not have to be.'

'What does not have to be?' demanded Ezekiel.

'Caliban does not have to be destroyed. With my help you can save your world. And the Lion.'

FAREWELLS AND REGRETS

Waking with a start, a burst of energy flooding what was left of his body, Telemenus opened his eyes and discovered that he was not alone. Three others stood around the life-support system, their bulk almost filling the rest of the small med-chamber.

He did not recognise them at first. It took prompts from the Emperor – who appeared as the reflection of a golden griffon in the glass pane of the door – to remind him of their names.

'Galadan… Caulderain.' He looked at the third and fond recollections rushed up from the depths of his memories. Telemenus smiled. 'Daellon!'

He had thought his squad-brother dead. His last memory before awaking on the *Penitent Warrior* had been of the gigantic daemon swatting Daellon aside with its skull-headed flail. He looked at the robe-clad warrior and saw no sign of bionics or serious injury.

'You saved my life, putting yourself in the path of the

daemon to take the blow meant for me. I can never repay the debt I owe even if I had all my limbs remaining. Would that I had the means to reciprocate.'

'My Terminator suit, praise its spirit, protected me from the worst,' Daellon said, guessing Telemenus's thoughts. He came forward and gripped his battle-brother's hand. 'If only your war-plate had been so faithful.'

'I live,' said Telemenus. 'It protected me just enough for that.'

He saw sadness in the eyes of his fellow Deathwing.

'You look as though you attend my funerary rites. Why so leaden with sorrow?'

They looked at each other, waiting for another to speak. Caulderain it was that took the lead, swapping places with Daellon.

'The Apothecary woke you for us, so that we might say farewell,' said the sergeant.

'This need not be farewell, brothers!' Telemenus raised his hand and attempted a shrug. 'This small form takes little enough life to animate. This does not have to be a last parting.'

'For us it may be,' said Galadan. 'The Rock returns to Caliban. Some devious plan of the Fallen that might see us all destroyed. The Deathwing go to war and you will not be counted amongst our number. Even if we survive, you will not fight beside us on the line again.'

The announcement struck Telemenus as hard as the blow that had cut him in half. He closed his eyes and looked away, his jaw clenched so that he made no sound of despair. Mastering himself in a couple of seconds, he looked back at them.

'I live to serve the Emperor and the Lion's shade. There are many that went to Ulthor and ended their duty there. I am grateful to continue in my service.'

'Other than the obvious, is all well with you?' Daellon looked concerned. 'Forgive my saying, brother, but you seem... humbler.'

Telemenus laughed. He saw a golden flash in the glass of the door as the vision of the Emperor regarded him with eyes of fire.

'It would be a break of faith not to learn from such a catastrophic experience. I understand my weaknesses and see why my behaviour vexed my superiors at times.' Telemenus's thoughts caught up with what Galadan had said. 'The Deathwing travel to Caliban? A momentous time, and a testing one also. I wish that I could fight alongside you, my time with such esteemed brothers seems woefully short now that it has passed.'

'I would have your keen eye in my squad,' said Caulderain. He glanced at the others. 'Your absence lessens us, the whole company, in strength and in spirit.'

'Perhaps you did not realise, but we took heart from your achievement,' said Daellon. 'To fight beside one with the marksman's honour gave us all pride. You allowed us to share in your triumph.'

That was not how everyone saw matters, thought Telemenus. He thought back to Sergeant Arbalan, trapped inside the daemonflesh of the city on Ulthor, and his last words to Telemenus.

'Do not make me beg,' growled Arbalan, staring at Telemenus from his flesh cocoon.

'Perhaps if we found a Librarian, he could cleanse the taint from you,' Telemenus suggested, though he knew it was a hopeless situation.

'Telemenus, come closer.' The Space Marine complied with Arbalan's request as Daellon stepped away. When the

sergeant spoke his voice was a whisper. 'There is more to being a great warrior than shooting straight. You have been a disappointment to me and to the Grand Master since you arrived. It is not patience or skill that you lack, it is humility, and that is why we have been scrutinising you so closely.'

'You think that I show promise?' Telemenus was confused, unsure whether Arbalan was praising him or criticising. 'The Grand Master pushes me harder than the others because he senses what I could offer?'

'No.' The sergeant's lips were almost nonexistent and his skin all but a mask but he still managed a dissatisfied expression. 'With training and armaments like yours, any warrior can serve with distinction in the First Company. Remember, you are not special.'

Telemenus recoiled as if shot, stepping away from the sergeant. He shook his head.

'Now, which one of you is going to end it for me?' The sergeant grunted in pain, baring decaying teeth and blackened gums.

'I will, damn it,' said Daellon.

'No!' Telemenus stepped in front of his companion and raised his storm bolter, aiming at Arbalan's face. He met the sergeant's stare, knowing that Arbalan could see nothing of his expression past the helm of Telemenus's armour.

'At least I know you can hit me from that distance,' Arbalan snarled, unrepentant to the end.

'You deserve this,' said Telemenus. 'I owe it to you.'

He fired.

He had thought about Arbalan's assessment in the few lucid waking moments he had experienced since being saved by Temraen and Librarian Ezekiel. The veteran had been correct, Telemenus was not special. He deserved no greater praise than any of the other thousand brothers of the Chapter.

'Thank you for coming to see me,' he said. It occurred to Telemenus whether such respect would have been forthcoming if he had not almost died at the hands of the enemy. Was it shameful that he had not died, lingering on as a burden to the Chapter? Would it not have been better if he had joined the ranks of the Honoured Dead? It seemed as though he heard the eulogy of his own funeral ceremony, but he tried to accept the thought as it was intended. 'It gratifies me to know that despite my behaviour at times I am remembered fondly by my brothers.'

There was little else that could be said that would not seem maudlin or ridiculous and the three Deathwing Space Marines made to leave with simple goodbyes. Daellon waited after Galadan and Caulderain had departed.

'There is no justice in what has happened to you, brother,' he said, looking Telemenus directly in the eye. 'I see the hurt, the wounds that cannot heal. Were it not forbidden I would grant the grace you gave Sergeant Arbalan. They are going to place you back into stasis, until your final duty is decided. I cannot imagine the half-life you will have to endure, but know that you were meant for a fate better than this, an end more remarkable.'

'We cannot all become Masters and legends, brother. Fear not for my soul, and feel no sorrow for me. Be content with the punishment of the enemy and know that I will always stand beside you in thought if not deed.'

Daellon took a deep breath and laid a hand on Telemenus's shoulder.

'Stay strong, brother.'

'Fight hard, die well,' Telemenus replied. He uttered the words without irony.

Daellon left him, though he spent a few seconds speaking with one of the medicae serfs, who looked at Telemenus several times, shaking his head.

He felt fresh drowsiness pulling him into a stupor and knew that when he awoke he would know the life ordained to him for the rest of his span. Sustained by elixirs and mechanical systems, his service would continue for several centuries yet.

'Are you afraid?' the Emperor asked, returning to the skull face He frequently assumed during their conversations, glimmering at the heart of the glow-globe above the table.

'They shall know no fear,' Telemenus replied. 'Did not Guilliman quote You in his famous speech? I dare not defy one of Your edicts, and so I shall know no fear.'

Despite these brave words, he could not deny a degree of apprehension as the Emperor faded from view and he slipped into the darkness.

PART THREE
CALIBAN

OLD ALLIANCES

'Circles within circles within circles,' Azrael said to Ezekiel, shaking his head. The two of them had met in the Hidden Chamber to discuss the next step in dealing with Cypher and Tuchulcha. 'The last thing our Chapter needs is more secrets, but there is no alternative. Sapphon and Asmodai were right to exclude the bulk of the Inner Circle from discussions about Cypher. The Hidden Masters, Sapphon calls us. And now, Tuchulcha. We cannot allow anyone else to know that the Rock has been harbouring some kind of half-daemon for the last ten thousand years! But I do not trust Cypher to–'

'Something has happened,' Ezekiel said suddenly, interrupting Azrael. He looked around the chamber, his good eye twinkling with golden power. 'We are no longer in the warp.'

The Supreme Grand Master had felt nothing, no soul-wrenching transition from the immaterial to the material. He knew better than to ask the Chief Librarian if he was sure.

'How is that possible?' he said instead.

'The sphere,' Ezekiel replied with a look of concern. He closed his eye for a few seconds, an auric glimmer shining through the lid. When he opened it, his brow furrowed even further. 'The whole fleet has been moved into real space.'

'Our Navigators reported that the warp was unusually calm, with a swift-running current that has guided us speedily to Caliban faster than any journey before. Do you think Tuchulcha was responsible?'

'I would suggest that the only way to be sure is to ask it, but I wouldn't advise that. We should spend no more time with the abomination than is necessary.'

'I agree. It clearly has some objective of its own, as does Cypher. What of the Order of Crimson Knights? They were supposed to follow us from the rendezvous at Arcadus.'

'They have been transitioned too. I also detected more ships, in-system and approaching through the warp. There's a lot of turbulence in the wake of our exit, it's impossible to tell distance or numbers.'

Both the Space Marines were fully armoured, as was standard protocol while traversing the perilous warp. Azrael activated his vox and hailed Master Issachar, who was the current Master of the Watch.

'Issachar, make your report.'

There was a lengthy pause before the Third Company Captain replied, somewhat hesitantly.

'We have dropped out of warp space, Supreme Grand Master. With all of the fleet. And we are far inside the system delineation for a tolerable warp jump. I don't know how it happened. We just… appeared.'

'Call all stations and ships to full battle-readiness.'

'Already done, Lord Azrael. The instant we emerged, the Master of the Forge detected several other warships in the system. Analysis shows that seven cruiser-class and larger ships are from the Consecrators Chapter, the others are unidentified, presumed hostile.'

'Transfer all details to the station in my chambers.' Azrael cut the connection and turned his attention to Ezekiel. 'How did the watch-monitors not detect a sizeable enemy fleet entering our hallowed system?'

'The monitors are attuned to detect warp emissions. Perhaps, like us, the enemy entered by means other than a standard warp breach.'

This answer added to Azrael's concerns as he stalked towards the steps that led past the Great Library to his chambers. He realised that Ezekiel was not following and looked back.

'I need you at my side at all times, brother. I cannot navigate the rough waters of this crisis without you.'

'As you wish, Lord Azrael.' Ezekiel caught up with his superior and looked up the steps. 'I would swear there are more secret stairs and passages in this place than those plainly known!'

'Very likely,' said Azrael, beginning the ascent. 'One might be tempted to think our forebears on Caliban had something to hide long before the schism.'

'Please, brother, do not joke about such things. We have enough conspiracies to occupy us already.'

They continued in silence, winding their way up through the Rock until they came to the corridor that held the Great Library and Azrael's rooms. Entering the command chamber of the Supreme Grand Master, they discovered Issachar's report waiting on a screen for them. Azrael scanned it quickly.

'The energy signature detected at the heart of the unknown fleet seems familiar,' he said. He activated the interface servitor wired into the back of the desk. It was nothing more than a head affixed to gimbals angled from a recess in the wall. A sallow-skinned face regarded him with blank glass eyes, coiled cables trailing from its temples.

'Input data criteria,' it droned from an artificial voicebox, lips sealed with loops of red wire. Azrael felt a quiver of distaste, reminded of Tuchulcha's puppet.

'Search archives, reverse chronology, seeking matches with latest scan report.'

'Searching.'

While the servitor accessed the depths of the archival storage banks, Azrael examined the status report in more detail. The Consecrators were on a trajectory taking them on a circumspect route around the system, keeping a long distance between them and the unknown fleet. The unidentified ships numbered between five and seven capital-class ships, with twice that number of escorts. They were coming around Caliban's star and were heading towards the former location of the Dark Angels home world.

'Cease search,' Azrael said sharply, remembering where he had seen the sensor readings before. 'Those energy outputs are the same as those that Belial uploaded from the databanks of the Streisgant citadel. He said it was identified by Astelan as the *Terminus Est*.'

'The plagueship of Typhus,' said Ezekiel. 'That is not surprising. His role in this crisis has yet to be identified but he is intimately involved. It seems that Sapphon and Asmodai were right. The capture of the Fallen, the ones we thought were architects of this plot, has not curtailed its execution. Others still at large continue the scheme.'

'Tuchulcha said that we could save Caliban, but I cannot see how that is possible.'

Ezekiel was lost in thought for several minutes while Azrael continued with the report. A vid-connection from Issachar flashed across the screen. The Supreme Grand Master stabbed an armoured finger onto the acceptance key, apprehensive of what the Master of the Watch might say.

'Report,' Azrael snapped.

'Unknown fleet is retiring, Supreme Grand Master. They are turning back from our axis of advance. Also, we have received a hail from Grand Master Nakir requesting a rendezvous.'

'Nakir is here?' Ezekiel said quietly, as surprised as Azrael by this news. Chapter Master Nakir of the Consecrators was something of an enigma even amongst the mystery-wreathed warriors of the Unforgiven. 'Your message has brought forth the Master of Souls from the catacombs of the *Reliquaria*. These must be dire times indeed.'

'Tell Nakir to make all speed for the Caliban nominal point, he is welcome to join us in the Tower of Angels. Extend the same invitation to Chapter Master Dane aboard the *Flame of Galandros*.'

Azrael silenced the link and moved from the command chamber to his office, Ezekiel on his heels. He sat down behind his desk, the reinforced chair creaking in protest at the weight of his war-plate, and rested his hands on wood polished smooth by generations of Supreme Grand Masters.

'What do we tell them? Dane and Nakir?'

'I suppose the truth is not an option,' replied the

Chief Librarian. Azrael raised an eyebrow, not sharing his companion's moment of humour. 'No need to mention Cypher or the warp-thing. Divinations have led us here. The *Terminus Est* and the importance of the location is enough of a threat to justify mobilising the Unforgiven in force. Dane will follow your lead and will not pry deeply.'

'I am surprised by his response almost as much as by the Consecrators' presence. They have suffered many casualties in their latest campaigns. Almost reduced to half strength by several accounts.'

'As I said, Dane is utterly loyal to you, Lord Azrael. He would lead his last warrior into the teeth of the enemy to uphold the honour of his Chapter in your eyes.'

'Let us hope that will not be necessary.' Azrael leaned back, rubbing his forehead. 'You are right, Dane is not the issue. Nakir will be more inquisitive.'

'The perils of allowing Interrogator-Chaplains to become Chapter Masters,' said the Librarian. 'They always want to delve deeper than is required.'

'You speak of divinations. What have you seen with your second sight, brother?'

'The Hooded Death, but such doom is a constant companion to the Dark Angels. Of late, little else.'

'Nothing?'

'Disturbingly so. I wonder if it is connected to the warp effect conjured by Tuchulcha. The flattening of the warp might isolate us from the ripples of astropathic signals and the swirls of events yet to occur.'

'We have enough uncertainty, adding the vagaries of warp sight to the list of obstacles we must overcome is unhelpful.'

It occurred to Azrael that there was another gifted

with prophecy who might have more to say about the unfolding events. Not another living soul knew about the existence of Luther, Ezekiel included. There were already too many threads starting to unravel from the Unforgiven's tapestry of lies to introduce that particular bombshell to the Chief Librarian.

'Do you need me for anything else, brother?' asked Ezekiel, noticing his superior's distraction.

'One moment more.' Azrael clenched his fists on the tabletop. 'I will not jeopardise the future of the Imperium to save this Chapter. We must hold higher regard for mankind. My instinct tells me that our enemies are seeking some means to reveal the nature of our history to opposing forces within the Imperium. If we fail here, if the true legacy of Caliban is made known, we must accept the judgement of our peers and allies.'

'You would allow the Dark Angels to be executed?'

'Not just the Dark Angels, all of the Unforgiven.'

'Let us hope it does not come to that pass,' said Ezekiel, shaking his head. 'Better to concentrate on achieving victory than worrying about the consequences of failure. After all, this entire incident is based on the tales of a self-admitted traitor and an alien warp-sphere. I am simply engaging each problem as it arises and hoping that we will see an end to both of these inconveniences.'

'Whatever Typhus desires here, we will deny it to him. Perhaps we have already succeeded. He runs now, afraid to test his might against the guns of the Rock. I do not expect he will find his bravery soon.'

'That may be so, but if he seeks something here, he will return. We cannot mount such a strong guard forever, he knows that our eye must be drawn elsewhere in time.'

'Why now? What circumstances have arisen that makes this plan, whatever it is, feasible now?'

'Who can say?'

'I was hoping that you might be able to.' Azrael forced a smile. 'You are my Chief Librarian, after all.'

'Conjunctions, both astral and cosmic.' The Librarian closed his eye and bowed his head. 'We near the end of the millennium, a time of great upheaval and devastation. Long in our minds has this time loomed, bringing darkness and destruction. But should we survive the trials ahead, should the soul and strength of the Dark Angels endure the onslaught, we shall emerge into a new age of light, renewed and redeemed.'

The thought that it was possible that the burden of so much secrecy might be lifted from his shoulders lightened Azrael's mood. There was always turmoil. There was always an obstacle to overcome. Such was the nature of penance. Redemption was not earned with words and deeds, but with toil and blood.

'Conjunctions, you say?'

Ezekiel opened his eye and nodded solemnly. Azrael stared at him, trying to pierce the inscrutable veil across his companion's thoughts. His gaze flicked from one eye to the other and back. He was not sure which he disliked the most. The bionic eye made him feel like a target. The other eye burrowed into his soul even when lit by dry wit.

'It is several days until we reach the Caliban nominal point,' the Lord of the Rock said to cover his unease, looking away. 'We will gather the full Inner Circle and apprise them of the plan.'

'Which is?'

'To hunt down Typhus and destroy him. Only then can we be sure whatever secret he seeks is safe from his clutches.'

Ezekiel accepted this without comment. Azrael could think of nothing more to say and dismissed the Librarian. Left on his own, the Supreme Grand Master turned his thoughts to the promises of Tuchulcha. Could it really be possible to save the Lion? And if so, what price was worth paying?

THE HONOURED HALF-DEAD

A piercing pain in the back of Telemenus's head shocked him into wakefulness.

In a box. More accurately, a metal coffin.

Without legs he had no means to tell how long the box was, but it was just a little wider than his broad shoulders. Steel pins pierced the flesh and bones of his arm and chest, holding him in place. He could feel something rubbing at the small of his back – or at least, where it had once been. Just about the same area where the interface of his black carapace used to connect to his battleplate.

His head was similarly fixed, he discovered as he tried to turn towards the sound of drilling just behind his left ear. He came to the conclusion that the irritating noise was the bit on his skull.

His vision cleared further, his focus extending beyond his immediate confines. Smudges of red resolved into Techmarines. Three of them, including Adrophius. The white robes of two orderlies from the apothecarion flanked Temraen, whose own overalls were covered in viscera.

The Apothecary noticed that Telemenus was awake and glanced down at the grey and red filth staining his uniform.

'Don't panic, we haven't removed more of you. The opposite, we've had to extend the nervous system and coronary network.'

'It hurts,' grunted Telemenus, feeling a stab of pain in his left shoulder. He could not see what was happening.

'Unavoidable,' said Adrophius, disappearing behind the Space Marine. 'We need the nerve endings active to get the best connection.'

'It feels like I have regrown my spine,' said Telemenus. 'It is not comfortable.'

'A feedback effect from the neural system. When we've made a few more joins you'll think you have arms and legs again. It allows for more stability.'

The pain returned, more severe than anything he had felt before, even the slash of the daemon's blade through his body and the fire of the tainted infection. Every part of him was nailed, stretched, twisted and bent, as though he was a rubber doll being stuffed into a space too small to contain him.

The Techmarines and orderlies busied themselves with ratchets and suction pumps, fleshwelders, saws, soldering irons and small spanners. One of them inserted a screwdriver under Telemenus's ribs and he felt his breastbone tightening. He hissed his disapproval and the Techmarine gave him an apologetic look.

'It will get worse,' warned Adrophius from out of sight. 'Once we activate the integration systems your whole body is going to come alive. Literally your whole body, even the parts you no longer physically possess.'

'I must warn you that there is a significant threat to mental stability,' added Temraen.

'You mean I might go insane?'

The Apothecary nodded and Telemenus wondered how bad could it really be? He had been sliced in two and dealt with the consequences. Being hooked up to a gunnery control system could not be so much worse.

And then he screamed.

Electricity pulsed through his brain, setting synapses afire. Blood vessels flared, atrophied matter brutally kicked back into activity. His eyes were fit to burst, the lights of the armoury bay a shocking white. His ears filled with such a clamour and wailing that he could not hear the rising shriek that passed through spittle-flecked lips that felt like they had been sprayed with acid.

The pain grew even worse, moving from the tip of his head down into his chest. His remaining heart thundered so roughly he thought his ribs would crack. His aorta seemed to swell to the size of the corridors of a battle-barge, the rush of blood surging through him making every artery and capillary vibrate with pain.

Rescued lungs filled with scalding liquid. He could feel a searing sensation moving down the bronchial tubes, coursing across the alveoli like an intense forest fire. He tried to breathe out, to extinguish the flame inside, but he had no diaphragm. Instead, pistons wheezed into life, ramrods pushing up into the flesh of his lungs, while intercostal muscles reinforced with bands of plasteel strained against the sudden pressure.

Telemenus felt something in his throat and coughed, the spasm sending ripples of agony down into his chest. A gobbet of phlegm the size of his fist flew out of his mouth. Taking in a deep draught of air, he smelled anti-infection spray. The taste of his battle-brothers' sweat rolled over his tongue like thick droplets. The iron tang of blood filled his thoughts.

Just when he thought the pain would subside, the technological phantom limbs returned, sending shockwaves back up through his nervous system. Two waves of agony met along his spinal column, crashing together to create new heights of pain.

Telemenus caught himself panting, taking hurried breaths between bellowed obscenities. He wanted to claw at his tormentors, to tear out their eyes and rip off their arms for what they had done to him. He thrashed at his bonds but he and the coffin were one and the same, indivisible.

The Techmarines and Apothecaries shared worried glances and spoke quickly to each other, but their words were lost in the roar of blood that filled Telemenus's ears. Through the din he thought he could hear alarms shrieking a two-tone warning. He did not know whether they concerned him or some exterior threat. Temraen reacted with a syringe almost as thick as Telemenus's thumb, jabbing a ten-centimetre reinforced needle into the Space Marine's chest.

For an instant cool water washed away the fire. Cleansing. Calming.

But only for an instant.

The pain flooded back, crackling along missing toes, shattering shin and thigh bones that only existed in his mind. His pelvis, now in memory, split apart with a harrowing *crack*, then turned to dust inside his flesh.

He started to lose sight of his fellow Dark Angels. A mist concealed them, scarlet, obscuring their faces.

A terrible foreboding filled him as the shapes of his brothers receded into the red fog.

He was alone, left to die in torment in a whirlwind of blood.

Telemenus tried to form words with lips that refused to obey. *Kill me.* He tried to beg. *Kill me.* He tried to howl. *Kill me!*

Despair gripped him, his mad anger becoming a terrible grief. Fear had been expunged by the attentions of the Tenth Company sergeants and the Chaplains. Hate had been poured into the void left behind. Hate for the enemy. Hate for the mutant, heretic and alien. That hate turned upon Telemenus now, left with no other course to follow.

Arbalan was correct, he was nothing special. Worse than that, he was a coward. A loathsome wretch of a hollow creature. He had failed as a Space Marine and brought shame to all that wore the colours of the Dark Angels.

'I cannot abide the selfish,' said the Emperor, appearing as a raven with wings of dripping blood, merged with the tornado that surrounded Telemenus.

'I am sorry,' sobbed the Space Marine. 'I am not worthy.'

'I choose who is worthy,' the Emperor replied.

The bloody whirlwind slowed and stopped, dissipating into a golden fog. The Emperor became an eagle during this transformation, wrapping His wings about Telemenus. His feathers soothed the pain that made the Dark Angel's limbs tremble.

Limbs.

Telemenus looked at himself, fully formed, created anew by the miracle of the Emperor. Where the wings passed, ravaged flesh became perfected. He felt the hot breath of the Emperor on his face, His golden beak centimetres from his nose.

'You will survive this,' the Emperor insisted. 'Prove to me that you are strong. Uphold your oaths.'

Telemenus relaxed.

In that moment his fears and cares and pain lifted like sparkling motes from his body, a shimmer of silver that drifted away with each breath from his lips.

His vision returned briefly, eyes still swimming with fluid. Telemenus thought he recognised the face of Belial staring down at him. It was either another hallucination of his madness, or the Deathwing commander had come to gloat at the final failing of his most disappointing warrior.

Even as these dark thoughts clouded his mind, Telemenus felt himself falling back into the grip of dread. He fixed upon the stern expression of the Grand Master, forcing himself to remember the first time they had met after Telemenus's ascension to the Deathwing.

He laughed. What a fool he had been. He had denied his faults in the face of the Grand Master, rather than accepting the truth of the accusations. Pride. Pride that Belial had seen. Pride that Arbalan had detested.

Where now was pride? In a ravaged body about to become the organic component of an anti-torpedo battery or lance array?

Pride made him fight. Pride brought the pain.

Telemenus released the burden of his pride with another silvery exhalation. It mattered not where he was, what he did. He was a Dark Angel. He would serve the Lion's shade and the Emperor in whatever way was required. It was not in his power to choose the noble fate.

He was no hero.

Telemenus realised his eyes were closed. At least, he felt they were closed and opened them. What greeted him was a complex vision akin to the telemetry display of his old Terminator armour. He could feel other senses – audio pick-ups, pressure gauges, kinaesthetic attitude relays – and somehow knew that he was standing.

He looked left and heard a whine of servos. He was greeted by the smiling faces of Temraen and Adrophius. Belial was with them, stern but not scowling for a change.

They seemed short. Smaller than Telemenus remembered. He assumed that he had been mounted in a high position on a wall or perhaps hanging from the ceiling.

Other sensations disproved this belief. He could feel limbs, just as clearly as he had felt them during the Emperor's caress. He felt strong. He felt whole.

'Can you hear me?' asked Temraen.

'I can,' Telemenus replied. He was shocked by the volume of his voice, thundering from an external address amplifier.

'We will have to perform more specific audio and ocular tests, but for now confirm that you can also see us,' said Adrophius.

With a thought, Telemenus zoomed in on the Techmarine's face. He could see the pores, the beads of sweat, tiny scars and abrasions from sparks let loose by forgework. His view flickered through several different spectral scopes and settled on x-ray. Adrophius's left arm was extensively rebuilt with bionic parts and there was a sheath cladding the upper part of his spine.

'I can see very well.' Telemenus enjoyed the rolling

boom of his new voice. 'What has become of me? What will my duties be?'

Belial stepped forward, looking up at Telemenus.

'You will continue to fight for the Chapter.'

Telemenus noticed the shadow he cast across the floor of the armourium. It swathed Belial in his Terminator armour. Blocky, at least four metres tall, almost as wide. His chemical sensor picked up the taint of exhaust on the air. He had no arms, not as a man might. On his right shoulder was a weapon with two long barrels. A twin-linked lascannon. The left mount sported a chamfered, armoured box which he now recognised as a multiple missile launcher.

'A Dreadnought?' he said, incredulous. 'You have placed me into the armour of a Dreadnought.'

'Yes,' said Belial. 'Such shall be your burden, to fight on for the Emperor and the Dark Angels.'

'Why?' Telemenus asked. 'You cannot believe me worthy, surely?'

'I can. You earned the marksman's honour, a remarkable achievement. The Chapter cannot waste such a skill. You have swapped bolter and storm bolter for lascannon and missile launcher, but I expect you to employ them with the same precision. You will support your brothers with these weapons, protecting them with your firepower as these plates of ceramite and adamantium protect the carcass you have become.'

Belial stepped back, and crossed his arms.

'More than that, you have proven yourself capable of upholding the honour of this armour. There are few with the will to survive the bonding process. Ezekiel vouched for you, after your ordeal at the hands of the daemon. It was your spirit that drove the warp-disease from your body. He said you would prevail and he was correct. Your battle-brothers brought petition unasked-for, so that you might fight with them again on the line. Brother Daellon in particular praised your tactical skills and awareness. He claims that he would not have survived Ulthor without your aid and insight.'

'I...' Telemenus was lost for words, which he knew must appear somewhat odd for a hulking war machine that could obliterate battle tanks and wipe out whole squads of troops. 'I will extend my gratitude to them, when I have the opportunity.'

'You will repay their faith with attention to your battle-duties,' Belial said sternly. 'You are still a warrior of the Deathwing, but much more than that. They will look up to you, even my Knights whom you have revered as heroes. You must lead by word as well as deed. Fight with honour at their side.'

'I will,' said Telemenus. It was almost overwhelming, but it would be dishonourable to dwell on such a boon. As Belial had said, the only true way to honour his brothers and Chapter was in battle. After such misgivings over what fate held for him, the thought that he would again walk the field of battle with his brothers brought a surge of happiness. He tempered it quickly, knowing that not only was he now a powerful engine of war, but also a figurehead that others would follow. He had become an embodiment of the Lion's will and the strength of Caliban. 'I will honour this armour with my oaths. I shall be the fist that breaks armies, whose blows topple fortresses. More machine than man, perhaps, but always a battle-brother.'

'Good. There is still much that must be done before you are battle-ready, and I believe that we do not have long to prepare. I will leave you for now, but will return soon.'

Belial strode away, leaving Telemenus to ponder what this meant. Daellon and the others had spoken of fabled Caliban, but Telemenus had no idea how long he had remained in suspended animation. It could have been days or years. He would need to learn what he had missed.

His thoughts turned to the Emperor, who had been his guide and shield throughout the whole ordeal since his wounding. He wondered whether his internment into the Dreadnought sarcophagus signalled the end of the intervention of the Master of Mankind.

He need not have worried. Where Belial had been moments before, the shadow of a great two-headed eagle stretched across the ground.

'I will never leave you,' the Emperor told him.

AN ENEMY REVEALED

Carried through the void by arcane engines, the Rock powered towards the zone of space that the metriculation systems claimed had once been the orbit of Caliban. The attendant fleets of the Dark Angels, Knights of the Crimson Order and the Consecrators spread out across several hundred thousand kilometres from the bastion of the Unforgiven. Eleven battle-barges, eighteen strike cruisers and more than three dozen rapid strike vessels, fast patrol destroyers, torpedo corvettes and other escort-class warships created a sphere of guns around the remnants of the Lion's home world.

As they advanced, the *Terminus Est* and the rest of Typhus's plaguefleet withdrew, maintaining a separation of at least five hundred thousand kilometres. It was clear that the traitor commander had no intention of leaving the system unless he was forced, but for the moment Azrael was content to secure the orbit of Caliban and plan his next move.

Over ten thousand years the asteroid remains of ancient Caliban had spread along the planet's former orbit, creating a dense field containing tens of thousands of pieces of planetary debris and a cloud of dust and gas that extended for several thousand kilometres further.

While the other ships maintained their cordon at a distance, the Rock ploughed into these crumbling remains, its navigational field flaring as it shunted aside the ancient planetary matter. Larger pieces of celestial debris still held haunting reminders that the swirling rocks had once been an inhabited world. Though pocked and cratered and cracked by impacts and collisions, after ten thousand years the void had not erased the towers and battlements of ancient fortresses. The tumbled ruins of arcologies kilometres-tall spun as moons around the splintered remains of their foundations. Bridges, roads, viaducts, canals, aqueducts and rivers still etched their lines across floating chunks of debris five kilometres across, like scratch-marked runestones of the gods.

The artificial gravity field powered from the innards of the massive fortress-monastery attracted the smaller asteroids. To avoid the nav-shields overloading from so many impacts, the aegis field was set to allow these through, whereupon they were blasted into atoms by point-defence turrets built to defend against gunships and landing craft – weapons that to this day, as far as Azrael knew from his readings, had not fired in anger for ten thousand years. Even so, by the time the Rock had pushed into the heart of the stellar field it was orbited by several dozen satellites ranging from fist-sized to a few metres across.

In a blaze of lasers and tracer bullets, thrusters letting

THE UNFORGIVEN

out plumes of white fire, the fortress-monastery of the Dark Angels came to a slow stop.

'Positional nominal null point established, Lord Azrael.' The Master of the Forge's voice blared from the command spire's speakers with a mechanical rattle. 'System orbital dominance established.'

Unlike the bridges of the starships around it, the Rock's central strategium needed no servitors to monitor the metriculation systems. In the first instance, everything was coordinated through the semi-cyberised mind of the Master of the Forge. A few Space Marines oversaw the offensive and defensive systems, aided by a small company of Chapter-serfs, while other unaugmented human auxiliaries attended to communications and scanner stations.

The spire was not quite at the pinnacle of what had once been the Tower of Aldurukh. The very summit of the edifice was a broken mess of toppled towers, blocked corridors and collapsed halls – a scar from the Age of Heresy left in place as a mark of honour to the fortress. Rumours abounded through the lower ranks of what might lurk in those lofty turrets and galleries. As he had risen to the position of Supreme Grand Master Azrael had slowly learned that there were far greater and more disturbing mysteries than the ghost stories of pre-transformation novitiates and Tenth Company Scouts.

Huge windows, each ten metres high, surrounded the octagonal command deck at the heart of the chamber. Massive columns held up the great vaults of the ceiling, each keystone forming the mount for a lantern as tall as Azrael, filling the space with a pale blue light. From his position atop a stepped dais at the centre of the strategium the Supreme Grand Master could see up into the void of space and out across the barren expanse of the Rock.

The fortress-monastery extended several kilometres from the Tower of Angels, incorporating the three central curtain walls of old Aldurukh. Like the other remnants of Caliban that now filled the view, the Rock was dotted with reminders of the ancient civilisation that had given rise to the Order and later sustained the Dark Angels.

Dormant gun towers and empty barracks blocks, outer defensive works, docks and ports, all had survived the great upheaval of the world, protected by the mighty Gorgon's Aegis – the powerful energy shield that had sheathed Aldurukh and its foundation during the cataclysmic battle between the Lion's followers and the Fallen.

Azrael could not help but turn towards the pinnacle of the tower and look upon the collapsed roofs and broken walls of the summit. There the Lion had battled Luther while war raged in orbit and on the surface of Caliban. How that confrontation had ended, not even Luther would say except to insist that the Lion still lived on, his shade haunting the Rock.

Azrael considered his last audience with the Dark Oracle.

The last Grand Master of the Order was calm, sat on his bench facing Azrael on his stool outside the cell. The Supreme Grand Master was not lulled into any confidence by the apparently cogent expression of his prisoner – there had been many times Luther's sedate exterior had broken in moments to reveal the madness within.

'It is coming quickly, the death of a world, the end of hope,' the Dark Oracle said quietly, leaning forward with his arms on his knees. His eyes were fixed on Azrael. 'The

vultures gather, each hoping to pluck a morsel from the corpse.'

'Whose corpse?'

'Fair Caliban's corpse, of course. We are but mites on her beautiful skin. A dermal infection. A parasite. We offended her, delving deep wounds into her flesh to fill with our nests. We thought to gouge her secrets from her and she turned on her children.'

'You destroyed Caliban, with your treachery,' Azrael snapped. Circumstances allowed him no patience at this time. 'What of Typhus? Why has he come?'

Luther was surprised by this question, sitting up with a frown.

'Calas Typhon, the seedbringer, the plough and the harvest. The circle of fecundity. He comes for me, but I am already here. Thrice-cursed, thrice-cursed, thrice-cursed. Why always thrice, dear Azrael? And now a new triumvirate of scavengers, picking over the devastation to see what prizes they can find.'

Azrael stood up to leave but Luther stood up also, eyes imploring.

'Let Caliban die...' he whispered. 'Leave her in peace.'

It had not gone well from there, leaving Luther a raving mess and Azrael none the wiser about Cypher or Typhus's plans. All that he had been able to gather from the madman's ranting was that Caliban was about to fall, just as he had said before. Looking at the broken pieces of the planet around him, the Supreme Grand Master knew that it was a warning ten thousand years too late.

A clarion rang out across the command tower, turning all eyes towards the main doors. The huge double portal wheezed open to reveal a striking figure clad in black war-plate and a long white cloak. He wore his helm, crested front to back with a red brush. The sigils on his shoulder pads were almost completely obscured by a plethora of purity seals made from crimson wax and streamers of script-covered parchment. More of the seals fluttered from his greaves as he strode into the command hall.

His armour was a mix of archaic marks from the time of the Imperium's founding and the Horus Heresy – pieces of Mark Three and Mark Four combined, studded with bonding rivets across the chest. A knightly helm taken from a suit of ancient Crusade Armour – officially designated Mark Two – completed the battleplate. What should have been a strange ad-hoc mix had been rendered into a beautiful suit of wargear by the artificers of his Chapter. The black enamel shone like oil, the gold that edged his breastplate and gilded the rivets sparkled in the lamps of the command tower.

Behind him came five Terminators, as black-clad as their lord save for helms of off-white to symbolise brotherhood with the Deathwing. Like their commander, their armour was a mix of styles and types, gathered from armouries and forgotten Legiones Astartes depots scattered across the galaxy. They bore with them the Chapter standard of the Consecrators, and several other artefacts from their hidden fortress-monastery known as the *Reliquaria* – chalices, sceptres and a bronze-sheathed staff topped with a winged blade.

'Grand Master Nakir,' Azrael called down to the new arrival. 'I bid you welcome to the Tower of Angels.'

With some unheard command, Nakir ordered his honour guard to remain where they were. He ascended the steps swiftly, and it was only when he reached the command platform that Azrael realised how tall the

Chapter Master was. He had twenty centimetres on Azrael, a difference that felt even greater with the swaying crest on his helm.

Nakir drew his sword and lowered to one knee. Taking the blade in both hands, he wordlessly offered it up to Azrael. The Supreme Grand Master examined the weapon keenly. It was of superb craftsmanship, and with surprise Azrael recognised the black material of the blade. It was the same as the weapons wielded by himself and Belial – the Sword of Secrets and the Sword of Silence.

'A Heavenfall blade?' said Azrael. Nakir stood and offered the hilt of his weapon. The Supreme Grand Master took it, the grip feeling comfortable in his fist, the weight as balanced as his own blade. 'Incredible. Where did it come from?'

'It was gifted to Grand Master Orias, first lord of the Disciples of Caliban.' The Consecrator's voice was quiet and gravelly, almost a growl. 'He fell in battle against the orks of the Quolon Pass. I recovered it three decades ago.'

'I have read of this weapon. The Sword of Sanctity.'

'I would return it to its proper master.'

'It has found its proper master,' said Azrael. He handed back the sword. 'It is not only yours by right of recovery, but you would bring honour to the cousin of my own blade.'

Nakir took the weapon and sheathed it with a nod. He glanced around the command tower and then reached up to remove his helm. It came free with a hiss of escaping air. Nakir's face was surprisingly young, gaunt to the point of skeletal. His eyes were a piercing blue, at odds with the mop of black hair on his scalp. His brow was tattooed with an Imperial aquila in black, and a broken blade in red adorned each of his cheeks. There was a scar across the front and right side of his throat and evidence of an implant – the wound that gave him his distinctive voice.

'I have longed to set foot in the Tower of Angels for my whole life,' Nakir said, looking around again, this time drinking in his surroundings, eyes wide with awe. It was a strange contrast to the severe figure he cut when wearing his helmet. He returned his gaze to Azrael and his expression hardened. 'A silver lining to the storm that brings me here.'

Nakir had been an Interrogator-Chaplain before his ascension to command of the Consecrators, the so-called Master of Souls. Even now a symbol of his past hung at his waist, a wooden rod in the shape of a small crozius arcanum, studded with six black pearls. Each was a trophy of a Fallen made to repent, a remarkable feat for any Dark Angel, and almost unprecedented in one of Nakir's short service. He led a Chapter dedicated to unearthing the secrets of the past. A penetrating stare threatened to strip away the layers of deceit in which Azrael was forced to wrap himself. He had dealt with the likes of Asmodai and Sapphon for decades, but felt himself being opened up by the Master of Souls.

'A dire time, but you have my utmost gratitude for your presence,' he said to move the conversation in a different direction. 'I must admit that it was a surprise, particularly to find out that you personally led the force.'

'When the Chief Librarian of the Dark Angels issues a rallying call on behalf of the Supreme Grand Master, it penetrates even the sepulchre of the *Reliquaria*. That the muster was to be at Caliban added even greater weight to the missive.'

'Of course.'

The Caliban System was technically protected territory of the Dark Angels, forbidden to enter without invitation even for the Successors. However, Azrael knew that there had been occasions when the Consecrators had sent missions into the remnants of the Legion home world in their quest for the ancient heirlooms of the Lion. Nakir probably knew more about those times than even Ezekiel. Azrael considered whether it would be profitable to see if Nakir knew anything about the existence of Tuchulcha, but dismissed the idea. It was too dangerous to invite any inquiry in that direction.

'Has Grand Master Dane arrived?' asked Nakir. 'Can the conclave begin?'

'He will remain on his battle-barge, commanding the fleet,' said Azrael. He had thought it better to host only one Chapter Master at a time. Dane was an accomplished fleet commander, and giving him control of the assembled warships allowed Azrael to concentrate on other matters. 'I expect your flotilla to follow his lead, in absence of any direct command to the contrary.'

'The Consecrators are a sovereign Chapter of the Adeptus Astartes,' Nakir replied soberly. 'We will consider any requests from yourself or Master Dane on their individual merits.'

'Of course,' said Azrael, and then caught the hint of a smile from Nakir. He responded in kind. 'Far be it from me to ever suggest that the Successors of the Dark Angels should be beholden to a cause beyond their own duties, or hold loyalty to any other than the Emperor.'

'Lord Azrael!' The shout came from Carlion, one of the Dark Angels overseeing the surveyor systems.

'Report,' Azrael replied, moving to the edge of the command dais overlooking the sensor consoles.

'The enemy fleet has changed course. New heading brings them directly towards us.'

'They are attacking?' Nakir held up a hand in apology as Azrael darted him an irritated glance at the interruption. 'Apologies, the instincts of command.'

'Good instincts,' said Azrael. He returned his attention to Carlion. 'Confirm course and speed, do they suggest an attack?'

'The enemy are still accelerating, it's not certain if they will settle at battle speed.'

'Signal Grand Master Dane to muster the fleet for defence of the Caliban nominal point. It could be an attempt to lure us away from where we are. The Rock will remain in position. Capital ships to form the main line of battle. I want escort squadrons arrayed to intercept any breakthrough.'

'Confirmed, Supreme Grand Master. Relaying your orders to Grand Master Dane.'

'Your last communiqué confided that the enemy fleet is commanded by Typhus,' Nakir said quietly. 'Even with the *Terminus Est* he is hopelessly outgunned. What does he think he can achieve?'

'I have no idea, but let us not be caught by surprise. You will remain here for the time being. Please defer command of your ships to Dane.'

'Of course,' said Nakir, his confusion obvious. 'Why am I not returning to my ship?'

'I must hold council with my Masters and I would leave you in charge of the Rock.'

Nakir's surprise was matched only by an almost childlike delight that crossed his face. It lasted only an instant until he tempered his response and slowly nodded with an attempt at gravitas. Even so, Azrael could see his companion swallowing hard, evidently coming to terms with the magnitude of what had been asked of him.

'I am honoured,' said the Consecrator. 'I will repay your faith in me.'

'I am sure you will acquit yourself with distinction, Grand Master.'

Azrael turned and had descended a few steps towards the lower level when the great doors slid open once more, revealing Ezekiel. The Chief Librarian entered without ceremony, expression agitated. Azrael met him halfway down the dais.

'What brings you forth from the Librarium, brother?'

Ezekiel cast a glance up to Nakir and then spoke, leaning close to whisper so that no other could hear what was said.

'Tuchulcha touched my mind a few minutes ago,' the Librarian said. 'It warned that we were not alone. I summoned a coven of my brothers and we performed a deep scan of the warp. There are nearly thirty warships in the immaterium close to the Caliban System. They are shrouded by some warp-spell, which blinded our usual sweeps. Definitely not friendly.'

'Thirty?' Azrael caught his voice rising in shock. 'Thirty warships. Why have they not broken from the warp? We are still seven or eight days from a safe transition point, they cannot be of assistance to Typhus, surely?'

'We also detected another dozen or more Successor ships, all within a few light years. If the enemy do break into real space, reinforcements are only a handful of days away at most.'

'This situation is rapidly escalating. But it still does not explain why Typh–'

Azrael stopped when Ezekiel took a step back, eye widening as it turned gold, a hiss escaping from gritted teeth.

'The warp spews forth its vile filth!' the Librarian snarled.

'Lord Azrael! Detecting massive interspatial break!' Carlion's warning came just a second later.

'On display!' Azrael bellowed, dashing back up to the command podium. He glanced back to check on Ezekiel. The Chief Librarian was following at a more sedate pace, his eye still ablaze with psychic power. 'Show me, now!'

Two of the windows darkened and hololithic projectors sprang into life, painting a view from the external visual scanners. The view moved left and right for a few seconds and then panned upwards to centre on a point a few thousand kilometres above the line of attack followed by Typhus, roughly halfway between the two fleets.

The starfield wavered as though water rippled over a lens. The pinpricks of light started to oscillate, some growing larger, others disappearing, a few becoming bright red. They swirled and danced, spinning around each other, leaving vermilion trails.

A tear appeared, the prismatic energy of the warp ripping through reality in a multicoloured blaze. Silhouettes wavered in the brightness, casting long shadows into the real universe that blotted out more stars. The gash lengthened and widened, as though invisible fingers prised open the edges.

'They are coming through,' snarled Ezekiel, reaching the top of the command dais. He leaned on the rail, one hand held to his temple, eye screwed shut. 'Something on Typhus's ship... A bridge between the warp and...'

He sank to one knee, golden tears running down his cheeks, face contorted with effort. Nakir took a step forward but Azrael pushed past and crouched beside Ezekiel.

'Where?' Azrael demanded, grabbing the Librarian's arm. 'Where does the bridge end?'

Ezekiel took in a shuddering breath, teeth bared. He pushed himself upright and opened his eye. In the golden orb Azrael saw a flicker of reflection – an immensely bloated daemonic creature with a dozen fanged maws and a thousand eyes. Yet beyond the daemon, inside its immaterial form, he saw a vast worm, coiled about the core of the daemon, feeding on its own tail.

'Here!' said Ezekiel, grabbing Azrael's shoulders, staring deep into him. 'Through the lens!'

Alarmed, Azrael spun back to the hololithic display. The shadows in the rift had resolved into the crude shapes of warships – cruisers and battleships that poured from the breach in two lines astern.

Some looked normal – several of them patterns of ships that Azrael had seen before, others that he recognised from the old databanks. Most were bizarre conglomerations of starship and warp-matter – vessels mutated by daemonic possession and twisted with Chaos energy. They followed the largest of these, a black star of filth-encrusted stone and metal in perverse mockery of the Rock, an anarchic mass of jutting towers, splintered spires and immense barnacle-like growths.

The outer edge of the Consecrators fleet was closest to the warp breach, their ships turning towards Typhus's vessels. The plague-star ploughed into the cordon of escort ships that had been protecting the capital ships.

Purple light flared from arcane weapons and void shields burned blue against the blackness of space. A destroyer detonated in a plume of plasma as its reactor overloaded.

Torpedoes raced towards the Chaos ship and weapon batteries sparkled as they opened fire in return. Nakir watched with fists held to his chest, lips tight, eyes narrowed as the ships of his Chapter tried their best to manoeuvre to counter this new threat.

'All ships, engage the new fleet!' Azrael bellowed. 'Transmit attack order to all vessels!'

'We have to go,' Ezekiel said, his composure returned. His intent stare conveyed his meaning more than words. *The lens.* Tuchulcha.

'Nakir,' said Azrael, but the other Chapter Master was fixed on watching the first stages of the battle unfolding on the main display. 'Nakir!'

The commander of the Consecrators looked round, clarity returning.

'You are in command. My warriors will already be responding to attack protocols. Coordinate with Dane and ensure that we do not get caught between the two fleets. Ignore what I said earlier, the Rock will directly engage the enemy. We need all of the firepower we can muster.'

'As you will it, Supreme Grand Master,' Nakir replied, saluting with a fist to his chest. He was about to say something else, perhaps to ask where Azrael was going at this critical moment. Nakir glanced at the Dark Angel and his Chief Librarian and thought better of it. 'The Lion shall guide my ire.'

'I am sure he will,' said Azrael as he hurried down the steps beside Ezekiel. He glanced at the Librarian. 'There is one that knows more than any of us, I am sure. Fetch Cypher. Bring him to the sphere.'

'Is that wise?' asked Ezekiel as they stopped at the grand doors, waiting for them to open. 'The two most unreliable elements in this whole crisis and you wish to bring them together again.'

'The Watchers did so before, I must trust to that thought. Have we any other choice?'

DARK TALONS

The emergency launch clarion continued to blare as Annael hauled himself up the steps onto the wing of his Dark Talon. He paused there and shouted across to Sabrael, who was climbing into the cockpit of the aircraft behind him.

'Any briefing?'

'Not a word from the Huntmaster,' Sabrael called back. 'Perhaps the Supreme Grand Master dropped something out of a window and needs us to pick it up.'

'Good to hear that penitence has not improved your wit,' Annael replied. Sabrael's canopy hissed closed around him. Annael looked around for Tybalain and saw the Huntmaster in a heated discussion with Grand Master Sammael. The Lord of the Ravenwing was very animated, his hands moving with rapid chopping gestures and thumping one fist into the other.

Annael stepped into the cockpit and lowered himself into the seat, an interface jack slotting into the spine of his armour where his backpack usually nestled. The thick armourglass canopy *snicked* into place around him, forming a pressurised cocoon.

'Vox-check.' Tybalain's voice was a snarl over the communicator in Annael's ear. The squadron sounded off one by one. 'Immediate launch. Interdiction and elimination. Destroy all available targets.'

Annael's hearts started to beat faster when he heard this. The Rock was under attack! He wrapped his fingers around the control column and started the aircraft's engine. There were no more pre-flight checks to make – the armourium deck crews kept every aircraft in the flight bays ready to launch at a moment's notice. Only one last system needed activation.

Annael flipped open the plastek cover of the rift cannon firing stud. This simple action connected the main reactor to the dormant warp core situated just beneath him. Though he had never seen or heard of an incident involving a malfunctioning core, there had always been rumours and stories. When he had moved to the Ravenwing his old squad brothers had joked that he would be sucked into the warp by a rift cannon misfire.

He had laughed back then. He was not laughing now as red lights sparkled into life across the display in front of him. Almost immediately they turned amber and after three seconds the rift cannon system was green across the board. He could feel the steady thrum of the coolant systems beneath him, slow and steady, like the Dark Talon's heartbeat.

While he had been doing this, the servitors and armourers had left the bay, leaving only the Dark Talons of the Black Knights. The lighting dimmed to a ruddy twilight, allowing the auto-senses in Annael's helm to adjust to low light.

A siren sounded, audible even through the canopy. The huge gate that held back the vacuum of space slid up, immense chains and gears cycling to either side. The exterior pressure gauge dropped as the air in the flight deck rushed out, taking with it a few pieces of machine-cult detritus – empty unguent cans, discarded rags stained with sacred oils, litany-papers that had been removed from ammunition belts and replacement parts.

The launch bay was located in the lower parts of the Rock, delved into the foundation stone itself, half a kilometre from the Gate of Woes where the Fallen were taken to the dungeons. The invisible wall of the Gorgon's Aegis was close at this point, extending only two hundred metres from the surface of the fortress-monastery. Annael had expected to see an expanse of stars, perhaps even the local sun. Instead, when the gate had fully opened he was confronted by a swirling melee of asteroids, panning and crashing together, some smaller than his Dark Talon, others several times bigger than the Rock.

'Lion's blood,' cursed Nerean.

'They want us to launch into this?' said Sabrael. 'That is a truly awful joke.'

'Cease the chatter, launch commands have been issued,' said Tybalain. It was clear from his tone that he had raised objections and been overruled by Sammael. 'Initiate launch sequences.'

The hum of the engines increased to a whine as the five Black Knights powered up vertical thrusters. Annael's craft lifted two metres from the floor, wobbling slightly as the systems warmed up.

Tybalain led the way, easing his Dark Talon forward, nose dipped slightly, the main engines glowing with a faint blue light. Annael slid into place next, followed by Sabrael, then Calatus, and Nerean took up the last place in line.

The Huntmaster hit the boost controls and white fire flared into life, powering the Dark Talon out of the bay. Almost immediately, Tybalain pulled his aircraft into a steep climb to avoid an asteroid just a few hundred metres outside the bay gate.

'Wait!' snapped Sabrael as Annael was about to hit the forward thrust ignition.

A jagged piece of rock spun past the opening, three metres across. Annael saw what looked like a pair of legs standing on a pedestal – the remnant of a statue.

He had no time to remark on this sight. There was a clear opening of several hundred metres ahead. The Black Knight fired the main engines and was launched out of the flight bay, his warsuit compensating for the immense acceleration.

The moment the display indicated he was free of the gate, he pulled back on the control column, guiding his Dark Talon after Tybalain. His eyes searched the surrounding space, taking in the unfolding spectacle.

Beyond the immediate asteroid cloud, the darkness was split with trails of plasma and fire while flickering traceries of laser lances crisscrossed the heavens. He could see the sparkle of gun batteries firing on distant ships and the azure halos of blazing void shields.

Rolling his craft, he looked back at the Rock. Gigantic trios of cannons, each capable of hurling macro-shells larger than his aircraft, pounded out their wrath, their thunderous ire silent in the void. Asteroids turned to dust as the bombardment guns cleared an opening through the debris, the explosions filling the Dark Talon's scanners with splashes of energy. Lance batteries projected slicing beams of red energy that slashed across the asteroid field, opening fire paths for massed torpedo tubes and rocket silos to pour forth their deadly projectiles.

In seconds he had reached the limit of the Gorgon's Aegis and ascended from the protective bubble of energy. The Dark Talon's proximity alarm shrieked into life, the circular scanner display almost whited out with signal returns.

Impact danger ahead
Impact danger to port
Impact danger ahead
Impact danger to starboard
Impact danger ahead

He silenced the whining of the collision detection system, stabbing at the runekey with a snarl. Relying on his boosted reflexes and the vector thrusters of the Dark Talon he followed the jinking twin blue stars of Tybalain's engines, rolling and curving around the intersecting courses of the asteroids.

He entered a trance-like state, his hand on the column and feet on the rudder pedals moving unconsciously in response to the data-stream entering his auto-senses, easing the Dark Talon through the gaps, ascending and descending, accelerating and decelerating as easily as if he were on foot. His head was in constant motion too, checking every angle, calculating the vectors of the incoming asteroids. The flash of firing thrusters illuminated spinning chunks of rock passing just a few metres from the canopy. Occasionally he unleashed bursts of fire from the hurricane bolter arrays under the wings, obliterating smaller chunks of rock and masonry that spun into his path.

A flash of blue to starboard caught his eye. Sabrael

accelerated past in a display of flying that matched his skill with a bike. Like an insect darting from one spot to another, Sabrael's Dark Talon thrust forward and then stopped, it spiralled and rolled, twisted on the spot, dropped and rose, every manoeuvre seamlessly woven together as though rehearsed a thousand times.

Annael tried not to think too much about his own more mechanical responses. Engaging his conscious mind would stunt his reaction time. Sabrael was showing off, and with good reason. There was no need to get drawn into some kind of exuberant contest that Annael could never hope to win. Rather than allow himself to be annoyed and distracted by his companion's antics, he let his Dark Talon drift in behind his battle-brother, making it easier to admire his dazzling skill.

Eventually they broke free of the asteroid cloud, accelerating into open space on plumes of plasma. Annael increased the magnification of his auto-senses to maximum and looked around.

Half the sky appeared to have been swallowed by a gigantic pulsing maw of multicoloured light. Annael's auto-senses flickered with static as they tried to interpret the impossibility of the scenes playing out beyond the split veil between reality and the warp. It almost blinded him with nonsensical swirls and flashes of black and white, forcing him to look away.

The closest enemy vessel looked like an armoured comet with jutting spines of gun batteries and pylons that crackled with unnatural energy. It was at the centre of a circling line of strike cruisers and battle-barges – their colours marked them out as coming from the Dark Angels and Consecrators. A quick glance at the scanning array confirmed that the *Implacable Justice* was amongst the ships tackling the immense foe. Annael spared a thought for the brothers and serfs aboard the Ravenwing's strike cruiser.

With it were several light cruisers, cruisers and battleships, and complex, interlaced lines of battle were forming as the vessels of both sides joined the fight, each trying to bring their greatest weight of guns to bear on the enemy. Salvoes of torpedoes glittered between the closing fleets, accompanied by the small sparks of interceptor engines and gunship plasma drives.

A second wave of renegade ships were circumnavigating the Space Marine fleet, ignoring the vessels attacking the doom-star and its flotilla to head directly for the Rock. An immense warship led this next attack, dwarfing the battle-barge of the Knights of the Crimson Order that moved to intercept with its attendant strike cruisers.

Obviously the enemy flagship, this vessel reminded Annael more of the daemon-city on Ulthor than a spacefaring craft. Though here and there he saw expanses of tarnished metal and cracked ferrocrete, the bulk of the battleship seemed to be swathed in an impossibly thick green-brownish-grey hide puckered with scars and lesions. Weapon batteries sprouted like fungal growths, and atop its dorsal ridge was mounted a turret like the bombardment cannons sported by many Adeptus Astartes vessels.

Most striking was the prow. It was split like the tusks of a gigantic beast, the launch bay between gaping wide in a rippling mouth lined with fangs, lit by a ruddy glow from within. Annael was sure he saw impossibly vast eyes squinting from wrinkled sockets above the opening, but his attention was quickly drawn back to the ruddy maw as something that appeared as a cloud of flies issued from its hellish interior.

Following the battleship was a line of cruisers of various sizes and designations, many of them as perverted as the ship that led them. They broke from their line-astern formation, spreading out behind their flagship, a few launching torrents of torpedoes towards the Rock. The flight bays on several others spewed out fighters, as yet too distant to make out individually, looking like sprays of bright spores unleashed into the void.

The Knights of the Crimson Order turned to face this threat, disgorging their own torpedoes, flights of Storm Talons and Thunderhawks issuing from their bays. Looking to the left and right, Annael saw other Dark Angels craft jetting across the void with the Black Knights – Nephilim fighters and Dark Talons piloted by his Ravenwing brethren, supported by Thunderhawks in the bone-white livery of the Deathwing and the dark green of the battle companies.

Everything the assembled Chapters could put into space was now converging on the approaching enemy fleet.

The initial waves of enemy fighters bypassed the escorts at the periphery of the fleet, as intent on the Dark Angels fortress-monastery as the ships that launched them. Tybalain signalled for the Black Knights to assemble in a delta formation, a spearhead with the Huntmaster at the tip, separated by just a few kilometres.

As they closed with the leading edge of the incoming cloud of enemy craft, Annael saw that there seemed to be a mix. Some were more like drop pods, roughly spherical with ribbed bodies, trailing streamers of flesh-like entrails. Spurts of gas from flexing valves and puckered orifices manoeuvred the craft, albeit poorly.

The clusters of blister-like protuberances at the tip of each pod put Annael more in mind of a bomb or torpedo than a fighter.

The other craft were definitely more akin to interceptors, although rather than thrusters and jets they had four splayed reflective panels shaped in the likeness of fly wings, their bulbous bodies striped red and black like enormous wasps. Scintillating Chaos energy propelled these craft, leaving glistening trails across the void like slugs.

'Attack order remains,' Tybalain told them. 'Follow my lead.'

The Nephilim were more suited to the interceptor role and sped past the squadrons of Dark Talons, missiles streaking from their wing mounts, lascannons flaring, Avenger bolters spewing rounds across the void.

Following Tybalain, the Black Knights climbed and rolled, avoiding the first clash of craft that erupted in bursts of purplish warp energy and the detonation of rockets and bolts. Glittering wings shattered and armour splintered as the squadrons swept past each other with a deadly exchange of fire.

'Target the pod-missiles,' Tybalain commanded, pitching down towards the wave of ordnance following the Chaos fighters.

The spore-torpedoes were not very manoeuvrable, each seven or eight times larger than a Dark Talon. It was simple enough for Annael to pull in behind one of them and target the hurricane bolters. He let loose a short salvo and watched the bolts disappear into the tangle of tentacles and flanges that flailed from the pod-bomb's tail. The scanner registered the detonation, but there was no visible effect. A few pieces of shell-like carapace bounced from the canopy, leaving mucus threaded across the armourglass.

Drawing a long breath, Annael powered up the rift cannon. He could feel the heartbeat of the warp chamber increase from its steady pulse to a bass throbbing. It felt as though the Dark Talon wanted to open fire, trembling with anticipation for the moment.

Adjusting his attitude to rise above his target by a few dozen metres, he modified his aim towards the front of the pod-missile.

'Imperator protectiva,' he muttered and pressed the rift cannon firing stud. *'Judicio magna Leo.'*

He felt a jolt surge through him as the warp chamber opened, flooding the focusing array beneath the nose of the aircraft with unnatural power. A scintillating beam of energy surged from the crystal-lensed muzzle of the rift cannon and shot across the void. Where it struck the spore-bomb a warp rift several metres across sprang into being. The impossible intersection of real and unreal dimensions shredded the crusted growths, tearing out the tip of the projectile.

Annael was already pulling up when a ripple of black fire exploded from the rift, growing into a cloud of purple flame that consumed the rest of the spore-missile and threw out a shockwave that reached the Dark Talon in less than a second. The expanding sphere of fire engulfed Annael briefly, throwing his craft into a yawing spin to port. Attitude warnings wailed while he wrestled with the column, the fire's passing wiping the debris from the canopy and leaving a greasy smear in its place.

A few seconds later and pieces of shrapnel-like shell clattered against the hull and wings, leaving centimetre-deep gouges in the ceramite that hissed as if burning with acid.

The other Dark Talons were thinning the number of projectiles streaming towards the Rock, but more flycraft were closing in, launched by the more distant Chaos ships. The iridescent detonation of rift cannons lit the void with flashes of blue and green and red, followed by the sickly detonations of the spore-missiles.

Annael's surveyor systems were warning him of the incoming enemy but he focused on the task at hand, targeting one spore-torpedo after another, firing the main cannon and moving on to the next target. Around the Black Knights, the Nephilim and flycraft duelled while Thunderhawks smashed through the swirling dogfight, their lascannons, heavy bolters and battle cannons scything through fighter and ordnance alike, thick armoured plates sparking with shell impacts and sorcerous energies.

In a brief lull while the sides parted and he searched for a fresh target, Annael checked on the whereabouts of the enemy capital ships. He looked up with concern as the gargantuan bulk of the enemy flagship blotted out the stars just a few hundred kilometres away. Smaller turrets that lined its necrotic flank like clusters of bristles opened fire with shells and plasma blasts.

'Break away!' snapped Tybalain. The jets of the Huntmaster's Dark Talon slid him away from the flagship with bursts of cobalt flame.

Annael did likewise, the vectored engines hurling the Dark Talon into a steep turn as he slammed a steering pedal, his power armour protecting him against the inertial forces pulling at the aircraft. The battleship's fusillade streamed towards the Black Knights and other craft of the Ravenwing as the squadrons split and peeled away from the incoming storm of fire.

A rocket almost as big as his aircraft sped past Annael,

passing just a hundred metres from his port wing. A second later he realised that its course took it directly towards Nerean.

'Nerean! Evasive action! You...'

The warning died on his lips as the proximity sensor of the anti-craft projectile activated, detonating its plasma warhead. Nerean's Dark Talon was engulfed by a flash of pale blue energy, the brightness of the miniature star darkened to a grey by the dampening of Annael's auto-senses.

In an instant it was gone, leaving half of Nerean's craft spinning away, its warp chamber fitfully spewing white and red sparks, sheared almost cleanly down the middle with the molten edge still glowing. Of the pilot, Annael saw shattered pieces of war-plate tumbling from the breached cockpit.

More projectiles were incoming. There was no time to mourn for their lost brother as the Black Knights powered their craft away from the vengeful cannons and missile launchers of the enemy battleship.

'Orders incoming from Chapter Master Dane,' Tybalain warned them. There was a pause of several seconds and then an unfamiliar voice crackled across the vox.

'All starside assets are to withdraw to close defence positions. The Rock is under attack. Defence of the *prima monasteria* is paramount. Show no relent!'

Rolling his Dark Talon so that he could see the fortress-monastery, Annael looked up and saw that several cruisers from the death-comet's fleet had broken through the line of the Consecrators. The Gorgon's Aegis was a crackling ovoid of crimson around the Tower of Angels as lance beams and macro-shells slammed into the energy shield.

Following close behind a wave of torpedoes, he could see the glimmer of landing craft and drop pods.

ONLY IN DEATH

Belial had not exaggerated when he had warned Telemenus that he would see action again soon. It had not been four days since he had regained consciousness in his new armoured form and now the Rock was under full assault.

He stomped into the main sally gate on the southern wall – it occurred to him only now that it seemed odd to refer to the Rock's original facings now that it was adrift in the void – and joined a contingent of two Predators in the livery of the Third Company, and a Redeemer-pattern Land Raider in the colours of the Deathwing. It felt strange to be considered part of an armoured counter-attack, though his new war-plate boasted defences the equal of a battle tank.

The inner gate slammed shut behind them, plunging them into a ruddy gloom. Telemenus would have drawn in an apprehensive breath had his lungs not been a maze of pumps and pipework controlled by the

Dreadnought armour's automatic systems. The lack of physiological response left him feeling calm, almost aloof.

Moving the focal point of his visual array to the left he raised his lascannons in a salute to the Land Raider crew. The sponson gunner on the near side saw the gesture and replied in kind, dipping the flamestorm cannon.

Telemenus felt the rumble of the outer portals splitting open and started to move forward. Light spilled through the widening gap, bright and flickering, stark shadows dancing across the cracked ferrocrete roadway that led out of the ancient fortress.

He stepped out beneath a sky of red lightning. The Gorgon's Aegis was an almost solid wall of power, rippling and buckling as the fire of half a dozen warships poured down onto the fortress-monastery. Banks of defence lasers unleashed searing white beams in reply and silos spat forth missile after missile, filling the sky with contrails. Anti-air turrets pounded out a steady beat of shells, the detonation of airbursts like black blossoms against a dawn horizon.

Dark blurs against the ruddy heavens fell fast through the vacuum. New constellations appeared as dozens of drop pods fired their retro rockets, their claw-like forms heading for the main citadel while slab-sided drop-ships descended steeply towards the barren ground surrounding the Tower of Angels.

The Predators sped past on the left, moving off the flat course of the rock, bumping over the rocky ground, their weapons tracking distant targets. The Land Raider peeled off to the right, heading to bolster the defence of the outer fortifications where its close-ranged weapons would provide invaluable support to the Devastator and Tactical squads holding the line.

Telemenus's role was very different. He headed along the road for half a kilometre, to where he found Sergeants Caulderain and Arloch with thirteen more Terminators waiting for him. The Deathwing warriors turned and raised their storm bolters and assault cannons to acknowledge the presence of the Dreadnought.

'A timely arrival, venerable brother,' said Arloch. Telemenus still felt slightly ashamed at the title, thinking it unearned, but it was as much an address to the Dreadnought suit as its occupant.

'A welcome return,' added Caulderain. The sergeant pointed with his power blade towards a jagged breach in the outer wall ahead, a hundred metres from the peripheral gate at the far end of the road. 'The enemy are moving on this point. We will defend it to the last. *Frater fidelis ad morbidum.*'

'Well met, brothers. I did not think I would see the day the Rock itself suffered the insult of enemy assault. It is our task to set right the affront and admonish the offenders.'

'The enemy are almost upon us,' said Arloch. 'Such sentiments of reunion can wait for quieter times.'

'They can, brother-sergeant,' said Telemenus. The automated guns on the towers of the gate ahead opened fire, slicing lascannon beams down into an unseen enemy beyond. 'The enemy are hasty for their punishment.'

The Dreadnought and Terminators made all speed for the breach, leaving a cloud of dust drifting in their wake as they lumbered up to the breached wall. The defence line was almost twenty metres thick, the storerooms and guard chambers within exposed by some catastrophic blast ten millennia ago.

The edge of the Rock was no more than a kilometre and a half away. The empty plain, that might once have been fields or training grounds, was alive with warriors and vehicles. Burning wrecks of drop pods and landers lit the scene with the glare of flames. Traitor Space Marines in livery of tarnished white formed squads and advanced on the Tower of Angels, their filth-encrusted vehicles lumbering from the holds of drop-ships beside them.

Telemenus's scanners told him that the sky above was relatively clear of objects. Chapter Master Nakir had been wise enough to order the close-defence turrets to secure the area behind the wall, destroying anything that entered the few hundred metres closest to the citadel. At least the Dark Angels only faced the foe to their front and did not have to fear an enemy dropping onto them or behind.

While the Terminators entered the ruin of the wall, seeking some means to ascend to the upper battlement, Telemenus strode into the breach itself. A crater several metres deep provided obvious cover, and he moved to the lip closest to the enemy, placing a broken piece of wall several metres long to his left, protecting his flank from attack in that direction.

His targeters were already filling his mind with an array of potential marks, both infantry and vehicles. Nakir's last orders had been to hold the line and buy time for the Chapter to muster. Telemenus mentally prioritised all armoured targets and suddenly his vision changed, the lascannon and missile launcher aiming reticules concentrated on the vehicles he could see.

He spied two enemy Dreadnoughts, each disgorged by its own drop pod three hundred metres away, slightly to his right. One was armed with a pair of heavy bolters and a crackling siege hammer, the other with a single multi-barrelled cannon and a flail that sparked with purple lightning as it swung back and forth. They would be the first into the breach if allowed, able to traverse the rubble-strewn crater to clear the way for the transports.

He fired both weapons at the cannon-armed Dreadnought. The lascannon struck instantaneously, slashing into the left leg of his target. The joint buckled and it swayed for two seconds before the limb gave way entirely. The anti-armour missile hit as the Dreadnought toppled forward, splitting open the armour of the enemy's cannon mount.

More missiles flared from above and to Telemenus's right – some of the Terminators had cyclone launchers mounted across the carapace of their battleplate and were sending streams of rockets into the advancing legionaries.

The enemy did not return fire, but concentrated on closing the distance as swiftly as they could. A spearhead of Dark Angels vehicles burst from the gate to Telemenus's right, their autocannons, assault cannons and lascannons concentrated on the Traitor Space Marines converging close to the road. The gates closed behind them and they formed up as a mobile fortification of their own, two Land Raiders acting as towers to the wall of Predator tanks between them.

It occurred to Telemenus that, but for Belial's intervention, he might have been interred into one of the gun mounts of that forlorn squadron. After a moment he corrected himself. He watched their firing patterns and realised that there were no crews aboard. The vehicles' machine-spirits had been left to operate independently.

He understood why as the weight of the enemy attack came to bear. Anything on or beyond the wall would be sacrificed for time. There would be no retreat. His auspex systems were overloaded with the number of signals – more than four hundred power-armoured warriors were advancing on this front alone, and the sky was still lit with stars of descending ships and drop pods. He felt rather than saw them, like prickles on his skin, an instinct of where his enemies were as natural as feeling the direction of the wind.

He fired the missile launcher in a full salvo. There was no point conserving ammunition, there would be no relent. He could not miss the column of enemy moving quickly towards the nearest gatehouse. A mixture of anti-tank and anti-personnel missiles detonated amongst the vehicles and Traitor Space Marines, punching through battleplate and tank armour, hurling shrapnel at vision slits and exposed workings.

The burring of the assault cannons of the Deathwing warned him that the enemy were getting close. It was time to use the lascannons for some sharpshooting. Adjusting his stance, he locked his legs and clawed feet in place, creating a stable firing platform. The second Dreadnought was one hundred and twenty-five metres away, spearheading a drive directed towards the breach. Its heavy bolters sprayed fire up at the rampart – the explosive rounds would be largely ineffective against the Terminators, as much as if they were targeted at Telemenus. There was a reason the heavy war-plate of the First Company was called Tactical *Dreadnought* armour.

Telemenus picked his moment to the tenth of a second, opening fire as the Dreadnought was transferring its weight from left foot to right. He had seen that the enemy engine had a limp, a motivator system suffering poor maintenance, which caused the body of the war machine to tilt slightly. Two lascannon beams sliced across the vacuum and through the exposed side armour of the main sarcophagus.

Telemenus had no further time to spare for his opposite number, now a charred corpse inside his battle-tomb. The legionaries that had been accompanying the enemy Dreadnought were moving into range, several squads strong, taking up covered positions among the rocks and debris. He detected the build-up of energy from meltaguns and the charge of the plasma cells.

Another salvo of rockets had cycled into place but he left them in the rack, waiting for a clear target. He contented himself with obliterating some of the smaller rocks with his lascannon, whittling away the cover of the enemy as they came within one hundred metres. A torrent of sparks swept both ways as the enemy fired their bolters in reply to the storm bolters of the Deathwing.

A feeling of throbbing drew his attention to the sky a few kilometres up. A ship was crashing down through the Gorgon's Aegis, leaving a trail like a meteor. No drop transport or pod, this was a proper voidship, half a kilometre long. The force field flared wildly as the ship smashed through, earthing great lightning bolts into the barren rock and flashing kilometre-long plumes of energy into open space.

Trailing fire and debris, the enemy destroyer was breaking up, but a significant part of the main dorsal structure remained intact even as the Rock's last line of defence turrets opened fire in a blaze of rockets and shells.

Moments before it hit the wall, Telemenus realised the ship was being crashed on purpose. Its descent was too controlled to be unplanned. Little more than a ball of molten debris, it smashed into the eastern gate, two kilometres to his left. A flash that blotted out all of his senses blinded him for an instant.

In the seconds after, as his auguries established themselves again, Telemenus was left with only the vox-traffic to know what had happened.

'Estimated forty to fifty per cent terminal casualties. Most of Fifth Company lost.'

'Reserves from Eight and Nine move to stem the gap. Calling Deathwing counter-strike.'

'Eastern flank heavily compromised. Second line forces stand by.'

'Do we hold?'

It took a moment to realise that this last question was directed at him from Caulderain.

'Our left flank protection is nonexistent now. Right flank will be overrun in time.' Telemenus could see nothing of the sergeant but Caulderain's voice was tense. 'Reserves are being redirected to the eastern breach. Do we hold this position?'

He knew what the sergeant meant. This would be the last opportunity to retreat to the main citadel unmolested. There would be no other Dark Angels coming to reinforce their position, or to cover them if they had to withdraw. In a minute or two, the enemy would be too close for a safe extraction. The sergeant was looking to share an opinion, not to be given an order.

Something flickered in the red sky just above the horizon. For an instant Telemenus thought it was a glitch in his scanner feed – a misinterpretation in the feedback from the Gorgon's Aegis. But it returned, clearer than before, and there could be no mistake.

Amongst the crackle of crimson lightning was an angel with a skull face, a sword held aloft in one hand, a broken crown in the other.

The Emperor.

The apparition broke into a shower of descending stars, which fell upon Telemenus in an auric flutter. A blessing, no doubt. An assertion of protection. A repayment of faith.

'The command was to hold the breach,' said Telemenus. The Traitor Space Marines were gathering for an attack. His targeting systems were the first back online and he fired the lascannons at a white-armoured warrior who was stepping out from behind a boulder. The warrior's chest evaporated in a splash of molten ceramite. 'Our brothers at the eastern gate need us to hold this flank for as long as we can.'

'I concur,' said Arloch. 'We must give the eastern force every chance to recover.'

'We are agreed, then,' said Caulderain.

Telemenus unleashed an anti-tank missile at a siege vehicle creeping along the road towards the main gatehouse. It exploded against the large-calibre cannon mounted in the front of its hull, piercing the stubby barrel.

'We are agreed,' said the Dreadnought pilot. 'For the Rock. For the Lion. For the Emperor. We hold or we die.'

BATTLE FOR THE ROCK

Not since the time of the Horus Heresy had any foe set foot in the hallowed halls of Aldurukh. For ten millennia the Tower of Angels, the Rock, had never known the insult of invasion.

That had changed the moment the first of the traitor drop pods had landed.

Belial was filled with an ever-present rage by the thought. He did not allow it to cloud his decisions, but it was there, an affront to every dignity he held to. The Dark Angels fortress-monastery was being violated. It was not just the physical offence that drew the Grand Master's ire, but the impudence of the slight.

The enemy *dared* to attack the home of the Dark Angels. The mere thought of such an act should have left any foe trembling with dread. That the enemy believed they were capable of inflicting this hurt, that they were somehow immune to the retribution of the Unforgiven, could not be discarded as folly. It was a calculated barb, a thrust spear piercing the pride of the Chapter.

Belial would demonstrate to the foe the immense error of their decision.

The loss of the outer eastern gate had been a blow. With the fleet engaged with the enemy warships, Belial believed he should have foreseen such an attack. Not that there was anything to be done – there was not a shield or gun on the Rock that could have stopped the suicidal impact.

From the inner gate he looked out at the blazing ruin of the curtain wall. It had been flattened for a kilometre to the south and north, lit by pools of burning promethium, scoured by plasma blasts. In scattered bands the Dark Angels that had miraculously survived the impact fell back to the Tower of Angels, battered but not broken. They raised ragged cheers when they saw Belial and his Knights standing before the gates, defiant to any attack.

The foe did not pursue with heedless disregard, but advanced in the wake of the disaster with careful manoeuvres. They were Space Marines, or at least had been long ago. Though they had thrown their fate into the lap of uncaring dark powers, they retained much of their discipline and fearlessness.

Belial had faced enemies such as this before. Heedless of injuries that would fell even a Dark Angel, immune to pain, they were worshippers of the Lord of Decay. Where once Legion banners had fluttered proudly – standards of the warriors recorded in history as the Death Guard – now there were raised icons of rusted metal and pitted bone, fashioned in praise to their insane god. Armour once white was encrusted with filth, the ceramite stained by millennia of disrepair.

Yet the centuries of poor maintenance seemed not to affect the functioning of the war-plate, as salvoes of bolts were shrugged off by the advancing columns.

Heavier weapons laid down shells and beams of laser energy, the detonations and blasts throwing up clouds of dust and pulverised rock. The gravitic field did not extend beyond the outer wall, so that clouds of burning metal and molten rock swathed the battlefield with a fiery smog.

Vehicles came with them, ancient patterns of Land Raiders and Predators, Rhino transports that had seen battle at the Siege of Terra. There were other war machines too, that owed no heritage to the Legions of the Emperor or the Mechanicus of Mars. Six-legged walkers with scorpion claws and battle cannons. Beetle-like armoured cars with plasteel-plated balloon tyres and barnacle-like pods sprouting heavy bolters and autocannons.

Corroded exhaust stacks spewed oily smoke that moved and veered like swarms of flies, swathing the approach with a misty gloom. Yellow headlights seemed to weep greasy tears. Holes left by missing rivets and joins between armoured plates seeped sap-like fluid, while hatchways and turret rings sprouted colourful fungi.

In the burning sky dragon-like attack craft with jagged wings swooped and circled, evading the batteries of anti-air guns that filled the heavens with airburst munitions and rapid pulses of laser fire. Belial thought he could hear the half-machine creatures screeching, in his mind rather than with his ears.

Around the helldrakes swarmed lesser craft – flyships with single pilots, kept aloft in the thin atmosphere by the blur of insectile ornithopter wings.

There were other entities too, reminiscent of the daemon-foes he had faced at Ulthor. Enormous slug-like beasts with howdahs slung in pairs, brimming with guns and armoured warriors. Fusions of tanks and bipedal monsters that lumbered along behind the infantry advance, crescent-shaped blades and fume-spilling censers swaying from dozens of chains hooked into their leathery bodies, claws and fangs sheathed with some exotic material that sparked and flared in the darkness.

So intent on the enemy was Belial that he had not noticed his Knights had been joined by other warriors. He turned to see five Terminators in the livery of the Consecrators standing to his left.

'Your duty would put you at the side of Chapter Master Nakir,' Belial told them.

'The Grand Master sent us to you with his kind regards,' replied their leader. He lifted an ornate power sword in salute. Even at a glance Belial could see that it was master-crafted, a beautiful weapon made by the best artificers at the dawn of the Imperium. Three blood-drop rubies glittered in the channel of the blade – carefully wrought power field lenses, he assumed. He wondered what other treasures the Consecrators owned, if such a marvel was in the hands of a sergeant, even one that was head of the Chapter Master's guard. 'I am Seneschal Maalik, and my sword is yours to command.'

'I cannot argue that I need the warriors,' Belial replied. He considered the current disposition of his forces and the lines of advance of the enemy, but came to a simple conclusion. 'I want you at my back. If my Knights fall, I want you to be ready.'

'As you wish, Master Belial.' There was a pause while

Maalik issued orders to his squad over their vox. The Terminators turned and filed back towards the gateway, leaving the seneschal with Belial. 'Gratitude, it will be an honour to fight beside you.'

Belial said nothing as Maalik joined his warriors. His thoughts had already moved back to the unfolding attack. The Death Guard had reached the break in the curtain wall where the eastern gate had once been. This brought them into range of the main defence batteries, which rained down artillery and plasma from fortified positions built into the Tower of Angels.

Into this maelstrom advanced the warped legionaries of the Death Guard, heedless of the danger. Where once had been a flat killing ground, marked by bunkers and gun pits that had held two hundred Dark Angels, there was broken devastation, littered with burning debris from the crashed ship and cracked remains of the curtain wall, which continued to fall like giant fiery hail across the wasteland.

Fire zones and crossfires had been blocked, craters and shattered blocks of masonry providing ample cover against the storm of fire. Sortie gates linked to tunnels beneath the bare ground had been sealed by the blast waves of plasma and thousands of tonnes of rubble.

The vox-link hissed into life, bringing the voice of Chapter Master Nakir. Belial did not know what other matters occupied Azrael nor why he had deferred to the Consecrator, but it was not the time to raise issues regarding the chain of command.

'We cannot allow the enemy attack to reach the Tower of Angels uncontested,' said the Chapter Master. 'The loss of the outer gate is a setback, not a defeat.'

'I concur,' said Belial. 'A counter-attack across the

western axis of their assault will turn their advance away for a while.'

'A diligent course of action, Master Belial, but I prefer a more direct approach. I have despatched armoured units to your position for a full assault across the battlefront. You will retake the perimeter of the curtain wall and establish the line of resistance from that position.'

Belial was left momentarily speechless by the audacity of the plan.

'To attack into the heart of the enemy assault could break the back of the attack in one move, Chapter Master, but we have already committed our reserves. If we suffer a reverse, the whole sector will be lost.'

'Would you prefer a slow death, Belial?' The Deathwing commander could not tell over the distortion of the vox whether Nakir was being humorous or not. 'Better to muster our strength into one retaliatory blow than wage a war of attrition we cannot win.'

The plan made sense in that context, but Belial was still reluctant to issue the order for an all-out attack. He had no basis for his reticence other than an instinct to marshal whatever forces he had to hand for as long as possible. Nakir's gambit, and it was a gambit, could throw away the fortress-monastery of the Dark Angels in one ill-considered move.

'I await your acknowledgement, Master Belial. Are your orders unclear in some fashion? Do you wish to make an alternative suggestion?'

'Orders received, Chapter Master,' replied Belial. Nakir was correct. Fear of losing the battle should not stay their hand. They were Space Marines, Dark Angels, and their fury could not be abated. Belial came to the conclusion that he was overcompensating for his anger. His instinct to strike out, to chastise the enemy with blade and gun, was driven by strategic logic not personal feeling. It was right that he recognised the Consecrator's insight. 'A wise command, Master Nakir. We will prevail.'

'I have no doubt of that. The Deathwing are the envy of the Unforgiven, brother-captain. I am jealous that it is my honour guard and not me that will participate in the glorious action.'

Again Belial wanted to ask what had become of Azrael. It was better that questions were not raised. It likely involved Cypher, of that there was little doubt. To make inquiries would only promote queries from Nakir as well.

As the Rhinos, Razorbacks, Land Raiders and Predators of the armoured column powered their way from the armoury garages, the leading elements of the Death Guard attack advanced into range. Heavy weapons squads with ancient plasma cannons, reaper autocannons and lascannons took up firing positions in the smouldering ruins. Belial directed his own Devastator squads to counter-fire and the battlefield was lit by the exchange of missiles and las-blasts, plasma bolts and hails of heavy bolter fire.

While this crossing fusillade continued, half a dozen enemy Rhino transports made a foray towards the west, outflanking beyond a line of burning wreckage several hundred metres long. There was little Belial could do to combat this advance, other than to signal to the defence batteries to concentrate their firepower against the attack. The thunder of the guns left a swathe of craters across the path of the flanking force, baulking it for the time being. Power-armoured legionaries spilled from the transports, slowed but not stopped.

He could spare no other response and had to hold his nerve. If he despatched any of his forces to reinforce the flank he would weaken his counter-attack. Now that he was readying for the riposte, it was imperative that the Dark Angels hit back with all the warriors they could muster.

Within two more minutes the column sent by Nakir arrived. Belial assigned transport duties and arrayed the tanks and troop carriers into a spearhead formation, with the Terminators in their various patterns of Land Raiders in the vanguard, and the brothers of the Third, Fifth and Seventh companies spread through the Razorbacks and Rhinos.

'I would be honoured if we could ride with you, Grand Master,' Maalik told him over the vox. 'We would not fight anywhere else than at the heart of the attack.'

'Of course,' Belial replied. 'Assemble at my position.'

He led his Knights towards the Land Raider Crusader *Lion's Fury*. Designed for urban assault, it lacked long-range weapons but would be ideal for punching a hole through the Death Guard line. Belial knew that he would be where the fighting was fiercest, his Terminators drawing the enemy ire like a lightning rod so that the other squads could reach their objectives.

The Deathwing Knights boarded the Land Raider while Belial waited on the ramp, taking a last look at the Tower of Angels. For centuries it had been his home, his fortress-monastery. He had hardly given it a second glance approaching by gunship or shuttle. He had always accepted that it would provide him with sanctuary and succour. The thought that it might fall – not just today, but ever – turned his stomach.

Maalik's Consecrators arrived and Belial waved them

onto the Land Raider with the Sword of Silence. No words were needed and he was grateful for Maalik's understanding as the Terminators assumed their positions in the bracing alcoves along the sides of the troop compartment.

The assault ramp hissed shut behind Belial as he joined his battle-brothers. Usually he would have attended to the command station behind the driver's position. This attack would be brutally simple, and he could rely upon Chapter Master Nakir to orchestrate the larger force. He took his place amongst his Knights instead.

'Hard fighting ahead,' said Barzareon.

'The best kind,' replied Cragarion.

'Seek and destroy,' added Galbarad. 'I always prefer the simple missions.'

'As do I,' said Belial. He activated the sensorium and his view merged with that of his companions. More than that, it felt as though his soul became one with theirs. An uncharacteristic urge caused him to share the feeling and he opened up his vox to a force-wide channel. 'My brothers, today might see all we have fought for laid low. Our armour may be broken. Our bodies may be crushed. Our fortress-monastery, the Chapter that gives us purpose, might be destroyed. We do not confront this challenge with heavy hearts, but with gladness. There is not a Dark Angel…' He glanced at the Consecrators. 'There is not a son of the Lion that would not give all that he had that he might fight with us today. We are not shamed that this battle falls to us. We are privileged!'

The Land Raider rumbled into motion, plasma-powered engines pushing the armoured behemoth across the uneven ground.

'I look at our foe and I see not the bearers of our demise. I see the manner of our glorious victory. They are cowards sheltering in the guise of Space Marines. They have given up all semblance of honour. So it is to our credit that we have been chosen by the Emperor to face them today. Trust in your brothers. Trust in the Lion. Trust in the Emperor. We shall prevail and seal our names amongst the greatest of the Chapter!'

DEFIANCE

With the Deathwing at the forefront, the Dark Angels column leapt from the shadow of the inner gates like a mastiff from the leash. The front line of Death Guard opened fire, their bolts and blasts sheering harmlessly from the armoured hulls of the Land Raiders leading the charge. Lascannons and assault cannons spat in reply, while the turrets of Predators and Razorbacks coursed plasma and heavy bolter salvoes through the enemy squads.

The armoured column ploughed into the thick fog, lamps cutting white and yellow wounds across the enveloping darkness. The smog whirled with the passing of accelerating vehicles, leaving strangely contoured faces and grimacing mouths carved into the unnatural fume.

Taken unawares by the unexpected counter-attack, the legionaries of the Death Guard were easily swept aside by the armoured fist crashing through their midst. Power-armoured warriors were torn apart by heavy weapons fire or forced to fall back lest they be crushed beneath a score of whirring tracks.

Heedless of the scattered enemies left in their wake, Belial's spearhead plunged on. They ran straight through the second line of advancing Death Guard, once more pouring such fire from their weapons as they could muster on the move, choosing momentum over accuracy. Return fire from bolters pattered from armoured hulls like rain. Redeemer-pattern Land Raiders left swathes of burning promethium from their flamestorm cannons, driving the Death Guard out of ruined bunkers and half-collapsed trenches. From amongst the Rhinos, Whirlwinds unleashed blankets of explosions with multiple missile launchers, blasting every scrap of cover used by the traitor legionaries.

The shock of the attack carried the Dark Angels into the first reserves of the invading forces. Coming upon armoured foes – ancient patterns of Space Marine vehicles and the half-machine abominations spawned by the warp – here the force split. Land Raiders and Predators with their anti-tank lascannons and autocannons peeled to the left and right, targeting their weapons against the self-propelled guns, slug beasts and carriers of the enemy.

Three Deathwing squads, each five warriors strong, deployed from the Land Raiders to provide close support. Heavy flamers and cyclone launchers scoured the surrounding ruins as the Terminators advanced outwards, their armour shrugging off the irregular bursts of fire from the Death Guard. The bone-white armoured figures dispersed into the miasma, their progress highlighted only by the spark of muzzle flare and the blaze of rocket trails.

THE UNFORGIVEN

From behind this storm of missiles, laser beams and rapid-firing shells, the remaining assault vehicles and transports pushed onwards, like the warhead of a missile ejected from its carrier housing, striking deep into the heart of the assaulting force.

The outer gate, or rather the smoking mass of craters and kilometres-long furrow that had been the outer gate, lay only five hundred metres ahead. There was no rearguard, just a smattering of isolated squads and the odd beast or vehicle that had been deposited by their landers or drop pods further from the attack. These sporadic encounters were easily dealt with, the hurricane bolters and assault cannons of the *Lion's Fury* and the storm bolters of the Rhinos equal to the task.

At two hundred and fifty metres from the objective, Belial ordered his remaining Deathwing transports to spread out, half a kilometre between each. The two Crusaders and Redeemer slewed to a halt, turning hard until their weapons pointed back towards the enemy to form a formidable bunker line, their armour a match for almost anything the Death Guard possessed. Belial's Knights, along with the Consecrators and two other Deathwing squads, dismounted from their vehicles, forming a line between the Land Raiders.

The transports carrying the power-armoured Dark Angels continued on towards the line of rubble and molten stone that marked the original border wall. The spaceship crash had exposed the inner guard rooms and subterranean chambers – a plethora of cover for the Devastator and Tactical squads to defend, while Assault squads found positions from which they could counter-attack against any enemy breakthrough.

There was a lull in the fighting as the Death Guard pulled back from the armoured thrust into the gut of their force. Belial waited, monitoring the sensorium feeds from the Deathwing squads stationed with the anti-tank line half a kilometre ahead of him.

'Bite, you pox-ridden filth,' he muttered. 'Here we are.'

'Pardon, Grand Master?' asked Barzareon, standing just to Belial's left.

'The eastern gate is all but unguarded,' the Grand Master explained. 'Let us hope that the Death Guard commander, or what passes for their leader, is either stupid enough to attack the enemy that has just humiliated him, or clever enough to want to rid himself of the enemy to his rear.'

'What if he is neither stupid nor clever, but merely competent?' said Barzareon.

'Then in thirty minutes we will be fighting to reclaim the Tower of Angels from him.'

This sobering thought silenced any further comment.

Initial reports were encouraging. The Death Guard did not press on towards the Tower of Angels but mustered to combat the Dark Angels force arrayed between them and their drop-ships. Evidently their officers were not wholly convinced they would take the fortress-monastery.

'Cowards,' said Belial. 'They look to secure their line of retreat rather than push wholeheartedly into the fray. Their lack of dedication will be their defeat.'

'Just as well we are not concerned about retreats, Grand Master,' said Decimus, referencing the fact that the Death Guard were now between the Dark Angels and their fortress. He was the replacement for Deralus, who had not survived the wounds inflicted aboard Anovel's flagship. The latest inductee to the Deathwing Knights was a fine warrior, but had a reputation for flippancy. Belial could not tell if he was joking.

'We have a collapsing defence,' growled the Deathwing commander. 'The first line falls back to this position. We all fall back to the objective. There we will stand. Not a step back.'

'Aye, Grand Master,' his warriors replied in unison.

The mists lit up again as the intensity of fire increased over the following minutes. The Death Guard were trying to turn around the southern flank to regain the line at the curtain wall, pressing forward with their Dreadnoughts and tanks. The Land Raiders and Predators were able to stem the initial thrust, but their repositioning allowed infantry squads to reclaim much of the ruins, almost encircling the Deathwing squads arrayed to protect the vehicles. Belial saw the developing situation and commanded them to reconvene with their transports pending the order to draw back.

On the other side of the battlefield, where the warriors of the other companies were stationed in the remnants of the wall, there were reports of fresh invaders arriving by a second wave of gunships. Squad portable support weapons such as Rapier laser destroyers and Tarantula gun platforms, controlled by sophisticated machine-spirits, assisted the defence, firing at anything that moved in the blasted wilderness beyond the Dark Angels cordon. The longest-ranged cannons of the Tower of Angels kept up a steady bombardment of the drop zone, but frequently had to turn their ire onto other areas to prevent the enemy breaking the curtain wall in various sectors.

Eventually the Land Raiders and Predators were on the verge of being surrounded. One of the Land Raiders had been nearly crippled by a hit on its engines. *Determinatus* limped back through the mists sputtering and choking, its squad of Deathwing marching alongside as escort. Two of the Predators had been abandoned, the crews taking sanctuary in the larger battle tanks.

It was time to bring the armoured column back together and Belial issued the order.

'The enemy will come at us hard, thinking that we are on the verge of breaking,' he warned his Terminators and the Land Raider crews. 'We will not discourage that thinking, but allow them to come onto our guns as close as we dare. We must lure them into a full commitment, to keep their wrath focused upon us and not the Tower of Angels.'

With these words in mind, the Deathwing chanted their catechisms and triple-checked sensorium and weapons systems. Maalik approached even as the lamps of the retreating vehicles grew brighter in the unnatural fog.

'Grand Master, I think these accursed mists afflict our foes as much as us,' said the seneschal. 'With your permission I will lead my warriors a little further out, to ensure the anti-armour task force is herded directly into your sights. The enemy will be taken aback that we are so close.'

'Two hundred metres, no more,' Belial said, seeing the sense in Maalik's plan. 'You have the rally point fixed, I leave it up to you when you choose to fall back.'

'Gratitude, Grand Master.' Maalik raised his beautiful sword in salute and then led his warriors into the swirling green fog.

The throb of engines and glare of yellow lanterns heralded the arrival of the Dark Angels vehicles. The tanks rumbled out of the gloom, each showing grievous battle scars but still mobile. Cracked ceramite plates hung from the side of the Predator called *Iron*

Lion, while the track links of the Land Raider *Bringer of Honour* were almost flying loose from a shattered track housing.

The bark of the Consecrators' storm bolters and the flare of their heavy flamer betrayed the presence of the pursuing enemy just two hundred metres behind the retreating tanks. Perhaps the Death Guard had hoped that the vehicles would bar the Dark Angels fire. As it was, they pushed on past the Terminators, the *crack* of bolters and glow of plasma guns sweeping to the left and right of Belial's position.

The line reinforced by the newly arrived vehicles and Terminators, the Dark Angels met the coming attack head-on. Belial fired his storm bolter over and over, picking out armoured warriors approaching through the mist. His bursts of fire bounced harmlessly from the power armour of the enemy for the most part, but such was the concentration of firepower from the assembled Deathwing that even ancient warplate occasionally succumbed. Meanwhile the heavy weapons of the vehicles and the assault cannons and cyclone launchers of the Terminators kept all but the heaviest enemy tanks at bay.

A few minutes passed, the exchange of fire escalating as the Death Guard manoeuvred for an angle to attack the Dark Angels line while the sons of the Lion poured out whatever firepower they could muster. Maalik emerged from the gloom, broadcasting his approach over the vox-link lest they be mistaken for enemies. All five of the Consecrators were still standing, but their once brightly enamelled armour showed dozens of cracks and chips, revealing the plain grey ceramite beneath.

The Death Guard appeared to be pushing to the left

and right, trying to get around the Dark Angels rather than going through them. It was possible that they were trying to link up with fresh forces being landed every few minutes. For some time, Belial resisted the feeling that he needed to redeploy his forces from the centre, but as time wore on and casualties grew, he was forced into a decision and despatched the two Deathwing squads to reinforce the eastern and western approaches, leaving his Knights, the Consecrators and the *Lion's Fury* defending the centre.

The alteration seemed to work, as the encroachments to the east and west stalled, baulked by the armour and weapons of the Terminators. Though the sensorium was limited in range, Belial followed the vox-traffic, creating a mental picture of the unfolding engagement. The cut and parry and counter-thrust between the plague-ridden warriors of the Death Guard and his Terminators appeared to be swinging in favour of the Dark Angels.

It was then that he was alerted to a sensor reading coming from Cragarion, who was positioned twenty metres ahead and to the right, and a moment later another from Zandorael on the similar watch position to the left.

Something was approaching through the fog.

Lamps lit up the miasma. Three towering Dreadnoughts whose hulls and limbs were decked in rusted chains, armed with scything flails and crushing morningstars. Their heavy bolters and autocannons had remained silent. Largely ineffective against the Deathwing, they would have betrayed the presence of the attack for no gain.

Silhouetted by the lamps of the war engines were several dozen Plague Marines, who had managed to close within fifty metres, shrouded by the cursed mist.

'Form shieldwall!' Belial bellowed, but his Knights had predicted his command and were already moving. 'Maalik, behind us!'

As the first rattle of bolts on Tactical Dreadnought armour engulfed the Terminators, they closed together, forming up to the left and right of their Grand Master. The assault cannons of the *Lion's Fury* roared into life, spitting fire and shells into the gloom. The Death Guard split, parting before the wrath of the Crusader as flesh before a keen blade. The gunner redirected the hail of shells to the Dreadnoughts, but the war engines marched on relentlessly, their heavy weapons opening fire on the converging Terminators.

Belial held firm, trusting to the artifice of the Techmarines to protect him against the surge of projectiles slamming into his war-plate. Ceramite splintered and paint flaked, but the bonded layer of plasteel and adamantium beneath held firm. Barzareon lifted his shield, covering the right side of Belial. Zandorael did the same to the left and the intermittent *crack* of detonating rounds turned into the hiss of their power shields intercepting the incoming bolts.

One of the Plague Marines stole forwards, a meltagun in his hands. Belial barked a warning to the crew of the *Lion's Fury* but it came too late. The housing of the twin assault cannons mounted in the upper hull disappeared in an explosive vaporisation of agitated particles, a cloud of expanding gas mushrooming into the air.

The fire from the power-armoured legionaries returned, slamming into the crackling shields of the Terminators in waves, sounding like rain thrown by flurries of wind against a window. Through this steady beat came frequent deeper detonations of the heavy bolters and the boom of autocannon shells.

The *Lion's Fury* pushed forward, activating its frag assault launchers. Explosive charges mounted on the fronts of the track arrays hurled shrapnel a hundred metres, the jagged shards cutting erratic gashes through the thick fog. The blast wave hurled back the closest Plague Marines, studding their armour with splinters of metal. Others were knocked to their knees while shrapnel broke weapons and slashed armour seals.

The hurricane system opened fire. Twelve interlinked bolters lit the mist with muzzle flare, the hail of bolts hitting two Death Guard standing directly in the line of fire. The armour was smashed from them piece by piece as the torrent continued, the sheer weight of rounds overcoming millennia-old battleplate. Corrupted flesh was torn apart, blood and pus spraying into the air as the mortally wounded Plague Marines staggered back from the onslaught.

And still the Dreadnoughts loomed from the fog, twice as tall as the Terminators, flickers of devastating energy lighting their rust-encrusted bodies, making them seem even larger.

'No retreat!' Belial bellowed.

SINS OF THE PAST

Azrael waited in the hall of Tuchulcha, not looking at the ragged servitor that stood slumped just a few paces away. He wanted to pace but refused to show agitation in front of the warp-construct. For the same reason, he had a micro-bead in his ear relaying the ongoing strategic situation from the control tower of the Rock. Nakir was wielding two and a half Chapters of Space Marines with aplomb. The initial landings had been contained and the enemy cruisers driven off, although the fight for the Rock continued.

The Chaos doom-star was holding position out of range, perhaps awaiting the arrival of the *Terminus Est*, which had broken through the joint fleet of the Dark Angels and Knights of the Crimson Order.

These facts occupied his thoughts, ensuring that there was nothing Tuchulcha could pluck from his mind concerning deeper misgivings about the whole battle. If Azrael concentrated on purely military matters, the more spiritual ones could remain hidden.

It was almost with relief that he heard footsteps echoing along the corridor and turned to see Ezekiel escorting Cypher to the chamber. The arrival of the Chief Librarian brought a welcome break to the effort of shielding his mind against any probing tendrils of Tuchulcha's power.

'What does Typhus want with the Rock?' Azrael demanded. He looked first at Cypher and then at the gold-flecked globe. 'Is it you he comes after, daemon?'

'I am not a daemon,' the servitor mouthpiece replied, almost petulant. 'I am far greater than some mindless facet of an incomprehensible entity. If you wish to see a daemon, cast your eye out to that abomination close at hand. This physical vessel is incapable of pronouncing its name, but it has been known by many titles by the generations of humans that have worshipped it. The latest was the Plagueheart, in the prayers of the people of Ulthor.'

'There are no people on Ulthor,' said Ezekiel, no doubt remembering the reports of Belial and Sammael.

'They were there,' Cypher replied. 'Your warriors did not recognise them. I have been to Ulthor also and saw them. Like shadows enslaved to the will of the Plagueheart. Souls damned to eternal servitude.'

'So this is a plot by the followers of the Lord of Decay?' the Librarian continued. Azrael was uncomfortable referring to the Chaos Powers even by euphemism and was content to let his companion deal with the discussion. 'Methelas was obviously corrupted. Typhus and the Plagueheart are conspiring to some advantage of their necrotic master.'

'They believe they are,' croaked Tuchulcha's flesh

puppet. There was a dry cough that might have been a laugh.

'I do not expect this... creature to tell me the truth or a straight answer,' said Azrael, glaring at Cypher, 'but what do you have to say on the matter?'

'You have been lured into a trap that has waited three thousand years to be sprung,' Cypher replied. 'I thought it impossible but the pieces of a key have been brought together. I did not realise until now what Tuchulcha is. It is the bridge between the Plagueheart and the Consumer.'

'Your words make no sense. Speak plainly,' demanded Azrael.

Cypher frowned, insulted, and shook his head disparagingly.

'It is not difficult to understand.' The renegade looked at Ezekiel. 'Perhaps you are more accustomed to discussions of this nature. This artefact, creature, call it what you will, was made to create pathways through the warp.'

'As we have witnessed,' said Azrael, annoyed at Cypher's dismissive tone. 'It brought us here swiftly and transitioned the whole fleet into the central system.'

'I am so glad you appreciated my work,' said Tuchulcha.

'But the warp does not just ignore the physical properties of space, it bends time.' There was a look of triumph on Cypher's face, whether from realisation or some deeper motive Azrael could not tell.

'A device that burrows through time,' said Ezekiel. His eye widened with recognition. 'Brought to Caliban!'

It took several seconds for Azrael to follow the Librarian's line of thought. When he had come to the same place in reasoning, the notion staggered him.

'Tuchulcha said we could save Caliban, save the Lion. We can send back a message, to warn him of the treachery?' He resisted the urge to grab the decrepit servitor and shake it until Tuchulcha answered. 'We can stop the schism?'

The thought silenced all present, save for Tuchulcha, who chuckled drily through its half-mechanical avatar. The corpse-puppet turned jerkily towards Cypher.

'Would that make you happy?' it asked.

'Wait.' Azrael thought about what Tuchulcha had said, and tried to figure how it was relevant to the plot that had brought the Dark Angels to Caliban. He felt pressurised by events to act and deliberately took some time to appraise the situation from a position of detached calm. 'Why would Astelan want to save the Lion?'

'He would not,' said Cypher. 'The Terran renegade had nothing but hate for our primarch.'

'Indeed. What would be Astelan's greatest revenge against the Lion?' Azrael did not wait for an answer. 'To steal his Legion from him.'

'What do you mean?' said Ezekiel.

'What if instead of us going back to warn the Lion of what was happening, Astelan and his allies went back ten thousand years and saved the Fallen from his retribution?'

'By bringing them here, to the present...' suggested Ezekiel.

'Tharsis was to be the home world for the renegade Dark Angels?' Cypher looked aghast at the suggestion, but soon he accepted the possibility. 'The recruits, the gene-seed... More than thirty thousand renegade Dark Angels. He was founding a new Legion, but not from scratch.'

Azrael suddenly recognised the warning that Luther had been trying to give him. The Dark Oracle had not been spouting madness about Cypher, or the Lion, but about Astelan.

'We have to stop him,' said Azrael. He looked at his two companions in turn. 'But I do not know how.'

'I do,' replied Cypher, his expression grim. 'But you will not like it.'

'I have to release you?' Azrael said. He had been wondering when Cypher's assertion that the Supreme Grand Master would let him go would bear fruit. 'Is this what you were waiting for?'

'There is something, was something, on Caliban. A dark core, an infectious madness in the heart of the world. It gave rise to the Nephilim and great beasts.'

'A Chaos taint?' said Ezekiel. 'Caliban was corrupted?'

Tuchulcha's living dummy laughed again, hands slapping limply together in a parody of clapping.

'They made us, the one split into three,' the puppet cackled. 'The essence of Chaos, refined and shaped. They thought they could tame the warp, use me to dig their tunnels and secret ways hidden from the eyes of the Powers That Rule. They did not know that they made something else. Something far grander.'

'Who? Who made you?' Azrael demanded.

'At the dawn of the galaxy, so far removed from humans they might as well be gods. But even they could not tame the warp, only corral it for moments at a time. But that which creates also devours, and I am the foundation of all that was, is and will be. I am the lens, the bridge, the doorway.'

Azrael pulled his pistol and aimed it at Tuchulcha.

'If you are the bridge, we only have to destroy you and the threat is over.'

'Your pistol will have no effect,' said Cypher. He looked as though he might lunge for the weapon, but held himself in check. 'Besides, even if you had the means to destroy this thing, you cannot.'

'Why not?' said Azrael, turning the pistol on his captive.

The vox buzzed and Nakir's voice interrupted proceedings.

'Supreme Grand Master, the *Terminus Est* has taken up station fifty thousand kilometres away, advance halted. The warp-comet has also ceased its attack. The rift is growing in power, doubling intensity every ninety seconds. What are your commands?'

Azrael was caught in two minds, his pistol veering between Cypher and Tuchulcha as his mind lurched from one problem to the next. He forced himself to analyse the situation as best as he could.

'Call the fleet to create a fresh cordon around our current position. All warriors on all stations prepare for void transport. All First Companies to muster at the Rock if possible. Tell the Master of the Forge to make ready to power up our full teleport capabilities.' Azrael cut the vox and turned on Cypher. 'Tell me why I should not destroy the sphere?'

'It exists across the entirety of its timeline. It is divorced from the normal turn of temporal matters. If you destroy it now, you will destroy it in the past also. It will never have been.'

'So?'

'In short, the Emperor will lose the war against Horus. The Lion used Tuchulcha to come to the aid of Guilliman in the Eastern Fringe, and in doing so forced Horus into attacking Terra before the Ultramarines could arrive. Without Tuchulcha, Guilliman and his allies would be slowly destroyed, cut off from Terra by the ruinstorm of the Word Bearers. Horus would attack at full strength and the Emperor would fail.'

'You cannot know that,' said Azrael, not sure he understood all of what Cypher had said. More convincing though was the memory of the vision from Luther returning to haunt him, of an empire burning, a Lion dying in the flames.

'Can we risk it?' said Ezekiel. 'Also, if this thing is the doorway back to the past, if we destroy it then we cannot use it to warn the Lion.'

Azrael shook his head, clearing away the distracting thoughts to focus on a single issue.

'We cannot allow Astelan to succeed. Whatever that takes.'

'Including allowing Horus to rule?' said Cypher. There was an intrigued look in his eye rather than horror at such a suggestion.

'Except that.'

'There is another way,' said Cypher. 'As I said. The taint of Caliban, the canker at its heart, must be close at hand. That is why the *Terminus Est* and Plagueheart are not attacking. The three elements of the ritual are within range of each other.'

'Ritual?' said Ezekiel. 'What do you know, that you have not told us?'

'I swear by the Emperor that this is all I know,' said Cypher. 'From Tuchulcha itself. One divided into three. It is the bridge, between the Plagueheart and whatever dwells in the core of Caliban. It is reuniting, becoming one again, tearing open reality to conjoin the material and immaterial as it was designed to do.'

'What happens then? It destroys us?'

'I can stop it. We can stop it.' Cypher implored Azrael

with his hands. 'I know the beast of Caliban, I can kill it. If we break one part of the triumvirate the other two will fail.'

'And this is where I give you your freedom?'

'Send me with guards, I do not argue against that. Just return my armour and sword and give me a gunship. By my honour, I will return.'

Azrael looked at Ezekiel and then the renegade. He clenched and unclenched his fists, knowing that he was being forced into making a decision but powerless to avoid whatever fate was awaiting him. To simply not act would hand victory to his enemies.

'I will not pin the future of the Chapter, of the Imperium, on the worthless oath of a renegade on a dubious mission.' Cypher seemed as though he might argue but a look from the Supreme Grand Master silenced the protest before it took shape. 'You will be released, but I will send Tybalain and his Black Knights to escort you. The enemy will intervene if they have any notion of what you are attempting, so we must give them reason to occupy themselves elsewhere. And, if the Emperor's spirit favours us, we might even vanquish the enemy in the act. The rest of the Unforgiven will attack the problem from the opposite end. We will seize the *Terminus Est* and kill Typhus, and Astelan if he is there.'

HONOUR REPAID

Incoming projectile warnings blared at the back of Telemenus's mind, but he was too preoccupied to take evasive measures. The rocket struck the left side of his sarcophagus, leaving a half-metre jagged crack in the ceramite shielding. Ignoring the damage indicators, the Dreadnought pilot slid his targeter onto the bulky form of a Rhino transport accelerating across the broken ground towards the gate.

Twin beams of light stabbed from his lascannons, slicing into the transport's left-hand track housing. Glittering metal spun into the air as links shredded against the twisted hull, throwing the vehicle into a wild skid. He unleashed a flurry of krak missiles as traitor legionaries piled from the hatches, the armour-piercing warheads slamming into their corroded and battered plate.

Eight surviving Terminators were valiantly holding to his left, their bone-white armour lit by the flare of cyclone rocket launchers and the muzzle flash of assault cannons and storm bolters. There were a handful of other battle-brothers to the right – squad remnants from the starship crash that had been forced south rather than back to the Tower of Angels.

Widening the scope of his appraisal, whilst sending another shaft of laser energy punching through the armour of a traitor, he saw that his brothers did not fare well at the eastern gate. The Death Guard were mounting assaults from three directions.

'We cannot remain here,' he told Caulderain, the remaining sergeant at hand. 'Master Belial requires our assistance.'

Caulderain did not reply straight away, his sword lashing out to meet the neck of a traitor as the Space Marine pulled himself towards the Terminators, dragging his stained armour over a chunk of broken masonry, knife and bolt pistol at the ready. There were others in the debris no more than ten metres from the line, their bolters spitting a constant hail of fire.

'If Belial needs our assistance, he will call for it,' the sergeant replied, kicking away the headless corpse. He fired his storm bolter. 'We cannot abandon our position.'

'The eastern line must hold or we all shall be lost,' insisted Telemenus. He let loose a flurry of missiles – he had only six remaining – and turned his huge body eastward. 'Our position is no longer tenable, we must relocate.'

He twisted the huge torso of his shell so that he could continue to fire at the Plague Marines, even as his legs trundled towards Belial and his beleaguered warriors. Caulderain followed, the Terminators covering their retreat with a heavy flamer blast and a salvo from the remaining cyclone launcher. Through the mist, the other battle-brothers hurried past, their long strides carrying them quickly across the ruined ground.

They reached a semi-intact bastion a few hundred metres from Belial's defensive cordon. The battle-brothers quickly took up firing positions in the ruins while Telemenus and the other Deathwing continued on. Seconds later the blast of a plasma cannon broke the fog as the Dark Angels gave the pursuing Death Guard a hot welcome.

The unnatural smog of the Death Guard played tricks on Telemenus's augurs, but he could sense the bulky Land Raiders forming a line a few hundred metres ahead, and the gloom was lit with constant flashes of plasma and the strobing of intense storm bolter fire.

Something as large as him stalked through the mist, one arm a crackling, swaying flail of barbed blades, the other mounting linked heavy bolters. The instant he detected the enemy Dreadnought, Telemenus was raising his weapons. He waited until both aiming reticules were centred on the target and opened fire, sending a krak missile flying a couple of seconds before unleashing the beams of his lascannons.

The missile struck the housing protecting the central sarcophagus, shattering the outer plates. An instant later the lascannon hit the same spot, punching straight through with a ruby shaft. The Dreadnought stumbled and toppled sideways, heavy bolter rounds detonating in its ammunition pods.

Another dozen metres on, Telemenus came upon the Grand Master and his Knights. Another Dreadnought loomed above the Deathwing commander and his companions, lashing out with its flail. The Terminators' locked shields sent out a storm of cerulean sparks with every blow. The Death Guard machine's autocannon chattered constantly, blazing shell after shell into the shieldwall, but it found no weakness.

A third Dreadnought was trying to circumvent the Knights' solid barrier, but there were other Terminators moving to intercept. He recognised the black livery of the Consecrators. Nakir's guard had hung up their storm bolters and advanced with greatswords, four blades shining like slivers of sapphire in the jade fog. Their sergeant led the way with power sword and shield, driving into the blasts of plasma erupting from the Dreadnought's cannon, risking himself to ensure his warriors reached their foe.

The Dreadnought swung a censer-like morningstar in a whirling arc towards the Terminators. It smashed into the closest, sending him reeling, but the others closed in, their greatswords rising and falling with lethal precision. The morningstar's chain was severed and the plasma cannon exploded as a shining blade thrust into its containment chamber, gouting fire over the Dreadnought and its assailants.

Telemenus opened fire on the Plague Marines surging up behind the Dreadnought assault, trusting that Belial and the Deathwing Knights would overpower the last of the war engines. With him Caulderain and the other Terminators scourged a wound in the packed mass of advancing Death Guard, pitted armour shattering, their encrusted war-plate and desensitised flesh no match for the raw firepower of the Deathwing.

After a few minutes of frenetic fighting, during which Telemenus had to use his lascannon as a lethal club on two occasions and stamp a Death Guard to a pulp, the pressure finally eased. The Dark Angels Dreadnought moved to stand close to Belial, heavy weapons watching over his Grand Master as the rest of the Deathwing regrouped.

'I think we have broken the impetus of the attack, brother-captain,' said Telemenus.

'I think you are overly optimistic, Brother-Dreadnought,' the Grand Master replied. He pointed his sword to the sky. 'They were simply keeping us occupied while other matters took their course.'

Telemenus directed his surveyors skyward, but could make no sense of the jumbled signals that came back. The whirl of contradictory returns reminded him of the insanity that had overwhelmed the sensorium when they had teleported on Ulthor. He cut out all but the basic visual suite of inputs and looked at the sky with the closest he had to normal eyes.

The Gorgon's Aegis had dimmed, but of the stars beyond nothing could be seen. The heavens were tearing apart, a three-way rip erupting across the ruins of Caliban. It was as though the star system was being pulled, the fabric of the material universe stretching and then shredding from the titanic pressures.

The wound appeared to be caused by three objects – the *Terminus Est*, the doom-star, and the Rock itself. As it opened wider, Telemenus saw another world silhouetted against the system's star. Just the edge, highlighted by dawn or dusk, it was impossible to say. In orbit over the world were hundreds of ships, a forest of glittering engines that obscured the field of stars.

The scene was impossibly close, as though he was in orbit with the ships, although at the same time he knew that a universe divided them.

As he watched there was a flash from one of the

orbital stations and moments later the telltale flare of void shields. Torpedoes flared in response and battle was joined.

AN UNLIKELY REUNION

As Annael came in to land, the sky beyond his canopy seemed remarkably clear without the coruscating energies of the Gorgon's Aegis to obscure it. To the south and east there were still some sporadic flashes of fire and bright explosions, but the battle for the Rock had, for the time being, been reduced to a few running skirmishes between the Dark Angels and the survivors of the traitors' assault force.

Annael's destination was a spear of rock and metal that thrust two hundred metres out from the base of the Rock, several hundred metres below the last line of stones that formed the base of the Tower of Angels. Hidden between two bulky cliffs on either side, the Gate of Woes was a glint of gold in the darkness. The landing spot was only a mark on the scanner display in front of Annael – a blinking rune to be lined up with blasts from the attitude jets. No other light indicated the presence of the docking station.

Manoeuvring closer between the outthrusts, Annael saw that there was a Thunderhawk already set upon the main area of the landing. Dark green, its bulk was almost lost in the shadow, its hard edges glinting in the navigational lights of the Dark Talon as Annael steered it towards the lip of the landing apron.

He put the aircraft down a few metres from the gunship and set the engines to idle. As their whine died to a grumble, he opened the canopy and hauled himself from the cockpit. There were no porting steps here, so he dropped down from the wing to the ground.

Looking around, he saw that Tybalain, Sabrael and Calatus were already there, waiting beside the open gate. They said nothing as he joined them.

When Sammael brought out the Black Knights' next 'mission' Annael shot a glance at Tybalain. The renegade who had called himself Lord Cypher stood beside the Ravenwing commander with one hand resting on the holster at his right hip, his winged helm under the other arm. The Huntmaster was impassive.

'I did not think that they came back out of the Gate of Woes,' said Calatus, staring at the Fallen in his full battle regalia.

'You will conduct the captive to the coordinates locked into the Thunderhawk's navigation system,' Sammael said, ignoring the comment. 'Expect physical resistance at the target site.'

'What sort of resistance, Grand Master?' said Tybalain, clearly unhappy with the whole idea.

Sammael glanced a look at Cypher and then returned the Huntmaster's stare.

'Unknown, but if you remember Ulthor you might not be far wrong.'

'What a delight,' said Sabrael. 'I was hoping for more filth and unnatural monsters.'

His flippancy earned him a glare from Sammael, as sharp as the sword at his hip. One hand on the Fallen's shoulder, the Ravenwing Grand Master led Cypher towards the waiting gunship.

'Annael, you will fly escort,' Sammael said, glancing at the Dark Talon next to the Thunderhawk on the landing pad behind them. 'It is imperative that you conduct this captive safely to the mission objective. Protect him at all costs but do not allow him to leave your sight.'

Sammael handed Cypher to Calatus. Sabrael drew the Blade of Corswain and lifted the sword in front of Cypher.

'Do not think that you will be able to elude our attentions,' said the Black Knight. Cypher gave him a lopsided smile.

'That is a very nice sword. I once knew someone who carried one just like it.' The renegade's expression hardened. 'Be sure you can live up to your boasts, braggart, because you certainly do not live up to the standards of your weapon.'

Sabrael sneered, but there was bravado in his look. The Black Knight waved for Cypher to move and Calatus led the captive up the ramp of the gunship with Sabrael behind.

Tybalain leaned close to the Grand Master and spoke quietly, but Annael's sensitive ears still picked up the exchange.

'What about after?' said Tybalain. 'Does he need to be returned?'

'*After* you are successful, his survival is no longer desirable,' replied Sammael. To his credit, the Grand

Master seemed to find the notion necessary but distasteful.

Annael turned to the Dark Talon but Tybalain called him back. Sammael was already heading towards the Gate of Woes, swift strides taking him into the darkness of the dungeon.

'Huntmaster?'

'This is unprecedented, but we must stay focused. Above all, the Fallen is not to escape. Do you understand?'

'I am not sure that I do, brother-sergeant,' admitted Annael.

'The Thunderhawk has its navigational systems locked in. If you see us deviating from that course in any way at all, we are no longer in control and you must act quickly.'

'You mean fire on the gunship?' The possibility gave Annael pause, but the hard expression of Tybalain put him in no doubt that he was being given a direct, incontrovertible order. 'I could probably disable the eng–'

'Take no chances,' insisted Tybalain, baring gritted teeth. 'A lot of Ravenwing brothers have died in the last few months because of this traitor. They were not the first. He does not escape his due punishment. If needed, you will be the executioner. Swear it.'

'I swear, by the Lion's shade and the Emperor.'

Tybalain stared at him for a few more seconds and then, evidently satisfied with what he saw, the Huntmaster turned and stalked up the ramp of the Thunderhawk. His eyes following the squadron leader into the interior, Annael saw Cypher sat between Sabrael and Calatus. His helmet was in place and he stared straight at the bulkhead opposite.

He fixed that image in his mind, of the traitor and not his brothers, as he pulled himself back up to the canopy of the Dark Talon. And Tybalain was correct. It was no coincidence that the Fallen had arrived when he had. From Piscina to Caliban, it was not difficult to lay the slaying of Annael's brothers at the feet of 'Lord Cypher' – and from the intimations of Tybalain, countless thousands before.

Something far more stark and personal crossed Annael's thoughts. Nerean, dead less than two hours. Sabrael, Tybalain and Calatus might be next. Someone had to end the legacy of death.

It would be easier to pull the trigger if that was the thought in his mind.

RETRIBUTION UNLEASHED

Two battles raged across the Caliban System.

The combined fleet of the Unforgiven Chapters cleaved towards the *Terminus Est* and the Plagueheart, the Rock at the centre of the counter-attack. Defensive shields alight with crimson energy, the fortress-monastery of the Dark Angels spat fire and destruction at any enemy vessel that remained in its path, splitting the renegade forces like an axe into wood.

Outnumbered but never outgunned or outclassed, the ships of the Dark Angels, Knights of the Crimson Order and Consecrators attacked in wolf packs. Gathered into small flotillas they pounced upon the opposing vessels scattered by the advance of the Rock, overwhelming and destroying the heavy cruisers and grand cruisers in swift and determined attacks, eliminating each target in turn before moving on to the next.

For their part the renegades and traitors seemed

unfocused, lacking direction now that their lords had opened the warp breach. The objective fulfilled, the combined might of the Unforgiven held at bay for long enough for the ritual to create the rift, the Death Guard and other traitors of the fleet were left to fend for themselves. Only the ships that had arrived with the *Terminus Est* showed any signs of coordination, withdrawing by squadrons to defend the massive battleship of their master.

As a backdrop around this cataclysmic exchange of plasma, las and shell, the break in reality showed glimpses of an entirely different war being waged. Through the tear in the material universe could be seen an immense fleet, dozens of ships, pushing into orbit over a world of grey and green while a ring of orbital stations hurled torpedoes and ground-based defence lasers unleashed their beams in rough welcome. The vox-channels were filled with static through which snatches of archaic voices could be heard, their accents recognisable but barely comprehensible. Distant alarms from the other reality rang in the ears of the combatants of both sides, alongside angry shouts and the cries of the wounded and dying.

On both sides of the widening breach between realities, space was filled with crippled ships and burning wrecks. Unexploded ordnance littered the inner reaches of the star system and rogue squadrons of fighters and assault craft, their home ships destroyed, flew between the fleets looking for sanctuary or revenge.

The surface of the Rock had been all but swept of enemies, the Tower of Angels' corridors and halls cleansed of the invaders. The apothecarions heaved with casualties, while the silent Chambers of Remembrance next to the Reclusiam of each company held the mortal remains of many more Space Marines. Nearly a third of the Dark Angels had been seriously wounded or slain. Out in the fleet the other Unforgiven had suffered similar devastation. It was impossible to reckon the tally of foes killed, but it numbered more than a thousand legionaries and ten times that number of lesser warriors.

Despite this heavy price paid for the defence of the fortress-monastery, Azrael's thoughts were not on preventing further harm, but actively seeking to inflict it. The Dark Angels had been caught unawares by the arrival of the Plagueheart, but they had weathered the storm and it was time to retaliate.

Unnoticed amongst the grandiose spectacle, two craft sped from the launch pad of the Gate of Woes, heading back into the maelstrom of rocks and debris that had been blessed Caliban. Around them, drawing the eye of the foe to the launch bays of the Rock and the flight decks of the fleet, the Unforgiven disgorged every craft they had still capable of flight. Dark Talons and Nephilim led the swarm, bulkier Thunderhawk gunships laden with Space Marines following behind.

Their target was the *Terminus Est*.

It was almost a relief to be free from Cypher. The decision to send the renegade on his mission, whether right or wrong, had been made. Only time would tell if Azrael had been correct. Similarly, it gave the Supreme Grand Master fresh energy to have quit the chamber of Tuchulcha. Trying to unpick the myriad courses of possible history and present, with half a mind to the potential benefits for all of the forces involved, had been a taxing burden.

For the time being he was free of such concern. He

had a target and a mission, the most straightforward Azrael's life had been for many months. There was only one decision left to be taken.

'I need someone to remain in command,' insisted Azrael.

'In command of what forces?' Nakir replied quietly. 'Everything we have is taking part in the attack.'

He stopped and Azrael felt obliged to halt with him. They were descending the last steps to the southern teleportarium. Ahead, Belial and his Knights continued along the passageway, moving out of sight, if not hearing. The thud of heavy boots and wheeze of Terminator armour echoed back to the two Chapter Masters. Azrael could empathise with Nakir's complaint, but he simply could not abandon control of the Rock to any lesser commander.

'You need every warrior available,' said Nakir, waving a hand at the three Consecrator Terminators following a few metres behind their leader. The honour guard had halted on the floor above, silently awaiting the conclusion of the debate. By all accounts, especially Belial's, the Consecrators had fought like cornered varglions.

'To defend the Rock,' Azrael said. 'There is no other in whom I would place this trust.'

'Then extend that trust now, Lord Azrael.' Nakir dropped his voice. 'Do not think me some naive innocent to be instructed to go out of earshot when the adults are talking. I do not know what has transpired with your Chapter of late and it is of no concern to me. But I have led my warriors down many secret paths, and the vaults of the *Reliquaria* are filled with answers to mysteries ten thousand years old and more. When Supreme Grand Master

Valafar instigated the hidden founding of my order to seek out and preserve our past, he entrusted unto every Consecrator a sacred duty and a secret burden. He allowed the Inner Circle to grow, so that the Unforgiven might be strengthened. If you would but share a little of his faith…'

It tore at Azrael's soul to hear such earnest petition. Yet he was bound to uphold the secrecy of both Luther's existence and the capture of Cypher. He could not, in all conscience, divulge what he knew to the other Chapter Master.

Yet did that prevent him allowing Nakir to accompany the attack on the *Terminus Est*? The Consecrator had already professed a studied disinterest in the events that had led to this momentous occasion. Could he be trusted? More to the point, could Azrael leave him behind?

'Very well, but your oaths of secrecy and those of your brethren extend to anything they witness today. Am I clear?'

'You have my word on my honour, as a Space Marine, as a Consecrator and as a son of the Lion.'

This last reminded Azrael that the Unforgiven were all the gene-sons of the same primarch and the results of the day's battle would affect each and every one of them. Nakir had no less right to fight for his future, even if he did not wholly realise the stakes that were in play.

'You will be no more than ten strides from my side,' commanded Azrael as he set off again.

'Of course, Lord Azrael. Where else would I desire to be?'

They rejoined Belial and the Deathwing Knights in the main teleportarium chamber. Unlike those of the strike cruisers and battle-barges, the Rock's teleportation halls were massive cathedral-like spaces that had once housed entire companies in the days of Aldurukh. Three more squads of Terminators were already waiting for them.

'Sammael, report on the void assault,' Azrael said over the command vox.

'Ready to make final run at your command.'

The Supreme Grand Master had no hesitation in issuing the order.

'All companies, attack! For the Emperor and the Lion, we shall be swift wrath!'

With a wave, he signalled for the veterans of the First Company and the Consecrators to assemble on the oil-black teleportation plate. Nakir was on his left, no more than a pace behind. Ezekiel entered from another archway. He approached in silence and the Consecrators parted to allow him to stand beside the Supreme Grand Master on the right.

From the shadows emerged several of the Watchers in the Dark. Out of the corner of his eye, Azrael saw the Consecrators looking at the diminutive creatures with interest, following their progress as they moved across the teleportarium. One bore a helm with high wings as a crest, another a scabbarded sword, the third an ornate combi-weapon of a bolter with a plasma gun mounted beneath.

First Azrael took the fabled Lion Helm and fitted it into place, the seals snug with the neck collar of his ancient armour. Reputedly worn by the Lion himself, it was the greatest symbol of leadership possessed by the Unforgiven. Around Azrael the Dark Angels lifted their weapons in salute while the Consecrators bowed their heads.

He next received the Lion's Wrath, the combi-weapon cunningly crafted in the years of the Scouring. Suspensors inside cancelled most of its weight, allowing him to lift the bulky gun with one hand. As his fingers curled around the grip the plasma chamber sprang into life with a blue glow and a hum.

Azrael bent forward and pulled free the blade. The Sword of Secrets, most revered of the Heavenfall blades. He looked at Nakir and raised the weapon's hilt to the snout of his helm. The Consecrator pulled free the sibling blade at his waist and returned the gesture of respect.

'Death before dishonour,' said Nakir.

Azrael did not reply. There had been little to make him feel honoured or honourable in recent events. There was barely an oath he had sworn that he had not broken, except for his commitment to protect the Dark Angels against all threats. That oath came before all others.

He felt the Rock trembling as all weapons that could be brought to bear opened fire on the *Terminus Est*. Unable to maintain the warp rift if his battleship moved away from Caliban's nominal point, Typhus could not manoeuvre to evade the oncoming Dark Angels – a mistake Azrael hoped would be fatal for his foe.

Led into the attack by their battle-barges, the remaining Dark Angels ships swept aside the attendant cruisers and escorts, bombardment cannons and gun decks pounding away with blistering fury. Heaving into range of Typhus's flagship, the fortress-monastery poured forth a storm of fire, every tower and battery lighting up the void with their ire.

Void shields sprayed purple and blue energy as the bombardment intensified, cocooning the *Terminus Est*. Torpedoes and missiles spewed plasma warheads and cyclotronic storms across the time-ravaged hull of the Chaos vessel, cracking open the ancient armour.

With a final blossom of energy, the last of the *Terminus Est*'s void shield generators overloaded.

At the heart of the Rock, enveloped in a mesh of digital and mechanical systems amongst the shrivelled corpses of his predecessors, the Dark Angels Master of the Forge sensed the weakness of the battleship. Artificial stars captured in the magnetic containment fields of reactors were siphoned into immense plasma turbines. Arcane generators that tapped into the warp itself for power sputtered into being. Ancient power grids laid down before the dawn of the Imperium crackled into brief life.

The Tower of Angels blazed with the unprecedented surge of power, its immense stained-glass windows casting rainbows out into the void, the Gorgon's Aegis shimmering around the fortress-monastery in a golden dome.

Inside, electricity crackled along metre-thick cables and the coils and pylons of the teleportaria burst into sparkling life. Around Azrael the air of the hall thickened with the tang of ozone and the coolant pipes burst their seams, flooding the chamber with steam.

'Full teleport!' he roared into the vox. 'Sons of the Lion, our vengeance is at hand!'

Boarding torpedoes slammed into the exposed hull of the *Terminus Est* and gunships blasted their way into the open launch bays of the battleship to disgorge hundreds of Space Marines. At that moment the teleportaria of the Rock simultaneously burst into activity, directed at the command bridge of Typhus's flagship, casting the entirety of the surviving Deathwing across the warp.

FOOTFALLS ON CALIBAN

The Black Knights ventured into the passageway they had discovered in the side of the kilometre-wide asteroid to which they had been brought. The suit lamps of the floating Space Marines passed over pitted ferrocrete, which formed an arched corridor five metres high. Behind them the Thunderhawk and Dark Talon had been secured by docking grapples to the sides of the jagged opening. Tybalain led the way, Cypher between Annael and Calatus, with Sabrael bringing up the rear.

'It looks like an arterial transport tunnel,' said Annael as he pulled himself hand-over-hand along a glistening metal rail in what he assumed had been the floor.

'Maglev monorail,' said Cypher. 'It used to link the arcologies of the Northwilds with the starport at Andaril.'

'Arcologies?' said Calatus.

'Mega-cities. You might call them hives.'

'We were told that Caliban was a world of deep forests and oceans,' said Annael. He eased himself over a buckled length of rail, the ground beneath cracked as if twisted by some massive hand. 'Not a hive world.'

'Once, in the depths of time. Had precious Caliban survived, the Imperium would have the last of the forests cut down, the rolling hills strip-mined, the deep caverns delved in the search for riches. Perhaps a hive world ten thousand years later, if the plunder of Mankind did not destroy the planet earlier.'

There was a wistful edge to the renegade's speech rather than bitterness. A melancholy of times lost forever.

'It is hard to imagine that these spinning rocks were once home to the Lion,' said Annael. 'That millions of people lived and breathed here before the ruin was unleashed.'

'Stay focused,' warned Tybalain.

Annael readied his bolt pistol and continued to pull himself with his left hand, allowing his momentum to carry him forward. Ahead, the passage became rounded, the lamplight reflecting from broken tiles on the curved far wall. As Sabrael adjusted his angle, his lantern beam caught on something that glittered.

The squad came to an immediate halt at a word from their Huntmaster. They played their lamps back and forth across the tunnel mouth. The light refracted from glistening crystal deposits that looked like trails left across the bricks and tiles.

'We must push on,' said Cypher.

'You are not in command,' said Tybalain. There was an awkward moment until the Huntmaster thrust away from the wall and into the tunnel. 'Follow me.'

Annael took a closer look at the crystals as he drifted

past. They were like faceted glassy beads, slightly puddled where they stuck to the wall. Turning to the left and right, he counted more than twenty trails all within a few metres. He tried following them, but they disappeared into the darkness, intertwining and overlapping but all of them either heading into or out of the tunnel.

'Do you think something came in before us, or tried to escape a long time ago?' he asked.

'It is waiting for us, I am sure of it,' replied Cypher.

'Movement ahead!' Calatus warned before Cypher offered further explanation. The Space Marine held out his auspex and panned left and right for a few seconds. 'Signal cannot lock. Definitely movement, but no life signs or heat signature.'

'Threads of the empyrean,' said Cypher. 'Projections of the beast we hunt made real.'

'Hallucinations?' said Sabrael.

'No.' Cypher pulled free his pistols. The glow from the containment chamber of his plasma weapon lit the tunnel with a cerulean glare. 'The warp manifested. Nephila. Daemonspawn.'

As they continued, they passed branching service tunnels and broken ladders that led up to maintenance ducts. A few hundred metres into the tunnel they came to a station. The rail ended a hundred metres away, a two-metre-high platform on their left. The cavern-like terminus swallowed the lamplight, marooning them on an island of light in a sea of blackness.

The silence grated on Annael's nerves. He felt not the slightest vibration through his fingers as he grabbed hold of the platform edge and slowly vaulted from the track. Twisting, he landed on the platform, legs bent. The wall was a few metres further on, crisscrossed by more of the crystal traceries. They converged or emanated from an exit arch halfway along the station.

'This way, I think,' he told the others, attracting their attention to the archway with a half-second strobe of his lamp. He felt his eye drawn to Cypher for confirmation despite Tybalain's earlier assertion of command.

The renegade looked around, the red gleam of his helm lenses bright as they turned towards Annael.

'It would seem so,' said Cypher, but offered nothing further, moving his attention to Tybalain.

'Stay alert,' said the Huntmaster. 'Close confines, single file. Mark your aim carefully.'

Passing into the exit corridor, the Dark Angels found that there was a metal underlay beneath the floor tiles. Activating the mag-grips of their boots, they were able to walk almost normally. The metronomic hiss and clank of their steps brought comfort to Annael. A dozen metres on they came upon a moving staircase, long since immobilised by lack of power. The crystal spoor did not lead them up, but on through another archway, presumably to another platform.

'What are we seeking?' asked Calatus as Tybalain led the squad onward. 'What is the mission?'

Before Cypher could reply, the tiniest reverberation alerted Annael that something had changed. The others had felt it too and froze where they were, weapons at the ready.

A second later, the archway ahead exploded with fanged, writhing shapes as the tunnel vomited forth dozens of serpentine apparitions.

The worms were translucent, pulsing with blackness inside white skin. Their eyes were like shards of coal, glinting black in the lamps of the Space Marines. Mouths gaped wide, large enough to swallow one of the Dark Angels helms whole, ringed with finger-long fangs. Thick slime drooled in ropes from squirming purple tongues.

Annael fired on instinct. The flash of bolt propellant was stark white in the gloom, leaving a phosphorescent trail from pistol to detonation inside the mass of worm-like creatures. As though a single entity, the flailing mass thrashed back from the archway as more bolts raked into them from the squad. In moments, the darkness and silence descended again.

A second passed, and another.

'Why do I get the feeling we haven't won?' Sabrael asked. He looked at Cypher. 'I don't suppose that was the objective?'

The station lurched. The whole asteroid, in fact, shuddered as though struck by an almighty fist. The mag-grip of Annael's boots could not hold him in place and, along with Sabrael, he found himself tossed into the air. The others swayed like comical puppets, their feet locked in place while the world spun around them.

Grabbing a light fitting in his spare hand, Annael swung his pistol towards the opening, expecting a fresh attack by the worm-wraiths.

Nothing appeared.

'Shut up!' said Tybalain, sensing that Sabrael had readied another quip. 'Calatus, watch our backs.'

The Huntmaster took a step forward. The floor and wall exploded, engulfing him in a torrent of broken bricks and a cloud of mortar. His black armour disappeared under the avalanche of masonry as something eldritch and terrifying heaved itself into view.

It was neither humanoid nor slug, but some strange amalgam of both, the visible portion so large that it smashed through the ceiling as it straightened, showering dirt and debris onto the squad. Its snake-like body ended with four ribbed tentacle-appendages, each tipped with half a dozen claws as long as a combat blade. In the gloom beyond, Annael spied many-jointed legs like those of a centipede, scrabbling at the ruin of the tunnel beyond the arch.

Amongst its upper limbs was a head-stump, little more than a bulge with a cluster of multi-faceted eyes that shone crimson in the reflected light of the Space Marines' suit lamps. A disturbingly human mouth, thick-lipped, twisted in a grimace of displeasure, completed the horrific visage.

'The ouroboros!' bellowed Cypher. The word meant nothing to Annael but it was obviously a name for the creature. The renegade fired his plasma pistol. 'Destroy it!'

The Black Knights needed no encouragement. They opened fire together, targeting the head-lump. Bolt-round detonations lit the tunnel, harmless against the blistered, cracked skin of the daemonspawn.

Tybalain shouldered his way out of the rubble pile, firing up into the creature's mouth from underneath its bulk. As the ouroboros moved, ridged underbelly scraping flags from the floor, Tybalain retreated. He dodged aside just as its enormous girth settled where the Huntmaster had been standing, the floor buckling under the pressure of the thing forcing its way into the hallway.

Blue light flashed as Cypher fired his plasma pistol again, the bolt of energy splashing against the face of the ouroboros. It reeled back, jaw widening even further. It might have howled, or roared, or squealed, but all Annael felt was another ripple of vibrations through the tunnel, the walls shedding grubby tiles like scales. Hauling itself forward, bony projections like scythes slashing through the exposed ferrocrete of the walls, the monstrous creature towered over the Black Knights.

'Time to end this,' declared Sabrael.

He drew the Blade of Corswain and leapt at the daemonspawn. The gleaming blade parted a tentacle flailing towards his face, leaving a trail of fluorescent green globules and a twitching stump. Another appendage snapped out like a whip, catching Sabrael across the side of his helm, leaving a white welt of cracked ceramite against the black enamel. With no purchase, the Space Marine spun head over heels back across the chamber, snarling curses.

Annael and Tybalain followed Sabrael's example, swapping pistols for corvus hammers. The head of his weapon left a bright arc as Annael swung at what he supposed was the beast's chest. The force of the impact unleashed a flash of power from the hammer, the immaterial flesh of the ouroboros rippling as though a brick had been dropped in a puddle. The immutable laws of physics had an equal effect on Annael, sending him flying in the same direction as Sabrael.

Tybalain was wiser, keeping his feet firmly rooted to the floor as he swung his hammer at the descending fangs. Teeth broke into shards, grey splinters embedding themselves in the Huntmaster's armour. He took a step back and swung again, the hammer pulsing with energy as it smashed into the daemonspawn's body.

Cypher moved left, leaping over a tentacle as it swept out to snap his legs under him. The traitor fired a flurry of shots as he glided, twisting slowly, towards the moving stairway, stitching a line of shots across the creature's eyes. Lenses fractured like glass but the ouroboros forced itself further into the chamber, slashing left and right with blade-arms and thrashing limbs.

The ceiling had corrugated, giving Sabrael a footing from which he launched himself like an arrow, his sword forming the tip as he sped past Annael. The blade punched into flesh a metre below the monster's mouth, more bright fluid streaming forth. Sabrael's momentum carried him sideways into the body of the beast, a lashing tentacle wrapping about his chest before he could push himself free.

'Emperor's blood!' he cursed. 'My armour is splitting!'

Calatus threw himself at the appendage, tossing aside his hammer to grasp it with both hands. Anchoring his feet against a ridge of blubbery flesh, he tried to prise the limb away. Cypher continued past the creature's visage, disappearing into the gloom of the burrow it had created, his crested helm silhouetted by the flashes of bolt pistol and plasma blast.

Annael stopped his backward flight by securing himself to a twisted stanchion jutting from the wall. He clambered around the support and kicked away, using the undulating surface of the wall to 'run' at the monster, hammer held ready. A tentacle swung towards him and he jumped, turning in midair as he was propelled towards the opposite side of the chamber. He timed the twist to land feet first against the broken masonry and pushed again, the fibre bundles in his armour hurtling him at speed towards the ouroboros.

Calatus dragged Sabrael free a couple of seconds before Annael reached his target. The hammer left a burning trail as he swung it into the maw of the creature with all his strength, striking upward. The blazing weapon smashed through the creature's upper lip, leaving a gaping, flapping mess of flesh in its wake, coating the Black Knight's armour in a layer of filth.

Like Sabrael, Annael could not stop himself slamming into the creature's flank. Unlike his companion, he was ready, and thrust away with his hand before he was crushed against the wall, tumbling further into the darkness from which the ouroboros had erupted. He slowed his progress with a hand against the broken tiles and came to a stop.

Annael was about to push himself back towards the others when he glimpsed the blue glare of Cypher's plasma pistol. He followed it down through the collapsed remnants of the tunnel, passing into another station that lay parallel to the one by which the Space Marines had entered.

The huge space glittered, every surface covered with the same crystals they had seen earlier. Cypher was making his way across a bed of the angular deposits, following the line of the ouroboros's body. At first Annael thought the daemonspawn's bulk disappeared into a transport tunnel, but as he followed the renegade his lamp revealed that it was connected to a mass of pustules and warty flesh beneath the carpet of crystals.

'We have to get back to assist the others!' Annael insisted over the short-range vox. He pointed his pistol at Cypher. 'You are coming back with me!'

'We have to destroy the heart,' Cypher replied without turning around.

'It has a heart?' asked Annael. His lamp moved back and forth across the huge tube of the daemonspawn's body, sickened by the undulating mass. 'Where?'

'Not here, of course,' said the renegade. He was looking down, at the crystals. Suddenly he stood back and let his lantern illuminate the ceiling. 'It's around us.'

Annael looked up and saw a ballooning outcrop of ridged grey flesh, forming the roof of the chamber. In places there were deeper shadows, which he realised with apprehension were splits, the gaps between the mass and other snaking protrusions.

'That is just a head, one of a dozen, disposable,' Cypher said, flashing his lamp towards the monster they had been fighting.

The renegade's words did not make much sense but Annael had no time to ask any further questions. The asteroid trembled, the shaking growing more violent with every passing second. The quake continued to intensify until masonry and shards of stone rained down on Annael and Cypher. The fleshy ceiling shifted, straightening, while the neck and head slithered back past the pair of Space Marines, luminous eyes regarding them briefly in the darkness.

The moonlet broke apart, scattering thousands of tonnes of stone into the void.

The ground splintered and dropped away beneath Annael, leaving him floating over a deepening chasm. And then that was also gone, reduced to spinning fragments that whirled away into the vacuum.

The Black Knights were cast adrift amongst the debris, some of them still attached to splinters of floor by their mag-grip boots. Annael, Cypher and Sabrael floated free, flotsam amongst the tempest of rock and ferrocrete. Tiny jets of air from articulated vents on Annael's backpack allowed him to stay his outward momentum. He took up a position between the renegade and his battle-brother.

The creature formed a huge semi-transparent ring, the light of the local star a pale orange through its body, darker shadows of organs throbbing and elongating. The claw-feet that extended along the necks unfurled strange skin flaps, looking like sails, or solar sheets catching the light of the star – appendages for navigating through a universe of the immaterial.

The ouroboros's massive form was tipped at either end by fronds of bulbous heads like the hydras of ancient legend, each jaw clamped around the neck of a head on the opposite end. All save the head that the Dark Angels had been fighting, which glared down at the Space Marines with malign intent.

It seemed to be suckling from itself, pulsing, darkness flowing from one end of the immense body to the other. The beast shuddered and its jaws opened together, freeing the cosmic daemonspawn from its self-embrace. It uncoiled, darkening, flesh becoming solid, skin hardening into a glossy black hide that was barely visible against the night.

'That is the body,' said Cypher. The renegade seemed oddly calm considering the circumstances. Annael's whole body was abuzz with adrenaline and stimulants from his battleplate, and the apparition of the ouroboros defied rational thought, numbing him even more. 'We need to find and destroy the heart. Not a real heart, of course, but the warp anchor in this reality, the seed of Caliban it devoured.'

Annael looked down at his pistol and corvus hammer and then back up at the vastness of the ouroboros that blotted out the heavens.

'How?'

A RETURN TO DARK PLACES

The Thunderhawk eased down onto the floor of the landing bay, the assault ramp in its nose already lowering before the landing gear touched down. Telemenus was at the ramp, his missiles refilled, patches of bonded ceramite and chunky rivet-welds covering the worst of the damage he had suffered during the battle for the Rock.

The cannons of the gunship had already cleared the enemy flagship's landing bay, littering the corroded decking with blasted bodies. Striding down the ramp, Telemenus detected only mutants and twisted human remains – no legionaries. They would be close, but not directly at the forefront of the defence. Better to soak up the initial momentum of the assault with expendable minions.

It was an understandable but deplorable strategy, devoid of all honour. The Dark Angels treated their unaugmented serfs with respect – many had once been novitiates that had for one reason or another failed later testing or had suffered harm as a result of training or the organ implantation process. They were servants to be protected, not a faceless resource to be expended like ammunition.

Tactical Squad Devorus followed the Dreadnought as he lumbered onto the flight deck. The interior of the *Terminus Est* was as unholy as the exterior. Every surface was crusted with corrosion, fungal growths and filthy grease. Flies flitted everywhere and there were already hordes of maggots crawling up through the decking to set upon the newly-dead. Fronds like hanging guts draped from the ceiling, pulsing with internal motions, intertwined with the machine parts of the ship.

Telemenus fired his lascannons at the launch bay door as he advanced. Reinforced to guard against the ravening vacuum of space and the impact of anti-ship missiles, it took four pinpoint blasts to remove the locking mechanism. Two of the battle-brothers moved forward and pulled the doors apart, revealing an arterial corridor beyond.

The roar of more jets announced the arrival of a second gunship. Without turning, Telemenus felt the approach of twenty Assault Marines, bounding quickly across the deck with blasts from their jump packs. To the left and right, above and below, drop-ships and boarding torpedoes were bringing in the entirety of the Chapter. Telemenus had only witnessed the whole Chapter deployed to battle once before, during the first scouring of Piscina Four in the wake of Ghazghkull's invasion.

Never had he thought a starship would be the target of so much effort. Whatever was aboard the *Terminus*

Est, the Supreme Grand Master was willing to exchange his entire command for its destruction. Thoughts of Piscina Four were not encouraging – despite the best efforts of the Dark Angels the world had eventually succumbed to internal divisions and the ever-resurgent orks. Telemenus hoped that there was a more satisfying conclusion to this attack.

As he left the launch bay, Telemenus found himself in a gullet-like passageway. Fifty metres to the left and the right blast doors had descended to seal the pressure breach. Brothers from the Assault squads leapt forward and placed their melta charges. Both doors were simultaneously vaporised, unleashing a blizzard of warm air, dead flies, bloated spore pods and mangled body parts as the pressure equalised.

Telemenus moved to the right, towards the bark of shotguns and the zip of las-blasts. The Assault Marines returned fire with their pistols, chainswords whirring as they charged along the corridor. Above their heads Telemenus picked out targets further away, sending beams of laser energy and single missiles screaming along the corridor.

The objective beacon led them on two hundred metres to a cross-junction, and a left turn towards the spine of the ship. A huge archway opened up from the passageway into a vaulted space between the dorsal gun batteries.

Reaching the threshold, Telemenus was taken aback by the cathedral-like space. It stretched up for three hundred metres, the ceiling lost in a green vapour that swirled and billowed as though from monstrous exhalations. The walls were thick with hardened filth, in places broken by jutting bone and misshapen rows of teeth. Suckered tentacles turned towards the Dark

Angels as they entered, eyestalks quivered and lipless maws moaned mournful warning cries.

The floor was carpeted with daemonic mites – a morass of small, boil-shaped bodies with glinting eyes and needle teeth, and green and black beetles with knobbled carapaces and strangely human eyes. One-eyed daemon-things hovered in the upper mists on the backs of huge flies, while more of their kind emerged in shambling lines from the shadows of the colonnaded hall. Slug-like beasts flopped and slithered amongst the surging tide, waves of rippling filth splashing over the mites and bugs.

Here were the traitors too, in their filth-slicked armour almost indistinguishable from the rotted mess around them. Gizzards bulged from rents in their warplate, distorted limbs and faces broke through ancient ceramite layers, revealing pustuled skin and leprous flesh.

To the left, no more than two-score metres away, an immense mound of green, pestilent flesh presided over the daemonic horde. Broad, yellow-veined eyes turned towards him, a look almost of sadness drooping the bulbous lips of the huge daemon commander.

Telemenus froze, engulfed by a memory.

Daellon laughed.

'Emperor-damned miracle, it is. A damned miracle!'

The two Terminators burst into a cavernous space easily a hundred metres high, veined and vaulted like some immense pulmonary chamber. Droplets of spattering fluid fell from open sores above and the uneven floor forced them to slow, lest they trip on one of the cartilaginous ridges and masses that protruded through the skin-like surface.

Telemenus's eye was immediately drawn to a figure in black Terminator armour and he recognised the markings of Brother Sapphon. With the Chaplain were eight other Terminators, almost surrounded by a crowd of humanoid, single-eyed daemons that crashed rusted blades against the Space Marines' armour, their bodies twisted and rotting. The Terminators blasted and punched their way through the group, lightning claws carving ruinous tatters in immaterial flesh, while Sapphon bludgeoned and decapitated with his crozius arcanum.

'Praise the Lion!' Telemenus called out over the short-range vox. 'A happy moment this is.'

Sapphon turned in their direction, skull helm half-covered with sickly ichor. He pointed at them with his crozius.

'Beware!'

Daellon and Telemenus pivoted at the Chaplain's warning. Dozens of the pustule-beasts boiled through the widening archway behind them, bursting out under the pressure of their numbers. Yet it was not these that had so concerned Sapphon. Behind them loomed something enormous, a bloated shadow that lumbered after its diminutive children.

Squeezing its bulk into the cathedral-like hall with surprising swiftness, the immense daemon was a hill of a beast, a mound of pestilent, torn flesh bloated with gas and fluids that bubbled from weeping sores in its green hide. It was nearly five times the height of Telemenus and Daellon, its broad shadow eclipsing both Terminators. Its wide, flat face was split by a slash of a grin, dagger-teeth discoloured and fractured. Broken horns jutted from either side of its head, dangling with streamers of entrails and foetid matter.

'Get back!' Daellon stepped in front of Telemenus and opened fire, stitching bolter detonations across the beast's chest.

The daemon swung its right arm, flab bulging and rippling, a flail of rusted chain in its fist, each of the three *massive lengths ending with a clutch of monstrous skulls. The flail slammed into Daellon. The whip-crack speed of the heads made them hit with a deafening crash, sending the Space Marine clattering a dozen metres across the floor, bouncing and twisting awkwardly over the uneven surface.*

Telemenus raised his storm bolter and fired but it was pointless. A rusty pick whose head was as big as his torso plunged down, its tip punching through the left side of his plastron. A thousand crooked nails dragged through his ribs and innards where the pick cut deep into flesh to erupt from the base of his back. Telemenus could not swallow the screech of utter agony ripped from deep within his soul as the daemon dragged free the weapon, the rusted pick chewing at his wounds like a million insects gnawing in his flesh.

He met the gaze of the daemon and tried to fire again, but the storm bolter had fallen from his hand without him realising it. The daemon pouted, brow furrowed, a look of sympathy more than anything else. Telemenus collapsed to his knees, looking as though he had fallen in supplication to its mighty form. Blood frothed from the wound and smaller daemons poured around him, forked tongues lapping at the spilt life fluid. Telemenus mustered enough strength to swipe them away with his power fist, leaving them as burst smears across his broken armour.

Telemenus fell forwards and was unconscious before his masked face slammed into the floor.

The daemon-curse was still in him.

He could feel the blackness seeping up from his heart, moving sluggishly along arteries into his lungs and brain. There was nothing he could do to combat the filth that had been unleashed in him. Not even the armoured body of a Dreadnought was proof against the sickness of his soul.

'Faith is your armour.'

It was a phrase oft-used by the Chaplains, but it sounded far more convincing spoken by the voice of the Emperor. The words were a confident assertion of a fundamental truth, bringing forth something from deep inside his soul.

The memory of his near-death flickered away, burned as though by a bright fire. White flames licked at the edges of Telemenus's thoughts, forming the image of an eagle, eyes of red, claws made of lightning bolts.

The Dreadnought fired, unleashing a storm of missiles onto the bulbous daemon's flesh. Telemenus's lascannon stabbed white beams into its face, turning gawping features into a slurry of broken teeth and melting eyes.

'Onward for the Lion!' Telemenus roared from his external speakers. He fired again, pulping the body of the greater daemon with las and missile, turning its torn flesh and scattered innards into a testament to the glory of the Emperor. With each beam and impact his confidence grew. Every shot was a smiting blow for the immortal Master of Mankind. There were no more doubts, no more questions. It was for this purpose that he existed. He gave an exultant shout from his address systems as another salvo of shots turned the remnants of the daemon's carcass into a spattered mess. 'Spare no wrath!'

From the other side of the massive hall two more Dreadnoughts appeared, laying about them with power fists and heavy bolters. Assault squads bounded through the fray, hacking and shooting, while Devastators laid down swathes of fire from the upper decks, their heavy weapons tearing into the Plague Marines.

Telemenus pushed on, heading towards the prow as

he had been commanded. He did not count the kills, but gloried in each and every one as though it was his first and last. Behind him the Dark Angels surged into the heart of the *Terminus Est*, laying waste to all in their path.

UNHOLY REVELATION

They were called the Grave Wardens, the most dedicated and skilled of Typhus's warriors. One hundred strong, clad in ancient Terminator armour, festooned with the marks and rewards of their unholy patron. For ten thousand years a scourge on the Imperium, and before that the greatest warriors of a whole Legion.

They stood between Azrael and his goal and he did not show a moment's hesitation or mercy.

While the rest of the Chapter overwhelmed the lower decks of the *Terminus Est* the teleport attack was ranged against the strategium of the huge battleship – the throne room of the Chaos Champion Typhus. The control chamber of the warship was larger than many halls of the Rock, the ceiling held aloft by three dozen pitted pillars, the crumbling vaults above encrusted with glowing growths and fan-like fungi.

As when the Plague Marines had assaulted the Rock, the air was thick with buzzing insects and a cloying miasma of sluggish brown and green clouds. Though a thousand lanterns blazed on hooks in the walls, the smog swallowed up their light, turning it into half-seen daemonic shapes carved from swirling mist.

On a broad dais at the far end of the chamber stood Typhus. Tendrils like lianas hung from the *Terminus Est*, connected to his massive suit of Terminator armour in the manner of umbilical cords. The swaying cables throbbed and pulsed with their own life, bulging and heaving.

Around him the Grave Wardens were arrayed in squads, bearing reaper autocannons, missile launchers, flamers, plasma guns and combi-bolters. For close assault they wielded an eclectic assortment of glaives, scythes, claws and scimitars that burned with unholy fire. Above them were tattered standards and icons of bone and rusted iron, proclaiming victories for ten millennia and allegiances to powers a million years older.

Of Astelan there was no sign, but the Lord of the Dark Angels did not allow this disappointment to temper his wrath.

'Death to the traitors!' he roared, breaking into a run as more Deathwing squads arrived around him, the air swirling with warp energy. 'Spare none their just execution!'

The command hall erupted with the bark of storm bolters and the *crack* of combi-bolters. Promethium spewed and missiles shrieked from one force to the other.

Wielding the Lion's Wrath in one hand, Azrael unleashed alternate blasts of plasma and hails of bolts. The flickering balls of energy punched steaming holes in the armour of the foe, the detonation of bolts splintering hardened bony growths and shattering ceramite.

He ignored the storm of fire that engulfed him, trusting to the arcane powers of the Lion Helm upon his head. Bolts were turned to ash, plasma splashed like rain and missiles burst into fiery blossoms centimetres from his body, but no harm came to the Lord of the Rock.

To his left Nakir fired steady bursts from his storm bolter. Each round unleashed flickered with its own fire and punched clean holes through the enemy Terminators – melta-warheads whose manufacture had been lost in millennia past. His armour was slicked with a gleaming field of gold that shifted aside every incoming projectile and beam.

On the right Ezekiel was wreathed in a black cloud that flashed with red lightning at every impact of bolt and rocket. Bursts of energy streamed from the blade of Traitor's Bane each time the Chief Librarian levelled his weapon at the foe. His helm was bathed in an auric glow of psychic power, its light burning through the clouds of flies and fog that filled the vile cathedral.

Three squads of Grave Wardens broke from the line, stomping forward to meet the trio of officers. Nakir met the brunt of the first squad, the Sword of Sanctity crashing against the swung spear of the closest Terminator, shattering the haft of the accursed lance. The point of the Heavenfall blade sliced off the top of the Grave Warden's head with one clean motion, exposing pustulent brain matter.

Ezekiel took the second squad, letting free a burst of ravening energy from his fingertips at the moment of their meeting. The floor beneath the Terminators erupted with black sword blades, piercing their legs and abdomens, slicing through their heavy-gauge warplate as though it did not exist. Traitor's Bane coursed golden lightning through their wounded bodies, exploding in forked energy from their eyes and fingers.

The third squad was left for Azrael. A scythe blade slashed out towards his throat but he caught it on the vambrace of his battleplate, turning aside the gleaming weapon. The Sword of Secrets felt alive in his grasp, lunging for the enemy as if possessed by a life of its own. It stabbed into the exposed armpit of the Plague Terminator and buried deep into the corrupted warrior's chest. Wrenching the blade free, Azrael ducked beneath a swinging fist and fired the Lion's Wrath, turning the head of another foe into a dissipating mass of vapour.

Blows rained down on the field projected by the Lion Helm but Azrael's thoughts were fixed on dealing death. The Sword of Secrets licked left and right in his hand, dealing cuts and thrusts without pause, slashing open millennia-old armour, exposing necrotic flesh and skin blistered with weeping sores.

Belial arrived half a minute later with his Knights. Shields locked, the Deathwing were like a battering ram at the gates of a castle. The Grave Wardens could not hold against their charge, their line breaking apart like shattered timbers before the maces and flails of the First Company's finest.

Azrael did not hesitate, but charged into the breach opened by Belial's attack. Ezekiel and Nakir followed, breaking away from their foes as more Deathwing Terminators reached the Grave Warden squads. As Azrael reached the steps leading up to Typhus's dais, Nakir turned towards the Grave Wardens, taking up a guard position to protect Azrael. Ezekiel ascended beside him.

Typhus was swelled with arcane power, larger even than the company of Terminators that served him, dwarfing Azrael. His armour was covered with a sheen of pale green mucus that glistened on plates scabbed like torn flesh, ceramite vambraces and pauldrons scaled like flaking eczema. In places ragged weaves of adamantium mail covered breaches in the plate, which sported a profusion of reinforced bonding studs. Bony growths grew through cracks in the plate.

His once-knightly armour was adorned with a single forehead horn, his cheek guards inset with two half-censer breathing gills that leaked olive-coloured vapour. Yellow lenses flashed as the commander of the *Terminus Est* turned his head towards the mortal creature stepping foot into his domain.

The Lord of the Rock paused a few steps from the top of the platform.

'"Thou shalt not suffer the unclean to live,"' Azrael raged, brandishing the Sword of Secrets. 'Do not think that you can intrude upon the demesne of the Dark Angels and not suffer consequence.'

Typhus laughed, a grating, rumbling sound that reverberated across the whole edifice of the strategium, making columns shake free clouds of dust. Cracked plaster and faded murals scattered flakes like snow onto the raging battle between the Grave Wardens and the Deathwing.

'It dares to come onto my ship and threaten me? What spirit!' Typhus turned his whole body towards Azrael. With a hiss like a nest of snakes, the pipes adjoined to the Chaos lord broke away, exposing puckered orifices and bony flues across the top and back of his armour. 'Welcome to the heart of the Destroyer Hive!'

Typhus raised his arms. In his right hand appeared an enormous scythe, its crooked blade a long shard of iron that shone with dark power. He laughed again, and as his body shook there came to Azrael's ears a buzzing sound. From the holes and chimneys of Typhus's war-plate spewed forth a cloud of flies with black bodies as large as a fist, their veined wings fluttering. Dozens, then hundreds and then thousands spilled impossibly from within Typhus's suit, surrounding Azrael with a solid wall of squirming furry bodies and multi-faceted eyes.

The living wall started to close on the Lord of the Rock, blocking out all of the light, plunging him into a throbbing, buzzing darkness.

Azrael remained calm, refusing to strike out in panic lest his blade hit Ezekiel. The flies were settling on him, their weight ponderous, his armour creaking under the pressure, but he held firm, enduring the deafening noise and the sickening feeling of being swallowed alive.

True to his belief, a few seconds passed and a chink appeared in the mass crawling over him, scourged by golden fire. More auric flames licked across the plate of Azrael, incinerating the flies with their touch.

Typhus continued to laugh even as his flies burned in their thousands, the wisps of smoke from their ashy remains drifting lazily back towards the funnels and orifices of the Chaos lord's armour.

'Finish him,' snarled Ezekiel, swiping the last of the flies away with a sheet of fire from Traitor's Bane.

Azrael wasted no time and leapt up the last few steps, swinging the Sword of Secrets at the head of the bloated Terminator. The haft of Typhus's scythe – Manreaper – met the Heavenfall blade, turning aside the ancient weapon with a sickening thud like a hammer on bone. Azrael struck again, cutting low, then high, each attack met with haft or blade of the daemon-infused scythe.

'I will not allow you to bring forth the evil of our past,' Azrael spat as he stepped back, seeking a fresh approach. He lanced his sword point-first at Typhus's gut but was again denied by the slashing blade of his foe. 'There is no place for it here.'

Typhus counter-attacked, smashing the butt of Manreaper into Azrael's chest. The blow took him by surprise, knocking him back several steps, almost pushing him from the dais.

'I do not care for your past evils,' Typhus replied, his humour gone. 'It is you that must be stopped. The Plagueheart will be freed.'

Azrael did not understand, and threw up the Sword of Secrets as the scythe blade cut towards his throat, deflecting the blow over his head. He riposted, lunging hard, but the edge of his blade simply glanced from the thick plate of Typhus's left pauldron.

'You deny your plotting with the accursed renegades of our Legion?' Azrael crashed the Sword of Secrets against Typhus's armour, ichor spraying from the wound it opened up.

'You bear the key to the Plagueheart's prison, so I allowed them to bring you to me.' Azrael leapt aside as Manreaper swung down, its blade carving a furrow through the stone where he had been stood an instant before. 'I will take that which was promised to me so long ago.'

Azrael turned aside his foe's next swipe and smashed his shoulder into Typhus's midriff, creating enough separation to cut the Sword of Secrets across the Chaos lord's chest. Armour split like stretched skin, spilling dark, thick fluid.

'Your lies are for nothing. When I slay you, the breach will close and the dead of the past will remain buried. I will not let you bring them back.'

'The breach is of your making, carved by the abomination you have held secret these many centuries. Do not think that you can save your primarch at the expense of the Plagueheart.'

Azrael stepped back several paces, confused by Typhus's accusation.

'You opened the rift with your sorcery,' he replied. 'You seek to bring forth Luther and his traitors to wage a fresh war in the forty-first millennium.'

Typhus's unexpected laugh stayed Azrael's next attack.

'My bargain with Luther died with him,' said the Host of the Destroyer Hive. 'Simply give me the key and you can leave him to rot again for all that the Lord of Nothing cares.'

Azrael circled, buying time to think. Typhus bided his time also. He turned with Azrael to keep Manreaper between him and the Lord of the Rock, but made no effort to close the distance.

'What do you know of the key?' Azrael demanded, assuming that the Chaos lord was familiar with Tuchulcha. 'How do you know of it?'

'How do you know of the Plagueheart?' countered Typhus.

'We saw it, at Ulthor, corrupted to the core. Why have you brought it here?'

'I did not.' Typhus sounded uncertain, his guard lowered for a fraction of a second, but Azrael did not exploit the momentary weakness.

'You and it are children of the same evil,' said the Lord of the Rock. 'Allies in your scheme to bring forth the corrupted warriors of Caliban.'

'Caliban will die again,' said Typhus. 'That cannot change. But the key will free the Plagueheart at the moment of destruction.'

'My lord!' Ezekiel's call broke through from outside Azrael's thoughts. 'The breach has almost reached the Rock. Kill him!'

'No!' Typhus howled the word, staggering as if struck. Azrael took two steps but the Chaos lord straightened, the blade of Manreaper held before him. 'No, it cannot be! We have all been tricked!'

'What trick? By whom?' Azrael knew Ezekiel was right. He had to strike down Typhus now that he had the chance, not just for his Chapter but for the future safety of the Imperium. But if he did, there would be no answers, only eternal questions. A little time could be spared. 'Speak plainly, foul one.'

'We have been lured here, three parts to make the whole,' the corrupted Terminator answered. 'The bridge, the key and the Plagueheart, all in this place at the same time. Not to release the Plagueheart, not to bring back your traitorous kin, nor to save your souls. Something greater awakens, dormant for aeons, awaiting the time when it could be brought back. No! Grandfather, I failed you again! The bridge opens again, denying me.'

Azrael felt a moment of connection from Ezekiel, as the Librarian opened his mind to the Lord of the Rock. For an instant Azrael saw what Ezekiel could see, felt what he could feel.

Above the breach, the warp bucked, once, as though it turned inside out. There was no tear, no ripping of realities, simply a smooth exchange of energies. Where before there had been empty void, there were now dozens of starships.

Warships. They blared their identifiers as alarms sounded across their decks and thousands of minds were seized by a sudden surprise.

The Successors of the Dark Angels that had been approaching Caliban. A fleet of the Unforgiven.

The only explanation was that Tuchulcha had brought them into the star system in the same way it had the Rock and the Knights of the Crimson Order. Azrael had no idea why, nor did Ezekiel. Whatever the motive, it seemed that Typhus had sensed the same.

'I will not be denied again!' he raged. Typhus lumbered into a run, barrelling towards Azrael. The Supreme Grand Master raised his sword to receive the charge. Teeth gritted, his eyes on the gleaming tip of Manreaper, he watched the scythe blade descend.

The world disappeared.

In the blink of an eye, Azrael knew that he was elsewhere.

The gloom of a deep cavern, a swirling of red marble and gold. The unsettling presence of Tuchulcha.

He was back on the Rock. Ezekiel was there also.

'It is done,' croaked the warp device's servitor. 'The plague-lord will no longer interfere. We will be remade.'

THE BEGINNING AND THE END

It seemed to Annael that the ouroboros's body had acted like a tether, somehow containing the power of the warp rift opening across the Caliban System. As the huge daemonspawn unfurled its body, the breach widened too, splitting the sky around the Black Knights. Looking up, all Annael could see was the shadow of the ouroboros. Looking down he saw a grey and green world, the sky filled with scatters of cloud. The flash of atmospheric entries and the blaze of defence lasers lit the crescent of night-time slowly encroaching beneath him.

He looked for his companions and saw that Sabrael was hurtling towards the nightmarish apparition, the Sword of Corswain glinting in the starlight. Cypher was retreating, moving away from the beast despite his assurances moments ago that the ouroboros had to be destroyed. Tybalain drifted not far away, as limp as a discarded doll though Annael could not see why.

Calatus was a few hundred metres away, tossed out into the void by the monster's obscene eruption.

Annael took all of this in at a glance. Cypher was heading towards the Thunderhawk, but whether to attack or to escape he could not say. He had only a couple of seconds to decide whether to go after the renegade or to aid Sabrael in destroying the daemonspawn.

After the events in Streisgant – the confusion of Sabrael's disappearance, the escape of Astelan and the capture of Cypher – there was no hesitation. The Hunt was more than a duty, more than a burden. It was a distraction. Annael had been crushed by his failure before the Chapter and the primarch, and he would not fail now.

The greater enemy was the ouroboros, and it had to be defeated.

The Black Knight powered after his battle-brother, using the main exhaust vents of his backpack like a thruster, pistol in one hand, corvus hammer in the other. A look at Tybalain as Annael passed confirmed that the Huntmaster was dead – his chest plastron was cracked open from sternum to abdomen, the wound filled with frozen blood, crystallized droplets floating around him.

The raw edge of the warp breach was bleeding towards the ouroboros, as though reality itself was being torn to tatters. Annael glimpsed immense space docks and orbital stations, the first spewing flight after flight of sword-like attack craft while the second unleashed torrents of plasma and missiles at half-seen starships not quite in view yet.

Against this backdrop he saw the Thunderhawk that had brought the others to the asteroid lighting its engines. Leaving azure plasma trails, it accelerated away, answering the question of what Cypher intended.

The vox blared in Annael's ear, receiving a sudden transmission that was garbled and panicked. He heard voices shouting, but could make nothing of what was said save for the occasional archaic curse word or ancient oath. Twisting in his flight, he looked back to see that the Rock was breaking away from the enemy flagship, which was turning away from the fortress-monastery.

Annael followed its movement, drawing his eye to a new sight.

Dozens of battle-barges, strike cruisers and escorts were arrayed across the heavens behind the Chaos fleet. Where they had come from, Annael had no idea. Magnifying his auto-senses, he could make out markings – sigils from the Angels of Absolution, the Repentant Brotherhood, the Angels of Redemption and the Angels of Vengeance.

'Lion's blood,' he swore. 'The Successors are here!'

The newly arrived fleet was wasting no time bending its course towards the Chaos vessels in an attempt to trap them between the Rock and their angle of attack.

A little further on, the second part of the Chaos fleet, which had assaulted the Tower of Angels, was breaking apart. The monstrous comet at its heart was glowing with power, enmeshed in a shimmering iridescent aura that Annael knew was connected to the ouroboros's emergence.

His eyes snapped back to the Rock. Beyond the ruddy glow of the Gorgon's Aegis, the fortress-monastery was shrouded in a similar veil of light. What it meant, Annael dared not guess. He focused his attention on the ouroboros, just a hundred metres away now, so vast it had become the sky. The light from the emerging planet behind Annael shone from thousands of freshly grown scales, each bigger than a Space Marine. Against this impossibly huge bulk, Sabrael looked like a gnat attacking a Thunderhawk, his shining blade a solitary star in the inky blackness.

The creature itself seemed indifferent to the Space Marines. Fully extended, its body hundreds of metres long, the ouroboros started to move, its neck-gills fluttering like fish fins in water. It was descending, moving down towards the rift beneath Annael's feet.

'All Dark Talon flights, all Chapters, this is a priority recall.' Lord Azrael's voice sounded impossibly mundane in the circumstances, wrenching Annael from his awed contemplation of the ouroboros. He could scarcely believe that anyone was issuing orders at all. 'All Dark Talons, I have a priority mission. Target rift cannons at dimensional instability centred on the Caliban nominal point. All Dark Talons that are able, you must target the opening breach. We must overload the tear before it engulfs us all.'

Annael caught up with Sabrael, who was gripping the end of an immense scale in one hand, trying to force the Blade of Corswain into the supernatural flesh beneath with the other. One might just as well try to slay a dragon with a pin, Annael thought.

He acted with more optimism than he had in his thoughts. Boosting himself forward with another exhaust burst, Annael swung his hammer into the pulsing flesh exposed by Sabrael's sawing. The power weapon slammed into immortal matter, the force of its blast parting pseudo-sinews. The scale tore free in Sabrael's grip and the Space Marine looked up in surprise.

'Annael? Did you not hear the Supreme Grand Master's order?'

'A poor joke, even by your standards, brother,' said Annael, hooking a boot into the flesh of the ouroboros to prepare for another swing.

'I am serious!' Sabrael jabbed his blade back towards the warp rift. 'This is a fool's errand, but if you can seal that rift, perhaps I won't have to hack my way into this thing's heart!'

Looking back, Annael saw that several Dark Talons were already speeding towards the rift. As he watched, he saw the telltale rainbow glimmer of rift cannons firing. Looking at the wavering gash in reality, and the beleaguered world beyond, he saw no substantial effect.

'They need every cannon they can muster,' Sabrael insisted. Annael could see nothing of his brother's face, but knew that he had never been so serious in his long years.

'What about you?' Annael asked. 'I won't abandon you again.'

'Abandon me?' Sabrael did not understand. 'What?'

'On Tharsis, I left you for dead. Not this time.'

'I am an idiot,' Sabrael said, with perhaps more conviction than he intended. 'I do idiotic things. If you think that staying here with me is the best course of action, you are an even bigger idiot! By the Emperor, brother, get back to your Dark Talon.'

Sabrael kicked out, pushing Annael away, turning him head over heels. Dumbfounded, Annael had no choice but to adjust his trajectory and head back towards the aircraft that was still clinging to the craggy promontory on which he had left it.

Venting all of the remaining exhaust gases from his suit, he covered the distance in less than a minute, before realising that he had nothing left to stall his inertia. Annael slammed into the side of the Dark Talon, breaking ablative ceramite plates on both his armour and the aircraft, the two of them careering through the remains of the asteroid in a rapid spin.

Annael hauled himself up to the cockpit release handle and pulled it hard. Anchoring bolts detonated, the canopy dropping away as Space Marine and craft continued to spin. It made no difference, his armour was just as secure against the hard vacuum as the seal of the cockpit.

Clambering over the lip of the cockpit, Annael ejected his armour's backpack. Warning systems screamed into life as his war-plate snapped into reserve power mode and backup environmental mechanisms took over from the air and fluid recycling structures now turning away lazily through space.

Even with his auto-senses operational, the spinning view was very disorientating as he lowered himself into the seat and secured his spinal aperture on the interface projection. Every few seconds he saw the warp breach sliding past, itself an impossible overlay of stars and world, dotted with the kaleidoscopic anti-explosions of rift cannon shots. There were half a dozen of the aircraft now, but it seemed the chasm between the realities was wider than ever, almost half of Annael's vision swept up by the impossible view of a dead planet being birthed into his reality.

The Dark Talon sprang into life as it connected with his nervous system, drawing on his bioprocesses to complete its activation circuits. A touch on the throttle brought the engines into full life, attitude thrusters burning to halt the erratic flat spin that had cast Annael and his craft dozens of kilometres away from the ouroboros.

Taking control, Annael looped the Dark Talon around on the spot, steering for the warp breach. It filled his view while the scanners wailed and bleated in protest at the spectrum of unfeasible signals being returned by their sensors. The display screen was awash with a white blur that seemed to funnel down into itself, reminding him of the ouroboros clinging to its own tail.

Powering towards the rift felt like he was going to slam into the atmosphere of the materialising world. Annael had to override his instincts as much as he did the Dark Talon's collision detection systems. He could not help but grit his teeth as he sped towards that amorphous boundary point.

He hit the counter-thrusters and opened fire the second the rift cannon was in range, though the horizontal distance to the breach was a wavering measurement, growing closer all the time.

Nothing particular happened. The detonation was inside the warp break, and showed in his auto-senses as a brief swirl of prismatic energy before disappearing. He waited for the cannon to recharge and fired again. His second shot seemed no more significant.

'Sabrael,' he called over the vox.

It took a tortuous second for the signal to reach his battle-brother and the reply to return.

'Still alive,' came the answer.

'It has been at least five minutes, have you not yet killed the beast?' Annael fired the rift cannon again while he waited for his friend's response.

'Not as such. Can't say that I've seen its heart. Maybe it forgot to bring it. Calatus is helping.'

Annael's laugh died before reaching his lips as something occurred to him. He had assumed Cypher was fleeing, but he quickly reviewed the Dark Talon's passive scan record on a sub-screen. The log showed the Thunderhawk disappearing at the edge of the warp chasm.

'The heart's not here,' he said to himself. He hit the transmit button. 'The heart's not here!'

'What? Where in all that is unholy does it keep it?'

Annael said nothing as another thought entered his mind. He looked at the sparkle of rift cannon hits, like droplets of water hitting the surface of the pool. They made a tiny impact and then dispersed, becoming one with the opening.

It was hard not to think of himself as one of those droplets, falling onto the Dark Angels, briefly existing and then dissipating into the mass. He tried to remember what it had been like when he had been a Scout, or a warrior in the Fifth Company. It was a blur.

There had been duty. And honour. Dedication to his brothers.

All of that had changed the day he had asked how the Lion had died. A simple question, answered with a lie. That much he had learned in the short time since becoming a warrior of the Ravenwing. Horus had not killed the Lion, as Malcifer had taught him. The Chaplain had later recanted this assertion, and told the Black Knights that the Dark Angels had turned on themselves.

Another lie?

It was impossible to say. It certainly was not the whole truth, of that Annael was certain. He could look up and see a world embattled. A world he was convinced had to be Caliban. Not a myth, not a hallucination, but ancient Caliban ten thousand years in the past, the tear in space linking two realities separated by ten millennia.

What had the Dark Angels achieved since that disastrous day in the last throes of Horus's uprising? What had he achieved? He had propagated the lie to his battle-brothers, and fought to deceive others.

Methelas, Anovel, Astelan, Cypher. The Chaos ships overhead duelling with the combined fleet of the Unforgiven. They were all connected, everything was a web of falsehood, betrayal and deception, interlinked in ways he could not imagine. He knew he would never understand it. He would be lied to again, and he would believe the lies. He had no choice. To think otherwise, to move against the will of the Chapter, would be the destruction of the Dark Angels.

This was the loss of honour, the burden of the Black Knight. To accept the shame. To accept the lies as the better of the two alternatives. There had been one occasion when Malcifer had not lied to him. Deeds mattered. The inner failure had to be masked by outer success. As a Black Knight, he was a foundation stone in the teetering edifice that was the Unforgiven. A resolute brick, that would take the weight and not shift. To do other than that risked the fates of all the sons of the Lion.

It was not his place to fight history nor shape the future.

A droplet on the pool. Inconsequential. A passing moment.

No more. He could bear the burden not a second more. Shame, not of Malcifer's teachings, but of a deeper sense of honour and duty, burned his soul. Was it weakness to succumb to the pressure? Or was it strength to break free of the shackles of his peers?

It did not matter. Deeds mattered.

'We need a bigger stone,' he told Sabrael. 'Sorry, my

brother. My friend. It seems I must rob you of the title of chief idiot.'

He hit the thruster controls, the Dark Talon bursting forward, accelerating hard. The scanners could not tell him where the immaterial and the material overlapped. Annael closed his eyes, trusting to his own instinct, to the repulsion of his mortal form to the immortal world he was about to enter.

While the Dark Talon powered into the breach, Annael disengaged the containment power feeds, turning the core beneath him into an unshielded warp engine.

His stomach turned somersaults and the pressure in his head threatened to burst his ears and snap his spine. Time slowed as he passed the threshold of the real and unreal. Now was the moment.

Annael pulled the trigger of the rift cannon.

A WORLD BROKEN

The air in Tuchulcha's hall shimmered, pulsing with light and dark until it formed an image, a window into the void beyond the Rock. Azrael looked around and saw that behind him were dozens of small hooded figures. Scores of Watchers in the Dark lined the walls, all regarding him with glowing red eyes.

Ezekiel was intent upon the vision, his force blade Traitor's Bane still bare in his hand, a witchglow emanating along its length.

'Impossible,' said the Librarian, shaking his head.

Azrael looked more closely. He could see the huge rent in space that hung over the remnants of Caliban, and through the tear a battle raged for another world.

'Is that...?' he asked.

'It is as I promised,' croaked Tuchulcha's avatar, limbs twitching as the old man rose to his feet. 'Caliban. The Lion's sons war upon themselves. Your primarch and

Luther are about to do battle. You could reach through and touch them. Which would you save?'

'The Lion, of course,' Azrael said without thought. His body trembled at the prospect. Ten thousand years of dishonour and pain, all of it wiped from history by a simple act. 'Save the Lion. Save Caliban.'

He felt a wave of discontent. Castigation flowed around him from the Watchers, but he ignored it. The Supreme Grand Master fixed his gaze upon the marble and gold sphere.

'Can you do it? Will you do it?'

'No!' roared Ezekiel, the Traitor's Bane scything through Tuchulcha's meat puppet, cleaving it from shoulder to groin. Like a dry husk, it fell to the earth in two pieces, a dribble of thin blood leaking from severed veins and arteries. 'Do not listen to its lies!'

'What have you done?' snarled Azrael, turning on the Chief Librarian, the Sword of Secrets in his hand. 'You have doomed us all!'

'We are not the only ones that can move through the opening,' said Ezekiel, taking a step back, his gleaming sword held down to his side. 'Look!'

Azrael glanced at the void-vision. At first he saw nothing, just the distant glitter of orbital weapons and the flare of torpedo launches. Then he spied a pair of bright blue dots. The engines of a Thunderhawk. He followed it for several seconds, and then moved ahead, following its trajectory into the edge of the warp break. There was only one gunship in the area.

'Cypher?'

He saw no sign of the Black Knights he had despatched with the traitor. The asteroid to which they had been sent had broken apart it seemed, but of their fate he could see nothing.

'The Plagueheart is moving...' Ezekiel's whisper betrayed an unease Azrael had never heard from his companion before. It unsettled him to think that the imperturbable Chief Librarian was worried. 'Astelan is there. I can feel him now, his thoughts of glory unfettered by the approach of victory.'

'We must hurry,' said Azrael, looking at Ezekiel. 'We have to block the breach. Move the fleet and the Rock to stem the tide until we can break through.'

The Supreme Grand Master started to pace, eyes locked on Tuchulcha. 'You cannot speak but you can still understand me. I need you to m–'

'Say no more!' Ezekiel swung his blade at Azrael's chest. Instinct caused the Lord of the Rock to raise the Sword of Secrets to block it. As the two blades clashed, the Supreme Grand Master looked into the psyker's eye, feeling himself drenched in golden energy.

Tell it nothing! Ask it nothing! It is cursed. Brother, we cannot save the Lion. It is not to be. The portal must be closed to stop the others. What if Astelan succeeds and brings back a Legion of the Fallen? What if Typhus spoke the truth and some even greater power seeks to be returned?

'No, we must try,' said Azrael, but already the strength was seeping from him. He swallowed hard and looked at the vision. Caliban was wreathed in las-fire and explosions, but all he saw was the lands of his genefather in flames.

Azrael slumped to one knee, head bowed, the Sword of Secrets falling from his fingers. He shot one last look at the vision and then turned his face away.

'What do we have to do?' he asked Ezekiel.

'Fight fire with fire. The warp with the warp.'

Azrael nodded and activated the vox.

'Command, this is Lord Azrael, I want an immediate

signal transfer to all void assets.' He received an affirmative and then heard the short tone as his war-plate's transmitter was siphoned into the massive broadcast arrays of the Tower of Angels. 'All Dark Talon flights, all Chapters, this is a priority recall. All Dark Talons, I have a priority mission. Target rift cannons at dimensional instability centred on the Caliban nominal point. All Dark Talons that are able, you must target the opening breach. We must overload the tear before it engulfs us all.'

A sense of approval washed over him from the Watchers in the Dark, a sensation more heartening, more encouraging than any words could make possible. He stood and retrieved his sacred blade, and sheathed it as he stepped next to Ezekiel. The two of them watched in silence as Dark Talons from across the fleets converged on the warp breach.

For several minutes the Dark Talons bombarded the opening with their rift cannons, but there seemed to be little visible effect. The Plagueheart was just a few thousand kilometres from the breach, ploughing into the hastily reassembled fleet commanded by Dane.

'It isn't working,' Azrael said, looking at Ezekiel. 'What can we do?'

'Nothing,' admitted the Chief Librarian. 'We have been tricked. Tuchulcha never intended to allow us back through the breach, and now we are too far away for the Rock to intervene.'

Azrael could not accept this, and stared at the apparition of the void battle as though his thoughts alone could close the rippling gap between universes. In his frustration, he almost missed another Dark Talon flitting across the void-gap. It had come from a different direction to the others and was accelerating hard.

Ezekiel took a step forward, hand stretching out towards the psychic display as if he might reach into it and snatch what he sought. His good eye widened with shock, sparks of gold erupting from his pupil.

'Brother Annael,' growled the Librarian. 'His warp core is exposed.'

Azrael did not fully understand as he darted a look back towards the ongoing event. A moment later a bright star burst into life at the heart of the breach. It looked as though it might flare and die out like the shots of the rift cannons, but it endured. After a second it had stabilised, like a shell hanging in the air.

After two seconds it started to grow. Lightning of all colours snaked across the reality tear, crackling out into the void and inward towards lost Caliban.

'What's happening?' Azrael demanded, not able to move his eyes from what was unfolding in the vision.

'The breach is feeding upon itself, imploding from both directions.' The Librarian pointed at Tuchulcha. The surface of the sphere was almost completely golden now, swirling madly with smears of scarlet. 'The bridge is collapsing.'

In the depths of the breach Azrael could see Caliban wracked by warp energy. The storm unleashed by the disintegrating warp breach coruscated across the atmosphere of the world. Ships were set ablaze and orbital stations turned to dust.

'No!' he screamed, realising what he was witnessing.

Caliban was breaking apart.

Fronds of swirling power vomited from the closing breach, like solar flares of green and purple and white. They lashed at the void shields of the closest ships, detonating in sparks of yellow. The energy within the breach was being expelled as both sides of the gateway sealed, looking for release in the present as well as the past.

'Tuchulcha!' he bellowed. 'Get us away from here!'

The sphere's colours whirled enigmatically in reply.

'I command you. Get us away. Get everyone safely away from the breach.'

A flutter of red and gold might have approximated a smile or might have been a random confluence of the shifting patterns on the warp device's surface. Regardless, half a second later Azrael heard the warp sirens screaming across the upper levels of the Rock.

The vision of the void showed him an impossible explosion of shapes and colours for an instant before it vanished. Another second and Nakir was barking in his ear.

'Another mass translation, Lord Azrael! What is happening? Where is the rest of the fleet?'

Azrael looked to Ezekiel for an answer. The Grand Master of the Librarius held out a hand, slowly circling from left to right until he had turned fully about.

'Safe,' the Librarian replied after several seconds, his eye dimming as he ended his scan of the warp around them. 'Scattered, but safe. So are the Plagueheart and the *Terminus Est*. Tuchulcha took you literally. It saved *everyone*. Boarding forces have been returned to the Rock as well.'

'Stand down from general alert, Chapter Master,' Azrael told Nakir. 'I will be joining you shortly.'

He felt a faint urging in the back of his mind and saw that the doors to the chamber were open. He walked out into the corridor with Ezekiel, his feet almost moving of their own volition. Stepping onto the worn flags of the passage, he looked back. The Watchers had surrounded Tuchulcha, the blackness of their robes appearing to rise up like a shadow around the strange device.

The doors shut with a slam before he saw anything else. He looked at Ezekiel, seeking an answer, but his companion simply shook his head. When Azrael turned back to the chamber of Tuchulcha, there was no sign of the great doors, only the unbroken stone of the Rock's deep corridors.

He felt sick, in a way his altered physiology should never have felt. A spiritual malaise that all his gen-hancements and doctrinal lessons could not suppress. He took off his helm and gulped in the stale air of the passageway, his mind whirling as he tried to process everything that had happened.

SECRETS AND LIES

They came together without the need for a command to be issued. The Hidden Masters, Azrael's closest confidants, gathered in the Hidden Chamber over the course of the following hours. They did not speak at first, but waited for the Supreme Grand Master to initiate the discussion. Azrael was not sure where to begin. Amongst the others only Ezekiel knew of the strange presence in the bowels of the Rock and the Lord of the Dark Angels was not willing to spread the knowledge further.

'Cypher has escaped,' he told them.

'How?' demanded Asmodai. 'What happened?'

'It does not matter,' Azrael said sternly. 'It is the eighth time such an event has happened, we should not be surprised.'

'And what do we say to the rest of the Inner Circle?' asked Sapphon.

'He escaped his cell during the Death Guard attack. The details are unknown.'

'He disappeared into the breach, it seems,' added Ezekiel. 'I might contend that he is dead, or was cut off when it sealed, but Cypher's history shows us that he is not so easily disposed of. Better that we tell the others that the Hunt continues and Cypher remains at large. It is probably true.'

'The same is true of Astelan,' said Azrael. 'Though I cannot say for sure, it seems that he might have used the expedition to Ulthor to make contact with the followers of the Dark Gods. He had his own agenda to fulfil, supported by the unholy power of that lost world. We can be sure that Astelan will continue to seek to hurt us whenever opportunity presents itself.'

'Much has happened today that will require answers for the battle-brothers. They have seen things that defy belief,' said Belial, the words almost a confession of his own discomfort. 'The same is true of the other Chapters that assisted us.'

'I will host a conclave and the matter will be discussed with the Chapter Masters. The masters of the Chaplains will devise a suitable programme of dedications and collective penances to ensure the Chapter tenets remain instilled in our warriors. The First and Second Companies have suffered much of late. Belial, Sammael, you will see that your ranks are replenished by the most suitable candidates from those that voice the gravest concerns. It will be arduous but normality will be restored.'

'As ever it has been,' replied the captain of the Second Company. Belial silently nodded in acceptance of the order.

Nobody said anything for almost a minute, before Sapphon broke the silence.

'What actually happened?' He looked at the others,

who shared his confusion. 'Some of this I can piece together, but much seems nonsensical.'

They exchanged glances and all eyes settled on Azrael.

'A plot by the corrupted followers of Chaos, led by dread Typhus,' answered the Supreme Grand Master. 'They sought to bring forth an army of abominations from the warp. We thwarted them. It is as simple as that.'

'Rarely are matters of Chaos simple,' said Asmodai.

'There is nothing further to be said,' replied Azrael with a hint of a snarl. 'We came close to the brink of annihilation but thanks to the bravery of those here and across the Chapters we successfully defended the Imperium from disaster. Battle honours for Caliban will be issued as required.'

The officers looked far from satisfied by this explanation but knew that they would get nothing further from their lord. One by one they paid their respects with bows and departed, until Azrael was left with Ezekiel.

'A three-way battle for Caliban's past,' said the Lord of the Rock. 'And none of us were victorious.'

'Four forces battled today,' the Librarian corrected. 'The device itself and whatever purpose it serves. Thankfully it was also thwarted.'

'Can you make much sense of what it was trying to do? What it claimed?'

'Very little, brother,' admitted Ezekiel. 'Perhaps it is better that we do not understand. It would only invite further difficulties.'

Azrael felt sick at the thought and knew that his account in the journals of the Supreme Grand Masters would be brief and unhelpful. He wondered about the previous entries concerning Cypher, their content and tone terse. There was much that was left unsaid and he had nothing to offer hope to his successors. Better that the entire episode was forgotten, lest a weak soul in the future think that they could wield Tuchulcha again. That, Azrael was certain, would be calamitous.

'Am I right? Did I witness what I thought I did?' he asked his companion, his voice a whisper. 'The destruction of Caliban. The scattering of the Fallen. The cause of our shame.'

Ezekiel pulled back his cowl, revealing a scalp pierced by cables and pipes linked to the psychic hood built into his battleplate. There was no hint of energy in his eye now, just his usual piercing stare.

'Not just witnessed, brother,' the Chief Librarian replied in a taut whisper. 'It would be much easier if we had been merely witnesses.'

ABOUT THE AUTHOR

Gav Thorpe is the author of the Horus Heresy novel *Deliverance Lost*, as well as the novellas *Corax: Soulforge*, *Ravenlord* and *The Lion*, which formed part of the *New York Times* bestselling collection *The Primarchs*. He is particularly well-known for his Dark Angels stories, including the Legacy of Caliban series, and the ever-popular novel *Angels of Darkness*. His Warhammer 40,000 repertoire further includes the Path of the Eldar series, the Horus Heresy audio dramas *Raven's Flight* and *Honour to the Dead*, and a multiplicity of short stories. For Warhammer, Gav has penned the Time of Legends trilogy, *The Sundering*, and much more besides. He lives and works in Nottingham.

READ IT FIRST
EXCLUSIVE PRODUCTS | EARLY RELEASES | FREE DELIVERY
blacklibrary.com

This anthology contains six short stories featuring some of the mightiest heroes of the Dark Angels as they battle against impossible odds to defeat their foes and complete their shadowy crusade.

WARHAMMER 40,000

DARK ANGELS
LORDS OF CALIBAN
GAV THORPE

Available from *blacklibrary.com*,
GAMES WORKSHOP
Hobby Centres
and all good bookstores